THE MARRIAGE
AUCTION

BOOK 4

Audrey Carlan Titles

The Marriage Auction
Book 1
Book 2
Book 3
Book 4
Madam Alana
A Christmas Auction

Soul Sister Novels
Wild Child
Wild Beauty
Wild Spirit

Wish Series
What the Heart Wants
To Catch a Dream
On the Sweet Side
If Stars Were Wishes

Love Under Quarantine

Biker Beauties
Biker Babe
Biker Beloved
Biker Brit
Biker Boss

International Guy Series
Paris
New York
Copenhagen
Milan

San Francisco
Montreal
London
Berlin
Washington, D.C.
Madrid
Rio
Los Angeles

Lotus House Series
Resisting Roots
Sacred Serenity
Divine Desire
Limitless Love
Silent Sins
Intimate Intuition
Enlightened End

Trinity Trilogy
Body
Mind
Soul
Life
Fate

Calendar Girl
January
February
March
April
May
June
July
August
September

THE MARRIAGE AUCTION 2

BOOK 4

By Audrey Carlan

The Marriage Auction 2: Book Four
By Audrey Carlan

Copyright 2024 Audrey Carlan
ISBN: 978-1-963135-33-6

Published by Blue Box Press, an imprint of Evil Eye
Concepts, Incorporated

Editorial team: Liz Berry, Ekaterina Sayanova, Stacey Tardif, Suzy Baldwin

Dedication

*To Amy Tannenbaum, because you listen to my dreams and help
me make them a reality.
You are one of a kind.*

Episode 87

Sink or Swim

NAOMI

"This is a bad idea," I mumbled while frantically pacing back and forth across Memphis' small living room.

"How so?" Memphis asked and plopped his large frame on the couch. His lips twitched as he covered a chuckle behind his hand, clearly enjoying my nervousness.

I gritted my teeth and inhaled sharply through my nose. "Because I'm going to screw it up."

"Baby, it's shopping with my family," he answered with humor in his tone, proving he thought I was being ridiculous.

My entire body trembled with anxiety as I waited to be picked up by a member of the female Taylor clan. And Memphis didn't understand. How could he? Simply put, Memphis was a guy.

The first time a woman spent time with her soon to be mother-in-law and sisters-in-law alone shouldn't be picking out her wedding dress. Did women even go with their in-laws to do such a thing? I had planned on going with my mother, but of course, the dinner from hell and Lucifer himself ruined that plan entirely. Then, when Robin Taylor overheard me telling Memphis I would be busy shopping for a dress today, she not only invited herself, she invited her daughters too. Claimed we'd make a girls' day of it.

So I paced, trying desperately to get the gnawing fear of letting my new family down out of my system. I don't have a sister to fall back on, nor a best friend to call and hash out every minute detail of what was to happen before these women arrived. I don't even have any real female friends that aren't employees of my company or jewelers I work with. It certainly made me realize how out of touch I'd become in my workaholic lifestyle.

Basically, I was on my own.

Sink or swim.

Memphis stood up and caught me mid-pace, tugging me against his body.

"Hey there," he whispered while cupping my neck. "My mother and sisters already like you. They are excited about being involved in our wedding. You're going to have a blast with them today. I promise you."

I slumped against him and rested my cheek on his chest. "You think so?"

He held me close. "Baby, I know so. Now you have got to relax. Besides, you'll finally meet Sydney. And she's already a fan of yours."

"The model. The second oldest. The one you are the closest to. That Syd?" I frowned as the nerves swallowed me whole.

Memphis chuckled and rubbed my back. "Yeah, that Syd. She's also the most down-to-earth person you'll ever meet. Plus, she lives in New York. That means, when we set up shop in NYC, she'll be there to help me get adjusted. I actually have some great news about that…" he hedged, leaving that juicy morsel dangling.

"Oh? I thought you were worried about the big move to New York from Georgia."

He shook his head. "Naw, not worried. More like concerned I wouldn't know what to do with myself. But my options may be opening up. I've got a meeting with the head of the sports division at Cornell University next month."

My eyes bulged and my mouth fell open in shock. My cool-as-a-cucumber man simply smirked at my surprise.

"That's an Ivy League school…"

"Yep. And they're looking to fill an assistant defensive coaching position. They want someone young and hungry to help the team win their division. Coach told me he believed having new blood on the coaching team could be their ace in the hole."

"And they are considering you?"

He nodded. "Actually, he said the job was mine…on one condition."

"Which is?" My mind ran rampant with ideas. Who did I know in the Ivy League circuit that I could pull some favors with, to ensure my man got the job he wanted.

"I have to finish up my degree this year so I can be ready for spring training. I'm shy some credits, which means I need to sign up for those classes this coming enrollment period in order to secure my bachelor's degree."

I pushed at his chest. "That's it? You take and pass those classes and you're guaranteed the job?"

"Well, not exactly. Obviously the in-person interview means a lot."

"But you're great in person. The interview will be a cinch! And I can reach out, make some calls to some people I know and put in a good word if you'd like me—"

He cut me off with two fingers pressed lightly over my lips as he spoke gently. "No calling in favors, Nay. I applied and did all the work for this prospective job myself. And I'm going to get the job based on my own skills and experience in the field. I do not need my very powerful, extremely connected fiancée to score me a job. I'm perfectly capable of doing that on my own."

"I didn't mean to overstep..." I whispered right before he dipped forward and kissed away my next words.

"I know what you meant, and I'm grateful to have my woman at my back. If I need help with this, I'll ask. Okay?" He looked deeply into my eyes, his kind and sincere.

I nodded. "I'm sorry."

"Don't be sorry, be happy for me. For us. Means I've got something worthwhile to look forward to in my career that wasn't there before. It also means things are falling into place for both of us. Me finding a great job at a well-respected university, with a stellar athletics department, only helps settle me into my new life in New York, with you."

That made me smile. "I'm happy for you."

"Thank you."

"I'm also proud of you."

"Thank you for that too." He kissed me again. The kiss went on until we were interrupted by a knock on the door.

Instantly my anxiety rushed back to the surface and my skin became flushed. "They're here." I gulped.

"Stop fretting. It's shopping, Nay. Something about how fine you always look tells me you are no stranger to shopping."

I smacked at his back jokingly as he went to open the door. "It's different, and you know it!" I whisper-yelled.

Memphis opened the door and the most beautiful woman I'd ever seen in my entire life turned around and smiled. Perfect white teeth gleamed against her summery, sun-kissed umber skin tone. Her black hair was pulled into a sleek, high ponytail, the long strands hanging over one shoulder. She wore big Jackie O sunglasses and a glittery pink lipstick. Her midnight-colored turtleneck blouse was tucked into a pair of skintight black leather pants. The platform suede stilettos made the already tall woman an Amazon in comparison to me.

"Syd!" Memphis called out with what could only be considered boyish glee.

"Big Bro!" Sydney squealed and flung herself into her brother's arms.

Memphis swung her from side to side then kissed her cheek before stepping back a couple feet. "Let me get a look at you. Damn, girl. You look like a million dollars."

"I know." She pursed her lips playfully in a haughty expression.

"Seriously though, NYC must be treating you good."

"I think so too. Best city there is." Syd slipped off her glasses and directed her gaze at me. "And this must be your fiancée."

I held out my hand. "Naomi Shaw."

"Oh, I know exactly who you are, and I'm so excited to meet you in person. I actually worked on one of your jewelry campaigns awhile back. Unfortunately, my face didn't make the cut, just the jewels on my neck and hands." She chuckled.

I started to laugh as she shook my hand, because how absurd. My team had the opportunity to show this angel's face with my jewels, and they chose to cut her out? I would be speaking to my marketing director at my earliest convenience.

"That's rather shocking. I can't imagine why they would do such a thing. You're...breathtaking," I said on a slight gasp.

She grinned as her cheeks pinked, and her eyes shimmered with joy. "The marketing director told me my face was competing against the beauty of the jewels, and he was in the business of selling jewelry. I told them as long as I got paid, I didn't care what made the final cut."

We both burst into laughter. "Well, in all honesty, he was probably right. Your beauty is unmatched."

"Uh, I beg to differ. My sister is gorgeous, even her own brother can see that. But my fiancée is no slouch in the beauty department either," Memphis interjected, his gaze tracing my form up and down as though he could eat me for lunch.

Today I chose to wear a pair of wide-legged trousers in camel with an off-white button-up silk shirt, open far enough to show the delicate gold lacing around the cups of my corset underneath. A huge solitary pearl hung down between my breasts on a gold chain and a pair of strappy gold Jimmy Choo heels accentuated the look. I'd left my long hair down so I could manipulate it when trying different style dresses.

I went over to Memphis' side and looped my arm around his waist. "Thanks, baby."

Sydney clapped her hands together. "Okay, I'm supposed to pick you up and then meet the others at the bridal store. You ready to take on the Taylors?"

"As ready as I'm ever gonna be." I sighed.

"Then let's go!"

* * * *

"There she is!" Robin announced as Sydney and I entered the bridal store. Robin held a glass of champagne as did Granny Althea. Odessa, Cheyenne, Paris, and Holland held what looked to be glasses of apple cider as the color in the flutes was far too dark to be actual champagne.

"Here we are," Sydney cooed. "Where's our bubbly?"

"Right here, ladies." A blonde woman wearing a pink business suit approached the two of us with filled glasses. She handed one to Syd and the last to me. "You must be the bride."

"I am. What gave it away?"

She grinned, her pretty blue eyes twinkling. "I've known Syd most of my life. If she were getting married, I'd know about it, seeing as I'd be the maid of honor."

"Hey now, don't be pushing her sisters to the side just yet, Jennifer. She could pick one of us," Odessa griped.

The bridal attendant made a frustrated sound at the back of her throat. "Dess, we've had this conversation a million times over the past twenty years. I am Sydney's BFF for eternity."

"And I'm her sister!" Odessa fired back, heat in her tone even though her body language and smile expressed this was a long-standing argument between the two women.

"Yes, but I'm her *soul sister*. Which means she *chose* me. She was stuck with you. Big difference. Besides, how does a woman pick between four sisters? She doesn't. She picks her best friend. And that, Dess…is *moi!*"

Odessa rolled her eyes and made a snarky miming action with her hand and lips as though a duck were quacking.

"I love you too, Dess. Now let's get back to the bride. I hear you've snagged the previously unsnaggable Memphis Taylor. The lone wolf of the Taylor clan."

"Unsnaggable?" I asked.

"Jenn, just because Memphis wasn't into any of your sisters or the women you tried and failed to set him up with, doesn't mean he wouldn't find the right woman on his own."

"We could have been related," Jenn sighed. "But it wasn't meant to be. Such is life," she said in a melancholy tone. "Unless maybe you have a brother or two?" Jenn's gaze snapped to mine.

"Uh, no. Fresh out. Sorry."

"Fine. I guess I'll have to find another hunky family man to hook my sister up with."

"Or you could just leave it alone," Granny added. "Not smart to stick your nose where it don't belong."

Jenn covered her chest with her hand. "Granny, that is not nice. Everyone is looking for love, which is why I have to help my sisters find it."

"What about yourself?" I queried.

"Married my high school sweetheart right after graduation and have been living in romantic bliss for the last four years. Bought this place just so I could get my fix of all things romance and weddings every day."

Syd nudged my shoulder. "Jenn is a hopeless romantic and knows her stuff. She won't steer you wrong on finding the perfect dress."

"Well, I'm all yours."

"Do you have any ideas about what you're looking for?" Jennifer asked.

"Something that will look appropriate in the Taylor's backyard garden."

"Awwww you're getting married at Casa de Taylor? How lovely. Sooooo..." She tapped her bottom lip. "Green, lush background, roses of varying colors, and a body that was made to be fitted for a gown..." She looked me over. "I already have some ideas. Drink your champagne and follow me to the dressing room. I'll gather what we need, and we can get started. Let's see if we can find you the perfect gown to marry your prince charming."

Sydney blessedly followed me into the dressing room.

"Your best friend seems nice," I offered.

"She is truly amazing. We've been friends since first grade. A couple girls were making fun of my hair and calling me names. Jennifer went right up to them and shoved one down and bit the other girl, leaving teeth imprints on her skin. When they were both crying and carrying on, she pointed at them and said, 'Mean girls get treated mean back!' and we've been best friends since. My girl may be blonde, blue eyed, and look like a fairy princess, but she's mean as a snake with the sharpest tongue when someone hurts those she loves."

"Good one to have at your side," I nodded.

"Exactly. Speaking of the devil," Syd said as Jennifer came in holding a stack of dresses in each hand. She hissed at Syd as she passed, making us both laugh.

"Okay, start with the most extravagant and work your way down. I gotta hit my own quota this week," she teased and winked.

I put on the most expensive "extravagant" dress first. It

was lace at the neck, down the long sleeves and all the way to the floor. It was stunning and very regal but didn't seem to fit the setting of a backyard wedding. Still, I dutifully walked out and stood on the riser in front of the Taylor women.

"Wow, that dress fits like a latex glove," Odessa called out.

"It's mighty fine," Granny said and sipped on her champagne.

"Don't you think it's a little…I don't know…old?" said fourteen-year-old Cheyenne. Leave it to the youngest of the group to lay down the truth.

"I agree. It's pretty but not really appropriate for a garden wedding," I admitted, hoping they weren't upset.

"Good point. Next!" Robin called out.

"Who do you gotta ask to get some more bubbly around here?" Granny lifted her empty flute.

"Hold your horses, Gran, and I'll fix you right up!" Jennifer hustled behind a short wall and grabbed a fresh bottle.

"You have my thanks, Jenny," Gran said.

"Oh, do you prefer to be called Jenny?" I asked as we made our way back to the room.

Sydney snorted through her laugh.

"No, I hate it. But Gran is the matriarch of all matriarchs. You don't mess with her. If she wants to call me Jenny, she can."

"But no one else," I confirmed.

"Right. Try on the poofy princess one."

I looked at the dress with dread. It was absolutely not my style in any way. Corset on top with mounds and mounds of chiffon falling from the waist in a big bloom. I hated it.

Once again, I walked out to show the crowd. Immediately Cheyenne and Holland started laughing. The rest of the group wasn't far behind so instead of stepping on the riser, I made an about face and went directly back to the room. Their cackling could be heard echoing throughout the entire store.

"She looked like an upside-down flower!" one of the younger ones blurted, and she wasn't wrong.

Instead of going through each dress, I filtered through to my favorite. It was a soft eggshell white satin with spaghetti straps and a cowl neckline over the breasts. The fabric was buttery smooth, and the fluid drape hugged my curves all the way to the floor. The back was completely bare all the way to my tailbone. It was sexy, sultry, and beautifully simple.

My heart started to pound, goosebumps rose on my flesh, and I couldn't help but smile as I stared at my image in the mirror. I'd never felt more beautiful. It broke my heart a little that I was seeing myself as a bride for the first time without my own mother in attendance. But I was a strong, independent woman and I could handle the disappointment of her absence the same way I had my entire life. With grit and grace.

Sydney gasped, her hand over her mouth as she stared in awe. "That's the one. Show them. They're gonna die when they see you."

I walked slowly back out to my audience with my head held high and my heart in my throat. I wanted them to like it more than my next breath.

I needn't worry. The second I came out and stood up on the riser, Robin started crying. Odessa whooped and high-fived Holland. Cheyenne cried out, "Heck yes!" while Granny smiled and nodded.

Jennifer watched everyone's faces and then turned to me with big teary doe eyes, her hands clasped in the center of her chest. "Are we saying yes to this dress?"

"Absolutely. This is what I want to wear when Memphis sees me for the first time as his bride."

Episode 88

To Be Continued

RHODES

I stared into Maia's soulful eyes, shimmering with unshed tears. Her bottom lip trembled. "You don't understand," she croaked and clung to my shirt. "She left a note. I had them read it to me."

Misery filled the air around us as we stood pressed together on the balcony of Alana's country estate. The cool wind across my arms and face sent a shiver down my spine.

"And what did the note say?"

"She told me things were worse than before... And to never come home," Maia whispered and then face-planted against my chest.

I tucked my face into the crook of her neck. "We're going to figure this out. All of it. Your family and mine. But first, I have to get Emily back home. It's what she needs to feel safe."

Maia nodded against my chest. "I agree, but my time to help my mom and siblings is running out. What if he's done something worse to them than what I experienced? What if Derrik is touching Maisie? What if my stepfather is physically abusing all of them? For my mother to make such a harsh demand that I never return…" Her knees buckled as a sob tore through her body, muffled against my chest. I kept her upright, a sturdy support she could lean on no matter what.

"While we're on the plane, I'm going to make some calls. Have a tech expert I know do some digging into the family. I'll have them pull bank records, medical records, school records, anything we can in order to secure more information. Then we'll head to Colorado for your grandmother's funeral once we get Emily settled."

Maia straightened. "But Emily…"

I cupped her cheeks and wiped away her tears. "Emily will be safe and protected in California. Besides, that's where Marisol is."

"Marisol?"

It suddenly dawned on me that I'd never mentioned Marisol, the other member of my household.

"Her nanny. My house manager. The woman behind the man." I chuckled, remembering how Marisol and I had met under the strangest circumstances. I'd taken a leap of faith in hiring her all those years ago, but now she was part of my family.

"Emily's going to be fourteen. She still has a nanny?" And there was the leeriness I had come to expect from my skeptical fiancée.

"It will all make sense when you meet her. Now come on. Emily is waiting for us in the kitchen, stuffing her face full of more—"

"Let me guess…crepes!" Maia snickered, her drying tears leaving a glimmer of a smile in their wake.

"Bingo," I murmured as I put my arm around her shoulders and led her inside.

When we entered the kitchen, we were greeted by Emily, Christophe, and Alana at the table. Much to my surprise, Inspector Antoine Moreau, was also there, merrily sipping a cappuccino, with a freshly made crepe on the table before him.

Emily was stuffing her mouth full of her favorite breakfast, her head down to avoid making eye contact with the inspector.

"I sure hope you're not interviewing my daughter without her parent present?" I asked with enough venom the man put his cup down and shook his head anxiously.

"Not at all. Just enjoying the kindness offered by the Toussaints. However, if you'd like to get the interview underway, I'm amenable. I've gotten most of what I needed from Mrs. Toussaint. Still, I'd like to go over everything Emily remembers. The slightest detail might help us catch Angus Sokolov more quickly," he shared.

I grunted and stood behind my daughter, resting my hands on her shoulders. I bent and whispered in Emily's ear. "You ready to talk about all this with the detective so we can go home?"

She nodded.

"I'm right here, Em. Nothing bad is gonna happen to you again," I reminded her.

Maia slipped into the chair next to my daughter and reached for her hand. Emily grasped the support, holding onto Maia while edging closer. Maia took the hint and scooted her chair right next to Emily's so the two were hip to hip, as close as possible. Then Maia glared at the inspector, ready to jump between him and Emily at the slightest provocation.

Pride in Maia's actions and Emily's bravery filled my chest to almost bursting. We were a family of three. A pyramid, each holding the other up. Stronger together.

"I'm ready. Ask me anything," Emily said, directing her question to the inspector.

Four hours later, the three of us had said our goodbyes to Alana and Christophe and were on the private jet I'd chartered, headed back home to Los Angeles, California.

* * * *

On the plane, I'd called Joel Castellanos' cousin, Bruno. Unfortunately, he didn't answer personally. My call had been rerouted to a man named Jonas, who introduced himself as Bruno's second-in-command. I explained my connection to Joel, which he already seemed to know. Since time was of the essence, I didn't mince words and told Jonas the entire story about Maia, how we met the same way Joel and Faith had, and that her family situation was dire. He cataloged all the information, names, places, and even the grittier details about Maia's abuse at the hand of her stepbrother, which seemed to not only anger Jonas, but set a fire under his fingers as I could hear the rapid-fire clicking of keys on a keyboard.

Once done, he simply told me they would look into it and that I'd have preliminary information by the time the flight landed in California. He also explained their services were not cheap. I responded that I had money but not the resources to get what I needed. Which was sensitive information about Maia's family members.

After we hung up, an invoice for a hundred thousand dollars appeared in my inbox. I transferred the funds immediately, then cuddled up with my girls and slept like the dead all the way to California. When we landed, there was a file in my email.

I ignored the document, wanting to get Emily situated and Maia introduced to Marisol and her new home before I dug into what Jonas sent. The moment the SUV rolled through my security gates and then up to our driveway in front of the house, Marisol was standing at the door waving with excitement. Two security guards were positioned a few feet away. I scanned the length of my property and saw several others walking the perimeter as my security advisor had instructed.

"Marisol!" Emily screamed through the car's open window. When the SUV stopped, Emily bolted out and raced into Marisol's arms.

The older woman rocked my daughter back and forth, thanking God while staring at the open sky. I'd had to tell Marisol what happened to Emily prior to our arrival. Since Marisol was like a grandmother to Em and had escaped her own version of hell back in Mexico, I knew she'd be another ideal person to help my daughter through her traumatic experience. Marisol placed her hands to the sides of Emily's head and kissed her entire face. *"¡Mi bebé! ¡Te extrañé mucho!"* *My baby. I missed you so much.*

"I missed you too, *abuela*," Emily gushed, tears in her eyes as she kept her arms wrapped around Marisol's round waist. She rubbed her face against the ever-present apron Marisol wore. The woman was always cooking or organizing special things to make us feel loved. . She'd slowed down over the years as she was now in her late sixties, so I hired a few staff members for her to manage. They do the day-to-day cleaning, laundry, grocery shopping and whatever else is needed. The transition to house manager was hard for her since she liked full control of everything, but she'd gotten the hang of it over time. Her once black hair was streaked with silvery white strands that accentuated her kind and pretty face. Still, the woman was a formidable force of good in the Davenport household, and I was thrilled to see her.

I folded out of the vehicle and held my hand out for Maia.

"Is Marisol Emily's grandmother?" she whispered.

"By choice, yes. Though she has six children and a dozen or so grandchildren of her own. They are all living beautiful lives up and down California. Being a single woman in her sixties with grown children, she lives here and is paid to take care of us. A job she has perfected over the past thirteen years."

"Wow, that's awesome," Maia breathed, her gaze taking

in the surrounding area. "You have a big house. Kind of like a mansion."

I chuckled and interlaced our fingers. "It's not as big as it looks. Only seven bedrooms, thirteen bathrooms, and a guesthouse."

Maia's mouth dropped open in pure shock. "Holy shit."

I lifted her hand and kissed the back. "Come, let's meet Marisol," I tugged on her hand until she jolted into action.

"Mari, I'd like you to meet someone. My fiancée, Maia. Maia, this is Marisol, a treasured member of our family. She takes care of me, Emily, and this home."

"*Hola*, Maia. I am happy to meet you. *Bienvenida*." *Welcome*, she made a sweeping gesture with her hand toward the entrance. The door was wide open.

"*Gracias*. I don't know a lot of Spanish, but I'd love to learn more," Maia shook Marisol's hand.

Marisol gifted her a beaming smile. "I shall teach you all that I know!"

"Be careful Maia, pretty soon she'll stop speaking English. One day in the future, when she thinks you know enough, she'll put you to the test," Emily shared.

"Shhh…don't give away all my secrets just yet, *mija*," Marisol winked at Em.

"Did you make lunch?" Emily hedged.

"*¡Por supuesto!*" *Of course!* She pretended to be offended in that endearing way Emily and I were used to. "I feed my family. Come!" She clapped her hands. "We eat, then I will unpack you," she commanded, nudging Emily forward.

"Did you make beef enchiladas?" Emily pushed.

"*Sí*." Marisol clipped. "I know what your favorites are," she harrumphed, continuing the charade.

"And rice and beans…" Emily added, asking for what she already knew was there, just to get Marisol's goat. It was playful and so normal my entire body started to relax, the tension and nerves about getting out of France and bringing my family home finally dissipating.

"*Sí*. It is not my first day as your *abuela*. Now, go wash your hands!"

"Okay, okay!" Emily turned to leave then suddenly plastered herself to Marisol. "I love you, Mari."

Marisol put one hand to the back of Emily's head and the other around her shoulders hugging her once more. Then she dipped her head and whispered, *"Te amo, mi preciosa."* I love you, my precious. "Now go clean those filthy hands. Airport muck, eeeeyyyyeeee!" She made a disgruntled sound.

Emily bolted down the hallway into one of the bathrooms.

"Mari, I'm going to take Maia on a tour of the house and show her our room. Did you have Esmerelda do her thing?" I asked, referring to Marisol's eldest daughter, a fashion stylist to the stars.

"*Sí*. Everything is there. She left notes and said she'd make an appointment with Maia to get more specifics and learn her taste."

"Specific taste about what?" Maia asked.

"Your preferences in clothing, fashion, and the like. I had Marisol set her daughter to work on crafting a wardrobe for you. During our shopping days in France, you didn't get more than a handful of outfits, and you salvaged so little from your place in Las Vegas. I want you to be entirely comfortable in California and I noticed you had no interest in shopping, so I had Marisol work out a solution with her daughter Esmerelda."

"I'm a problem now?" Maia pursed her lips so she didn't give away her smile, but I saw through her shenanigans.

I pulled her against my body, lifted her chin, and pecked her lips. "No, you're the woman in my life. My fiancée and that position holds some influence."

She grinned. "Oh?" Her hands went from resting on my hips to reaching around and grabbing my ass.

I hummed against the sudden swelling of a certain appendage as she ground against me. More than anything I wanted to carry Maia upstairs bridal style, toss her on the bed, and have my wicked way with her, but I needed to make sure I kept an eye on my daughter too. Taking the less chivalrous road, I kissed Maia hungrily, tasting her sweet mouth and allowing her spicy vanilla scent to invade my senses. I was hard as a rock when I ripped my mouth away and rested my forehead against hers.

"Tonight, when Emily is sound asleep, I'm going to eat you alive," I warned.

Maia sighed dreamily. "I think I'd like that very much."

"Oh, you're not only going to like it, you're gonna love it. I'm going to fuck you so hard and for so long, you'll be walking bowlegged tomorrow."

"Holy hell, Rhodes," Maia whispered as she pressed her belly against my erection. "Are you trying to get me all hot and bothered?" She wrapped her arms around my neck and pecked my lips twice in quick succession.

I smiled a devilish grin. "Now you know how it feels. I take one look at your beautiful face or that tight ass of yours in the jeans you wear and I'm rock hard. It's your turn to burn with no fire extinguisher in sight," I bit her bottom lip then soothed it with a swipe of my tongue.

"Rude," she groaned but continued to rub her little body against me in all the right ways.

"Seriously? We've been home like two seconds and you're already making out?" Emily griped from several feet behind us. "Mari, you see what I have to live with? You should feel sorry for me," she complained, heading toward the kitchen. "And that sorry should come with a *Friends* marathon after lunch in the movie room," she called out as she disappeared from sight.

"Whoops. Guess we got caught." Maia giggled.

I slid my hands from her ass along her hips, over her

waist and just under her breasts where I dragged my thumbs over those erect little berries hiding behind her clothing. I loved sucking Maia's breasts because she was incredibly sensitive there. My mouth watered at the memory of her taste, and I couldn't help but palm her small tit. "Fuck I want to taste these right now," I dipped my head and nuzzled along the V of her shirt, slicking my tongue along the tops of her breasts.

Maia mewled and gripped my hair before she arched back, serving up her body as if it were the most natural thing in the world to her.

I lifted up the hem of her shirt, shoved down the cup of her bra and plumped up one juicy breast. Without further thought, I bent my head and swirled my tongue around the pert nipple, sucked it hard, and let it go with an audible *plop*. With my thumb and first finger, I pinched the tip until Maia's eyes rolled back, and she gasped.

"I could make you come right here, right now, just by sucking on these beautiful breasts." It was an erotic threat but one I was perfectly ready to carry out, right in the middle of the entrance to our home.

"Rhodes, please. Emily…" she reminded me.

It was as though a bucket of ice-cold water had been dumped over my head. My cock ached behind my restrictive clothing as I covered Maia's breasts and shook my head free of all carnal thoughts and put my mind back on the matters at hand: Emily's comfort and Maia's homecoming.

"Damn, I got a little out of control there," I admitted and could feel my skin flushing with the knowledge.

Maia grinned wickedly. "To be continued?" She cocked a brow.

"To be continued." I cleared my throat as I readjusted the steel pipe between my legs. "Let me give you the tour then meet Em and Mari back in the kitchen for her shredded beef enchiladas. She's an incredible cook. I hope you like Mexican food because we eat more than our fair share around here, by request. Marisol actually likes cooking an array of international cuisine, but Emily constantly asks for homemade Mexican, and I love it, too, so I don't discourage her."

"I will never turn down free food. Liking it has never mattered to me. Food means survival. I learned early on to be happy about whatever I was given." Maia shrugged. "I'm easy."

I shook my head and clasped her hand. "You're anything but easy, but I understand what you mean. With enough time feeling safe and secure in your new home, I'm sure you'll figure out the foods you like and dislike. Marisol will have fun trying to learn your preferences. I'll enjoy watching her stumble through that process the way I did into your heart."

"But you did…"

"Did what?"

"Stumble into my heart and set up shop there." Her cheeks turned rosy as she quickly looked away and pretended to study the art on the walls.

"Are you saying you like me?" I swung our arms as I showed her the living room, the den, the game room, and so on.

"I more than like you," she said under her breath.

"I'm sorry, what was that?" I pulled her into one of the many bathrooms and pressed her body up against the vanity. "Say it again."

She licked her lips to give herself time to figure out what to say. I watched that slippery tongue like a hawk tracking its prey.

She firmed her jaw and lifted her chin. "I said, I more than like you."

"I more than like you, too, Maia." I stared deeply into her eyes. "I've more than liked you for a while now."

"Oh?"

I cupped her cheeks. "You being here makes me so

happy. I didn't know what to expect after all that we've been through, but just having you in this house with my daughter and Marisol, it finally feels real. You and me, *it's real*. It feels right. Do you feel it?"

She nodded. "You're the only thing that has ever felt good and right."

I reminded her of the truth I'd shared on her birthday. "I love you, Maia, and I'm not going to let anything get between us. Not Portia. Not some criminal with a vengeance against Alana. Not anything. If you're not there yet, it's okay. We have all the time in the world…"

Her body trembled in my arms, and her gaze pierced mine as though she was pained by what she was about to share. "But I am in love with you…and I'm so scared I'm going to lose it."

"No, sweetheart, no." I hugged her so hard I wished I could merge us into one. "I'll battle the devil himself to hold on to you and your love."

Her breath was warm against my neck as she whispered, "I hope you mean that, Rhodes, because you might have to."

Episode 89

Practice Makes Perfect

JACK

I poured a couple glasses of red wine as Summer got TJ settled into the toddler crib provided by the resort. The Johansen's didn't spare a single dime, booking all of us in lavish suites overlooking a pristine snowy landscape and the mountains beyond. Based on the weather report, we wouldn't have much luck seeing the northern lights tomorrow, but the forecast for the next night looked clear. Due to that information, we decided to let everyone have a night to themselves. The ladies had plans to go shopping in the town tomorrow during the day and we men were going to take TJ to play in the snow and swim in the resort's heated pool. Then we'd all meet up for a family dinner.

Before Summer put TJ down, he'd asked about his mother again. Each and every time he called for his mother, my heart ached. The agony of losing her was always hiding under the surface, and it felt like any little thing made it swell and throb painfully. A consistent heartburn I couldn't shake.

A pair of slim arms wrapped around my waist from

behind as Summer pressed her front to my back. She rubbed her face between my shoulder blades. "He makes me so happy and so sad at the same time," she said, her words muffled against the fabric of my sweater.

I turned around, shifting her to my front where I hugged her fully. "Me too."

"It's brutal when he asks about Ellen. And when that bottom lip starts to quiver after I have to tell him Mommy isn't here..." She sucked in a ragged breath.

"It's the same for me. Just when I think I'm making progress, smiling and laughing, I remember that I'll never hear Ellen laugh, and I'm devastated all over again. I'd just come to terms with Troy's loss and now Ellen. When will it stop?"

"Hurting?"

I nodded.

"Oh honey, I don't think it ever stops hurting. When you love someone like you did Troy and Ellen, the pain of their loss never goes away. I believe it morphs into something else. The sharp edge of grief eventually fades, but a dull knife still cuts and so does loss. It creeps up on you. Just when you think you have a handle on it, a reminder pops up. A scent they shared, a song they adored, a good memory you had with them, maybe even a bad one, but that's all part of the process of letting go. Of being able to eventually think about the people you lost as a beautiful part of your own journey and what they brought to enrich it, instead of the pain of no longer having them. But that process takes time."

"You make it sound so *natural,* but none of this feels natural. It feels like my sister and brother were robbed of a beautiful life together with their son."

"Jack, you're going to spend years and years missing Ellen and Troy. As you should. They hold a big piece of your heart, and always will. They deserve all your tears and sadness because you loved them. Right now, you're still angry. And that's perfectly okay. I'm angry on your and TJ's behalf. But we both realize that this is our new reality. I know you're edging toward acceptance, especially by jumping into raising TJ. Another step in that direction will be putting Ellen and Troy to rest together. Once that is done, we'll find a routine that works for the three of us. Let's just take it all one day at a time for now."

"My fiancée… Compassionate, beyond beautiful, and wise. How did I get so lucky?" I murmured against the top of her head.

She shrugged then eased her upper body back, her nose crinkled. "Ouch, what's this lump I just rubbed my cheek against," she palmed my chest.

A wave of misery flooded my entire body as I dug at the neck of my shirt and pulled out a slim chain. Two wedding rings dangled heavily at the end.

Summer looped the chain through one finger and inspected the rings.

"Are these…"

"Troy and Ellen's wedding rings? Yeah." I slumped against the kitchen counter as the weight of two precious heir-looms slid against her fingers while she inspected them. One was a single diamond perched above a dainty gold band; the other was a larger, thicker, textured style men's ring.

"The funeral home gave them to you?"

I cleared my throat. "Ellen apparently wore Troy's around her neck. I didn't know what to do with them, so I added hers to his and put them around my neck for now. I'm sure TJ will want them down the road."

"That's really sweet, you keeping them together like that."

"Their love was unreal," I smiled solemnly. "They wouldn't be happy if they weren't together."

"Yeah?" She reached for the untouched glass of wine and took my hand. I grabbed my glass and followed her over to the fireplace where the flames were already warming the entire room. Summer tugged on my hand as she sat on the cushy sectional in front of the hearth. "Have a seat and tell me about them. We've talked a lot about how they left this Earth, but not much about how they lived. I want to know Troy and Ellen through your eyes."

She pulled her legs up underneath her, sitting sideways. I followed her lead and got comfortable next to her, one of our knees touching.

"Well, I told you we were childhood friends. We met in the orphanage first, then added Erik to the mix through our school connections. Ellen was at the girls' orphanage and Troy and I at the boys. Since we went to the same school, we all became fast friends. Troy was gone for Ellen from the moment he laid eyes on her."

"Total insta-love, my favorite romance genre," she replied with a dreamy gaze.

"I'm not sure I'd describe it like that, but he certainly would. Ellen was a harder nut to crack. Like most orphans, trust didn't come easy for us. But Troy was determined to prove his intentions. From the time they held hands to their first kiss, he swore to Erik and me that he was going to marry her. His confidence never swayed, not even for a moment. We thought he was girl-crazy, but he would just tell us he was crazy for Ellen. No one rose above her. She was the stars, the sky, the sun and the moon. We were mere humans compared to her."

"When did they get married?"

"Right out of high school. The second they could, they did. The Johansen's helped plan a small affair, being the only nurturing adults in our lives. They even let all of us live with them after we aged out of the orphanage. Erik and I went off to university, and Troy went to flight school while Ellen attended community college. Erik got heavily into the science behind brewing beer while getting a degree in business. I went further, going for my masters. By the time I finished, Erik's beer business had blown up. He needed help, and I needed a job. Together, we grew the company year by year. Eventually we were so big we needed a regular pilot. That's where Troy came in."

"Sounds like the plot to a movie. And TJ?"

With that question, my smile stretched so large my jaw ached. "Ellen had been feeling under the weather for a couple months. Every time we saw her, she looked pale and, frankly, rather gaunt. Erik and I reamed Troy. We told him we knew something was wrong with her, and we were upset they were hiding it from us. We were truly worried. We thought maybe she was very ill. Turned out she was pregnant."

Summer sighed merrily and pressed her free hand to her cheek, her elbow braced on the back cushion. "How did they tell you?"

"It was so cheesy." I laughed out loud, remembering the moment like it was yesterday.

Summer wiggled in her seat. "Tell me!"

I grinned, took a sip of wine and thought back to that night. "Well, we were at Sunday dinner, something we'd done for years. If everyone was around, we'd eat a meal together on Sundays. That day, Ellen was pushing food around her plate instead of eating it. Again, the woman looked like shit but didn't seem unhappy in the least."

"Because they had a secret." Summer waggled her eyebrows.

I chuckled at her eagerness. "At one point, I put my fork down and stood up in the middle of dinner, demanding that they either share what was going on, or I was leaving and not coming back. It was an empty threat, but I'd had it with whatever secret they were keeping."

"Ellen told me to sit my ass down and wait. Then she went over to the Christmas tree—it was a couple weeks before the holiday—and grabbed two brightly packed boxes and handed them to us."

"What was in the present?" Summer breathed, caught up

in the story.

"At first, I didn't want the present. I wanted to know if my best friend was sick. Ellen pointed at the present and said our answers were in there. Both Erik and I ripped open the packages and found a picture frame with a black image and a blurry white blob. The frame was garish with little plastic jewels glued all over it. The words "Best Uncle" had been painted on the top."

"Oh my god! That is sooooooo cute."

"Neither Erik nor I had any idea what we were looking at, never having seen an ultrasound picture before. We stared at the picture like a couple of idiots until Erik was brave enough to ask what we were looking at."

Summer started to laugh, covering her pretty mouth as she did so.

"Ellen pointed at the frame and told us to read the words. When we still looked at her like idiots again..."

Summer was chortling and snorting through her laughter.

"Ellen finally put us out of our misery stating they were pregnant, and that we were going to be uncles. She explained that the image was the sonogram of the baby. They had wanted to wait to surprise us at Christmas but realized pretty quickly that we did not miss how sick Ellen had become."

"That's awesome," Summer said.

"I still have that picture sitting on my desk in my office in Oslo. I'll show it to you sometime."

"I'd love that. And to see your workplace."

"Speaking of work, everything okay in California?"

Summer pressed her lips together and looked over at the fire. "Mmm hmm," she said without looking me in the eye.

"*Solskinn*, you don't ever need to withhold the truth from me. Whatever it is, you can always tell me."

She sighed deeply and sipped on her wine, while staring at the crackling flames. "Dad said there were some problems back home but nothing he couldn't handle from here with the team we have in place."

"Oh, what kind of problems?"

"Some activists picketing in front of the road to our farm."

"That doesn't sound good."

She ran her hand through her golden hair. "No, it doesn't, but it happens every year or two. There's still a major stigma about the recreational use of cannabis, even though it's been legal for years in California. Usually, it's just a small group of religious right-wingers that believe we're growing the devil's drugs. Eventually they burn out after a few days of screaming their views, receiving no attention from the media or us, and then everything goes back to normal."

"And this time is different?"

She bit into her bottom lip. "Apparently a couple of them jumped the fences at night and trashed one of our smaller outside gardens by pouring some kind of chemical over the plants. We lost over two hundred plants before they were caught."

I sucked in a sharp breath. "Is that going to be a steep hit to the business financially?"

Summer shrugged one shoulder.

"Do you not know?"

"Honestly, Jack, I don't really care right now."

That had me abruptly sitting upright and paying close attention. So much so, I set my glass of wine on the coffee table and grabbed hers and placed it next to the other one. Then I clasped both of her hands in mine.

"Summer, what do you mean you don't care? This sounds like a major problem that needs your attention as the owner. Or at the very least, your father's."

She shook her head. "I know I should care. I really should. But after what happened with Ellen and my new role as a guardian...as a *mother* to TJ...I find I'm just not as interested in Humble Buds as I was before all of this."

Fear, as nasty and ugly as a pus-filled wound rippled through me. "Summer, you cannot start giving up things that matter to you because our circumstances have changed."

"I can't?" She tipped her head to the side. "Honey, I already have. I spoke to my father at length over the past week. The things I find important have shifted. My job now is to protect, nurture, and love TJ and you."

"That doesn't mean you have to give up your dream," I blurted, uncertainty making the hair on my forearms rise.

"I'm not giving up my dream. I just realized my dream has evolved into something new. Now when I picture myself, I don't see myself grinding away day in and day out on the farm. Of course I'll spend time there and work part-time, but until he's in school, I see myself with TJ. Showing him the world. Making a home for us the way my parents did. You see, my mother and father didn't give up anything when they had us. They did change though. Mom lost interest in the things that took her away from me and Autumn. Instead, she spent her time teaching us and building memories. She contributed to the family the way she and my dad agreed upon. He'd make the money; she'd keep the house and home running."

"Summer, I need you to understand that, as my wife, you will have all the help you could ever need. We can hire a nanny, a cook, a housekeeper. Whatever is necessary in order for us to have our careers and our family."

"I know that, Jack. I do. I can afford all of those things myself, but I don't want them." She lifted her hand and cupped my scruffy cheek. "And I will find a healthy balance between work and family, but you and TJ need me present right now. I'm not going to have a stranger raise him. He needs us more than anything, and I'm happy to be here. What I will need, is your expertise in hiring a CEO. One that can take Humble Buds where it should go, while realizing that my dad and I are the brains behind the company's success. We handle the plants and will never give up that portion of it. I can do the work I love, with TJ by my side or with him hanging out with Grandma while I knock out a few hours here and there. It's literally her dream to watch her grandkids while her daughters build their lives. And I imagine, if we're here in Norway, we'll have plenty of backup with the Johansens too."

This woman was a living dream come true. I don't know what I did to deserve her, but she's everything I could have ever wanted. Still, this is a big decision, one that shouldn't be made lightly.

"I want you to keep thinking about it. I can step down from Johansen Brewing too. Between the two of us, we have enough money to live multiple lifetimes. Neither of us needs to work, but we're both committed to these companies because it's part of who we are."

"And it's our legacy to TJ and our future children."

Future children.

At the talk of having more kids with Summer, my heartbeat thrummed like a base drum against my chest. Imagining her rounded in pregnancy, TJ clinging to her leg, not only filled me to bursting with love, but also lust. Plowing into Summer's gorgeous body, impregnating her…

"Fuck," I stood abruptly and adjusted my hardening shaft.

Summer's eyebrows rose up toward her hairline as her gaze took in my not so little problem. "Looks like someone likes the idea of having kids with me." She got up onto her knees and licked her lips. "Should we try right now? The odds are not in our favor yet, but practice makes perfect."

I stood there like a raging bull staring down a matador waving a red flag. My fingertips throbbed with the desire to touch her when I watched her breath hitch, her pupils dilate, and her nipples become erect against the sexy little cotton nightgown she worn.

Before I could say a single word, she stood up, lifted the hem of her nightgown and pulled it over her head. She was blissfully naked underneath. Her skin glowed against the flickering firelight.

"I'm getting cold. You gonna stare at me all night or come warm me up?"

My gaze danced from her perfect full breasts, rounded stomach, nipped in waist and curvy hips. She was the sun, pure radiance, and light. I was the darkness that sometimes eclipsed that light, but never completely, because she was so bright, her brilliance would always shine through.

"I'm going to spend a lifetime loving you, Summer."

"A lifetime is too short. I'm shooting for eternity. Now get over here and show me how good eternity is going to feel being with you."

"My pleasure, *solskinn*."

Episode 90

Blissful Ignorance

MADAM ALANA

The morning after our kidnapping had been brutal. Watching Emily give her statement to Inspector Moreau ripped my heart into a million tiny pieces. No child should have to go through what she did yesterday, nor should she have to experience the pain of sharing that trauma with the authorities. I will admit that Detective Moreau was kind, fair, and gentle with his interview. Emily did cry, however, which made Rhodes stiffen, but he didn't stop the interview.

What none of us were prepared for was how angry Maia became at seeing Emily's discomfort. At one point she flat out looked at Emily and said, "If this is hurting you, we can stop. I don't care who this information helps. You want out? Your dad and I will make that happen. Right Rhodes?" Maia had looked at Rhodes with such determination and grit, it was almost as if she dared him right then and there to override her claim.

He did no such thing. He actually nodded and squeezed his daughter's shoulders and said, "Maia's right. You've been through a lot, honey, and if this is too much, we stop now. I'll contact our lawyers to do the talking for us."

Emily's bottom lip had trembled but instead of taking the easy way out, she shook her head and told them she'd like to tell the inspector everything she could. She said she hoped it would help Moreau and his team catch the bad man before he hurt anyone else. Pride filled the room as Emily proved just how brave she could be.

After the interview, Rhodes, Maia, and Emily packed up their things and were gone within the hour. I was relieved when they left. Rhodes claimed he had a team of people to protect them and felt strongly that he needed to get his daughter back home to California. I couldn't have agreed more. This wasn't about Emily and Rhodes. Even though Maia's place had been trashed, I still didn't believe it was about her either. It was about me, Christophe, Celine, and Angus.

When we were kidnapped, they made it clear they were only taking Emily because they wanted my cooperation. Angus didn't make a single mention of Maia when we spoke yesterday. That makes me believe that Maia was insurance. My guess: I was being watched back in Las Vegas, and those people informed Angus how fond I'd become of Maia.

But why did a woman make the request to threaten Maia?

Where is that woman now?

The only person who knows the answer to that particular question is my morally dubious contact in the Latin mafia… Diego.

"Mrs. Toussaint, before I leave, I must insist that you and your husband come with me and allow the French authorities to put you in a safe house until Angus Sokolov is caught." Inspector Moreau's gaze and tone were pleading. He seemed genuinely worried that Angus was going to come after me at any moment. I had the same concerns.

"I agree, Alana," Christophe added.

I narrowed my gaze at my husband. "Mr. Moreau, can

you give us some privacy please?" I asked.

"*Oui*, of course. I'm going to speak with the security team. Please think about the safe house. It really is the best option for everyone involved." With that parting comment, the inspector left the room.

"Darling, we need to do as the inspector says. It's the safest plan," Christophe pushed.

"You know," I crossed my arms over my chest and leaned against the kitchen counter. "We wouldn't be in this predicament if you'd just left well enough alone all those years ago."

Christophe winced as his shoulders slumped, and he closed his eyes. "That isn't fair Alana, and you know it."

Seeing his pain made my own heart physically ache. Christophe and I didn't carelessly harm one another. Since the beginning of our relationship, we had always been one hundred percent honest with one another in all things… except this, it seemed. Which, truthfully, was more upsetting than anything else. I wasn't angry at him for doing what he did, I was hurt by the fact that he didn't share it with me. For years I'd lived in blissful ignorance.

"But is it true?" My voice shook as I admitted the ugly feelings bubbling in my soul and soiling the trust I'd always had in him.

"I will admit that I should have told you what I'd done. Now, I regret that decision, but would I have made the same one again?" His gaze shot to mine, and I could see straight through to the open, honest, beautiful soul beneath. "I'd do it again. For Celine…but mostly, I'd do it again for *you*. He harmed the one person I vowed to love, honor, and protect until my last breath. I wouldn't be the man you love today if I'd sat back and let him get away with carving scars into your heart the way he did. Celine has always been a part of you. I know that. You wouldn't be the woman I'm devoted to without carrying around a piece of her. And he helped take a piece of you away. Lost forever. I could not in good conscience allow that to go unpunished. And if that means I'm going to spend the rest of my life making up for it, then that's what I'm prepared to do. Because you, Alana, own my entire heart. You are my everything."

Tears fell down my cheeks as a broken sob tore through my body. My knees became weak, and my legs felt like jelly as I lost my footing and crumbled toward the ground. The pain of it all had become too much. My knees never touched the floor because Christophe was there, lifting me up, holding me in his warm embrace. Proving time and time again that he'd always be there for me. Even when he was the source of my anger, he was still there, protecting me from harm.

"I love you so much, Christo. I can't stay mad at you. I can't live with this hideous feeling of betrayal between us."

"You can," he murmured into my ear. "Be mad at me for as long as you need. Punish me in whatever way will help you trust me again. I will still be here, ready to catch you if you fall. Ready to take whatever hits are necessary to make amends."

"Hearing the rationale behind why you chose that path…" I choked on a sob. "I understand. If I'd had the opportunity to double-cross Angus after his part in Celine's death, I might have made the very same decision. No. I *would* have made the same choice. She was my family. My chosen sister. The only person in the world who loved me before I met you. I can see that, when given the opportunity, you had no choice but to do right by her. I only wish I'd been a part of it."

He cupped my cheeks and wiped away the tears that kept falling. "Celine didn't deserve what happened to her. You didn't deserve what happened to her. I made a choice to act on behalf of both of you. I don't regret that. But I can promise you right here, right now, on my life and yours, that I will never keep a single thing from you again. Can you ever forgive me?"

I lifted one hand and put my palm over his heart. The other I placed at the back of his neck and looked deeply into his eyes. "I forgive you."

Tears shimmered in his eyes as he dipped his head and took my mouth in a deep kiss. It lasted a long time and said everything we'd left unsaid.

I missed you.

I trust you.

I love you.

It was reaffirming and exactly what I needed to get myself back on track. Until a loud blast and the sound of shattering glass ripped through the room, bringing us back to the real world. Christophe slammed my body to the floor, covering me completely with his bulk.

Inspector Moreau bolted into the kitchen, gun drawn, right as another few gunshots exploded through the balcony glass door. He slid to the ground and crawled over to us.

"Are either of you hurt?"

We both shook our heads.

Moreau grabbed a radio from his belt and yelled commands into it. "Back garden. Shots fired through the balcony window. Look for a sharpshooter in the trees. Hurry!"

Another couple bullets whizzed through air, piercing the upper cabinets across from where we were huddled behind the island.

We could hear answering shots fired outside by those I assumed to be the authorities.

"One man down. Sniper rifle in hand. We got him, but he won't be sharing any intel," came a rushed voice through the radio.

"Let's go. Now!" Moreau demanded. "We cannot keep you here. It isn't safe."

"And you know a place that would be safer?" I asked as I crawled across the kitchen floor toward the back staircase that led to the second floor. "These men snatched us in a public place after killing our security team. They have the balls to attack us in our home while the authorities are present. You are not a deterrent for them," I snapped. "I'm sorry, inspector. I don't believe for a moment you can keep us safe." With that, I climbed the rest of the stairs, Christophe in tow. We both crouched down and headed toward our room where Aurelie had already packed our bags.

I sat on the floor next to the bed, out of the view of the windows, just in case, and pulled out my phone.

"Who are you calling?" Christophe asked.

"The one man we know who can probably help us out of this mess."

Christophe's eyebrows rose but he kept his mouth shut.

Moreau entered the doorway and crouched low. "My team hasn't found another shooter. We should be okay for now."

I ignored the inspector and dialed the number I should have called the second we were freed yesterday.

"*Hola señora.*" Diego answered on the first ring. "I am surprised you are among the living. Sokolov doesn't tend to leave loose ends."

"I'm starting to see that. I'm calling in my marker."

"How can I help?"

"We need a new safe house," I started.

"Done. And?"

"We need a way to get to that safe house. We were just shot at in our home by a sniper in a tree."

"Sounds about right. There will be more than one sniper. Angus doesn't do anything by halves," Diego shared.

I directed my next words to Moreau. "My friend says that there will be more than one shooter. Have your men look again."

"Who's your friend?" Moreau asked.

I looked at Christophe and listened to Diego breathe through the receiver, not saying a word. Now was the time to choose sides. Who did I trust to keep me and Christo alive? Someone who followed every rule in the book, or someone who threw the book out and wrote their own.

"None of your business. Please have your men do another check of the premises."

Moreau scowled and his nostrils flared. "You know, I can't keep you safe if you don't tell me the whole truth," he growled and then left the room, barking more orders into his radio.

"Wise decision, *amiga*. Six blacked-out identical SUVs will arrive within an hour. Each one will pull into your garage for a total of three minutes a piece. Get into the fourth vehicle. Do not take a minute more or less before exiting. We're going to play the shell game with Sokolov's men. Two of the SUVs will go in a different direction at the same time. You and your husband will be driven to a parking garage where both SUVs will go in and come right out. The two of you, however, will get out in that garage and enter the trunk of another vehicle. That car will leave thirty minutes after the SUVs depart and head to another garage where you will do the same thing. Are you listening?"

"I've heard every word. Do you really think this will work?" Fear pressed against my temples making my head throb.

"There's only one way to find out. *Vaya con Dios, señora.*" He said and hung up.

Quickly I explained all that Diego planned to Christophe.

"Well, what do you think?" I asked my husband.

"I don't think we have any other option than to trust the mafia boss. He helped our friends."

"Yeah, and a lot of people died," I reminded him about the situation with Joel and Faith and the warehouse full of men that lost their lives when they were trying to save Faith.

"Our only other choice is going along with the authorities," Christophe explained, and he was right. Either we go with the advice of Inspector Moreau or the mafia boss with a positive track record for handling terrifying criminals.

"I'd rather take my chances with Diego," I whispered.

"Me too," Christophe said and then pecked me on the lips as though sealing the deal.

As outlined by Diego, an hour later, six SUVs showed up. The authorities still hadn't found anyone else on the property, but I believed Diego. He had no reason to lie to me. I explained the plan to Inspector Moreau. He didn't like it, but I gave him no alternative. He couldn't make me go with the authorities, but he could help make sure we got away, which is what he agreed to do.

When the first black SUV pulled into the garage, we waited the three minutes as instructed and watched it leave while the second SUV rolled in. Before the first SUV even reached the gate to exit, we could hear bullets flying.

It took everything I had not to get into that second SUV. Still, we stayed strong, hidden in the corner of the garage no one could see from any direction as the second left and the third, and finally the fourth SUV rolled in. The moment the garage door came down, we bolted over to the back of the vehicle and Christophe and I climbed inside with our small suitcases.

"There's a blanket back there. Cover yourselves," the driver demanded in heavily accented English. "The car is bulletproof. The tires are not. Cross your fingers we make it out the gate," he said and then waited for an alarm to go off before we heard the garage door go back up.

The gunshots slamming into the vehicle were like golf-ball-sized hail hitting the SUV as the driver backed out of the garage at top speed just like the others had before him. He swung a U-turn as though the car was driving on rails and then punched the gas, jolting forward at top speed. I was too afraid to be seen so I kept my eyes closed, my head covered by the blanket and held my husband's hand. Christophe whispered words of comfort against my cheek. His breath was hot and his cheek sweaty, but I clung to those words with my entire spirit.

Soon we were racing down the country roads.

"We've made it out. That's step one," the driver announced. "Stay hidden."

We did everything we were told. Even got into the terrifyingly small trunk of a Peugeot and waited in the pitch-dark trunk for thirty minutes before we felt the car start and head out onto the road again.

As promised, we were driven to another carpark where we were let out of the Peugeot and instructed to get into the trunk of a new blacked-out SUV. This time, we didn't have to wait. It was getting dark, and I knew by the time we arrived wherever the safehouse was, it would be well into the evening. My stomach rumbled and Christophe squeezed my hand.

"I'm sure we'll be there soon," he murmured.

A full hour later, after what felt like endless twists and turns, the SUV finally came to a stop. We were let out into a huge warehouse sized garage with at least a dozen extremely expensive European cars all lined up, shining under the bright fluorescent lights above.

"Come," the driver instructed.

Christophe grabbed our two small suitcases and we followed our rescuers into what turned out to be a luxury home. We entered a massive kitchen where a petite full-figured older woman of Latin descent was actively cooking a feast. The scent of spiced meat and Spanish rice filtered through the air and made my mouth water.

"*¡Hola amigos!*" a man said in a deep voice from somewhere behind us. We both turned around and were shocked to see Diego Salazar in the flesh. "Welcome to my European home." He pointed to the woman cooking. "That's *Mamá.*"

She turned around, spatula in hand and said, "*Espero que tengan hambre,*" and pointed the cooking utensil at us both before going back to her task.

"*Mamá* says she hopes you are hungry. She likes to feed people."

"Diego? What are you doing here?" Christophe asked, for which I was grateful because I was honest to God speechless.

He was absolutely the last person I'd expected to see.

"What?" He held out his hands and grinned like a maniac. "And let you have all the fun?"

Episode 91

Only a Matter of Time

JULIANNE

My head hurt like a bitch when I slowly came to. Bright white, red and yellow lights flashed across my vision in a kaleidoscope of blurry streaks of colors. People were screaming commands as though they were speaking through a bullhorn. I was jostled around on what I believed to be a stretcher.

"Suspected blunt force trauma, deep laceration on the forehead, abrasions and first degree burns on forearms and hands," a man in a medical uniform hollered as I was rushed through a series of hospital doors. Glaringly white walls blinded me, and I closed my eyes again.

"Miss, try to stay awake. Listen to my voice. You're in the hospital. We're going to take good care of you. Can you tell me your name?" a dark-haired woman asked. She was wearing scrubs and was using a stethoscope to listen to my chest. She spoke, but her words morphed and changed, sounding garbled and hard to follow. It felt like the sounds around me were getting louder and then fading away.

"Giovanni..." I whispered. My mouth felt as dry as the

Sahara Desert, making it difficult to speak. "Hus-band," I managed to get out.

"Two men were brought in with you. They are receiving help now. Let's focus on you," the doctor said, and I swear it was as if she'd screamed it right into my ear. I winced and tried to lift my hands, but they hurt too much.

"Gio!" I croaked finally putting the pieces back together of what happened.

We were at the office. My brother was being an asshole as usual. Then we heard that ominous beeping sound. Gio pulled me away from Brenden and pushed me down and underneath him. Then everything went black.

I need to get to Gio!

"Gio!" I felt myself open my mouth to scream his name but could only manage a guttural whisper.

Someone was putting pressure on my forehead. It hurt, sending fire bolting through every one of my nerve endings. My heart beat so hard I thought it might explode outside of my chest, and I couldn't catch my breath.

Suddenly, everything around me became hazier and more blurred until I passed out.

* * * *

When I woke up the second time, I was in a hospital bed. The room was dimly lit. A dark figure approached.

"Gio?" I rasped.

"Sorry Julianne, it's me, Bruno," he said as my eyes acclimated, and his features became distinct. The wavy curls of his layered hair. The scruffy beard and mustache combo. The tight expression on his handsome face.

"Gio?" I croaked.

"They're both in surgery. Gio's being treated for a compound fracture in his arm, a series of lacerations from the explosion and second-degree burns along his back and legs.

The doctors wouldn't tell me anything, so I had my guy Jonas hack the system. I'm sorry to say it doesn't look good for Brenden, Julianne. He received the brunt of the explosion. We don't know Gio's full prognosis yet, but based on what a doctor on my team read in his file, he will likely make a painful but full recovery." He squeezed my ankle for emphasis.

The wave of relief hearing Gio would ultimately be okay brought tears to my eyes. "Thank you." I looked down at my arms. They were wrapped from forearm to fingertips in bandages. "And these?" I held up my arms the best I could.

"I'm sure the doctor will go over the details with you, but from what we gathered in your chart, those are first-degree burns. You should heal up just fine. Though you received a concussion and a nasty cut on your head from smacking into the wall where a glass picture frame was. They stitched you up and gave you some medication for the pain."

I winced as I lifted my right hand to my forehead and felt the bandage wrapped around my head.

"What happened?" I asked Bruno.

He shook his head. "Best I can tell, someone broke in and placed the bomb prior to our arrival. Based on the fact that the bomb was attached to Brenden's office door, a door that was clearly marked as his, tells me he was the target of that explosion, not you or Giovanni."

"You think Bianca wanted to kill her own husband to get the insurance payout?"

Bruno tilted his head. "You seem surprised. We're talking about the same woman that sexually assaulted Giovanni, cheated on her fiancé at their rehearsal dinner with his best friend, married that friend, and is pregnant with one of their babies? Who also was magically released from jail and fled the country. I wouldn't put anything past her," he said while rubbing his chin.

I let out a long sigh. "I know, I know. It's just that Brenden has backed her every step of the way. He chose her over his best friend and even his own sister." I gulped against the need to swallow the emotional pain that went with that truth.

"Unfortunately, it doesn't mean she had the same loyalty to him," he replied gently.

"No, it doesn't." Why I would think evil people could be loyal was beyond me. "If he dies from this explosion, she gets the payout right?"

He nodded. "Twenty-five million dollars to be exact. Provided there isn't proof that she planted it. And seeing as she was nowhere near the offices or in the same country, it sure gives her a pretty ironclad alibi."

I closed my eyes and breathed in through my nose and out my mouth for a full five breaths, trying to get my anger under control. I needed to think all of this through, but my brain felt foggy, my thoughts all muddled together.

"Look, you rest. I'm going to touch base with my guys. I've got a couple members of my security team keeping an eye on your room, just to be extra cautious."

I nodded. "Thank you. When can I see Gio?"

"I don't know. I'll look into it." He walked over to the table then filled a cup of water for me. He added a straw and held it to my lips.

I drank greedily until some dribbled down my chin. Bruno lifted the cotton blanket and patted the water away. "You need to rest up. I don't imagine things are going to get any easier for you. I'll have the doctor come in to speak with you."

"Thank you, Bruno." I reached out until he took my hand, tightened his grip, and then let it go.

"You're welcome." He moved to leave my room.

"Bruno," I called out.

He turned, his hand on the doorknob. "Yeah?"

"Please find her. I want justice. No..." I swallowed the torturous emotions swelling and ebbing throughout my body.

"I *need* justice."

"I'll do my best." He said the words as though they were a vow. One I had to hold onto with my entire being in order to keep myself together.

Bianca would get hers.

It was only a matter of time.

* * * *

Two agonizing days later, Giovanni started coming back to me. He had been on heavy pain and agitation medication but was finally making progress. He was lying on his side due to the patchwork of injuries the doctors had to mend on his back, not including the burns. Thankfully, right before the explosion, Giovanni got us mostly around a corner wall leading to a hallway. That wall protected us more than anything else. Had he not, we both would have been injured far worse. We'd be in a medically induced coma fighting for our lives like my brother was. I was discharged the morning after I arrived but had been at my husband's side ever since.

Things did not look good for Brenden, and the doctors made it clear it would take a miracle for him to survive the next couple weeks. I wasn't sure how to feel about his condition. On the one hand, he'd put us through absolute hell. On the other, he was my blood. My brother. My family. At least he was before Hurricane Bianca tore through our family and shredded us to bits. Now I wasn't sure what was left of us.

"Hey," I spoke low in case Gio was having the same sensitivity to sound that I was. I put my hand on his cheek, delighting in feeling the renewed warmth there. He'd been so cold the last two days.

His glassy eyes stared at me, flicking from one point to another on my face before doing it all over again. Those grey orbs filled with tears and my heart broke as they fell down his cheeks, relief evident in his gaze.

"I thought you were dead," he rasped.

I smiled through my own tears. "You're not getting rid of me just yet, Mister," I teased then dipped my head to rest my injured forehead lightly to his. I winced but breathed through the pain. "Don't ever scare me like that again," I whispered and licked the salty tears from my lips. "Not ever again, Gio. I can't do this alone."

"I'm sorry," he murmured.

I cupped both of his cheeks. "You saved us. You have nothing to be sorry for."

"Brenden…I could only save one. I chose you," he muttered. "I'll always choose you, Jules."

A sob tore through me. "I'll always choose you too." I gently pressed my lips to his.

He lifted one of his hands to cup the back of my head, keeping me in place as he held the firm kiss. Then I felt the weight of his hand slowly slip away as he let go, his body easing back to the bed as his eyes closed. He fell back to sleep.

I ran my fingers through his hair at the crown of his head. The back layers had been singed by the explosion. He'd need a haircut when all this was over, but I was grateful the bulk of his luxurious black locks were still in place. I traced his brow, cheeks, and lips as he slept, needing to feel him alive and breathing underneath my fingertips. He had quite a long way to go before he would be well enough to leave the hospital, but him waking on his own was a good sign.

In the meantime, I needed to touch base with Bruno on the search for Bianca.

Thinking of the devil must have conjured him because right as I was about to pull my phone out and call him, the man himself appeared at the doorway. He was just about to knock, his knuckle poised against the wood.

"How's he doing?"

"He woke up for a couple minutes. Doctors say he'll

sleep a lot over the coming days, but they've taken him off the harder drugs while still managing his pain."

"Do they know when he'll get to go home?"

I shook my head. "Too early to tell."

Bruno nodded as he rubbed his hands slowly together and looked down at the floor. "I have news but it's not good news."

I frowned. "Okay..."

"You remember how, before the explosion, my team tracked Bianca down to a small town in France?"

"Yeah, Mouroux. We were worried about how close that was to my godmother Alana."

Bruno's jaw firmed and he pursed his lips. "Julianne, I had my men go to the Toussaint estate in France."

Dread, thick and doughy covered me in a blanket of fear. "What did they find?" I pleaded.

"Fuck Jules, I don't know how to tell you this," he grated through clenched teeth.

"Is she...is she..." I started to tremble as my vision became spotty, imagining the worst.

Bruno came to my chair, kneeled down, and took my hands in his. "Her home was shot up with multiple rounds from what could only be assault rifles."

I pulled one of my hands from his to cover my mouth as I gasped.

"A few days ago, Alana and a young girl by the name of Emily Davenport were kidnapped from a tourist attraction. The Palace of Versailles to be exact."

"Bianca has them?" I asked, remembering the girl who attended my wedding. Emily was her name.

She was so young. Barely a teenager if memory served. I knew her father, Rhodes, but only in a business capacity. Rhodes had primarily worked with Giovanni for the most part, securing land purchases for the high-rises and resorts he was known for building. And I recalled Alana mentioning she'd gotten close to the man over the years, especially since he'd designed and built their first home. That still didn't answer why Bianca would have them kidnapped.

He shook his head. "I don't…just listen. There's more. After the last auction, Alana and one of her candidates received threatening messages. Rhodes Davenport was the bidder and winner for that candidate, who is named Maia."

"Now Maia I know, because we met in person at the auction…"

"Maia is more than just a candidate of Alana's. Apparently, Alana had taken a liking to the young girl. I had a call with Jade Lee, Alana's protégé, who claimed the Madam doted on the young woman, but she didn't know their history."

"Then why didn't I know her better? And what does this have to do with Bianca?"

"I can't answer that. Only Alana can. However, the good news is that Alana and Emily were found and taken into custody along with several men. Most notably a man by the name of Dimitri Volkov. Do you know that name?"

I shook my head.

"He's the second in command of a very violent Russian militia group the authorities have been trying to take down for the better part of two decades."

"Okay…and this is connected to Alana and Bianca how?"

"Bianca Cameron is actually Bianca Volkov, the real wife of Dimitri. However, before that she was Bianca Sokolov."

"And this information is important because…"

"Bianca is the daughter of a man named Angus Sokolov. Does that name ring a bell?"

The hair on the back of my neck rose at the mention of the one man I knew my godmother hated. I'd even used his name and memory as a taunt to get her to put me in the auction. Threatened to actually call him for help if she didn't put me in. It was a fucking joke. I'd never do that. I wouldn't have even known how to contact that man.

"He was the person who originally brought my parents into The Marriage Auction before Alana took it over. They were her very first contract…a true love match."

"Well, that just notched a piece of the puzzle right into place."

"How so?" I asked as my mind spun with all the information Bruno had shared.

"Motive for one. Alana took away the thing that made him a lot of money. Your parents were the first big payout he lost, and it was big."

"Where is Alana now?" I needed to know if she was okay.

"We don't know exactly. As I said, there was some type of showdown at her estate. The French authorities stated in their reports that they'd interviewed everyone, and that Rhodes, Maia, and Emily had gotten on a private plane to Los Angeles. They're being watched not only by the police but by a team of guards Rhodes hired."

"Okay, that's good news, kinda. What about Alana?"

"The showdown at her estate happened after the Davenports left, once again proving the clear target was the Toussaints. The authorities noted taking down two armed men with sniper rifles during the firefight."

"Were Alana or Christophe hurt?" I swallowed down the fear of losing yet another member of my dwindling family.

He shook his head. "No. That's where it gets tricky. They escaped with the help of a very powerful man."

"Jesus. This is getting crazier by the minute."

Bruno stood up and ran his hand through his curls. "Oh, that's only half of it," he claimed in a weary tone.

"Why?"

"Because I was informed that the person that helped them escape was Diego Salazar, the leader of the West Coast Latin Mafia."

Episode 92

Just When Things Were Looking Good

MEMPHIS

I entered my parents' house to the sound of female laughter coming from the kitchen. I'd received a text earlier from Naomi, saying she'd found the perfect wedding dress, would be hanging out with the ladies for the rest of the afternoon, and to meet at their house for dinner. I followed the sweet sound of my family's voices, cackling and screaming over one another. In a house with five sisters, my momma, and my granny, Dad and me, the house could get noisy on a normal day. Today, the decibel level was turned way up. It became clear why they were all hyped up when I entered the kitchen and saw my woman, head tilted back and laughing like a hyena right along with my sister Syd.

Naomi's gaze came to mine as I approached.

"Baby!" she said at a volume astronauts could have heard in outer space.

I scanned the room and noted my mother, my gran, and Syd loaded up with huge glasses of wine. On the table were a couple of empty bottles.

"Don't you worry, I got more comin'," my father announced as he entered with not one but two fresh bottles of vino.

Naomi stood and clapped. "Baby, we found the most perfect dress, and you are sooooo gonna wanna bang me when you see it!" she slurred a bit and then hiccupped.

"Damn straight!" Syd hollered. "You'll be giving momma a grandbaby right away!"

"I'll drink to that!" Momma lifted her glass, and braced herself against the kitchen island as she did so.

"From your mouth to the good Lord's ears!" Granny quipped, slugging back the remains of her glass and holding it out to Dad, who promptly added more. "Such a good boy, my son!" Granny cooed in a silly voice.

I shook my head. "You're all drunk."

"As skunks!" Syd blurted, and all four of them burst into laughter.

I went around the table to Naomi, who flung her arms around my neck and planted a kiss to my lips. "Hi, baby!"

"Hey, gorgeous. I see you've been bonding with the ladies, yeah?"

"Your family is sooooooo fuuuuun." She let the words drag out far longer than normal, clearly allowing the alcohol to do the talking.

Sydney held her glass up in salute. "We're gonna be your family too, sis."

The elder Taylor women did the same. "To Naomi joining the family! Whoo hoo!" Syd hollered, and the rest of the ladies followed.

Just then, my other sisters came bumbling in, talking a mile a minute.

"And Nay says she's going to have one of her fancy friends read through my grant letters to make sure they are really good so I can score as much grant and scholarship money as possible," Paris was saying to Odessa. Both of them were holding three large pizzas from our favorite spot in town. Cheyenne and Holland followed behind, one carrying a bag of sauces, the other with a couple two-liter bottles of Coke.

"Yeah, well, she promised me she'd get me a walk-through at New York-Presbyterian Hospital and a meet and greet with one of their top surgeons! I might even be able to watch a real-life procedure from one of their teaching amphi-theaters," Holland gushed. Holland wanted to be a surgeon one day, so I knew an experience like that would score huge points with her.

I cuddled my woman and kissed her neck, whispering in her ear. "Did you bribe my sisters with things they want in order to score points?"

"Absolutely!" She giggled against my chest.

I couldn't suppress a laugh. "Nay, you don't have to do, say, or give anyone anything to like you. They like you just as you are."

"I know, but a little sweet can go a long way," she whispered, even though no one was paying us any attention, what with their focus locked on the pizzas landing on the island. "And I want your family to know I'm in it for the long haul," she continued.

I cupped her cheeks and stared into her pretty brown eyes. "You are something special, lady. You know that, right?"

"Love you too." She rose on her toes and kissed me rather indecently in front of my family.

Catcalls and whistling commenced as expected.

"All right everyone, let's eat," Momma directed once the plates were set next to the pizzas.

"We're having pizza!" Naomi bounced up and down, her expression filled with excitement. "I can't remember the last time I had pizza."

"We usually have it a couple times a month, and this pie is the best. Did anyone order meat supreme for me?" I called out.

"Of course. What? Do you think it's our first day having you as our brother? Pssshhhhh," Odessa made a rude noise as she answered with all the sass, per usual.

I let Nay go and walked behind Odessa, then kicked the bottom of her shoe the second she lifted her foot to take a step. She stumbled against Dad, her face smooshing right against his arm pit. I held her head there for not even five seconds as she wailed and flung her arms. "Let me go!" she screeched, but it sounded more like, "Wet me dough!"

Finally, I released her, and she took a huge breath as I backed up, grinning. "You earned that!"

"You. Are. So. Dead!" Odessa yelled, as she raised her hands and came at me like a manic bear.

I caught her as she jumped at me, turned her around and tickled the hell out of her ribs until she was on the floor laughing so hard she'd curled up into a little ball.

"That'll teach ya!" I stood to full height and brushed off my shoulders.

"Must you antagonize your sister, son?" Dad chastised with a smile pulling at his lips.

"She started it," I said at the same time as Odessa said, "He started it."

We both cracked up. Some things never changed.

I helped my sister up, tucked her against my chest, gave her a big hug, and kissed her forehead. "Love you, Dess. But you're still a punk," I teased, yanking out her scrunchie and flinging it across the room.

"You suck, you know that?" she growled, playfully pulling her hair out her face. "There better still be some veggie left or I'm coming for you." She pointed two fingers at her eyes and then at me as I let her go and retrieved two plates.

"Nay, what kind of pizza do you want? You've got lots to choose from." I held up an empty plate.

"Surprise me with a couple," she said, back in her seat next to Sydney. Their heads were close together, looking at something on Syd's phone. It warmed my heart to see her getting along so well with the women in my family.

As I glanced around the room, there was nothing but smiles. Everyone was happy and enjoying our time together. I watched as Momma approached Syd and Nay then leaned over my woman's shoulder. Momma pointed at the phone and said something that made Naomi glow with happiness. My mother and my fiancée clinked their wine glasses and took a sip, then turned to focus on whatever had their attention.

My heart filled to the brim with joy as I loaded up my plate with four slices of meat lovers and then picked a slice of pepperoni and vegetarian for my girl. I went to the table and put the plate in front of her.

"Ooh, it looks so good!" She immediately picked up the veggie and took a huge bite, moaning as she did so.

"Bro…where's mine?" Syd pouted as she gestured to the plate I'd brought Naomi.

"Get your own, squirt." I snorted.

Sydney rolled her eyes. "Oh, I see how it is. Hook up with a hottie and then the rest of us are chopped liver."

"Basically." I grinned.

"Whatever!" She groaned and got up, wobbling when she finally stood straight. Then I heard rather than saw her kick off her insanely high shoes, taking her height down a few inches. "Whew! That's better. Let's try this again," she mumbled, holding on to the back of the chairs as she swayed from side to side.

"How much did you guys drink?" I chuckled.

"Well, we started with champagne at the bridal store. That Jennifer chick was badass!" Naomi said. "Wish she could have come tonight," she frowned. "But she's coming to the wedding."

"We talking about your best friend?" I called out knowing Syd would answer.

"Yep!" Syd hollered.

"Did she and Odessa get into it?" I asked Naomi.

"They totally did," Naomi whispered as she leaned closer over the table as though it were a secret. "My money is on Jenn though. That woman owns a room when she's in it."

"Sounds like you respect her."

Naomi nodded avidly while munching on the pepperoni slice. "Mmm hmm. She's in love with love."

"There are worse things in life," I added then finished off one piece, already lifting up another to tackle.

"True, like mean-spirited overlords who think they can control everyone's lives," Naomi bit out.

"Talk to your father today, did you?" I snickered.

"He called while I was buying the dress. I told him I couldn't be bothered to speak to him as I was buying my wedding gown and spending time with my new family. Then I hung up. Serves him right!"

"You didn't!" I blurted, not at all surprised that she would be so bold. Still, I knew that her family not agreeing with our marriage was hurting her. It would upset any child to not have their parents' acceptance.

I just hoped that the love my family and I could give her would help offset some of that loss. And then perhaps, in the future, when they've seen how much I love and cherish their daughter, they could find a way back to being a family, with me as a new addition.

"I did. He even tried to call back and I ignored it," she gushed, clearly proud of herself.

"Damn, baby, looks like you had an eventful day."

"And this pizza, and the memories I'm building with everyone have made it awesome," she breathed, emotion cutting through her tone.

She cleared her throat, and I reached out and took her hand. "I'm glad you had a good day, Nay."

"Me too."

"Also, we have a surprise for the two of you." Dad

braced his hands on his hips, chest puffed up. "When we're all finished in here, we'll show you."

Momma grabbed the lapels of her sweater and held them close to her chest. She smiled beautifully, snuggling up to my father's side. He wrapped an arm around her, then kissed her forehead. They never hid their affection and love for one another. Always demonstrating to us kids that, when you loved someone, you showed it. I wanted to raise my kids exactly the same. With them knowing how much I loved their momma.

An hour later, everyone was finished and the kitchen cleaned of dinner debris. The ladies were coming down from their wine high after some food in their bellies and Dad forcing each of them to drink water in between refills. Everyone was in a happy food, drink, and laughter haze. Gran was in her favorite rocker on the front porch, chatting up the neighbors that walked by, as she did every night. My younger sisters had retired to their rooms to get ready for the new school week, leaving me, Naomi, Syd, Odessa, Mom, and Dad.

Dad was twitching with anticipation as he approached Momma, who had just dried and put away the last dish.

"We ready now?" he asked, clearly eager to get the surprise underway.

She lifted her hand, cupped his cheek and smiled. "You betcha. Let's get the lovebirds," I heard her murmur before giving Dad a peck on the lips. "Such a softie," she teased and kissed him again.

Naomi squeezed my hand and nuzzled my shoulder.

"Come on, son, Naomi. We've got something to show you," he boasted, pride in his tone.

I stood and helped Naomi rise from the table. We followed my parents out back, Dad leading the way. His limp was there, but I also noted a lightness to his footsteps. They led us around the biggest section of the yard. At one end stood a wooden riser with a brand new beautiful wooden arbor.

My mouth fell open in shock. "What is this?"

I'd never seen the arbor before, but it was obvious it had taken many hours, possibly weeks to craft. Even from a few feet away, I could smell the scent of the cedar the creator had used to make it. There were carved leaf etchings across the front facing beam that must have taken forever to whittle. The entire piece was sturdy and intricate. Each new bit added more splendor to the whole.

"Your father made it," Momma said with extreme pride.

I gasped. "No way."

"When he was let go from the trucking company and eventually got better use of the leg, he started working on this in the little shed off the garage. He's been super hush-hush about it for the past year. At first, I thought it was just for me, but then I realized why he made it."

"So my children could all get married under something I made with love from my bare hands. What do you think, son? Will you and Naomi do me the honor of starting your life together right here, under this arbor?" Dad asked, his voice filled with hope.

"It is incredible." It was more than that actually; it was breathtaking and absolutely perfect for my wedding to Naomi. Though I wanted my fiancée to have a say. "What do you think, Nay?"

Her eyes were glassy with unshed tears, but she powered through, stepping up onto the riser and evaluating each detail up close. I could already imagine her there standing in a white dress, saying *I do* before me and all my family.

"I say yes, but I need to confirm one thing before we get married underneath this beautiful piece," she hedged.

"And that would be?"

She stepped down and went right up to my father. "I'll need someone to walk me down the aisle."

A muffled sob left Mom as she dabbed at her teary eyes with a handkerchief.

Dad looked down at his shoes for a full breath before lifting his head and looking Naomi straight in the eyes. "I'd be so honored to have the gift of walking you down the aisle."

Momma lost it, her loud sobs filling the air.

Dad opened his arms and Naomi crashed against his broad chest. She looked so small and fragile I often forgot that she wasn't ten feet tall and made of steel. My woman was strong, but she was soft too, and likely crushed by the fact that her own parents weren't accepting of her choice in marrying me. It broke my heart to see her in pain, but Dad put it back together as I watched how easily he gave her the comfort she would likely never receive from her own father.

We hugged one another and took silly selfies in front of this incredible heirloom my father had made with his own hands. The future felt big and bright as we headed toward the house.

"Dad, you've got an important call from Mr. White. He says it can't wait until tomorrow," Odessa called out to us from the backdoor off the kitchen.

"Who's Mr. White?" I asked my father.

"He's our loan adjuster for the house. Works down at the community bank. He's also part of my poker group. A good man, and a friend. He's been helping us with the liens on the house."

"Liens?" I asked. "What do you mean?"

Dad waved me off and went to answer the phone while my mother put her hand on the ball of my shoulder. "I'm sure it's nothing to worry about."

"Mom, what did Dad say regarding liens on the house? That sounds worse than being a couple months behind on the mortgage, which I told you I'd planned to help pay down once I got married."

"We didn't want to burden you."

"Yeah, Ma, but having liens against your house is worse than just being behind. How far in the hole are you?"

"Honey, I'm sure your dad has it covered. Mr. White has been helping us set up a more reasonable payment plan, but it's hard with the double mortgage and the fact that we're six months behind."

"Six months!" I barked. "Why the hell didn't you tell me?"

"Baby, calm down." Naomi pressed herself against my back, her hands on both of my arms.

"I can't calm down. My family is about to lose their home!" I yelled.

"Not about to, we're being foreclosed on," my father said from the patio door. "My friend was fired from the bank. Some big wig called and had our account investigated. He was let go for allowing us to get so far behind without imposing the appropriate fines and deadlines." Dad's head dropped forward, his demeanor sullen.

"I'm sure there's something we can do," Naomi said. "I know a lot of people in the banking world. I'll make some calls…"

"Yeah, apparently you know one very powerful person," my father said, his words coming off curt.

"What does that mean? What are you saying, Dad?"

My father lifted his head, shame and anger all over his proud face. "I'm saying our house was foreclosed on and sold out from under us to one very insistent company."

"Who?" I demanded.

"Shaw International."

Naomi gasped and shook her head while backing up. Tears fell down her cheeks as her eyes widened. "No…he didn't. He wouldn't dare…"

"I'm afraid so. We have to move out in fourteen days," Dad whispered, shoulders slumping in what could only be seen as defeat. "I thought we had more time. I'm sorry, Robin.

I failed the family," he croaked, his voice tight as he covered his mouth with his fist.

"This isn't right," Naomi said and wiped her tears. "I'm going to fix this, Mr. and Mrs. Taylor," she grated and stomped to the side of the house that led to the front where the car was parked.

"Naomi, what are you going to do?"

"Well, first, you're going to take me back to your place. And tomorrow, bright and early, I'm getting on a plane to New York. Then, I'm having a meeting with my father."

Episode 93

The Lesser Evil

MAIA

Why in the world did I tell Rhodes I loved him?

The simple answer is because I do, in fact, love him.

He's everything I could ever want in a man. Kind. Gentle. Unbelievably considerate and compassionate. An amazing dad. A devoted fiancé. Hard worker, as can be seen by the mansion I'm standing in today. Not to mention, he's ridiculously attractive. Truly, a smile, a glimpse of his chest, the sound of his voice, and I'm swooning like some damsel in distress. And maybe that's part of my problem.

I'd worked so hard to not be someone else's baggage. Yet there I was staring into a closet half full of expensive clothes made by designers I'd never even heard of. I walked the length of my side of Rhode's closet, that was larger than my entire studio apartment back in Vegas. The fabrics had a wide variety of textures and colors that were very appealing to the touch and the eyes. But I didn't do anything to earn them. Rhodes knew I needed additional clothing and set about supplying them for me. It was part of that considerate and thoughtful nature that constantly blew me away. He was always worried about the ones he loved.

But did he love me?

He'd said he was *falling* in love with me, not *in* love. Though stupid me, had to go whole hog and drop the love bomb before him. I'd never told a man I loved them before. Not ever. Probably because I'd never trusted a man long enough to have those feelings. I absolutely did for Rhodes. After only such a short time, the man had become important to me. Important to my future happiness. He and his daughter Emily. For the first time, I felt like part of a family.

A *real*, loving, caring family.

And I was terrified of losing it.

"There you are," Rhodes said as he entered our closet. "Checking out your new duds?" he asked while hugging me from behind.

I nodded. "There's just so much of it," I whispered, scanning the long rows of women's clothing.

Rhodes kissed my neck and hummed as he inhaled. "God, you smell delicious."

A shiver ran down my spine making my heart beat erratically.

He placed his hands on my shoulders and then ran his fingertips down my arms. "Have I told you how gorgeous you are lately?" He clasped my hands with his and lifted my arms above my head and behind his neck. I arched my towel covered body as he slid those fingers down the underside of my arms until he reached my breasts. He cupped them over the towel and squeezed, eliciting a moan from me.

"You know... Emily is in bed." His breath was warm as he kissed down the length of my neck.

"Already?" I sighed as he continued teasing and plumping my breasts.

I wanted to yank the towel from my body and feel his hands on my skin directly, but decided to let him lead, preferring to enjoy his touch.

"Marisol knew she was tired but didn't want to leave her, so she suggested they continue their *Friends* marathon in her bedroom. Emily was out before the credits finished rolling." He chuckled and then bit down on the space where my shoulder and neck met.

"Rhodes, please." I gasped.

"Please what?" he murmured, then moved my hair to one side so he could rest his chin on my shoulder and look down the front of my body.

"Touch me," I mewled.

"I am touching you," he whispered, while one of his hands left my breast and slid down my belly over the towel until he made it to the apex of my thighs. My breath caught as he teased his way under the fabric to boldly cup my center.

"Yes," I cried out softly.

He rubbed my sex with his entire hand, his fingers becoming slick the more he played.

"Like this?" he bit down on the ball of my shoulder and inserted a finger.

"Gawd, yesssss!" I moved my hips, arousal tearing through my body at a rapid pace.

He wedged another finger inside and the fullness caused me to rise up onto my toes and press against him, trying to force him deeper.

His hand started to move faster, fucking me harder.

"You're so wet for me. I can't decide if I want to fuck you or eat your cunt right here in the closet." He growled and doubled his efforts.

I clung to the back of his neck and bucked wildly, riding his hand. I was so close to coming.

"Rhoooodes, please, please," I begged, for what, I didn't know.

I just needed more.

More of his hand working my sex.

More of his filthy words.

More of him.

"Fuck it, I'm taking both," he rumbled on a whispered growl before pulling his hand away, spinning me around, ripping off the towel, and dropping to his knees.

His mouth was on me in what felt like a nanosecond. I cried out at the extreme sensation of his assault on my over-sensitive flesh. I grabbed the back of his head, gripping his hair by the roots, and bore down on his face feeling nothing but beauty.

His hands came around my hips to my ass where he dug his fingers into the plump cheeks. His tongue was everywhere at once. Gliding the length of my sex one second and then fucking me as deep as he could the next.

Blindly, I reached my arm out and grabbed one of the closet rungs as desire tore through me, shredding my nerve endings with powerful bursts of pleasure. I was a stick of dynamite that had been lit when Rhodes took the experience to a whole new level.

"Don't fucking come!" he demanded as he adjusted one of my legs, lifting it up and over his shoulder, opening me fully to his perusal. "I want you coming on my dick not my tongue, but I'm not done," he leisurely flicked my clit as his gaze trailed over my naked body then up to my face. "You hear me?"

I nodded, my breath sawing in and out of my body.

"Good girl," he smiled salaciously and went to town on my pussy.

I had to bite down on my forearm in order to not scream as wave after wave of sheer bliss cascaded in every direction.

I pulled at his hair, trying to be good. The pleasure was so intense, I couldn't escape it. I shook and rocked my hips as I moaned wantonly. It was filthy and so hot watching his pink tongue glide all over my glistening clit and swollen sex. It was carnal. It was raunchy. It was Rhodes, losing himself in me.

"I'm gonna come. I'm gonna come." I rocked my hips hard, forcing his tongue with more pressure against the tight bundle of nerves that could make me sing.

Rhodes pulled his head away and caught me when my legs could no longer hold me up. I fell directly on top of him. He was still in a white t-shirt and a pair of grey sweatpants, a large wet spot from his hard cock soaking the fabric near his waistband. I straddled his thighs and pulled his thick cock out. I didn't even wait to remove his pants or his shirt before I got up on my knees, centered the wide head of his dick at my entrance and slammed home.

"Fuck!" he roared as I arched my entire body, coming instantly.

The orgasm seemed to go on and on as I rode him like a wild bucking bronco. I wanted him to feel every inch of pleasure he'd given me and then some.

"Jesus, fuck, yes!" He grated through clenched teeth, his hands clinging to my hips as he thrust up on my down strokes.

I rode him with everything I had in me. All the pent-up worry, fear, and anxiety coming out in a flurry of mind-blowing sex.

Before I could finish him off, he sat up, wrapped me in his arms, then kissed me as he rolled me underneath him. His tongue tangled with mine as one of his hands hiked my knee up and toward my arm pit. He ground his cock against my center, crushing my clit in the process.

Another orgasm coiled low in my pelvis, getting larger, almost ready to burst as he fucked me harder.

"God damn, I can't get enough of you, Maia. I just want to keep fucking you," he hissed, seemingly pained by continuing to hold off his own release.

I cupped his face, our lips knocking into one another as he pistoned into me.

"I'm going to come again," I whispered. "I love you, Rhodes. I love you, baby." I chanted as he curved his arms under my back, cupped my shoulders from underneath as I wrapped both of my legs and arms around him, holding him close.

"Fuck yeah, you're going to come again. All over my cock, baby. You squeeze me so good. God, I fucking love you. Maia." He jackhammered into me, his energy seemingly renewed by his admission. "You hear me…"

"I do. I hear you," I took his mouth in a deep kiss as he swiveled his hips, the crown of his cock suddenly bumping against that special place deep inside me.

"I. Love. You." He accentuated each word with a deep thrust against my g-spot.

I lost it. My entire body convulsed and locked down around him as I came and came hard.

Finally, he planted himself to the root and groaned into my mouth, his release spurting hotly inside of me.

We stayed on the floor, connected for a long time. So long his length softened and slid out of me. I was as limp as a cooked noodle, every one of my muscles having been overused. Sated didn't even come close to the bliss I felt in that moment.

At some point, Rhodes placed a series of sweet kisses all over my face, down my neck, over each breast, and down my stomach. When he got to my sex, he spread my legs, butter-flying them.

"I love seeing a part of me inside you," he said with reverence. He teased my slit with a finger, sending little pinpricks of arousal zipping and zapping through my body once more. "Just looking at your cunt like this makes me hard all over again," he grunted, palming his half hard cock.

It should be nasty, his words, and the way he played with me. Somehow it wasn't. He stared and touched this part of me as though I was a treasured piece of art that he couldn't help but put his hands on, or in this case, *in me* again.

He licked his lips as he pushed two fingers deep. "I can

still taste you on my tongue…"

I moaned, starting to get with the program. If he wanted to go for O number three, I could rally, even though my eyes were closing of their own accord.

I must have dozed off while he played, because the air changed, and I opened my eyes to find I was being carried from the closet to a huge king-sized bed.

"Do you want to sleep with a part of me inside you, or should I get a cloth?" he asked.

I yawned. "You worried about another wet spot?" I gestured to his sweats where he'd made a mess.

He grinned. "Not even a little bit."

"Then come snuggle me. After a nap, you can give me O number three," I murmured already falling into dreamland.

"Sounds like a deal," he said.

I barely felt the bed shift when he got under the covers. He must have removed his clothing because his body was bare and scalding warm when he spooned me from behind.

"I do love you, Maia. I'm sorry I didn't say it earlier when you said it. I just didn't want you to think it was because you admitted it first. But I do love you, and I've never been happier to have you here, in my bed, within my arms." He snuggled my neck.

"I love you, too," I whispered and then fell asleep.

* * * *

It was dark. He was touching me again. I could feel his hand cupping my breast, squeezing rhythmically. His naked body was plastered behind mine. His breath smelled of cigarettes.

My eyes opened instantly and I went completely still, taking in the unfamiliar dark room.

There *was* a body plastered to mine. A huge one, not small and gangly like a teenager who hadn't gone through puberty yet.

The hand around my breast was…firm, in a pleasant way. Like it had a right to be there so casually.

My breathing sped up as reality and the nightmarish world of my past collided together, both fighting for supremacy over my brain.

I inhaled deeply. There was no cigarette smell, only the combined scent of my bodywash, Rhode's cologne, and the musky notes of the sex we'd had earlier.

Rhodes.

I lifted my hand and covered the one holding my breast. It was dry, with a light dusting of hair across the top. *Not free of hair with spindly fingers.*

I smiled as I realized that I'd woken naked in Rhodes' arms and didn't scream or jump out of bed like a scared kitten. I'd been a little frightened, and uncertain of my surroundings, because we'd forgotten to leave a light on, but I could hear the sound of Rhodes breathing. It was distinct. Like a large bear at rest. A soothing purr. And his hold around me was intimate and protective, *not searching.*

I laid there long enough to enjoy the feeling of waking within the arms of the man I loved and not freaking out. It was a first. A really good first. It meant I was healing. Rhodes was helping me heal. Through his care and his love. It made me feel like the luckiest girl in the world.

Unfortunately, luck couldn't stop the fact that I desperately needed to use the restroom.

With care, I extricated myself from Rhodes' hold. In his sleep, he stretched out his arm as though reaching for me. Ultimately, he tagged my pillow and tucked it against his chest while continuing to snooze away.

I went to the bathroom and took care of business before slipping into the monster sized closet to find some comfy clothes. The towel I'd worn was still on the floor in a rumpled heap. My cheeks heated as I remembered all that we'd done last night and the many times he told me he loved me. Just hearing those three words from him gave me such an incredible sense of peace.

All of this was new to me. This life. Being a stepmother type figure. A fiancée. And today, after all that we'd survived, including the beautiful things we've shared, I could finally say I felt comfortable. Confident even. I was madly in love with a man who loved me in return. My relationship with Emily had grown and evolved into something special. And I believed she genuinely cared about me as much as I did her. Sure, I'd need to get to know Marisol, but there would be time for that once we dealt with my mother and siblings.

The reminder that I had unfinished business in Colorado threatened to ruin my good mood, but I forced that problem down and pushed it aside. Rhodes promised we'd go to my grandmother's funeral at the end of the week and that's when we'd figure out what exactly was happening with my family. I had to trust that he would help as promised, and things would eventually get better. After all that we'd been through, it had to, right?

If history was anything to go by, nothing would go as planned. I needed to be careful not to set my expectations too high. I had no idea what we were going to find when we arrived in Colorado. I just had to pray that I wasn't too late.

Feeling antsy again, I decided to go check on Emily. It was her first night at home and the last couple evenings she'd slept with us by her side. Last night, Marisol stayed with Em until she'd fallen asleep, but I knew all too well what it was like waking up after a traumatic experience. I'd been dealing with my own demons for a decade. I didn't want Emily to feel alone when she woke.

Quietly, I padded out of the primary bedroom on socked feet down the hall to where I'd been shown Emily's room. It was still very early in the morning, and the sun wasn't up yet. Her door was open a crack, as was the door to the room across from hers, which I remembered was Marisol's. It was lovely that Marisol kept her door open in order to be available to Emily if she was needed.

Before I entered, I heard the tiniest of whimpers.

I acted immediately, pushing the door open. "Hey, Em, honey, it's me, Maia. You okay, sweetheart?" I approached her bed where she'd had the blankets pulled all the way up to her face. Her wide, frightened gaze broke my heart.

She nodded but didn't speak.

"Did you have a bad dream?" I asked and came to sit on her bed. I didn't touch her because when I was in the middle of a nightmare, or the aftereffects of one, I usually didn't want to be touched.

"I-I w-was b-back in that car…"

"Okay. I know that was a super scary time," I said softly. "Do you want to talk about it?"

"He had a gun on me and Auntie," she whispered squeezing her eyes shut.

"Can I lay down with you?" I asked, needing to be closer to her, but knowing it had to be her choice.

She eased the covers back in invitation.

I crawled in and pulled her into my arms. "Tell me everything that is scaring you."

"Will you tell my dad?" she whispered.

"Not if you don't want me to," I said automatically, but it was a big fat lie. If I had to involve Rhodes in something harming his daughter, I'd take the hit to our relationship in order to ensure she received the help she needed. It was the lesser evil.

She told me her dream. It was terrifying and with each new revelation, I held her tighter. Eventually, she talked herself back to sleep.

Not willing to leave her, I closed my eyes. It felt like only a minute of sleep but was probably hours, before the door to Emily's room flew open, the handle hitting the wall with a loud bang.

I sat up, instantly awake, and put myself in front of Emily who'd also heard the sound and screamed at the top of her lungs.

"Who the fuck are you and why are you in bed with my daughter?" screamed an angry, gorgeous blonde woman dressed in a skintight dress and stilettos.

"Mom?" Emily croaked, white as a ghost with tears streaming down her cheeks. "What are you doing here?"

Episode 94

Winter Weddings & Funerals - Part 1

SUMMER

"Sunny, quit fidgeting," my mother scolded as she zipped up the back of the dress I hoped I'd be marrying Jack in tonight. Provided he didn't think my idea was insane.

Planning to pair a wedding with what could technically be considered a funeral, wasn't exactly a normal person's idea for the perfect time to trade nuptials. Good thing I'd never been considered normal.

Autumn swiped blush on my cheeks as I glared at my mother in the mirror.

"The dress wasn't altered," I sighed. "We didn't have time." I groaned as I stared at myself in the dress I'd chosen back in California. We'd purchased it for the wedding we were planning on our property but when we got the call about Ellen, all that changed, and we jetted to Norway.

I scowled at the image I presented in the mirror.

Something just didn't feel right.

"Maybe if you suck it in? Inhale really big and then Mom can yank it up," Autumn suggested.

I shook my head and shucked off Mom's prying hands.

"Just stop!" I snapped. "We can't make all of this"—I gestured to my ample curves—"fit into a dress a full size too small. It's just not going to work. I'll be miserable." Not that I wasn't miserable right then. "Maybe this was a bad idea…" I hedged, second guessing everything.

"I mean, who really wants to get married at a funeral, right? It was a stupid idea anyway." I sniffed, shoving the emotions way down as I realized how, once again, I'd bulldozed forward on one of my wild, harebrained ideas without truly thinking it all through.

"Well, there is one other option," Mom volunteered with a sly smirk.

"And that would be?" I flopped into the chair in my parents' room. "Jack and TJ will be waiting in the lobby for all of us in less than a half hour.

I watched as Mom entered the closet in the palatial room. A few seconds later, she exited with something I had not expected to see in a million years.

Her wedding gown.

"I know you said you wanted to do your own thing for your wedding with Jack, but I was your size exactly when I married your father and…" She ran her hand down the front of the champagne-colored beaded wedding gown. It was magnificent. As little girls, my sister and I used to fight over who would get to wear Mom's wedding dress first. Then, we got older and formed our own personalities, and that concept went right out the window.

Staring at the gown now, I wondered why I'd ever thought something else would be better.

"Mom," I gulped, "I can't believe you brought it."

She shrugged. "Honestly, right before the flight, I prayed to the ancestors that all would happen as it should for you and your new family. Then I felt a pull toward my closet and this dress. You know how it is, you never question—"

"You never question the ancestors," Autumn and I said at the same time.

"Exactly. And lookie here. You need a wedding dress you connect to. Something that feels genuine and was made and embroidered with love. Your own grandmother hand stitched and beaded this entire dress. I can't think of anything more fitting than marrying Jack wearing this gown."

I stood up and let the other dress fall into a heap at my feet. Wearing nothing but my undergarments, I grabbed Autumn's hand as Mom bent low so I could step inside the gown. She pulled the heavier fabric up and my bust fit perfectly. The shoulders were capped, and the front opened to a deep V that made my cleavage look incredible. Beading flowed in a chevron design across my breasts, pointing like arrows at the waist. The beads continued on a sheer overlay of lace and tulle from the waist, all the way to the floor, flaring out a couple feet. My golden blonde hair was curled and cascaded down my back and over my shoulders, catching the light and making me feel like a goddess.

I'd never looked more beautiful in my entire life.

Mom gasped, tears in her eyes as she fiddled with my hair. "Baby, you are so gorgeous, you steal my breath away."

The dress fit perfectly. No alternation needed. Per usual, my mother was right all along. She'd suggested her gown when I told her we were getting married, but I'd pushed back, thinking I wanted something that was only mine. I was so wrong. Nothing else could have made me feel this good.

"She is not lying, sis. Look at yourself in the mirror. That is what a bride looks like on her wedding day."

"Maybe wedding day," I whispered, taking my image in while praying Jack would appreciate the wild idea I had.

"How are you going to drop getting married today on him?" Mom asked as she approached with the velvet cloaks we'd purchased yesterday on our girls shopping day. Mine was white, for obvious reasons. My mother's cloak was a dark navy that made her blonde hair look like she was bathed in a golden halo of light. A deep rich emerald green set off Autumn's hair making it look as though it had caught fire and complimented her mossy eye color perfectly.

"I hadn't thought that far in advance. I figured the timing would present itself," I answered. "If the universe and our goddesses want us to get married today, it will happen. If they don't, well, that settles it don't you think?"

Mom nodded. "Makes perfect sense to me."

I lifted the hood of the cloak and set it on my head, then closed the ties to prevent anyone from seeing the dress underneath until just the right time.

"All right, let's go lay Jack's friends to rest and maybe get married!" I chuckled, disbelieving I was actually going to attempt to marry Jack on the mountains underneath the Northern Lights.

"Sunny, aren't you forgetting something?" Mom asked as I made it to the door to leave the room.

I looked down at myself. "Not that I can think of…"

"Honey, you're not wearing any shoes. How are you going to hike through the woods in the snow without shoes?"

I lifted the dress and the cloak and wiggled my pink-painted toes on my bare feet. "Okay, so maybe I forgot one thing."

* * * *

My nerves were at a thousand as I held Jack's hand and we tromped through the snow. It was technically nighttime but the moon was so bright, it lit up the snow well enough to see our little group make our way to what the guide claimed was the perfect spot for seeing the lights and setting our friends' souls free.

"You sure you're warm enough in that cloak?" he asked.

"It's lined with faux fur and satin. I'm good. Besides, it's not the cloak that matters, it's what's underneath that is important."

Jack's eyebrows rose toward his hairline. "Oh? Can I expect to find you bare under there?"

I burst into laughter. It felt good to laugh since my anxiety and stress were at an all-time high.

"That is a stellar idea, and I promise to surprise you with such a thing in our near future," I chuckled.

"You've been acting a little strange the last couple days. Is it the funeral?" Jack asked. "Or…" He swallowed as though he was worried about something important.

"Or what?"

"The other night you told me you were going to take a step back from your business to focus on TJ and me. I wouldn't be upset if you'd changed your mind."

I squeezed Jack's hand and shook my head. "I have never been more sure of anything in my life. I want to be there for you and TJ. Honestly, I don't feel as though I'm giving up anything. You promised to help me find a CEO who could take the brunt of the work. I trust you to do that. Do you trust me to be TJ's mother?"

Jack stopped in his tracks. A few of the others did too.

"Go on ahead. Summer and I will follow in a minute," he waved his hand for our families to follow the guide.

Erik and Savannah passed us with a smiling TJ. Erik had our boy on his shoulders. He was babbling nonstop in Norwegian, pointing to different things that were of interest to him. Erik being an eager new uncle, dutifully took in each thing and shared his thoughts.

Jack waited until the others were out of hearing distance before he cupped my cheeks. "You are the only woman I trust to mother TJ. Savannah is sweet and will probably be a good mom to their children. Your mom, Irene, Autumn, all really wonderful people that I'm glad are in TJ's life. But you…you have already become his touchstone. He looks for you in a crowd of people. He calls out for Sum Sum more than anyone else. You've made yourself his person during a very hard time. And I don't know how I could ever be more grateful or feel more love for you than I do today."

Now was the time.

The wind blew the hood off my head, and I felt a little nudge on my shoulder, but no one besides Jack and me were there.

The ancestors.

"I want to get married," I blurted.

Jack smiled wide and nodded. "Soon as we can, we will." He looped his arm around my waist and brought me flat against his chest.

"No. I want to get married today. Now. On this mountain."

"What?" His entire expression was one of confusion.

"When we get to the spot where we set Ellen and Troy's souls free to spend eternity together, I want my mother to marry us. Right out in the open, under the lights, in nature, with only the family we've chosen present."

His gaze traced my entire face. "You're serious."

"I am. It's the only way we can be sure Ellen and Troy are with us. The three of us. I'd like to have their blessing."

The kiss came out of nowhere.

Jack's mouth crashed over mine so fast and so hard I almost lost my balance. But Jack was there to hold me up. His tongue tangled with mine in a dance as old as time.

The kiss went on and on until he ripped his mouth away, sucking in air.

He pressed his forehead to mine, both of us winded.

"You are the best fucking thing that has ever happened to me. You hear me, Summer? Before you, I was cold, alone, and empty inside. Every day I'm with you I feel…full. Full of life, of love, of hope."

"Jack," I croaked, putting my hand over his heart, comforted by the rapid beat against my palm.

"All the years I grew up with no family to call my own. Practically every year until I was put in the boys' home, I had a new family to get used to. One that never stayed. Sure, I had the Johansens, and my best friends, but they weren't mine. They didn't belong with me. You...you're mine. And I'm yours. And I know with my whole heart not a single soul could ever take that away from me. You prove time and again that you aren't going anywhere."

"I never want to be without you, Jack," I stated with as much grit and confidence as I could muster.

"And you never will. I don't care what I have to do, you and me are forever. So if you want to get married here, in my home country, with the people we care about most present...while we still have Ellen and Troy, I say we do it. I can't imagine a more perfect union."

"I love you, Jack."

"Love is too small of a word to express how I feel about you, Summer." Jack said and then kissed me softly. "Let's get married!"

Jack tugged on my hand and together, we ran through the moonlit snow toward our future.

Episode 95
Winter Weddings & Funerals – Part 2

JACK

This woman…

I shook my head and chuckled loudly as we tromped through the snow at a fast clip toward our family and friends. Summer gripped my hand tightly and kept pace with my longer legs. Adrenaline flooded my veins, warming my blood and filling me with a majestic energy that fueled my excitement.

Today I'd become a married man.

A family man.

I couldn't wait.

With every step we took, I got closer to the future I'd always desired. Sure, it looked quite different than what I'd envisioned over the years, but I had no complaints. Summer was it for me. She challenged me at every turn. Her thirst for life was unmatched. And the way she'd taken to TJ as if he was her own child…*priceless*. I'd honor her commitment and sacrifice until the day I died.

So when she came up with the idea to get married

tonight, here, with everyone we loved present, even Troy and Ellen, I jumped at the chance to make her mine forever.

We climbed up a hill that was around ten meters, following the multitude of footprints in the packed snow. Once we crested the top, we both stopped and took in the view.

As far as the eye could see were purple, pink and green swathes of light, painted across the sky like God was using a brush against a midnight-colored canvas.

"It's breathtaking," Summer gasped.

I squeezed her hand and took in her profile. Her sun-soaked hair glowed against the white velvet of her cloak. Her skin seemed luminescent as the swirling colors moved through the night sky above us. I watched as a single tear slipped down the pearly skin of her cheek like a diamond falling from the heavens.

"It's so beautiful," she breathed, her voice trembling.

I looped my arm around her waist and nuzzled her cheek. "You're beautiful. The sky pales in comparison, Summer."

She smiled and turned her head. "And you're charming, husband-to-be."

I scanned the entire horizon and felt an enormous sense of belonging and peace.

"This is the place. This is where we lay Troy and Ellen's souls to rest. This is where we become a family."

Summer smiled, and it was as if the sun had come out at night, just for me.

She was my light. My sun. My *solskinn*.

"Family," she whispered. "I like the sound of that. I can't wait to be Mrs. Summer Larsen."

My eyebrow rose toward my hairline. "You're taking my name?" It was the one thing I had to give from my beginning on this Earth. The only thing my biological parents ever gave me.

Summer cupped my cheeks and kissed me softly. I could taste the wintery mint ChapStick she wore.

"Jack, I want every part of you," she whispered and kissed me again.

"Let's go tell the others," I gestured to our group who were down in a little valley not far from the bluff we'd stopped on.

A stream trickled along the entire plain, disappearing alongside the mountains in the distance, likely headed to the coast. The sky was beyond anything that could be captured by a photograph. It was perfect. The air seemed thick and filled with magic.

This was it.

I stretched out my hand and she placed her smaller one within.

Together we made our way toward our friends and family.

* * * *

I didn't hear a single word Summer had said to our group when she told them the plan. None of it mattered. My focus was on my bride-to-be as we stood under the Northen Lights and the full moon, with the people we loved most in the world in attendance. Summer and I thought it was important to include TJ in the ceremony so we both held one of his little hands. Surprisingly, he seemed content to listen and watch while swinging our arms.

Ann had suggested our group form a circle around us. Then she proceeded to remove items one at a time from the pocket of her navy cloak. She walked around us in the center of the circle while chanting something under her breath, then stopped abruptly when facing north.

"We honor the element Air. May your marriage move and glide with the wind, always adapting to life's challenges." She held up a bird's feather and let it go. The breeze instantly lifted it up and into the sky, taking it away, destination unknown.

"Ooohhhh," TJ said watching intently.

Ann lifted her arms as though hugging the sky as she walked to the east. Once again, she put her hand into her pocket and transferred what looked to be flower petals into both hands. Then she walked around us dropping the petals.

"We honor the element Earth. May your marriage and love be as stable as the mountains and as grounded as the earth beneath your feet," she said, dropping the petals. They looked like pink, red, and yellow confetti against the white snow.

"*Blomst!*" *Flower.* TJ giggled, the rest of us following his adorable lead.

Ann smiled and continued to circle us. She stopped in front of Autumn who was facing south.

"We honor the element Fire," Ann's voice rose as Autumn lifted her hand, holding a lighter. She flicked it, and the flame rose higher as if by magic. "May your marriage be filled with passion, long life, and boundless energy." Autumn entered the circle and walked around Summer, TJ, and myself, the flame never going out until she made it back to her spot where she closed her eyes, whispered something then blew out the flame.

My heart started beating wildly as Ann continued her walk, finally stopping at the west.

"We honor the element Water." She bent in half and picked up a handful of snow. "May your marriage adapt and evolve, melting like snow into the rivers, providing sustenance and growth to the family you've become."

Tears filled my eyes as the realization that through all of the heartache and sacrifice I'd suffered up to this point, I was finally getting everything I'd ever dreamed of and wanted.

My own family.

As I stared into Summer's soulful eyes and held the hand of the little boy I loved, I knew it had all been worth it.

"Hold up your hands," Ann instructed. "You too, grandson," Ann winked at TJ.

Summer sniffed, tears falling down her cheeks as the three of us held out our left hands while holding onto TJs much smaller one. I could hear gentle whimpers from each of the ladies around the circle, maybe even from my soul brother Erik too. I glanced at him, and sure enough, he was wiping his eyes and smiling, joy clear in his expression.

Ann reached out and grabbed a long red ribbon that her husband Bernie held aloft. I had no idea where or when she'd accumulated these items, but I surmised that my clever bride had made a plan for the evening in advance.

Ann lovingly wrapped the three of our hands, binding them together.

"Both of you repeat after me," she instructed.

We nodded, waiting for her to start.

"Heart bound to heart, and soul bound to soul, I am my own but also yours," she stated.

We repeated it.

"Our union grows of kindness and caring, of trust well-deserved and love unerring."

We spoke the phrase together, our words and cadence matching exactly.

"Heart bound to heart, and soul bound to soul, this love is a home of our own." Her voice wavered, emotion coating every syllable.

We stared into one another's eyes repeating every word, our voices harmonizing, caught in a moment of pure love.

"As your hands are joined, so are your lives forever-more." Ann leaned forward and kissed the top of each of our hands. "I bless this union."

Slowly she unbound our hands. "You are now husband and wife," Ann put her hands to her chest and bowed. "Blessed be."

Everyone cheered, and TJ jumped up and down.

"Wait!" I croaked, everyone coming down from their

highs. "I'd like to add one more thing that's important to me and my faith."

"Anything," Ann whispered.

The two rings felt like a burning weight lying against my chest. Something inside my soul, or hell, I don't know, maybe it was the magic of the night, or my best friends blessing me from the beyond. Whatever it was, I moved into action, pulled out the chain I held and yanked it off my neck. The two gold bands fell into my palm.

"Summer, I love you. I will always do my best to put you and TJ first in all things. Our little family starts today, and like this perfect circle, it will last forever." I held up my hand and she placed hers within it. I gripped Ellen's ring and slid it on Summer's fourth finger. "I think us wearing Ellen and Troy's wedding rings while we raise their son and show him the love they didn't get to give would provide them both the peace they need."

Summer stifled a sob as she nodded, accepting Troy's ring to complete the gesture.

I held out my left hand.

"Jack, you and TJ are my home now. Where you are, I want to be. I love you. I will do everything within my power to be a good partner and loving mother to TJ. Like this perfect circle, my love and commitment is unending." She slid the ring on my finger. Shockingly, it too fit perfectly.

"Now, I bless this union." Ann chuckled. "Blessed be."

"Blessed be!" everyone hollered as I pulled Summer into my arms and kissed her.

Joy, love, and hope filled my entire being as I tasted my wife's lips.

"My wife," I whispered against her lips, awe lacing each word.

"My husband," she responded, eyes twinkling, her lips still glistening from my kiss.

* * * *

Congratulations were shared and pictures were taken against the backdrop of the moon and Northern Lights to capture the moment. Still, we had come here for a different reason, and it was time to set my friends' souls free.

Once we settled down, Erik reached for the bag that held two urns.

"It's time, brother," Erik clapped me on the shoulder and squeezed. Then he reached into the bag and pulled out a silver urn and passed it to me. "Ellen," he croaked, his voice raw and jagged like our emotions.

I held the urn like I would a newborn babe, with reverence and love.

Erik removed the copper urn. "Troy," he whispered as though his heart had been ravaged by even saying our brother's name.

I swallowed the lump forming in my throat.

Summer picked up TJ and held her hand out. Savannah passed a small, thimble-sized brass locket hanging from a silver necklace. She'd taken it upon herself to handle securing a small amount of ashes from both Troy and Ellen's urns and sealing them into a locket. This was so that TJ would always have a piece of his parents close. It was an incredible gesture and a gift I hoped the child would treasure.

Our group walked to the riverbank. The Northern Lights seemed even brighter here. The moon shed its light like a beacon of hope.

"Ellen, you were loved. By Troy, me, and Erik. We were the three musketeers from the day we met. I'll always mourn the loss of my brother and sister. You represented everything good and right in the world. I can already see that goodness in your son. TJ will know nothing but love because you and Troy showed us the way." I couldn't help the sob that tore from my body.

"Troy, our brother, our friend. You showed us what it meant to be a brotherhood. You showed us what true love looked like through your love for Ellen. We will miss you both for the rest of our lives but will remember you and honor you through the love we give to your son. We are grateful for the years we had." Erik let out a broken sigh.

"Please open the urns," Ann said, also instructing us on this process. "Spread the ashes as you set them free."

Erik and I did as we were told. Together, we tipped the urns and let the ashes fall into the stream. The group watched in silence as the ashes mingled and flowed along with the current.

"Now you are free to be together forever." I whispered as Summer sidled up to my side, TJ on her hip.

The three of us watched the river until our noses were red-tipped and our bare skin was bristling against the cold.

"They're gone." I gulped, staring at the dark water as the colorful sky and moon reflected off its inky surface.

"But never forgotten," Summer said, cuddling TJ who'd fallen asleep against her chest.

"Now we live for them." It was a statement and a vow.

Summer smiled as I reached out and cupped her chilly cheek. "I love you, Mrs. Larsen."

She grinned wide, her smile imprinting on my mind, body, and soul.

"I love you too, Mr. Larsen."

I kissed the side of her temple and then the top of TJ's head. "Come on, I need to get my family somewhere warm so we can celebrate."

"Lead the way," Summer encouraged and rested her cheek to my shoulder.

I held my family close as we followed our loved ones back home.

Episode 96

Whatever Will Be, Will Be

MADAM ALANA

"Diego? What are you doing here?" Christophe asked, clearly as shocked as I was to see the mafia boss in what was supposed to be our safe house.

"What?" He held out his hands and grinned like a maniac. "And let you have all the fun?"

I opened my mouth and then closed it, doing my best to compose myself.

"Fun? You think we're having fun? My wife and niece were kidnapped. Four of our guards killed in cold blood, for no other reason than they were assigned to protect us. Our home was shot at by, not one, but multiple snipers. We just spent the day in and out of the back of vehicles, our vision impaired and our bodies battered and bruised as we were tossed around like a box of rocks to an unknown location. And you think we're having fun? Are you insane?" Christophe roared, finally letting his rage explode.

Diego smiled manically. "Sounds like a regular day for me, *amigo*."

"Jesus Christ..." Christophe blurted, his hands sliding into his messy hair as he closed his eyes and let out a deep groan.

"Are you not safe now?" Diego said nonchalantly as he walked over to the stove where his mother was cooking. He boldly stuck a finger into whatever sauce she had bubbling. Lightning fast, she struck his hand with a wooden spoon. He snatched his hand away and put the finger into his mouth, humming.

"*¡Ayeee, Mamá!* Just a little taste..."

"No!" she snapped and pointed at the table, then spoke something in fiery Spanish.

Diego nodded and held up his hands in supplication. He proceeded to the opposite side of the room, where he pulled out a stack of plates from a cupboard and took them to the table.

"What are you doing?" I asked.

"Setting the table. *Mamá* says it's ready. Sit."

I let out a long sigh, my stomach twisting even though I was desperately hungry, not having eaten all day.

"*Señor* Salazar, we need to talk about what's been happening and what to do moving forward," I started.

He waved his hand in the air like he was a butcher cutting sharply through bone and meat. "We break bread, enjoying what *Mamá* has graciously cooked for us, then we discuss business." His dark gaze sliced straight through any retort I may have had.

Christophe pulled out a chair, and I sat gently into it, my body aching with the effort. I needed a shower, a stiff drink, a massage, and a good night's sleep to recoup after the day we'd had. But more than that, I needed information.

A plan.

The only thing we had going in our favor was that we were alive, and the others had made it safely to Los Angeles, far away from Angus and his minions. For that small gift, I was grateful.

I sat numbly as I watched other individuals stroll into the kitchen. All seemed to be of Latino descent and male. Each individual that entered went straight to *Mamá* and kissed her cheek before approaching the table where they took their seats.

Diego helped his mother serve everyone a heaping plate filled with Mexican delights I hadn't sampled in years. Likely since the last time Christophe and I were vacationing in Cancun.

The plate was steaming with savory chunks of steak—or possibly pork—slathered in the most delicious smelling red sauce, Spanish rice, refried beans, and fresh tortillas rolled up and resting on top of the rice.

Christophe did not have to be told twice. My husband tore into his food with gusto, stuffing his mouth with meat while unrolling a tortilla and making a burrito with the beans and rice. He hummed around the second bite he'd shoveled in.

"*Oh mon dieu, le paradis!*" *Oh my God, heaven!* he moaned openly.

Mamá gifted him a huge smile before she went back to the stove and scooped up another heaping spoonful of the meat and sauce, then added it to Christophe's plate. He nodded and hummed, much the way an eager puppy would. The man was shameless when it came to his food.

I waited to eat until both Diego and *Mamá* were seated, he at the head of the table, she to his right. Something I found rather odd. He had his mother here cooking for what I guessed were his family or soldiers, but no woman.

"And where is Mrs. Salazar?" I asked, gesturing around the table filled with men, us, and *Mamá*.

Diego pointed at his mother and tipped his head in query.

"No, your wife. The mother of your children? Joel said you had a wife and children, *oui?*" I asked, while spearing a chunk of meat and putting it into my mouth.

The flavors were extraordinary, bursting across my tongue. Famished, I chewed and swallowed quickly in order to get another scrumptious bite. "*Ouah!*" *Wow,* I gasped in disbelief. The meat was savory and melted in one's mouth like the finest filet mignon. It was smothered in the most delicious red sauce I'd ever experienced. I picked up my tortilla and slid it through the sauce, adding more of that incredible flavor to my second bite.

"My compliments to the chef." I nodded at *Mamá,* whose chest puffed with pride as she took in the eight of us at the table, hunkered down, focused solely on her impressive meal.

Diego grinned salaciously. "I have no wife, Madam. I had been in a relationship with a woman who blessed me with two princes and one princess."

"And where is she now?" I continued to eat, staring him down. If we were going to pretend that my world hadn't imploded, I was going to get as much information about the mysterious mafia boss as I could.

"*Vaca inútil…*" *Useless cow, Mamá* hissed under her breath. I didn't fully speak Spanish, but the words were similar in French. Apparently, Diego's mother wasn't fond of the mother of his children.

Diego chuckled then wiped his mouth and sat back in his chair. "I do not bring my children on dangerous missions, Madam."

I frowned. "And yet your mother is not exempt from this danger?"

He glanced at his *Mamá.* "No one tells *Mamá* what to do. She goes where she goes. Always her choice."

"And if your enemies were to find her amongst your hideouts?"

His nostrils flared. "*Mamá* was raised in the life. Her father led us, passed down from her grandfather, and his before that. I am her oldest son and took over the business when my father passed."

"I see. The family business."

His head dipped, and he smirked. "*Sí, la familia lo es todo.* Family is everything." He translated into English. "These"— he gestured around the table—"are my brothers. Some by name, all by *blood.*"

Based on that statement, I wasn't sure who was his actual biologic relation, and who fought and killed with him to earn the status of *brother.* Coming from a man like Diego Salazar, I didn't think the difference mattered.

The point was *they were family.*

Diego picked his silverware up once more and continued eating. Discussion over. I followed his lead, stuffing myself full of one of the best homemade meals of my life.

* * * *

When dinner was done, the four brothers picked up the plates and proceeded to clean the kitchen while *Mamá* called out orders in Spanish. They worked together like a well-oiled machine, each having their primary task and completing it efficiently.

"Come to my study," Diego instructed.

"*Gracias, Mamá,*" I dipped my head to the older woman as I passed.

I started to follow Diego and noticed Christophe stopped in front of *Mamá.* He reached for her hands and took them both within his own before he bowed. "*Gracias.* Dinner was exceptional."

Mamá preened under his praise before turning her head to the side and pointing at her cheek.

Christophe chuckled before he bent in half and dutifully kissed her cheek like the brothers had when they'd arrived.

"*No te preocupes, te engordaré,*" she said as she lightly smacked his cheek a couple times, then pointed at me.

"*¡Demasiada flaca!*" she tsked and shook her head.

"What did she say?" I asked as Christophe joined us.

Diego grinned. "She said she was going to fatten Christophe up and that you were too skinny."

"That's quite rude," I whispered.

Diego burst out laughing. "That's *Mamá*. You'll learn to love it."

I highly doubted that. I didn't plan on being here long enough to build a close relationship with the woman.

We followed Diego to a beautiful den that consisted of wall-to-wall books. A full library from floor to ceiling. A large cedar desk sat in the center. A single leather chair befitting a king sat on one side, two smaller leather chairs directly across from it.

"Have a seat," Diego said as he slumped into his own chair, kicking his feet up on one end of the desk.

Christophe held on to the back of one chair as I sat, then took the remaining seat.

Diego opened a wooden box and pulled out two cigars, passing one to Christophe, who took the item with glee. He offered me the other, but I shook my head. He shrugged and clipped the tip, then lit his stogie before passing both the cutter and the lighter to my husband, who repeated the process.

For a full thirty seconds, the two men puffed their cigars as though they didn't have a care in the world, while my insides were bursting with the desire to find a way out of our predicament with Angus. Still, I sat quietly. Having worked with powerful men from all walks of life, I learned quickly to be patient. Things were never solved with heightened emotions and knee-jerk reactions.

"Drink?" Diego lifted his chin toward a bar cart in the corner.

"*Oui*, thank you. I'll get it," I offered, needing to do something.

I went to the cart and poured three glasses of top shelf whiskey, passing out the two before I slammed my first glass in one go, hissing at the burn that scalded my throat. It wasn't the most ladylike thing to do, and something I normally would detest, but I needed the liquid courage more than I needed my next breath. I filled the glass with another two fingers of the glorious alcohol and went back to my seat.

Diego lifted his glass. "To taking down the enemy," he toasted.

We didn't clink his glass in cheers; this wasn't a party or a celebration. This was two people needing to figure out a way to survive, while the third laid out what he could offer by way of assistance. I just hoped the cost wouldn't be too high or something I wasn't willing to give.

"*Señor* Salazar…" I started, unable to delay the inevitable any longer. Fear was like a rash I had no ointment for, itching and twitching along my skin, with no relief in sight.

"Diego," he corrected. "I think after what we've shared, we can go by first names…*Alana*."

I let out a long, tortured breath. "Diego, we need your help."

"Have I not already fulfilled my marker by getting you out of a very sticky situation and bringing you to the safest home possible?"

I licked my lips. "*Oui*, and we are very grateful, but Angus will not stop. And you have yet to share all you know about the woman who hired you originally to destroy Maia's home and threaten her."

He puffed on his cigar, watching the smoke rise and waft around the ceiling.

"She is his daughter."

"The child he mentioned to me?" I recalled what he'd said during my kidnapping. That he'd lost ten years of his daughter's life when he went to jail for his part in Celine's death.

Diego nodded but gave no more.

"She would be around thirty now?" I tapped my chin.

"*Sí,* and she is a viper. She charms her prey while circling around them, cutting off their air before striking with her venomous bite," Diego grunted.

"She sounds awful." I bit down on my lip.

"Worse, she lies in wait for you, her hatred far surpassing that of her father's."

"But I don't even know her."

Diego's eyes flashed with something I couldn't name.

"Ah, but you do know her. She's been slinking around your extended family for quite a while, finding just the right moment to hurt you most, to take the killing bite."

"Who?"

"Her maiden name is Bianca Sokolov. You know her as Bianca Myers."

Christophe and I gasped at the same time. The revelation shocked me straight to my core. My entire body overheated instantly, sweat beading at my temples and behind my neck.

"You mean to tell me, the woman that was once Giovanni's fiancée, later Brenden's wife, is Angus Sokolov's biological daughter?" I gulped, my hands quaking.

So many things came together in a flood of information, pieces connecting left and right. "She worked for the attorney Falco & Myers used for their shared business for years. She dated Giovanni for a year and a half before she conned him into marrying her. Then she cheated on Giovanni with Brenden, one of my oldest friend's sons."

"And now she's carrying the heir to either the Falco dynasty or the Myers' fortune. If I didn't despise her father, I would tip my hat to her ruthlessness."

"We have to warn them!" I stood up, my drink splashing over the wooden desk as I quickly set the glass down. "Where's my phone…" I remembered leaving the traceless phone in my coat pocket when we entered the house. Inspector Moreau had given it to me since the authorities had taken our phones into evidence.

"It's too late," Diego frowned.

"What's too late?" I breathed.

"My sources looked into the connection between all of you. While you were kidnapped and dealing with Angus, your family was on the receiving end of Bianca's wrath. It is why I felt compelled to come to France."

I tightened both my hands into fists, my nails digging into my palms as I imagined the worst... That Julianne and Brenden were dead. Possibly even Giovanni, though that was less likely. Gio was a force all unto himself.

"Tell me," I croaked. "Tell me everything."

For the next thirty minutes, my heart broke in half as I listened to Diego share the horror story of what had been happening in New York. Giovanni had been sexually assaulted, Bianca going to jail, only to be released on bail, now holed up in a cottage close to my home here in France. The last was the worst part. That Diego received word that the physical office of Falco & Myers had been bombed, while Gio, Julianne, and Brenden were still in it. Their medical status was listed as confidential, but Diego had his sources working on retrieving the information. We had no idea if they were alive or dead. He claimed he'd have more information in the morning.

I slumped back into the chair, no longer capable of holding myself up.

So much destruction and turmoil.

"This is all my fault..." I shook my head, my voice quivering.

"No." Christophe's voice grated, his tone raw and jagged. Suddenly, he was kneeling directly in front of me, his hands on my kneecaps, his eyes piercing straight into my soul. "This is all my fault, *mon coeur.*"

I closed my eyes, tears falling down my cheeks.

"No, it is ours. For taking over The Marriage Auction all those years ago."

It all started then. Thirty years ago. When I myself was a candidate in The Marriage Auction.

"*Lo que será será.*" *Whatever will be, will be.* Diego sang, sounding much like the song, his nonchalance grating on my last frayed nerve.

"That's easy for you to say, Diego, you have no skin in this game. You haven't even shared whether or not you will help us get through whatever this is and take down Angus for good," I spat, the ugliness inside of me spilling out into the beautiful room.

He grinned and puffed on his cigar, looking very much like the cat that ate the canary.

"I will help you take out Angus. But it will cost you a great deal and even more trust."

"Anything! We are desperate," Christophe demanded as he stood and faced the criminal that had somehow become...a friend.

"My first demand—we kill Angus. Do not kid yourself into believing he will go to jail and justice will be served. If I am involved, he will be dead, because for men like Angus and myself, it's kill or be killed. There is no *justice.*"

I swallowed back the bile gliding up my throat as the ramifications of our situation became brutally clear.

Christophe stood behind me and squeezed my shoulders. "This revenge of Angus' is ultimately my responsibility. It stems from my actions snitching on him to the authorities regarding his part in Celine's death. I will take his demise upon my heart and soul and wear it like a badge of honor!" Christophe sneered.

Diego lifted his chin, accepting Christophe's claim with an air of dignity.

"There's more," Diego issued. "When me and my men take him down, we will acquire his empire. When one giant falls, another rises to take his place."

"We don't care about his empire. I want nothing to do with the man," I added, and Christophe nodded.

"Good. The last thing I want, and this one is entirely on you...*Madam Alana*," he spoke my title as though it were coated in velvet.

"Anything." I said the word but also feared what it might mean to a man like him.

"A bride."

"Excuse me?" I frowned, uncertain I'd heard him clearly. He couldn't possibly want me to match him with...

"I want a wife. A woman that can handle my unique life-style. A woman who will look the other way. A woman who will mother my three children as if they were her own. A woman who will take my name with pride and honor. A woman who will share my bed and only my bed...*for life*."

Episode 97
Play Dead

GIOVANNI

Pain. Bone melting, excruciating agony tore across my back and legs like I was being burned alive for the second time. Tears soaked the pillow I silently screamed into. I held my hands into fists, my belly to the hospital bed as I tried not to pass out.

It was too much. I'd never survive days or more likely weeks of this.

Every single one of my nerve endings felt as though they were being ripped from my body with dirty tweezers.

"Fucking hell," I roared and bit into the cotton pillow as the nurse cleaned my wounds, whatever solution she used sluicing over my destroyed back and legs like a waterfall of pure acid. The heavy pain meds and nerve blocker I was on supposedly dulled the worst of it. The medicine didn't come close to assuaging the absolute torture I experienced every time they changed my bandages. The doctors urged me to accept stronger pain infusions, but I refused as it would require my admission to the ICU. I'd spent days lost in the ugly haze of my nightmares due to sedation. I'd rather deal with the pain than feel nothing at all.

"Okay, Pookie," the nurse cooed, patting the bottom of my foot. It was probably the only place she could touch me without adding to my suffering. "You did better this time. The burns are healing really well."

"Awesome," I grumbled. She said that every time she changed my bandages. "Maybe I'll sign up to run the next New York City marathon," I added dryly.

She chuckled, and it sounded like birds chirping. Maggie was her name. Short for Margaret, she'd explained, but absolutely not Peggy. She hated that common nickname and made it clear she wouldn't be answering if anyone called her by it.

Maggie was the only nurse I could tolerate. Mostly because I was a terrible patient. She put up with my bullshit when the others gave up, calling for orderlies and a doctor's assistance. The grey-haired nurse somewhere in her sixties was a sprite compared to me, with a quick wit that also could withstand my angry outbursts. When I got out of hand due to the endless pain, she treated me as though I was a screaming toddler, hence the nickname Pookie. She claimed if I was going to act like a toddler, she'd address me as such. It didn't phase her that I was a six-foot-two, built man that could knock her out with one punch. Instead, she used kindness, sarcasm and humor to push through my anger. For some reason, with her, it worked.

Julianne knocked on the hospital door and peeked her head in. My heart beat rapidly, my skin buzzing as the worst of the pain eased at simply seeing her face.

"The yelling stopped. Can I come in now?" She asked Maggie, not me.

"Oh, he was a rascal today. Weren't you, Pookie? Ripping up his pillowcase with his teeth like a wild beast!" She patted my foot again. "Don't worry, I'll get you another one and throw away the evidence. None will be the wiser." She winked, as if what went on between us in this room when I lost my shit would stay between us. I appreciated the favor.

By my own decree, Julianne was kicked out of the room ever since my first experience with my injuries being cleaned while I was awake. I refused to have my wife see me sobbing like a baby every time my wounds were tended. It was demoralizing. I hated it and everything about being in this fucking hospital. I wanted out.

Today.

Julianne had other ideas. Wanting to follow along with the doctors' orders regardless of what I knew I needed.

"What did they say?" I hissed. They meaning the doctors.

She was supposed to be on an errand to get my doctors to agree to allow me to go on home healthcare. It was the only way they would consider letting me leave these four walls.

"They recommended you transfer to a special burn facility where you could get more expert care," she said gently.

"Fuck that!" I growled. "I want to go home and sleep in our bed. It's the only way I'm going to get any real rest."

"Here, here," Maggie cheered from across the room as she typed something into a rolling computer she dragged around from patient to patient as she performed her duties.

"Dr. Cline jokingly said the only way you could go home is if you had a full-time nurse and regular in-home doctor visits. He also sent your chart and images of your burns to a plastic surgeon who specializes in severe burns for a consult."

"Great. We'll set it up," I answered automatically, used to getting my way.

Maggie snorted, and I glared in her direction.

"Something to share from the audience?" I called out.

Maggie turned around and smiled evenly, completely unfazed by my shitty attitude. She was used to it by now.

"It's not so easy to get round-the-clock care."

"It is when you have more money than God," I huffed,

wincing as my lower back muscles pulled at the tender ravaged skin with each of my movements.

She tilted her head to the side, her lips pursing. "I guess that would do it. Not that you'll be able to keep 'em. Your attitude leaves much to be desired."

"She's right, honey," Julianne pushed a lock of my hair away from my forehead as I slowly eased from my front to my side to face them, using the leverage from my palm on the mattress to shift without adding too much additional pain.

"That's why I'm hiring you, Maggie," I blurted surprising myself, but then realized I'd meant it. She was the only person I'd listen to.

"That's sweet, Pookie, but this is my last year of service. I've already been conned into doing another year past my retirement."

"How old are you?" I asked.

"I'll be sixty-six this year. Was supposed to retire last year but with Covid and the shortages in staff, I stayed on to help."

"So you will get your retirement pay regardless of when you leave?" I concluded.

She tapped on her lips with her pen. "I suppose so…have plans to head to Florida near Boca Raton with my best friend this coming January. We found an affordable retirement home in Mission Bay about thirty minutes from where we'd really like to be, which is by the beach, but it's good enough for us."

I smiled wickedly.

"Gio…" Julianne warned. "I know that look…"

"How about you quit here, live out the rest of your time in New York with us, helping me heal for triple your current pay. Then when I'm better, I will pay for you and your best friend to live in a five-star retirement home on the fucking beach in Boca Raton until the day you both die of old age."

Maggie gasped, her hand flying up to her chest. "You couldn't possibly afford something like that."

"Try me," I growled, the idea already planting roots in my mind.

"He can more than afford it," Julianne responded with a sigh.

"And Maggie will be responsible for finding me the best doctors to treat my burns and manage my care." I smiled, loving this plan already.

"I already know all the best doctors in New York. I've been a nurse in just about every hospital in the city over my forty-five years of service." She puffed up with pride.

"See, it's settled," I grated out, my back throbbing with every breath I took. "Jules, love of my life, please, do this for me. Make this happen. I need to be home."

"I'll let you two talk, but if what you say is true, Pookie, I'd be an idiot not to take you up on your offer. And my momma didn't raise no fool. I'll be back this evening to check on you. Try to rest."

"I'll rest when I'm home."

Maggie laughed out loud, the birdlike sounds following her out the room.

"She's something else," Julianne whispered when the door clicked shut. "And Pookie?" She snickered. "I didn't think I'd ever see the day you'd allow someone to call you that."

I groaned under my breath. "She reminds me of my grandma."

"That woman looks nothing like Grandma Falco," Julianne countered.

"No, but she has that take-no-shit attitude and inner strength. Besides, she makes me laugh." My gaze lifted to my wife, and I swallowed the lump in my throat. "She also makes me believe I'll get through all of this and come out on the other side of it whole again."

Julianne cupped my cheek. "Oh Gio, you will. The worst of it, including the pain, will fade. You may be left with scars, but you survived. That's all that matters. And don't forget— you saved my life."

My gaze flicked down to her wrapped hands and fore-arms and the stitches scaling across her forehead and into her hairline. Her burns were fewer but no less damaging to my heart.

"I couldn't lose you. I'd rather not live in a world you weren't in."

Tears filled her pretty blue eyes as she leaned forward and kissed me softly. "Me either, so we'll just have to go on living."

"Actually, I'm going to suggest the exact opposite," came a booming voice from the doorway.

Bruno entered wearing all black, a grim expression, and more swagger than he should for a man visiting a patient in the hospital.

"What do you mean?" I asked.

Right then Julianne's cellphone rang.

"That would be your godmother, Alana. Turns out we've been fighting a similar battle as they have but on different continents," Bruno explained.

"I don't understand," Jules said.

"Answer the phone. You're not going to believe anything I have to say until you've spoken with her," Bruno claimed cryptically.

I watched as Julianne pulled out her phone and put it on speaker. "Alana?"

"*Dieu merci!*" Alana's cultured voice spoke in rushed French.

"Alana, where the heck have you been? So much has happened…"

"There is much to discuss, *chéri.*"

* * * *

The information Alana shared regarding her kidnapping, Angus, and more importantly, Bianca could have been the plotline for a suspense/action movie. These situations didn't happen in real life. Not only was Bianca married to a man named Dimitri, who was currently in jail for kidnapping Alana and Emily Davenport, but she was the daughter of one of the most wanted criminals across the globe. The same man that was the catalyst for including Julianne's parents into the original Marriage Auction.

In turn, we explained what happened here regarding the assault, Bianca being jailed, getting bailed out and the bombing of our offices. Lastly, we shared our various injuries, including the fact that Brenden was still in a medically induced coma.

My head spun with each new detail she revealed.

Bianca had played the long game. Weaving herself into our lives until she could handpick the many ways in which to screw us all over, likely making her criminal daddy proud.

It was all so twisted and jacked up that I had trouble keeping track of the details. Then again, that could be because of the plethora of pain meds, antibiotics and muscle relaxers I was on, but nonetheless, it was unbelievable when shared out loud.

"What are we going to do? Where are you now?" Julianne asked.

"Christo and I are in a safehouse in France, with…um…a friend."

Bruno grunted, seeming to have more information about this *friend* than we did.

"What friend?" Julianne snapped. "You need to come here. Be with family. We can protect you."

"I'm sorry, *ma petite fleur*, it is too dangerous for us to come to you. We would simply be bringing the devil to your doorstep, and I won't put you, Brenden, or Giovanni in jeopardy any further than what you've already experienced."

"That is not your decision to make," Julianne hissed, her

foot stomping on the floor like a petulant child. Alana always brought out a more immature side of Julianne. It seemed to fester and grow after we lost our parents. Which made sense that Alana would take on the role of matriarch in Julianne's eyes.

"It is my decision and I have made it. I will stay in France and deal with Angus and Bianca myself."

"You can't do that! She's insane! Look at what she's already done to get back at you and the family," Julianne switched from angry child to devastated family member in an instant. "They want you dead. They want us all dead. Don't you see?"

"I do, my darling one. I truly understand the stakes are very high, but me and my friend have a plan. And that plan starts with you."

Julianne batted away her tears. Her hands shook as she clung to the phone between us like a lifeline. "W-what c-can we do?" she croaked, jutting her chin out, firming her jaw, and pressing her shoulders back, readying for battle.

God, this woman made me proud. She'd been knocked down and hurt repeatedly, yet she still found the strength to fight.

"You need to play dead," Alana stated as clearly as one would state. "It's nice out today."

"I don't understand."

"Bruno?" Alana called out to the man that had been leaning against the wall quietly, letting everything play out as we caught up.

"I'm here," he pushed off the wall and came closer to the phone. "What Alana is suggesting is we report to the media that the three of you were killed in the office bombing."

Julianne and I both frowned.

"Why?" I asked.

"Because that takes you out of the equation as a current target. Levels the playing field to the fight in France."

"Wouldn't they already know we'd survived? It's been days since the blast occurred."

Bruno shook his head and grinned wickedly. "My hacker may have edited all of your patient files after the three of you were initially hospitalized. Brenden has been treated under the pseudonym Jim Johnson. You are Giorgio Albertino, which is why the nurses and medical team have picked up calling you Gio and you didn't notice. Julianne was listed as Juliet Smith."

"This whole time we've been receiving medical care under pseudonyms?" I laughed and then winced as even the slightest movement tugged on my wounds.

"Didn't you think it was odd that you weren't interviewed by the authorities?" Bruno smirked. "You're welcome by the way." He crossed his arms over his chest, a smugness filling the air.

"Why do I think your kindness will cost me?" I muttered.

"Because it does. You owe me a fortune, but I know you're good for it."

"Thank you, Bruno. For protecting my family. I will happily pay you for your services," Alana's voice cracked through the line, but I interrupted her.

"Absolutely not, Alana. I pay my own debts, thank you very much. What I need to know now, before I break the hell out of this hospital, is what are our next steps?"

"You need to go into hiding until Bianca and Angus have been handled," Alana instructed. "Have your most trusted employee issue death announcements for all three of you. Make sure that Bianca is listed as the heir. That ought to close up any possible loose ends she feels she may have left in New York."

"And what about you?" Jules asked, her voice sounding small and childlike once more.

"I'm jumping into the pond with the big fish. This ends with me, one way or another."

"I don't like the sound of that, Alana," Jules whispered.

"You're one of the only family members I have left."

"I know, *chérie*, and I will do everything in my power to come back to you when this is all over."

"Why does that sound like goodbye?" Julianne cried softly.

"Because I'm ending this call. I love you, Julianne. Always and forever, *ma petite fleur*. Your mother would be so proud of the woman you've become. So strong and resilient. Hold on to that strength. I fear you will need it in the days to come."

"Alana," Julianne sobbed. "I love you too!"

Nothing more was said as the line went dead.

Julianne hiccupped through her tears and stumbled into the seat next to my bed.

I reached for her, clenching my jaw as the sudden movement flared across my back like white-hot fire. I didn't care, needing to touch my wife and soothe her soul.

"Baby," I gripped her shoulder.

She turned her head and slumped toward me, her face pressed against my chest as she let go. I cupped the back of her head, looking over at Bruno who stood as still as a statue.

"What now?" I barked.

"We break you out of here and notify the world of your deaths. Then I hightail my ass to France."

Episode 98

The Nail in the Coffin

NAOMI

Memphis held the car door open for me as I exited the taxi. I looked up at the skyscraper that I despised with every ounce of my being. Shaw International, the building, was as ostentatious and unwelcoming as my father himself. It stood sixty stories into the sky, shimmering glass sticking out from the earth like a titanium blade. It was my father's pride and joy. To own something so monumental in the city that never sleeps was the highlight of his career. To a man like Abraham Shaw, it meant freedom, glory, and power.

At one time, I was also impressed. Until I realized how my father's company had become the albatross around my neck and future. He believed it was my birthright. That I owed him my fealty and a lifelong service to the cause. Instead, his cause wasn't just or meant to change the world for the better; it was selfish, driven by greed. He saw himself as a king. This eyesore, his castle. His office was the entire penthouse floor. Designed so he could lord over what he saw as his kingdom and the people of New York simply peons beneath him.

I hated it, and at the moment, I hated him, for what he'd

done to the Taylors.

This would not stand.

I gripped Memphis' hand tightly, looked him in the eyes and nodded succinctly before I let go and strutted forward like I owned the place. He followed dutifully behind me, understanding this was my mission. He demanded to be here for support but that was as far as I'd allow. This was my battle. My kin purposely hurt and threatened the livelihood of people I cared deeply for.

Again, this would not stand.

Memphis rushed ahead and held the door for me. I didn't even stop to thank him; instead, kept up the ruse, pretending I was in complete control. I did, however, wink at him as I passed by, enjoying his corresponding smirk and head shake.

I didn't stop at the reception desk either, lifting my hand and chopping at the air. "Notify my father I am here," I barked with conviction. "Memphis, this way," I ushered him right past security who didn't move from their station. Everyone here knew exactly who I was and wouldn't dare stop me for fear of getting fired by my father. After this visit, he would probably terminate my all-access pass, but I didn't plan on ever stepping foot back in this building again if I could avoid it.

"But you don't have an appointment," the receptionist cried out as we made our way to the elevator.

"He's my father; I don't need one. Please notify his secretary I'm on my way up," I bit out and then entered the elevator without so much as a glance back.

The doors closed, and Memphis instantly started laughing. "Damn baby, I can't wait to get you home. That take no prisoners, take charge attitude has me feelin' some type of way." His voice was low, mimicking that sexy timbre he often used in the bedroom.

I chuckled and then cleared my throat. "Stop it! I'm all business right now. I don't need to be imagining you naked while I'm in boss mode."

He lifted his hands. "As long as you know I am all the fuck in on you having your wicked way with me. Just please, keep the heels on. They are sexy as fuck." His gaze traveled down my body taking in my fierce business attire as though he was envisioning removing each item from me...*with his teeth.* I'd dressed to play the part. Black silk blouse. Black leather pencil skirt, and matching heels. My hair was parted down the middle and slicked back into a low ponytail. The ponytail hair extension skimmed my ass, giving me the boost I needed to feel fierce and ready for battle. The only color I wore came from the red soles on my sky-high stilettos he clearly fancied.

"Just sayin' if you need to boss someone around after this...I am your man."

"Noted." I smirked and then watched the numbers. We were about to hit the top floor. The elevator doors opened. "Show time," I whispered and exited, my father's secretary, Desiree, waiting.

"Hello Ms. Shaw. Mr. Shaw is on an important call and asks that you wait until he's finished." She gestured to the seating area near her desk.

"Thank you, Desiree, but I'm not waiting," I clipped, leaving her in my dust as I stormed down the hall, Memphis bringing up the rear. When I got to the double doors for my father's office, I swung them both open with a flourish, loving the fact that they slammed against the wall on either side as I entered.

"I'm going to have to call you back. My daughter is here unexpectedly," my father said before slamming the receiver down. He stood, automatically buttoning his suit jacket, ever the gentleman. But he wasn't a gentleman. It was all for show, and he played the part well. "What is the meaning of this?" he demanded.

"What is the meaning of this?" I parroted back. "You're outta your mind, old man. Isn't my attention what you were hoping for with the stunt you pulled?"

He crossed his arms over his chest and leaned his ass on the front of his desk, attempting to prove with his pose and stature that he had the high ground when he absolutely did not.

"I don't know what you mean. Speak clearly, daughter. Have you forgotten your Ivy League training and vast vocabulary, or has slumming it in Georgia already rotted your brain?"

"Say what now?" Memphis barked and started to move in front of me to give my father a piece of his mind.

I extended my arm to stop him from passing. His nostrils flared as he ground his teeth. "I'll just be over there," he grated, gesturing to the seating area. He was clearly angered by the cheap shot, but also understood this was my battle, not his.

"Be careful, Father. Whatever it is you want is hanging by a thread, along with my fury. So let's speak in a manner with which you are familiar. A business negotiation, if you will."

He dipped his head, waiting for me to speak. It was a business move he taught me. Let your opponent hang themselves by putting all their cards on the table first.

"What will it take for you to sell me the Taylor property?"

His eyes lit up with excitement, the thrill of the kill already at his fingertips.

"Oh, I don't know. I'm pretty fond of that holding." He tapped his bottom lip with one finger, his tone sarcastic.

I clenched my teeth while I tried and failed to wait him out. It was all part of his sick and twisted game.

"Instead of going back and forth, we both know what we want." I seethed internally, using all my energy to appear unfazed and calm on the outside. "You are going to give me back that property, and I'm going to graciously apologize on our family's behalf to the Taylors once you do and transfer it back to them free and clear. The only reason I am here today is to find out what you want for it, because I'm not leaving here without it."

That's when my father smiled. "There's my girl. Mind as fast and dangerous as lightning, just as I taught you."

It took Herculean effort not to roll my eyes, lest it piss him off, preventing me from getting what I wanted.

He pushed away from his desk and walked around to his chair. "I'll sell you the property back…on one condition."

"I'm waiting," I stood still as a statue.

"You end this farce of an engagement, and you marry Malik."

"Not happening," I snapped at the same time Memphis rose and barked, "Fuck that!" I lifted my hand to stop Memphis from interfering. "Baby, please. I got this." I put everything I could into one look, hoping he could see all that I tried to say without speaking.

I love you.

Trust me.

"Next offer," I snapped.

"There is nothing else I want," he claimed, lying through his teeth. This wasn't about Malik or even Memphis. This was about me not choosing to accept the life he'd built for me and refusing to fall in line like a good little soldier.

I grinned. "That isn't true. Never go into a negotiation without having a backup plan. You taught me that. What's your backup offer, *Dad*." I enunciated the last word as a taunt.

His lips twisted and he tilted his head to the side as though assessing whether or not the rattlesnake before him would strike.

Spoiler alert… I bite.

"Anytime, *Dad*," I taunted again.

He leaned over his desk, placing both hands to the glass surface. His gaze was that of a world champion boxer, ready to take me down with one punch.

"You come work for me. Take your rightful place as

second-in-command, and you can marry whomever you want." His gaze flitted to Memphis. "Even if he is a gold-digging jock with no future and little to show for the life he's already lived."

I winced, wanting desperately to defend Memphis and his honor, but it would only hinder getting what I wanted. "If I accept this offer, the first rule of us working together will be that you never speak of my future husband in that manner again," I spat.

His gaze slid to Memphis once more.

"Don't even look at him. Look at me. Eyes on me. I'm what you want." I pointed to where I knew Memphis was sitting, likely falling into a hole of his own mental misery after my father's nasty comments. "That man…he doesn't exist for you. He and his family are one hundred percent off limits. You no longer hurt them to get to me. Do you understand me?"

My father's smile disappeared, and the hardened asshole came to the forefront. "What you don't understand, Daughter, is you do not tell me what to do. I am your father," he banged his hand against the glass desk the same way a judge would a gavel.

I slowly moved closer and stopped when my thighs pressed against his desk, the only thing separating us. Every part of me wanted to jump across that surface and strangle him where he stood, but I wouldn't stoop to his level. No, I'd beat him at his own game.

"I will come work for you in three months' time…"

"One. Or the deal is off the table," he purred manically.

"Fine, I will work for you in one months' time. Today, not tomorrow, not next week, but *today*, you will transfer the deed of the Taylor property to me," I growled.

"Agreed."

"You will leave them alone. You will stay out of my romantic relationships from this day forward," I added curtly.

"Fine. If you want to ruin your life by marrying beneath you, go ahead," he said with an air of nonchalance.

I inhaled sharply, letting that ignorant jab roll off me. It didn't, however, prevent me from feeling the rage filled energy coming from the seating area behind me. I knew Memphis hated everything I was agreeing to, but I had a plan, and this was only the first part of it.

I extended my hand, and my father looked at it, then at me, a devious smile plastered across his face. He thought he'd won.

We shook hands.

"Well, now that is over…" He said it so flippantly it was as though we hadn't just been facing off. "Your mother would like to discuss the wedding with you. She's been devastated since we left Georgia. I'll expect you for dinner tonight."

I stepped back and shook my head. "I'm sorry, Mr. Shaw, but dinners are not part of my working contract."

"Excuse me?" he blustered. "We just made a deal."

"For employment, yes. You are about to be my boss. If you think for one minute you kept a relationship with me as part of your business deal, you are sorely mistaken. I am no longer your daughter. You will never be invited to our home. You will not be walking me down the aisle, nor attending my wedding, as that privilege is reserved for people who love and care about me, not those who think they own me. You will never look upon the faces of your biological grandchildren. After what you've done, the decisions you've made, you are no longer my father. He's dead to me."

His hands trembled as he slumped into his seat. "Naomi, please, let's be reasonable."

"You've made your bed, Mr. Shaw. Now you have to lie in it. And don't call me Naomi. When I return to start work a month from now, you will address me as Mrs. Taylor."

On that parting *fuck you*, I turned around, allowing my hair to fly out behind me like a superhero's cape. "Memphis, we've got a wedding to plan," I announced as I dug the hole an inch deeper into my father's psyche.

Memphis jumped up and followed me to the door. I walked through, my head held high. Memphis, as it turned out, had some parting words for the man I would no longer acknowledge as my father.

"You know, it didn't have to be like this, Abraham. Your decisions, your actions, lost you a world of future happiness with your only daughter. I pity you." Memphis shook his head, then followed me out of Abraham Shaw's office and out of his life forever.

* * * *

Neither Memphis nor I said a single word as we rode the elevator, walked out of the building and hailed a taxi. He did, however, hold my hand every step of the way.

When we made it to my penthouse apartment in Soho overlooking the waterfront, he followed me in.

"Welcome home, baby," I whispered and then burst into tears.

He pulled me into his arms as I sobbed, letting it all out in a tide of emotional trauma.

"It's okay, Nay. I'm here. Let it all out. You were fantastic in there. You socked it to him good, baby," he whispered against my hair. "We'll find a way to get you out of working for him. I mean forcing your daughter to work for you can't be legally binding, right? We'll figure it out."

I shook my head and pushed back. "Oh no, I fully plan on working for him."

Memphis frowned. "But you have your own successful business. And more importantly, you don't want that life."

I sniffled and wiped my snot on the sleeve of my silk blouse. Fuck it, I could afford a new one.

"I fully intend to hold up my side of the bargain. However, I never agreed to a specific term. There is no employment contract, though he might try to pull a fast one and get me to sign something, which I will ignore."

"Soooo what? You're going to work for him for a little while, and then just quit? And you think he'll let that fly?"

I wiped at my wet eyes, hating that I was even giving that man my precious tears. He didn't deserve them or the utter devastation I was feeling after cutting him out of my life for good.

"No, he wouldn't. But I'm not going to just start and quit. That would be too easy. My entire life he put me through hell. Questioned and demeaned me and my choices at every turn. Forced me to obtain a degree I wasn't interested in but will now put to good use against him. He even prevented me from having real friends because their families weren't in my parents' social circles. Well, I'm going to go work for him, then I'm going to ruin him from the inside. Find out every secret and shady business deal he's ever made, because I've heard the whisperings of deals gone wrong. When I was with Malik, he used to get drunk and share all kinds of things that my father did to get ahead. What I need shouldn't be too hard to find, especially when you're not expecting the threat to come from the inside."

"Okay, I'm trying to follow, babe, but this is convoluted as fuck."

"Basically, I'm going to take his company from him, destroy the sham of a reputation he spent his life building, and leave him a sad and lonely man with no family to speak of."

Memphis' mouth fell open with what I assumed was shock. "Damn, Nay. Remind me never to get on your bad side."

I moved back into his arms, pressing my face to his warm chest. "I don't think you could ever be on my bad side. Because all your sides are nothing but good." I lifted my face and rested my chin against his chest. "Will you stand by me while I take my father down?"

"Naomi, I'd stand by your side and jump off a cliff, if you asked me to. Woman, my faith and trust in you is endless. I'm just really sorry you feel the need to do this, and all because of what he did to my family."

I shook my head. "No, him stealing your family home out from underneath you was the final nail in the coffin. This is all about him. Like you said when we left, it didn't have to be this way. He could have left well enough alone and let me live my life by my terms. Instead, he schemed, threatened, and hurt me and the people I've come to love. All because he wanted to control me like some perfect little robot. Now he has to suffer the consequences of his decision and actions. He's going to learn he should be careful what he wishes for. Because ultimately, I'm the one that will be his demise."

Episode 99

One Thousand and One Chances

RHODES

"Who the fuck are you, and why are you in bed with my daughter?" I awoke to the sound of my ex-wife's shrill screech.

I bounded out of bed naked as the day I was born. "Fuck!" I hissed, searching my bedroom floor where I'd dropped my sweats. I tugged them on as fast as humanly possible and was out the door and down the hall.

"Mom?" my daughter croaked, her voice terrified. "What are you doing here?" I was just about at the door when Portia's body went flying backward and banged into the opposite wall. Like a Tasmanian devil, my little fiery fiancée had slammed into Portia with her own body. Before I could intervene, Maia was already swinging.

Maia punched Portia in the face, then reached around Portia's neck, and pulled her lithe body forward as she kneed her directly in the stomach. If I hadn't been in complete shock, I would have intervened sooner. Alas, Maia yanked Portia to the ground and was on top of her, straddling her and about to rain hellfire down on Portia's face.

My belated reflexes finally kicked in, and I bolted into the fray, looping my arm around Maia and physically lifting her up and off of Portia. She was scrappy as fuck though, kicking and punching, trying to get more shots at Portia.

I shifted Maia away and plastered her to the wall with my body. I cupped the side of her face as she wailed like a gladiator in the middle of a battle. Her eyes were wild, her snarl feral. She wanted to rip Portia into pieces.

"Maia! Stop!" I barked while looking straight into her terrified eyes. She was lost in the haze of what I suspected was a full-on panic attack, the same way she'd been that first night in Paris when we'd shared a bed. Portia apparently triggered her fight or flight response. But instead of running away, escaping and saving herself, she stayed and fought to protect Emily.

Maia's gaze went from me to Portia bleeding on the floor, rolling from side to side.

"Emily," she growled like a wounded animal, still pushing against my chest, a mama bear ready to protect her cub.

"Emily's fine, Maia. She's okay." I bodily turned us so she could see my daughter in Marisol's arms. She was crying, nuzzled against Marisol's chest as tears ran down her cheeks. Marisol, on the other hand, looked murderous, her gaze laser focused on Portia.

"What the fuck!" Portia cried, blood seeping from her torn lip and busted nose. She gingerly sat up then crab crawled backward until she was leaning against the wall. "How dare you attack me in my own home. Rhodes, do something!" she whined. "I need help, and she needs to be restrained. I'm pressing charges."

I ignored her blathering to focus on the precious woman now trembling in my arms, her eyes wild, still seeming scared and ready to strike out. "That's my ex-wife, Portia. We'll get to the bottom of this, but no one is going to hurt, Em. Not ever again. There's no threat here. See? Em's okay. You protected her, Maia," I cooed. "She's safe."

"Safe." Maia whispered, and suddenly, her rigid body relaxed, and her bottom lip quivered.

I kissed her forehead. "Emily, honey, come here." I gestured for Em, and she let Marisol go, avoided her mother entirely, and as I moved back, Maia reached out and enfolded her within her arms.

"I'm o-okay. Just…just got scared for a minute."

Maia nodded against Emily's neck but held on. "No one will ever hurt you again. Not as long as I'm alive," she promised Emily who cried harder and held on to my woman.

While they held one another, fury tore through my body. It took me a full minute to wake up and figure out what had happened.

"Hello? Bleeding over here? I was the one that was attacked," Portia complained, her blood staining my carpet a bright crimson.

"Mari, please get some wet cloths and the first aid kit," I instructed.

Marisol simply nodded and then mumbled something profane at Portia as she passed.

"Are you going to help me up, or what?" Portia extended a slender arm.

I crossed my arms over my chest and stared down at her. "How did you get in?"

"I have a key," she rolled her eyes.

"How did you get past my guards?" I demanded, knowing I would be having an unpleasant conversation with each member of my protection unit.

"Frank was at the gate. If you remember, I hired him," she smirked. "One wave from me and he buzzed my car right through. Why all the questions? This is my home and that's my daughter. Though you wouldn't know it for how little she obviously cares about her mother's pain," she snarled, then winced when the gesture pulled at her split lip.

"I warned you that Emily had been through a traumatic experience. One I planned to discuss with you when we got settled. You never answered any of my numerous calls about the situation before. When I finally got a hold of you, we confirmed we'd have dinner in a couple weeks. Did we not?" I growled.

She shrugged and then groaned in pain. "I decided I wanted to find out what happened now. Then I come in to find my daughter in bed with a woman I've never met, that same woman sleeping soundly as though she had a right to be there."

"Portia, you have no idea what any of us have been through. You being here, reacting the way you did just pushed back Emily's healing once again."

"I'm her mother." she fired back.

"You haven't been her mother her entire life! Maia's been more of a mother to her in mere weeks than you have in all her thirteen years!" I bellowed, my anger taking over. "This is not your home! You shouldn't even have a key anymore. We've been divorced for years, Portia, and you pull this shit? Do you ever want to see Emily again?"

"She's my daughter!"

"Do you think a judge in their right mind is going to give you any custody when you broke into my house, frightened my daughter, and tried to press charges when you were attacked for breaking and entering? Maia was protecting her soon-to-be stepdaughter. What were you thinking? Coming here at the crack of dawn, using your ex-boytoy Frank to access my home on the sly? I knew I should have fired that fucker when I had the chance. At the time I only cared that I got rid of you. That's not a mistake I'll be making again."

"Rhodes, I'm sorry. I got excited you guys were coming back to LA. I told you, I was going to do better by you and Emily. Show you how I can be a good wife and mother. If you'd only give me the chance…"

I huffed and shook my head. "Portia, I gave you chance after chance. And I haven't thought about you romantically since the divorce. You and I are long over. And yeah, I'd hoped you'd get your head out of your ass and make more of an effort in your daughter's life, because she needs a female figure to look up to. Then I realized, I don't want Emily to be anything like you. And now she has women in her life who mean something to her. They treat her with respect. Give her their time, attention, and love."

"*Alana.*" She hissed the woman's name as if the five letters were poison on her tongue.

"Yeah, Alana. A woman who has chosen to be in Emily's life since the day she took her first breath. Someone who has always been there. Not missed important days like her fucking birthday or her first play at school. Was her mother anywhere around? Nah, she was too busy having her picture taken in a bikini while she fucked the photographer and planned to marry him. What is it, the fourth or fifth proposal since we were divorced?"

"Sixth, Daddy," Emily added, still in Maia's arms.

"Six. Fuck me. You need to leave. I'm calling my lawyer. This last stunt you pulled is it. You're done. If you want to see Emily from here on out, you're going to need to request that through the lawyers. I'm taking you back to court."

"Rhodes, no! Please, don't do that. I can be better. I can. Let me try…"

I shook my head. "I've heard this crap before, Portia. You never follow through, and right now, Emily needs the people in her life who are devoted to her. Willing to do what it takes to help her through recent events. That means visits to a therapist. Being present in her life. Talking to her daily, not once a week in between shoots for a couple minutes. That's not what a mother is."

"I can be that." Her pleading blue-eyed gaze went from

me to Emily. "Baby girl, I can. I can be there for you. I swear this time. I'll stay in California. I won't miss my scheduled visits anymore. I'll change. For you, I can change," she begged, and it did sound genuine, but I couldn't risk my daughter's wellbeing on a maybe.

I ground my teeth. Emily shouldn't even be here for this conversation, especially after what she'd been through.

Marisol came back with the items needed to patch up Portia. Instead of helping her, she set the things on the ground next to her. Marisol despised Portia.

"*Ven conmigo pequeña*," *Come with me, little one*, Marisol gestured for Em to follow.

Maia kissed the top of Emily's forehead and let her go to Marisol. She spoke a bunch of Spanish as she led my daughter down the hall.

"Can we have huevos rancheros today?" Emily asked, obviously uninterested in spending any time with her mother.

"Anything for *mi chica*," Marisol smiled, her arm around Em as they went downstairs toward the kitchen.

"Maia, why don't you go take a shower and get cleaned up and join Emily and Marisol while I talk to Portia?"

Maia nodded, lifted her chin and proceeded to walk past Portia as though she wasn't even there. Suddenly, she stopped and turned around.

"You know, you should be ashamed of yourself. You're lucky I didn't do more damage. Sneaking into your ex-husbands house. Slamming doors open. Not only is it criminal, it's terrifying to a child who's experienced the worst week of her life. Being kidnapped at gunpoint isn't a fucking joke. But you know what is a joke? You." Maia sneered and then turned on a heel and left, disappearing into our bedroom.

"Kidnapped?" Portia croaked. "Emily was kidnapped?"

"Yeah, Portia. You would've known all about it if you'd answered any of my dozens of calls, texts and voicemail messages this past week."

"I was on a job! We shot in several locations."

"A job that prevented you from having access to your phone?" I snorted. "You're pathetic. Emily is a toy to you. One you only want when someone else is playing with it."

"That's not true. If I'd had known, I would have—"

"You would have what? Left the job? Held her hand through each interview? Laid in bed with her when she screamed in the middle of the night, afraid she was still living that nightmare? People died right in front of her. She was interviewed and had to give her statement, re-living everything that happened. And you know who was by her side? Maia. Emily clung to my fiancée as though she was a life raft. Her savior. Why? Because she was there. She calmed her down when the nightmares were too much, which is why I suspect she was in Emily's room. We've had to sleep with her the last couple nights because the fear was too much for her. Not that you'd care."

"And why was she kidnapped in the first place? Something having to do with your business or your money? The fact that you're a billionaire and try to pretend like you're just an everyday Joe. I warned you to get security when you were out and about, but no, I was being ostentatious and overbearing."

"Fuck you, Portia. Fuck you and your weak excuses for not being in our daughter's life. I've told you what's going to happen. Now get the fuck out of my house. You can use the bathroom to clean yourself up but that's the end of it. You, me, and Emily are done. You're more damaging to her life when you attempt to be in it for five whole minutes. We'll be fine without you. Actually, we'll thrive without you."

"Don't say that. Rhodes. Please. Don't take my daughter away from me." She stood up, one arm curving around her belly where Maia had kneed her good. "Look, I know I've been a shit mom. I know it. But I truly do want to change. To be a better mom. I came here today to surprise Em. I even have gifts for her from Prague."

I started to shake my head.

"No, no, please. I swear I had Emily's best interest at heart when coming here. I also have a mother and daughter spa day booked for this weekend. My weekend. You said I need to be in her life. This was my first step."

"You can't just break in and offer Emily gifts and a spa day to get on her good side. She's not five anymore, Portia. She's going to be fourteen soon. You think your crap has gone unnoticed by her? You know, when I introduced Maia as my fiancé, Emily was excited about the idea that she'd finally have a woman in her life every day."

"Not like she hasn't had Marisol," Portia griped under her breath.

"Marisol is like a grandmother. Fucking hell." I laced my hands behind my neck and breathed through the anger bubbling in my gut. "You see, it's this type of thing that proves you are not capable of being unselfish. You should be so happy Emily's had Marisol because she didn't have her mom! At least she had a mature feminine example but again, the thing you don't seem to get is she didn't want another woman. Emily wanted you! Her mother. And Marisol has been great, but she has a job to do. She isn't spending all her time bonding with Emily. She's running the house, doing the cooking, cleaning, laundry, the bills, taking and picking up Emily from school. But when the day is done, or the weekend comes along, she's spending time with her family. You'd know all of that if you talked to your own child for more than a minute at a time."

Portia's shoulders fell and she leaned against the wall, completely deflated. "I know. I'm a bad mother. But I really do want a second chance."

"Second... More like a thousand chances."

"Okay, fine, you've given me a thousand chances. I'm asking for one more. Please. I'll do whatever it takes."

That's when I remembered I needed to take Maia to Colorado this weekend for her grandmother's funeral. I had no idea what we were going to encounter with her stepfather and stepbrother but I knew it wasn't a situation I could bring Emily into. I'd planned on leaving her with Marisol and a dozen guards, but this might be a two birds one stone situation. With Marisol here, along with Portia, Emily could get the one-on-one time with her mother under Marisol's supervision. I'd pay her double to stay the weekend. After what happened today and last week, I didn't think Marisol was planning to be too far away from Emily anyway.

I clenched my teeth so hard my molars ached. "Fine. Against my better judgment, I'm going to give you your thousand and one chance. On Friday, Maia and I have to go to Colorado. Her grandmother passed away. After what Emily's been through, I'd rather not have her travel or attend a funeral."

"No problem. I'll take her for the weekend."

"You'll come and stay in the guest house, starting Friday until I come back. It may take a few days to settle things up with Maia's family. If you are the mother you say you want to be, you will cancel everything you have on your schedule and focus all of your time and attention on your daughter. Marisol will be here to supervise."

"I don't need someone to supervise me taking care of my own daughter." The sass oozed from her mouth.

"Well, seeing as you've never taken care of your child a day in her life, I view things differently. Emily trusts Marisol. She wants to trust you. Right now, she needs people that love her at her back. It's what *she* needs, *not you*. Do you understand?"

"Fine. But can I still take her to the spa day?"

"If you take her, you will also take Marisol and no less than four members of my new security team. Frank will not be included in that mix. As of today, your fuck buddy will be out of a job."

"Seriously, that's not necessary. It was years and years ago, Rhodes."

"What you don't understand is this: I don't give a fuck. He let an unauthorized person into my home. Our daughter had been kidnapped, Portia. Taken by gunpoint and held for hours before I was able to get to her. Emily's safety matters more than anything. Now, the next step for you is to clean yourself up. Go and apologize to Emily and Marisol for what you did. I'll see if Maia is interested in hearing your apology."

"But she's the one that attacked me! I'm bleeding, for crying out loud. And she better not have scarred me. My face is my moneymaker."

"No, the fact that you're my ex-wife and I'm a decent guy who pays you an exorbitant alimony is how you make your money. Let's not get it twisted."

"You're a real bastard, you know that?"

"Yeah, I'm also the bastard who decides whether you go or stay in your daughter's life. The bathroom is there, in case you've forgotten," I directed and then stormed toward my bedroom.

I heard the shower running and knew I needed to burn off some of this frustration before I went down and talked to Emily.

When I entered the bathroom, steam engulfed me. Maia was under the spray, hands braced on the wall, head down.

Sizzling need raced through my veins as I shucked off my pants and entered the shower stall taking in her strong body and luscious ass.

When Maia turned around to greet me, I grabbed her around the ribs and hoisted her up. Her legs automatically wound around my waist. I was already hard as I prodded at her entrance.

Her eyes widened in surprise.

"This okay?" I grated through my teeth, the head of my

cock resting between those pouty velvety lips.

She nodded succinctly, and I thrust all the way to the hilt, both of us crying out at the mind-blowing pleasure. I pressed her against the wall, fully imbedded, as I lifted my hand and wrapped it around her throat, my thumb holding her jaw. I felt wild and untamed, energy flowing through my veins as I stared straight into her soul.

"You protected our girl." My nostrils flared, my cock throbbing inside her.

"She's my family," she whispered, her eyes already dilated, her nails digging crescent shaped moons into my back while I could feel her pussy lock down around my cock.

"You would do anything for her." It was a revelation, not a statement. One so powerful I closed my eyes and breathed, sharing air between us.

"I'd die for her. I'd die for you." Each word was whispered against my lips as though we were both tasting her truth.

"Nothing's ever gonna come between us, Maia. It's you, me, and Em to the end," I growled, flicking my tongue against her plump bottom lip.

"To the end," she whispered.

I started to thrust, painfully slow, our gazes locked on one another, our mouths grazing as I made unhurried love to her. Putting everything I couldn't say into our lovemaking. And when she sailed over the edge of the cliff into bliss, I followed her. I'd follow her anywhere.

Episode 100

Sky's the Limit

SUMMER

TJ slept against my chest the entire way back to our winter wonderland resort getting in a very late nap. We should have put him to bed, but we didn't want him to miss out on the first time we'd be celebrating as a real family.

We entered the lobby of the resort as a group sporting bright pink noses from the cold, overflowing with boisterous laughter, and smiling faces. A man in a pristine suit approached our group and went straight up to my dad.

"Mr. Belanger, your private room has been set up and staffed exactly as you asked." He bowed formally. "If you and your party will follow me," he encouraged.

"Dad, what's going on?" I asked.

My father beamed with joy. "You'll see," he taunted with a sweetness I knew meant he was about to surprise me. Dad loved surprises. I mean, who didn't? More than that, though, Dad loved to *give* surprises to those he cared for. And I have to admit, he was really good at it.

Jack offered to take TJ, who was now awake and babbling

away. Some words were in Norwegian, and others were English. Regardless, everything he said was cute as all get-out.

I passed off TJ, and Jack put him on his hip like an experienced parent, then reached out his free hand. I took it and held on, the three of us following right behind Dad, the rest of our group behind us. We were led to a set of double doors where everyone abruptly stopped.

"Congratulations, Mr. & Mrs. Larsen," the manager said and opened the doors with a flourish.

The room beyond was decked out in formal finery. Candles and flowers gave the room an intimate glow and the pleasant floral scent wasn't overpowering. In the center of the space was a long rectangular table with plush dark green velvet seats and golden armrests already set up for ten. One of the chairs was a highchair. Champagne bottles were chilling in buckets of ice in each corner of the room along with large standing flower arrangements. A brilliant chandelier hanging several feet above ran almost the entire length of the table, it's dangling crystals shooting rainbows across the table in every direction. There were gold chargers under fine porcelain plates, gold flatware along with crystal wine goblets and water glasses, each place setting with a forest green napkin folded in the center. Flowers in shades of white, with green leaves and gold accents made the room look like a bona fide small wedding reception.

I let go of Jack's hand and bolted into my father's arms. "Thank you, Dad. I love it so much. It's absolutely perfect!" I gushed through the emotion threatening to turn me into a teary mess once again. But I'd cried too much today; it was time to celebrate. Time to soak in the good cheer we wanted to share with the people who meant the most to us.

"My daughter deserved a proper wedding reception. This was the best I could do after hearing you were dropping a surprise wedding on Jack. Your Mom and I wanted to make sure it was beyond memorable." He swallowed and cleared his throat, his eyes glistening with unshed tears. "I'm so happy for you, Sunny. You deserve a man who loves everything about you with his whole heart. And I do believe you have found that in Jack."

I cuddled against his chest and nodded, my gaze on my husband, who was looking at me as though the very moon had risen tonight in my honor. "I've never been happier."

Jack smiled and kissed the top of TJ's head. Our little one was kicking his feet, his eyes bulging at all the different things in the room to explore. Jack laughed and put him down. My mother immediately went to TJ and took his hand, walking him around the room, pointing at the different things he might find interesting. She was going to be an amazing grand-mother.

"Mr. Belanger, shall we start the drink service?" the manager asked my father.

"Absolutely. Champagne for everyone!" he called out, squeezed me tight, then let me go.

Autumn ambushed me with a huge hug. "I'm so happy for you, Sis. You deserve all of this and more!" she said while untying my cloak. "Turn around," she whispered in my ear. "I want Jack's eyes entirely on you when he sees you in this dress."

I did as instructed as she removed my white cloak.

Jack's mouth dropped open and he gasped. His gaze took in my dress from top to toe and back. My chest rose and fell under that heated look. He approached as though in slow motion. When he got to me, he held out his hand, and I put mine in his.

"Spin," he instructed, a guttural rasp I swore I could feel running down my spine like a fingertip.

I slowly turned in a circle, my hand still in his above my head as I did so.

"Jesus, you've never been more beautiful. I'll imagine you just like this our entire lives together."

"You like?" I bit into my bottom lip as he plastered me to his chest enfolding me in his embrace.

"I don't like. *I love.* The dress. Our ceremony. This reception. You. It's all more than I could have ever imagined. What we shared this evening, it was beyond my wildest dreams. Thank you for choosing to stay."

I chuckled. "It's you who chose me, remember?" I said, referring to the auction.

He shook his head. "No, I don't believe that for a second. Something bigger than us was involved. I don't know if it's the Universe, God, destiny, or fate. Whatever it is, we were meant to be right here, right now in this moment, experiencing a love that will never fade. We'll take it with us into eternity. Just as you claimed."

"Oooh, is my normally rational, science-over-spirituality type husband talking witchy to me?" I shifted my lips into a kissy pout. "That deserves a reward."

He laughed out loud then pressed his mouth to my exposed neck, layering a line of kisses from my clavicle to the space just behind my ear. His hot breath fanned that sensitive erogenous zone, and I mewled under his attention while clinging to his muscular back.

"There's only one thing I want," he whispered.

"And that would be?" I breathed, my heart rate rising along with desire.

"You. Naked. Spread out on our bed for me to ravish as I please." His voice was a deep rumble I felt race through my body and settle hotly between my thighs.

I squeezed my legs together as I swallowed against the sudden dryness in my throat.

Where the hell was that champagne?

"Okay," I croaked. "So now then?" I suggested, without any concern for the eight other guests here to celebrate with us.

Jack burst out laughing even harder than before, relieving

the sexual tension that could have been cut between us with a knife. "Later, my darling. Later."

I frowned, and let out a little miffed *harrumph,* which only made Jack laugh harder and more obnoxiously.

"Come, my boy," Henrik gestured to the empty seat in the middle of the table. "We're waiting for you two to sit so we can toast."

I followed Jack to the center of the table and took the chair he'd pulled out for me. He then sat in the seat to my left. Once we were settled, everyone took a seat. TJ was across from us, in between the grandmothers, something I was pretty sure they maneuvered intentionally. Probably to give Jack and me a break, but I knew my mother. She was getting in as much kiddo time as she could, especially since we hadn't decided what our plan was regarding where we were going to settle down permanently. I honestly still didn't know. It was such a huge commitment on both sides. But Jack and I would have those conversations once we were back in Oslo.

The waitstaff handed each of us a filled champagne glass. Henrik then stood and gestured for Irene to stand at his side. He put an arm around her back as he held up his glass over the table.

"Jack, you are like a son to us," Henrik spoke, his words strong and proud. "Irene and I have always tried to show you that you were welcome in our home and our lives as part of the family."

Jack nodded. "You did. Absolutely. I wouldn't be the man I am today without your guidance throughout the years. I'm eternally grateful."

Irene let a tear slide down her cheek and patted at her eyes while Henrik smiled in return. "Now, as you embark on your own journey, creating a family with Summer and TJ, we both want you to know how loved you are. We are amazed at all you've accomplished and are inspired by the man you've become. We know you'll make an excellent father to TJ, and husband to Summer. We're proud of you, son. We hope you, Summer, and TJ, and any other children you may bring into the family have a wonderful life filled with love."

"Cheers!" my sister shouted.

"Shears!" TJ lifted his sippy cup, trying to emulate Autumn.

Erik and Savannah lifted their glasses into the air along with Summer's parents. Then my parents stood. Dad held out his glass, grinning from ear to ear.

"Summer, we are thrilled in the choice you have made to marry Jack. We can see how very much he means to you and vice versa. Sometimes love smacks you upside the head and shows you the way. I believe that's what happened for the two of you. And after all you've been through these past weeks, your mother and I believe this will be a marriage that can withstand anything life throws at you. We love the woman you've become and can see that you are both in good hands with one another. May you be blessed with a long and happy marriage."

"And lots more grandbabies!" Mom quipped, and we all laughed.

After Mom's outburst came a quick toast by Erik who spoke of brotherhood and finding one's true love. Then, Jack stood and turned to face me more than our family.

"Summer, you have changed my entire life. All for the better. I used to think true love was improbable for a guy like me. Someone who didn't really believe something of that magnitude could be mine too. I thought it was reserved for the few like Irene and Henrik and Troy and Ellen. But after seeing my brother Erik enter the auction and find the love of his life in Savannah, my tune changed. I started to believe I could find the right woman for me in the auction. Which I did, but that wasn't when you ensnared my heart, was it?" He shook his head, and I gifted him a devilish smile.

"I never thought the day I walked into a building and got

stuck in an elevator with a woman who stole my breath and challenged me at every turn would be the start of my new life. Yet here we are."

"But, of course, I gave him the wrong phone number when he asked for mine," I shared with the group.

"No way!" Autumn gasped. "What number did you give him?"

"The pizza place in town," I grinned.

"That's hilarious! Bet sexy businessman didn't expect to have to chase after you." Autumn teased.

"Very true," Jack answered good-naturedly. "But low and behold, who was standing up on that stage looking like the sun had just come out to shed light on my very dark life? None other than my dream woman."

A collaborative, drawn out "Aww" soared through the room as tears filled my eyes.

"I love you with my whole heart, Summer. I'll always put you and TJ's happiness first, and I'll never forsake the bond we've built. I can't believe I get to spend my life with you." His tone was filled with emotion that I could practically taste.

Instead of clinking our glasses, I jumped up, grabbed both of his cheeks and laid a fat smackaroo on him.

The sweet "Aww" from our group turned into catcalls and hoots and hollers as the kiss went on. I didn't care.

"I can't wait to spend my life with you either." I pecked him lightly on the lips once more. "Sky's the limit on our happiness."

"Sky's the limit," he repeated. "Now, who's ready to eat?"

"Oh, my goodness, I'm starved!" I agreed.

Dad waved at the waiters to get things moving, and before I knew it, there was a plethora of platters set in the center of the table with a mix of vegan dishes and what I learned were traditional Norwegian foods. There was *Røkelaks,* a smoked salmon dish Jack was excited to see offered, and *Brunost,* a sweet brown cheese that was to die for. Of course,

Dad ordered a couple of vegetable-based dishes, including pasta, but there were many things to choose from, inspiring a unique discussion between the families about their food preferences. Sometimes I forgot that we were two unique groups of people with vast spiritual and cultural differences. We had a lot to learn about one another, which was another exciting part of this new journey.

When the food was demolished and TJ crashed out against Erik's chest this time, the resort manager came in with a traditional Norwegian spirit called *Aquavit*, which I was told was usually shared on special days and holidays such as Christmas.

"This drink is referred to as the 'water of life' and is often shared with loved ones. It's known for being Norway's national drink," Henrik announced to the group.

"Water of life? That sounds like my kind of spirit," Mom gushed.

The waiter filled each person's small crystal cocktail glass with the liquor as another staff member brought in a volcano-shaped dessert. It looked like at least a dozen or so cake rings that sat on top of one another, each ring smaller than the previous one, creating a pyramid-like structure. There was white icing drizzled all over the cake, and it smelled divine. Notes of almond and sugar wafting in the air made my mouth water.

Jack puffed up with pride as the unusual wedding cake was placed on the table between us.

"This is a *Kransekake*. A traditional Norwegian wedding cake also called the Lover's Ring Tree. The cake and its structure are meant to symbolize everlasting love." He picked up one of the extra pieces lying around the base of the cake, also drizzled with frosting and held it up to my lips. "Taste it."

I took the bite he offered, keeping my eyes open as the almond and pastry flavors exploded on my tongue. I hummed as I chewed. Jack's expression was bursting with love and joy as I grabbed a piece and offered it to him.

He slowly took it from my fingertips, swiping his tongue along my thumb as he did so. A shiver of arousal swam from the tips of my fingers, up my arm, and settled in my chest. His pupils dilated, desire swirling in his heated gaze.

Suddenly, I was ready to be done with dinner, and I made my intentions known to the room. "Welp, I think that's about all the celebrating I want to do here…"

"Atta girl. Go get your man," Mom said as Jack and I stood.

"You cool with taking TJ for the night and morning?" Jack asked Erik.

"Would be our pleasure," Erik confirmed. "Besides, he's crashed out anyway. We've got the diaper bag already loaded with everything he needs. Tomorrow, after breakfast, we'll take him to play in the snow and have lunch out in the town. Give you both a full day together."

"That would be lovely, guys. Thank you," I said.

"No problem at all," Savannah waved her hand. "We want to get in as much time with TJ as we can before we head to Montana. The twins will be here soon, and I really want to be there for Dakota and help out as much as possible."

"I can totally see that," I agreed. "If Autumn were preggers, I'd be all over Auntie duty."

"Fat chance of that happening any time soon. You and Jack will probably have a couple more kids before I even get married. Ugh." Autumn slumped in her chair, seeming rather sad.

"I thought you had a girlfriend," Savannah asked.

Autumn shrugged and looked away.

My heart stopped. "Did you finally break it off with Raquel?" I said with far too much enthusiasm.

"As a matter of fact, I did. Don't be so thrilled with my relationship ending. I'm still bummed about it. I hoped she'd be the one."

I held my breath, doing my best not to react insensitively. I fucking hated Raquel.

Autumn glared in my direction, likely seeing through my expression I wasn't unhappy about this breakup. "Just because you found Prince Charming over there doesn't mean we all do. Sometimes it's just not in the cards."

That time my mother snorted. "It's always in the cards." She reached into her purse and pulled out a tarot deck.

"I'm the one that has the sight, Ma, and I've never seen myself walking down the aisle to the person of my dreams, male or female."

"Do you want to be married one day?" Savannah asked.

"Honestly…more than anything. I would love to share my life with someone special. Someone who gets me, and of course, all of this chaos and family drama, I mean loyalty." She grinned and gestured around the room.

Autumn was right. We did have an unorthodox family that only got more complex with the addition of Jack, TJ, and all of the Johansens. We were a lot. Our spiritual beliefs. Our culinary needs. The way we made a living. The average person might shy away from all that comes with our group. I'm just glad Jack wasn't scared off.

"You know, you could always enter the auction," Erik suggested. "Seemed to work out aces for me and Jack."

Autumn's eyes widened before she looked at me, then at Mom and then at Dad. "Holy shit, I could totally enter the auction and let fate decide who was my destiny. That's a brilliant idea, Erik!"

"Whoo hoo!" Mom jumped up and clapped while dancing around the table and calling to the ancestors.

"I think that's our cue," Jack whispered.

"Wait, what's going on now?" I blinked in confusion as Jack helped me up and around the table. We both kissed TJ's head as he slept through all the noise like a champ. This boded well for our future sex life with a little one around.

"Come, darling, we have a long night ahead of us." He growled under his breath, and we both waved as we exited the room.

Jack led me down the hallway and up the stairs. Each staff member we passed on the way to our room congratulated us on our nuptials.

By the time we made it to our room, my head was spinning with all that had happened that day but especially regarding that last part involving my sister.

"What just happened in there?"

"You mean after our reception wound down?" Jack asked, tugging his black cashmere sweater up and off, leaving him in a white V-neck t-shirt. Before I could comment, he whipped the t-shirt off, gifting me a perfect view of his golden, muscular chest. I wanted to lick him everywhere, from his waistband up and over every abdominal hill and valley, over his steely pecs and all along his tasty neck.

I nodded silently as I watched my husband undo his belt and pull it through the loops on his pants and drop it on the floor. I jumped at the sudden sound; my gaze focused entirely on each new bit of skin that was revealed.

"Your sister just decided to enter The Marriage Auction."

I was about to respond when his pants and underwear hit the floor. Instead, I attacked him with my mouth. Anything else would have to come later.

Priorities and all that.

Episode 101

Angel of Death

MADAM ALANA

The shower was not hot enough as I pressed my forehead to the cool tile, letting the spray crash over my sore and battered muscles. Being bounced around in the cargo space of one car to another for most of the day yesterday had been murder on my body. Regardless, it wasn't as bad as the heaviness within my heart. Knowing it was my choice thirty years ago that had set this entire mess into motion felt like the weight of the world rested on my weak shoulders. I was no longer built for such strife and sacrifice. I had been born into it, lived a tumultuous life my first eighteen years on this Earth, but not since Christophe purchased me in the auction. Since then, we'd lived a beautiful, rather pampered lifestyle. Something I wouldn't apologize for as both Christo and I worked tirelessly over the years to get to this point.

"I can hear you thinking in there, *mon coeur*. Care to share?" Christophe's sleepy voice filtered through the sound of the water spray and my turbulent thoughts.

I lifted my head and peered through the steamy glass.

Christo stood in a pair of silk pajama pants and nothing else. His bronzed chest with a smattering of greying hair across his pecs still as welcoming and heart-stopping as it was when we first met, if a little softer and less muscular with age.

I turned off the shower and wiped the water out of my eyes, then ran my hands through my hair, squeezing the water out of the longer locks at the end. When I opened the shower door Christophe was there, holding a big fluffy white towel open for me. I went willingly into the center of his arms as he wrapped it around my body and held me locked against his chest. He pressed his face to my wet neck and shoulder.

"You know none of this is your fault, Alana. Living our lives and stopping a monster from hurting more people the way he did Celine was not a bad thing. Think of how many women were saved from a similar horror Celine suffered when that man went to jail."

I nodded against his chest while listening to his words along with the comforting beat of his heart.

"It doesn't change the situation we are in now. Or that of Julianne, Brenden and Giovanni." My voice cracked as the trauma they'd suffered due to Bianca ran rampant through my mind. And to find out she was Angus' daughter the entire time? I winced against the knowledge, rubbing my face against Christo's chest, trying to escape the ugly emotions plaguing my every thought.

"No, it doesn't, but we will get through this as we have gotten through every trial in our lives. Together. Today, we'll sit down with Diego and work through whatever plan he's concocted." He ran his hands over my body, drying and comforting me at the same time.

"And what of his demand?" I whispered, leaning back, needing to look into his steely gaze.

"About finding him a wife?"

I nodded, my heart in my throat.

"It is what you do best, is it not?"

"*Oui*, but what he wants does not fit into any terms or contracts I've negotiated in the past. He wants a wife for life. Someone who is accepting of the man he is, including but not limited to looking the other way on his criminal activities. Is that not the same as helping a man like Angus?"

"Do you believe Diego would harm a woman you paired him with? Because I get the impression that whoever he chose would be worshipped by him and his men. If the way they respected and adored Deigo's mother was anything to go by, she'd be a queen."

"But what of the danger involved with being connected to a man like him?"

"Full disclosure would be necessary. The woman that might be best for him wouldn't be similar to one of your average candidates. She'd need to be...*special*. Have a strong constitution. Be able to look the other way on what the man does for a living. Or, alternately, be like him, possibly having had some dalliances of her own with the authorities in the past."

"I wouldn't even know where to start," I admitted.

He rubbed his hands along my bare arms and hugged me tight. "We'll brainstorm it. I have complete faith in your matchmaking abilities. You have a stellar track record, *chérie*. And you always rise to any challenge."

I nuzzled his warm skin and sighed. "*Je t'aime*, Christo. Without you and your love, I would be nothing. I'd still be on the streets without a penny to my name and no family to speak of."

He chuckled and squeezed me tighter. "I don't believe that for a second. You are extremely resourceful, intelligent and have a unique ability to understand the true nature of people. This would have taken you far in life regardless of my involvement."

I rose onto my toes, wrapped my arms around my husband's neck and kissed him. He instantly opened his mouth, allowing me entrance. Our tongues tangoed, a dance we'd shared more times than I could ever count. I put all that I had into that kiss. My broken heart, my undying love for him, and my fear of what was to come. He took it all and gave me back his loyalty, his strength, and endless belief that when we braved things together, we'd be okay.

Once the kiss ended, he pressed his forehead to mine. "I would like to continue this on the bed, alas, we need to meet our host to go over his plan. I want this done and over with as soon as possible. For us, for those we love in New York and California, and for Celine, once and for all. Angus is finally going to get what he is owed, and I, for one, am eager to get the ball rolling."

I pecked his lips once more. "Give me thirty minutes to get ready for the day."

"You shall have it." He gripped my bum cheekily and then winked before letting me go.

"Christo?" I called out when he reached the door to the guestroom we were staying in.

He turned around, and I took in all that was him. Strong shoulders that could weather any storm. Kind eyes that melted just for me. A broad stature and body that had aged over the last thirty years but still got my heart pumping and desire soaring through my veins every time he said my name in that breathy manner I adored. More than all of that, I saw *him*.

A good man. A loving man. My soulmate. My other half.

"You are more than I could have ever dreamed up for myself. The life you've given me. Our love. It's better than any dream or love story I've ever heard, because it's real, and it's ours."

He smiled and shook his head. "Get ready, Alana, or we're going to be late for our meeting. Something tells me the leader of the Latin Mafia wouldn't take too kindly to that."

I chuckled. "Something tells me he'd make it a point to be crass and tease us endlessly about our not being able to keep our hands off one another."

"This is probably true," he agreed.

"I'll be out in thirty," I said and then shut the bathroom door so I wouldn't be distracted by my favorite person in the entire world.

Today we'd decide how we were going to deal with Angus and Bianca.

* * * *

Apparently, our meeting meant we'd have another meal together, prior to our chat. Once again, Diego's mother was making a feast. My stomach, however, did not agree with the idea of food, which garnered me dirty looks from *Mamá* along with hand gestures to her curves and the lack of my own. The woman I ended up finding for Diego would have to win over *Mamá* too. I made a mental note to keep her in mind when I started the process of finding Diego a bride once this was all over.

Provided I was alive when it ended.

For thirty minutes, I snuck food onto Christo's plate when *Mamá* wasn't looking, hoping to appease her. Christo ate with gusto, even though a worried expression crossed his features when he noticed I was pushing all my food to his plate. Blessedly, he rolled with my quirks as he always did. It was our way. But the look he gave me after said we'd be discussing my lack of appetite in private.

Just like last night, the men thanked the matriarch and cleaned up the dishes as Diego led us back to his study. I was too wired to sit, preferring to stand with my arms crossed over my chest as I leaned against one of the empty chairs in front of his desk.

Diego sat, leaned forward, then pressed a button on his

desk. The air changed and Christo and I whirled around to face the long wall of bookcases. Shockingly, a four-foot-wide section popped out about a foot or more and then slid to one side. Behind it was an entire room, with a wall of flatscreen TVs on the other side of it, a long control panel and several other desks and computers. There were four men in front of the wall of screens pressing buttons, their heads moving as though looking from one screen to another. There was yet another man on a computer looking at what seemed to be data or records of some kind. Behind all of them, walking the perimeter of the room, his gaze tracking from the screens to the desktop computers and back was another man, this one oozing authority. I pegged him as the boss in that space.

"I want more detail on that location." He pointed to a screen. "She was seen having dinner with a man matching Angus's description there. Get me everything you know about that restaurant and the camera footage along those streets, whether it be traffic or private businesses. Hack whatever you need to."

"Welcome to my European command center," Diego announced to us. "Angel," he called out, and the man turned around and calmly walked into the study.

He was younger than Diego and scary handsome. Rather frightening in his serious mannerism, chiseled facial features, and meticulous appearance. More like a handsome devil than an angel. His dark gaze was cool and calculating. He wore all black from head to toe. Tailored slacks and a fitted black dress shirt that he'd buttoned all the way up. The shirt, however, did not take away from the large neck tattoo I spied when he lifted his chin. A phoenix rising from the ashes, its wings stretched out along the sides of his neck as if the bird was still in flight. Everything about him was sharp lines and dark edges with a heavy dose of mystery. He had the same black hair as Diego, only his was cropped tight to the scalp with intricate meticulously cut lines around the face that could only have been done by a barber. His coal black eyes seared straight through me, a chill surfacing at the intense way he assessed me, Christo, and then Diego.

"Brother." He dipped his chin and lowered his gaze with what seemed to be respect.

"Angel is my baby brother, head of my security, my top advisor, and most skilled assassin. Don't let the good looks fool you. If you lay eyes on him, that means you are in the inner circle. *Parte de la familia.* It also can mean you are about to lose your life as he is known as *Ángel de la Muerte.* The Angel of Death."

I gasped and stepped back. Christophe immediately left his seat and came to stand at my side, slightly in front of me.

"Not to worry. We do not invite outsiders or our enemies into our home to stay and have meals with *mi familia.* You can relax. Please," Diego gestured to the seat in front of him. My legs felt wobbly as Christo led me to the chair. I sat in it, while he stood behind me, his hands on my shoulders, always there for support and to keep me safe. Christophe might be a lover more than a fighter, but he'd do what he had to in order to protect me. Even risk his own life.

"Update," Diego clipped.

"Bianca has moved away from the location close to the Toussaint estate," Angel stated. "They both have been sighted at a villa in The Gros Caillou, located in the *7th arrondissement.* We've scouted the location before. We have had eyes on it for a while now. My men have been able to confirm both Bianca's entrance into the building last night and Angus' earlier that afternoon. We believe they are scrambling to locate Ms. Toussaint's whereabouts."

"What are our next steps?" I interrupted, doing my best to keep my voice from showing any emotion. I was on pins and needles, ready to get my life back.

"The building is well guarded. Two men at every

entrance. Several rotating around the entire building. The windows on the lower levels have bars with more guards inside the home. There are also snipers on the neighboring roofs, ready to fire at a moment's notice."

I gritted my teeth. "Then how are we going to get to them? You can't send in your men knowing they'll be slaughtered immediately," I put my hand over my chest, my skin becoming clammy at a visual of the men I'd just had meals with being shot down in cold blood, all because of me. "I won't have it. My life is not worth theirs."

Angel crossed his arms over his chest and gave me what I believed was a smile but looked more like a cold, calculated sneer. "I'm glad you feel that way, *Madam*. It will make our next request more palatable to you."

"A request? I'll do anything to help get out of this predicament. My godchildren have been blown up and are right now having their people inform the American press they are all dead while going into hiding and healing from their injuries. One is in a coma with over half of his body burnt to a crisp. My niece was kidnapped and is traumatized for life. If you have a plan, I'm happy to participate."

"It will be dangerous." Diego tilted his head. "Are you truly willing to risk your own life to end this war between you and Sokolov?"

"Alana…" Christophe warned, knowing me all too well. I'd jump in with both feet if it meant no additional harm would come to those I loved.

"When do we start? What do I have to do?"

"We know Angus well. He'll need to believe he has the upper hand," Angel shared. "Our plan is to have you call one of your most trusted attendants at your estate and tell them your whereabouts. We know your phones have been tapped not only by the authorities, but most likely by Angus' team. We will cut off the transmissions to the authorities, so they'll be none the wiser, while Angus' team gets the tip and comes to the location we're controlling. That location being a hotel in a small city about an hour drive outside of Paris."

I frowned. "Okay. And then what?"

The Angel of Death did smile that time, the cruel curl of his lips almost beautiful in its brutality.

"Then we offer you up as bait."

Episode 102

There Is No "I" in Team

JULIANNE

"Listen to this crap," I hissed as I held open the latest edition of *The New York Times.* The media was once again reporting whatever the hell it wanted, not the statement that we had released by Gio's assistant and jack-of-all-trades, Muriel. One of a handful of people who now knew we were, in fact, alive and hiding out at the same lake house Gio had disappeared to when Bianca starting pulling her shit and our parents had died.

"Do I even want to hear this?" Gio groaned while he propped on his side in the king-sized bed, pillows shoved against his chest so he could lean on them. Since we'd arrived yesterday, he'd completely changed. In the hospital, he was angry, filled with complaints, and looked half on his death bed. There were still slight dark circles under his eyes from lack of sleep, but now that he'd had a full night's rest in a bed he was used to, with me by his side, he looked more human and alive than he had since I first saw him in the hospital last week.

I cleared my throat. "Quote: It has been revealed that

business mogul Giovanni Falco, the heir to the Falco dynasty and his new bride, Julianne, were two of the three persons that perished in last week's mid-town explosion. The other victim was real estate magnate Brenden Myers. Falco's net worth was estimated to be around forty billion, Myers around five hundred million. Falco leaves no family behind. Myers leaves behind a wife, Bianca, who it is believed will inherit the empire. This tragedy has rocked the business world in New York. This story is evolving and will be updated as more information becomes available. Unquote."

"I literally got a three-word mention. *New bride, Julianne.* That's all I am." I slapped the paper down on the bed and flopped backward into the cloud of pillows leaning against the headboard.

Gio reached out and took my hand. "The media is packed with nothing but assholes. Never read your own press. It's created entirely on supposition and sensationalism. None of if it tells the real truth."

I pouted like a child not getting her way, but it really irked me that my entire life's work to date was whittled down to one thing… being *Giovanni's wife.* Blech. "See, this is what's wrong with the patriarchy. This is why women lose their shit. I have more work and life achievements than my brother, and he's the one recognized."

"Jules…"

"And don't you dare get me started on you. My scores and honors in college were far higher than either of you, but because I married a man with more money than God, I'm relegated to 'wife' status. My life and achievements don't matter."

Gio patted my unburned palm, and I snarled, getting more wound up by the second.

"You matter to me, Jules. You're all that matters to me. I could lose every dime I have and not give a flying fuck. As long as I get to keep you for the rest of my life, everything else can disappear. We can stay dead for all I care." He paused, staring at a spot only he could see. "Actually, it's not a bad idea…" His finger teased the sensitive skin of my inner arm where I hadn't been burned, easing my irritation. The top of my forearms and hands had been scalded from the fire, but the rest of me faired far better. I was the lucky one. My head wound still had the line of stitches Maggie was keeping her eagle eye on, and the headaches were lessening each day.

Giovanni and my brother were an entirely different story. Both had received some pretty gruesome burns. Though the doctors were convinced that with the right treatment and commitment to his medical care, Gio would come out of it less scarred than we'd imagined based on what the burns looked like at the start. Brenden's outlook wasn't as optimistic. The doctors didn't hold out hope he'd ever wake from his coma if he made it through at all. They said if he survived the next couple weeks it would be a miracle and urged us to get his affairs in order.

I didn't allow myself to even consider the thought that I'd lose Brenden forever, especially after having lost our parents so suddenly. And because we were in hiding, Brenden had been shipped to the nation's best burn center under the pseudonym Bruno had given him. He'd set up a payment system for Brenden's care that couldn't be tracked back to us. At least I knew he was safe from Bianca for the time being, though I worried for my godmother. Alana didn't share much in her last call with us, but I knew her well. She'd do whatever it took to end this once and for all. I just prayed she'd come back to us whole.

"Knock, knock, you two! Time for me to clean and bandage the big guy!" Maggie called through the door as she banged on the wood several times.

"Already?" Gio groaned.

"Come in!" I hollered. I was fully clothed in lounge wear, whereas Gio was completely naked lying on top of the sheets, hugging the satin pillows while his backside received some fresh air.

"Ooh! I see you're following my orders to the letter. I love when my patients do that. Good boys get rewards," Maggie cooed as she entered wearing scrubs. We'd explained she could wear what she wanted, since this would be her home for the foreseeable future, and she told us she was more comfortable in scrubs than anything else. Today's outfit had cat faces on them.

"I'm loving the cats." I smiled at the older woman.

"Aren't they the cutest? Got 'em at half price during the holidays," Maggie gushed.

"Well, they're awesome, right, Gio?"

"Fucking great. Can we get to my reward?" Gio grouched.

Maggie narrowed her gaze. "I was going to show Julianne how to help you bathe so that it wasn't me cleaning your dangly bits, but if you're going to get snappy with me..." She let her words fall away.

"I'm sorry, Mags. I'd love to have my wife help me."

"I'm ready to be trained. Whatever you need, Maggie, I'm all ears." I got up onto my knees, kicking the paper to the floor. Fuck that thing. I didn't need the love and respect of strangers. I just needed my man to be happy and healthy. And for Bianca to fall face first off the nearest tall cliff and land on very jagged rocks. But being able to help Gio be more comfortable during his recovery was also high up on my list of desires.

"I thought so. First, go on and get the wash bucket and fill it with soapy warm water. I'll tend to the burns first," she said.

"Yoo hoo," another knock came from the open door as Muriel walked in. "Oh, sweet baby Jesus!" the older woman said and turned around abruptly.

Maggie snickered. "What? You squeamish? It's just burns."

Muriel shook her head. "No, I...perhaps someone could have told me that Mr. Falco wasn't wearing any clothing."

Giovanni burst into laughter and then moaned in pain. "Shit that's funny." He winced and chuckled at the same time. "You did that on purpose, leaving the door cracked, didn't you?" Giovanni surmised. "What is with you two anyway? I figured two strong, mature, independent ladies like yourselves would get along famously."

"Well, if Missus Big Business would keep your work away while you're healing, maybe we'd get along better. But you are my patient..."

"And he is my boss!" Muriel snapped, something I'd never seen her do in all the years she'd worked for us. Usually, Muriel was the epitome of class and professionalism. The woman spun around, her gaze shooting lasers at Maggie. "I'll have you know, my job is to keep his empire running smoothly while he's playing dead. You may not know this, *Nurse Ratchet*, but he is responsible for over sixty businesses, ten of which he is on the board of directors for."

"So? Like I give a fig what goes on in the corporate world." Maggie twirled her hand in the air in a whoop-dee-doo gesture. "My goal is to get him healed with as little scarring and pain as possible. Your health is your wealth."

"And my goal is to ensure the lights stay on, and for the hundreds of thousands of employees working for him to get paid on time. Or would you like to answer those calls from angry CEOs he's made dozens of promises to?"

"Oh shit, Pookie. You are rich rich. Way to go big guy!" Maggie congratulated.

"Yeah," Gio let out a long, tired breath. "Muriel, you're doing a wonderful job. Feel free to come back in an hour when I've been poked and prodded and bandaged up like a mummy. Thank you."

"Make that two to three hours. After your sponge bath, you're taking a nap."

"All I've done is sleep since we got here," Gio complained.

"You heal when you sleep. Besides, you'll be taking the muscle relaxer, and I don't believe you want to make important business decisions while under the influence of medication. In my vast experience, those two things don't really go well together."

"Two to three hours?" Muriel croaked, her face becoming tight with tension.

"Jules, love of my life, can you help Muriel run the show while I'm incapacitated? Be my second-in-command?" Gio asked.

"Uh, yeah. Whatever you need. We can table anything I don't know for sure, which will probably be most things, but I can certainly try."

"Darling, I have the utmost faith in your abilities to make well-informed decisions. Muriel will advise. Let's not make things sit on the backburner until we return from the dead. As Muriel said, the bills must be paid, and you're a co-signer on all my bank accounts. The banks will process anything we sign until a death certificate is provided as proof of our passing. It's business as usual until then. And since we didn't die, nothing has to change."

"Wait...what? I'm a co-signer? I thought we had separate accounts."

He shook his head. "No darling. When I married you, I married you. That means my dynasty is now yours. Congratulations, your net worth just went up about forty billion."

"For fucks sake, do you think you could have mentioned that?" I gulped, stunned he'd be so reckless. Then again, it absolutely said a lot about how he feels about our marriage.

"When? During our Vegas wedding, Bianca's assault, the fight I had with Brenden, the lawyers working on the contract stuff, or the explosion? We've been a little busy. Besides, I just assumed you knew."

"Well, what about my twenty million?" I taunted, pretending to take affront.

"You can take it out anytime you want. Transfer it today if you'd like. You have access to everything. Isn't that right, Muriel?"

She nodded. "Yes. Mr. Falco asked me to make the adjustment to all of his holdings and bank accounts the morning after you were married. It's all set."

"You're insane, you know that, right? No man worth what you are marries a woman without a prenup." I fully expected his lawyers to follow up with all of that once we were settled, but then I forgot about it.

"I'm insanely in love with you, yes. If you want to rob me blind, that's your prerogative," Gio hissed as Maggie ignored all of us and started cleansing his wounds.

"And what about the money I bring to our marriage?" I asked. I didn't have a lot available to me in liquid cash, but I still had the business and outside investments, not to mention half of my parents' estate now that the wills defaulted back to the originals. And even though the papers noted Brenden as the real estate "magnate" I was the one that now owned seventy-five percent of Falco & Myers.

"Do with it what you want. It's yours."

"But your money is now mine too?" I tilted my head and crossed my arms over my chest.

"Didn't you just say fuck the patriarchy a minute ago? You now have complete control over every detail of our lives. Be happy."

I slumped forward. "I am happy, but you could have told me," I whined and crawled on the bed, putting my face close to his.

"Jules, baby, it's just money. I need you to help Muriel keep our employees from jumping ship. Can you do that for me?" He gritted his teeth as Maggie tended to a particularly sensitive spot.

I held his hand. "I can do that. I'd do anything for you," I whispered and leaned forward and kissed his lips.

He kissed me back for all of a second before he grunted, his body trembling as he worked through the painful process of having his wounds cleaned.

"I'm going to go help Muriel for the next little bit and then I'll come back to learn how to sponge bathe you."

"Can't wait," he grated through his teeth and then let out a long-tortured breath when Maggie paused.

"Darlin', we're about to get into the worst of it," Maggie said, her gaze gentle. She knew he didn't want me to see him in pain, even though I wanted to be there for him. Regardless, I respected his decision for his own body and well-being.

"I'll be in the study," Muriel stated and then left the room.

I cupped Gio's cheek. "Be strong, baby."

"For you, always." He offered me a weak smile as I crawled off the bed, careful not to shift him, then headed for the door.

"You're the bravest, strongest man I know, Giovanni. You've got this!" I called out and then shut the door.

The moment I heard him cry out in pain, I let the tears fall. After taking a moment to catch my bearings, I swiped the tears away, lifted my chin and headed to his study where I knew Muriel would be waiting.

"I'll be the best damn second-in-command you've ever seen," I whispered, ready to take on whatever was needed on my husband's behalf. Because a good wife had her husband's back, and I wanted to prove I deserved the trust Giovanni had in me.

We are a team and there was no "I" in team.

Episode 103

Where in the World is Alana?

MEMPHIS

"Yeah, Ma, you and Dad own the house free and clear. You don't ever have to move. You'll need to pay the property taxes each year, but outside of that, your mortgages have been paid off."

"I can't...I don't...I don't understand, son. How is this possible?" Mom's voice shook after I shared the good news.

I grinned as I thought about how incredible Naomi was, battling against her father. I was still worried about what she planned to do about working for him when the month was up, but ultimately, we came to New York to get my family's home back.

"It was all Naomi. She went to war with her father and came out the victor. Their relationship, however, did not survive the battle."

"Oh no, I'm sorry to hear that. After meeting her parents, I could tell there was some bad blood between them, but I had hoped when the two of you left to discuss the situation things would have gotten worked out. I'm happy to have our home back darlin', don't get me wrong about that. I'm eternally grateful to Naomi for having our family's best interests at heart, but not at the risk of losing her parents. I can't live with that type of unrest on my heart. Tell me you believe things will ultimately work out between the three of them?"

"Momma, I honestly don't know. Some pretty harsh words were said between them, and I hate to admit it, but she disowned him outright. He's going to force her to work for him at his company even though he knows her heart isn't in it."

"Good Lord, that's awful."

"I agree. But ultimately, Naomi's happiness is what's important to me. She has plenty of time to work on her relationship with her family. For now, we've agreed we're focusing on our future, the wedding and my new job opportunity. And now that you own the house free and clear, we can get married as planned."

"That is music to my ears, son. And what of the job? Did you meet with the university?" she asked, nosing into my life as usual.

"I met with them this morning. They offered me the position, provided I finish my coursework before spring training. I've already got things in motion on that front too. Scheduled my online class and made sure the rest of my credits were in line with receiving my bachelor's degree. I start the class next month. Which means, after the wedding, Nay and I will have a couple weeks to honeymoon, and then move me to New York."

"Babe, I was thinking about your apartment in Georgia. We should keep it," Naomi interrupted my call.

"Ma, hold up for a sec."

"Of course, I'll be right here, listening in," she teased.

I chuckled and turned to face Naomi, who was at the table working in some design program that she used to create new jewelry.

"What were you saying, baby?" I asked.

"I know we talked about having you move to New York, and that's still the plan, but I like your apartment, and we'll need somewhere to stay when we visit the family. I imagine you'll want to take trips down to Georgia often, right?"

"Well, yeah, but...you like my place? It's a dump compared to this." I gestured around the palatial home we currently lived in.

She gave a little shrug and pursed her lips. "I like it. Reminds me of the you before me. Besides, I got used to spending time there. I don't see any reason to make a change. We can afford the yearly rent. Plus, Syd can use it when she visits too."

"Well, I think that's a dynamite idea!" Mom had clearly overheard our conversation.

"You're the boss," I winked at Nay as she rolled her eyes and shook her head, then went back to her work.

"Anyway, we'll be home in a couple days to help with the wedding plans."

"Speaking of the wedding, I'll need to know the number of guests Naomi is inviting from her side." I was about to butt in when she continued, "I know we're keeping it small. Just your sisters, and any relatives that live close, as well as the handful of friends you've mentioned, but I need a final tally from Naomi."

"I'll get back to you on the guest list once I've confirmed things with Naomi." My phone beeped, and I glanced down at the screen. It was Jade Lee from The Marriage Auction calling. For some reason, that made me excited and nervous at the same time. "Hey, Momma, I'm getting another call. I'll hit you back later. Love you."

"And I love you, son. Please tell Naomi she has our gratitude for returning our home to us. And I can't thank you both enough for paying off the mortgage in full. Your father and I…" she croaked, "we're just so appreciative and so damn proud of you, son. That's all. Talk soon. Love you. Bye." My mother hung up so fast I couldn't even respond.

I hit the button to accept Jade's call. "Hi Jade, to what do I owe the pleasure of your call?"

"I'm RSVPing for your wedding. I will be attending on behalf of The Marriage Auction."

I frowned. "Jade, I invited you because we're friends, not because of your job."

"Well, be that as it may, I have to inform you that I am attending as your friend but also on Madam Alana's behalf. She has a situation she is handling in France that prevents her from attending. Though she sends along her well wishes for a long and happy life together."

"Okay, now that you've got the work part out of the way…it's me Jade. You can speak freely. Is she okay?"

Jade sighed. "I don't know. I'm worried about her. She left for France with someone having threatened her and one of the other candidates."

"No shit? Who?" I started running through the list of my candidate peers, attempting to guess but coming up empty with someone who may have a shady side.

"Maia Fields," Jade answered. "But I could get in trouble for saying anything, so keep it to yourself."

"I know anything we discuss about The Marriage Auction is confidential. I'm not super familiar with her. She didn't speak much during the whole process. Dang, now I wish I'd connected more with her. She was threatened?"

"Yeah, and her place was trashed. Her bidder swooped her off her feet and they are supposedly fine now, but I know there's more to the story than what Alana has shared. She was really cagey and curt in her correspondence with me last week. She's even given me the go ahead to start working on the next set of candidates and bidders by myself."

"That's good news, right? It means she trusts you."

"Or she's got something keeping her away that she doesn't want me to know about."

I started laughing. "Seriously, Madam Alana is beloved by everyone. I can't imagine a single soul having a beef with her. It's probably one of her admirers gone rogue. I'm sure Christophe will take care of her. But in the meantime, I'll reach out. I'm actually surprised she hasn't been checking in."

"Wait a minute... She hasn't been checking in weekly with you?"

"Nah, I haven't heard a single word since we left Las Vegas."

"You see? That right there is proof something strange is going on. She always checks on the candidates. When I first started, I even offered to do the weekly check-ins, and she said she needed to hear their voices herself. Make sure every candidate was okay. Now you're saying she didn't check in."

"Maybe it's because she knows me better than the others? I'd contact one of the other candidates to see if they've heard from her. Is she responding to communications?"

"We haven't had anything pressing in the last week, so I didn't need to reach out."

"Give her a call and maybe check in with Julianne. That's her goddaughter, right?"

"Oh my God!" Naomi screamed. "Memphis, you need to see this!" Naomi was pointing at her laptop. "Put the phone on speaker. It's important." Her eyes were wild and her face pale.

"What is it?" I got up from the barstool I was perched on in the kitchen and went to the table.

"I got bored of designing so I thought I'd read the latest news..." She pointed to an article in *The New York Times.*

My heart started pounding as I read the paragraph out loud.

"It has been revealed that business mogul Giovanni Falco, the heir to the Falco dynasty and his new bride, Julianne, were two of the three persons that perished in last week's mid-town explosion. The other victim was real estate magnate Brenden Myers…"

"What the fuck! Julianne and Giovanni are dead? Jade, Jade, did you hear that?" I slumped into the chair next to Naomi. Visions of Julianne's bright red hair and big blue eyes flooded my mind.

"I need to go," Jade's voice was barely a whisper. "I need to get in touch with Alana now," she said and hung up.

"Baby…" Naomi reached for my hands. "I'm so sorry. I knew Giovanni as an acquaintance in business, but we weren't close. Were you close to Julianne?"

I shook my head. "Not really. I mean, she was in the auction, but more than anything, I'm worried about Alana. From what I understood, Julianne was her goddaughter and Giovanni her friend. She'd be devastated right now, and what's worse is Jade hasn't really talked to Alana in over a week. And the fact that Alana hasn't been doing her check-ins. I mean, has she called you at all?"

Naomi shook her head. "I know she mentioned that calls and pop-ins were likely, but frankly with all that we had going on, I'd forgotten about it entirely. I'm so sorry. This is awful."

"It is. I just can't believe it. The story says it was an explosion."

Naomi got up from her chair and slid into my lap sideways, her arms around my neck. She hugged me, and I held on to her for a solid few minutes, letting all the information we'd just received soak in as I tried to make sense of it all.

"I need to call some of the girls. Dakota, Faith, Ruby, or Savannah might have an idea of what's going on. Plus, they'll want to be there for Alana as she's grieving. Shit, we should probably go to the funeral. Did the article say anything about a funeral?"

Naomi shook her head. "No, it didn't, but these were

really rich people. If they announced where the funeral was taking place, a bunch of whackos might try to attend, to find a way into the family."

"Seriously?"

"Money brings out the weirdos, baby. I don't know what to tell you."

I kissed her pretty lips and then patted her thigh. She took the hint and got out of my lap. "Do you want a drink? I sure could use a drink after hearing all this."

"Yeah, I'm thinking a beer and a shot."

"Tequila or whiskey."

"It's definitely a whiskey moment."

"You got it." She bent toward me again and pecked my lips. "I'm really sorry to hear about your...um...coworker?" Her lips puckered. "No, that isn't right. Your peer. I'll send up a little prayer that they find peace at the foot of God."

"I love you, Nay."

"I love you, too. Now call your *girlfriends*." She used a silly high-pitched voice when saying the word "girlfriends."

"They are my friends that happen to be girls, not my *girlfriends*. I mean, they are but... Ah, shit, you know what I mean. You're twisting it up for the fun of it."

"But you're no longer frowning, so that means I win. Call your friends. I hope they have some answers about Alana too."

I pulled up my contact list. I would have called Ruby first because I know her and Alana became really close, but the time difference in London would put them in bed right now. So I pulled up the next best person I could think of and dialed.

"If you think I'm dragging this ginormous body all the way to Georgia to attend your wedding to 'God's answer to beautiful women', you've got a screw loose."

"Hey, Dakota, how's pregnant life?" I quipped.

"It fucking sucks. I can't wear any of my clothes, I've

taken to wearing my husband's sweats and flannels."

"You know, there is this thing called maternity clothes…"

"And waste money on clothes I'm never going to wear again? You're outta your mind." She huffed. "God, I wish they'd get out of me already."

"How much longer do you have?" I asked.

"Next question!" she snapped.

I chuckled at her outburst. "All right, little mama, I'll leave it be. Are you really not coming to the wedding?"

"Ugh, I'm not allowed," she whined. "Sutton put the smack down because the doctor says it's dangerous to travel in my third trimester. I planned on making that fancy wife of yours send a plane."

"She would absolutely do that, but I'm with your man. Doctors are doctors for a reason, my friend."

"But I can't even make fun of you in your penguin suit. Another con to pregnancy! Add that to the tally," she hollered. "And while you're at it, can you make me a peanut butter sandwich with Lay's potato chips in the center. Peanut butter on both sides!"

"Woman, you just ate lunch," I heard Sutton gripe from somewhere in the background.

Oh Lord, he was risking his life…

"Yeah, and that meal fed one of your children. There's still me and Baby B, so hop to it!" she demanded.

"We don't have anymore Lay's. Will Ruffles do?"

"Are you honestly asking me that?" Dakota hissed.

"I'm headed to the store now. Anything else you and our girls need?" Sutton murmured.

"Not at the moment, but if I think of something, I'll text. Wait…as a matter of fact, gummy bears. And make sure the package has a lot of red ones. Those are the best."

"For fucks sake." I heard Sutton grumble then the sound of a kiss.

She finally came back to the call. "Sorry, these cravings

are ridiculous, Memphis."

"Sounds like it."

"So, yeah, no to wedding attendance. And I doubt Savannah and Erik can come because they're in Norway with Jack and Summer doing the whole adopting their friends' kid thing."

"Shoot. How is all that working out?"

"Jack lost a friend and is now a dad to a two-year-old. How do you think it's going?" Dakota said dryly.

"Good point. Hey, subject change. I was wondering if you'd heard from Alana lately?"

Dakota groaned and whispered, "Calm down, your sammie is coming, little bug," before she got back to my question. "You know, it's weird, she usually calls or texts me daily. The damn woman always wants me to send her a weekly picture of the twins. Which means a picture of me looking fat and bloated in my ill-fitting clothes. Now that I think about it, it's been a couple weeks. Weird."

"Okay, no big deal. I'll check in with Faith and Ruby. Wanted to get a count for the wedding," I lied. The last thing Dakota needed was to worry about Alana when she had two small humans growing inside her, demanding all of her attention. "Keep me posted on the twins. I fully plan to be a regular part of their lives."

"You building a house in Montana too? Jeez. Seems like everyone else is. We've got homes being built for Alana and Christophe, Irene and Henrik, Savannah and Erik, might as well start a commune."

"I don't know about all that, but I'll run it by my fiancée and get back to you," I laughed. "Take care of yourself and don't be too hard on Sutton. The guy is trying."

"Um, hold the fuck up. You're my friend first. You're on my side. But I hear you. He is doing everything for me. Waiting on me hand and foot. It's annoying as fuck. He doesn't want me walking too far. Won't let me ride the horses.

He's even uncomfortable with me using the ATVs to get between houses. Says I need to use the truck. To hell in a handbasket. I'm pregnant, my legs aren't broken."

That had me laughing harder. "Boy, does he have his hands full with you."

"And there is so much more of me too!"

"Stop it! You're killing me, lady," I chuckled louder.

"Hey, you happy, Memphis? This Naomi woman treating you right?"

At that moment Naomi set a double shot of whiskey in front of me with a cold bottle of beer.

"Oh, she's taking care of me alright," I grinned up at my beautiful woman.

"Are you happy? Do I need to kick some ass? Don't let my size or disposition fool you. I'm an ace at gutting fish and have a lot of unchartered property to hide a body…"

"Fuckin' hell! Yes, D, I'm happy. She's everything. The whole damn package. I can't wait to spend the rest of my life with her."

"The rest, eh? Not just the three years?"

"Nope. We're marrying for love and life. The contract means jack shit at this point," I confirmed.

"That's what I was hoping to hear. All right, well, send Barbie my best."

"Barbie?" I looked Naomi up and down. She was made exceptionally well.

"Have you looked at your woman? She's absolutely perfect, so yeah, Barbie for the win, you lucky fucker."

Naomi slapped her hand over her mouth because she could hear what Dakota said and couldn't hold her laughter back.

"Good point. Take care of you and those babies, and tell them Uncle Memphis loves them."

"Will do. Now I gotta text Sutton. I'm suddenly in desperate need of a big package of Funyuns to go with my peanut butter and Lay's sandwich."

"Gross. Good luck!"

"To you as well. See you when these girls make their appearance."

"Wouldn't miss it for the world."

I ended the call smiling.

"So, all it takes to get you smiling is a pregnant woman? Gives a girl some crazy ideas." Naomi lifted her shot and I did the same. "Bottoms up!"

I made a few calls and left messages for Faith, Ruby, and Savannah and of course, Alana. There was nothing else I could do but wait and get shitfaced with my Barbie, while I wondered where in the world was Alana?

Episode 104

One Lucky Man

JACK

"What just happened in there?" Summer asked as we entered our hotel room.

I had trouble following where her mind had gone; mine had been entirely on getting my beautiful new bride to our room so I could show her in great detail how very much I appreciated, loved, and would soon worship her.

"You mean after our reception wound down?" I started removing my clothing, eager to get to the wedding night portion of the day's festivities. I had been blown away by Summer's suggestion to get married out in the open on the same evening we said goodbye to Ellen and Troy. It couldn't have been more magical. Having them and their son TJ a part of it all was perfect, just like the woman I married. She was absolutely everything I could ever need or want in a woman. And now, here she stood, wearing the most incredible wedding gown.

I was one lucky man.

Summer watched as I removed my sweater and undershirt. She licked her lips, her blue eyes zeroed in on each new bit of clothing I removed. When Summer was interested in something, she was laser focused. I removed my belt and dropped it to the floor. Her entire body jolted as though she was in a trance.

I answered her initial question, but I could tell she was no longer paying attention. "Your sister just decided to enter The Marriage Auction."

She came forward silently, and her mouth went straight to my chest where she pressed her lips. It felt like a brand, and I wanted to sear that press of her lips into my skin for eternity. Her hands glided down my chest along with her mouth as she eased slowly to her knees before me.

I stood still as a statue, watching her get into one of the sexiest positions of all time. Her hands shook as she unclasped the button of my pants, and I let out the breath I was holding when she eased my pants and underwear down at the same time, freeing my erection.

She licked her lips and glanced up at me. "Any last words?"

The humorous question broke the sexual tension for a moment. "Why? You going to kill me?" I chuckled half-heartedly.

Summer's gaze lit with desire as she flicked her tongue against the weeping tip of my cock and moaned as though she'd just sampled the tastiest treat. I had to fist both of my hands in order not to tunnel them into her hair. This was her idea, her move, and I was eager to experience all of it.

"No, but I do plan on blowing your mind, so anything intelligent you want to say, now's your chance," she taunted before dragging the flat of her tongue all over the tip.

"Fuck me," I hissed at the sudden burst of pleasure.

"That's the plan, baby. Enjoy the show," was the last thing she said before she took me down her throat. My cock bumped against the back of that tight, warm haven, and I had to tighten my ass cheeks and hold my breath to prevent myself from coming like a novice.

I couldn't hold back at that point, my fingers threading into her silky hair, giving me something to hold on to lest I fall to the floor where I stood.

My wife was a vision on her knees before me.

"Look at you, so beautiful," I growled as she took me deep and proceeded to swallow, my tip being squeezed so tight within her throat I reflexively gripped her hair and thrust deeper. She gagged and then went to work on blowing my mind as she'd promised. Summer seemed as turned on by sucking me off as I was in receiving it.

Her tongue dragged back along my length repeatedly, her movements paired to my thrusts.

"I have never had better. Fuck! That mouth…Jesus, so good. I'm gonna come so hard." My breathing picked up as my movements became jerky and uncoordinated. "You gonna swallow all of me, baby. Taste what you do to me…" I gritted through clenched teeth.

She moaned and picked up the pace, almost savage in the way she allowed me to fuck her mouth while gripping her hair and burrowing down her throat. She took it all, everything I had to give and then some. My entire body was electrified, pleasure gliding through my veins like hot lava. Stars blinked in and out of my vision as I dropped my head back and stared up at the ceiling. My balls drew up tight when Summer slid her hands around me to grip my ass, digging her nails in as she took me deep. I could barely breathe against the onslaught of sensation cascading from my groin and out through the rest of my body.

I could no longer hold off against the unbelievable bliss that tore through me like a freight train as I gripped her hair, thrust hard, and came, calling her name.

She gobbled me up, swallowing my release until I was a useless ball of noodle-like limbs.

I eased my half-hard cock out of her mouth, and it slapped wetly to my thigh. She lifted her head, and there were still a couple tears spilling from her soulful eyes. I reached out and cupped her face, wiping those tears gently, *reverently*, away with my thumbs. Her cheeks were a bright rosy hue, her lips cherry red and swollen. She was a goddess on her knees, and though I was unworthy of such a gift, I had our entire lives to become the man she deserved. For now, I'd remember the way her face looked, the passion she held, and her gorgeous loving gaze for years to come.

"Summer, I…that was…I don't…I can't even…so good…" I couldn't even speak a full sentence. She'd sucked every last intelligent brain cell straight through my cock, leaving me a babbling fool.

She grinned and then got to her feet before turning around. "Can you undo my dress please?"

My hands shook as I attempted something so simple as unzipping a dress. Eventually I got it undone and expected Summer to turn around and show me all the goods so I could return the favor and pleasure her, but instead, she looked at me coyly over her shoulder.

"Go ahead and get in bed. I'm going to go freshen up. I'd love some more champagne."

"Your wish is my command, *solskinn*."

She sashayed to the bathroom like a model on a catwalk, all confidence and sass. When she got to the doorway she shifted to the side, holding up the front of the dress at her chest so it wouldn't fall off her. "Don't fall asleep. That was only a preview of things to come. A little something to take the edge off." She bit her plump bottom lip, her gaze running all over my naked form.

I wobbled on my feet, my pants and underwear still around my ankles. I hadn't even taken off my shoes or socks before she overwhelmed me with her mouth. Not that I was complaining because that was the best blow job of my lifetime. And it sure as shit didn't stop my dick from taking notice of what she said, stirring from its short rest.

"I-I...won't," I finally managed to croak.

She smirked. "Be right back."

When the door closed, I took a few long deep breaths, getting my equilibrium back. Once my brain and body could talk to one another, I toed off my shoes, kicked my pants into the corner and tossed my socks on the growing pile. Then I went to the dresser and pulled out a pair of black satin pajama pants. After I was semi-clothed, I bolted to the small bar in the living space of our suite and pulled a bottle of champagne out of the chiller. I grabbed two crystal flutes and brought the items back to the bedroom.

I set them on the nightstand and proceeded to light the many candles around the room. These weren't here before we left, nor were the small bouquets of flowers on each nightstand or the rose petals on the bed. It looked like the hotel manager had made additional effort to make our room more romantic for our big night. I'd be sure to thank him personally before we went back home.

The room glowed a rich golden topaz and smelled divine when I was done with my task. I'd just picked up the champagne bottle to uncork it when the bathroom door opened.

Summer stood there one arm above her head, her body arched seductively, every wonderous curve backlit by a halo of light behind her. The glow from the candles just barely graced the skin on display. Her white satin robe had been left entirely open over a white lace bra and panty set that left nothing to the imagination. Her nipples showed through the fabric in a way that made my dick instantly hard and my mouth water for a taste.

As my excitement bubbled to the surface, so did the pressure in the champagne bottle, launching the cork out across the room until it hit the opposite wall. I jerked and fumbled the bottle just slightly, a bit of the fizzing drink spilling onto the floor.

"I guess you're happy to see me," she snickered sweetly.

"Uh, that would be an understatement, *kone*."

"*Kone?*"

"It means wife."

Her lips lifted into the biggest smile. "I love the sound of that almost as much as *solskinn*. What's husband in Norwegian?"

"*Ektemann*," I whispered, hoping for years that the right woman would say those very words to me someday.

"*Ektemann*," she repeated in a sultry timbre.

My dick became painfully hard at hearing that word from her succulent lips while a wave of dizziness swept through me. I stumbled to sit on the bed as my heartbeat thumped against my chest. Chills raced down my spine as an avalanche of emotions ripped through me.

Love. Fear. Pride. Gratitude.

I was so moved by her, by everything that had happened today, I could no longer bear the weight of it all. I had to take a moment to regain my bearings a second time. My elbows went to my knees as I cupped my head and breathed.

"Oh, my goodness, Jack!" Summer cried out. Then she was in front of me cupping my face and easing my chin up. "What's the matter, are you okay? Are you hurt? Should I call a doctor?" she fussed, her face a mask of worry and concern.

My lips trembled as I took in the face of my future.

With a quickness I didn't know I possessed, I looped my arm around her and pulled her onto my lap. She straddled me, both of her knees caging my sides. She hugged me to her as I planted my face between her glorious breasts and breathed in her wildflower scent. I just needed to breathe her in, commit this to memory. For a few beats, I basked in the warmth of her scent and the feel of her skin touching mine, settling my soul in a way I could never have imagined before tonight.

Her fingers ran through my hair soothingly. "Jack, what's happening? Talk to me," she whispered against my hairline.

I held her tighter, needing to be closer.

"I'm sorry, Summer. I just…I-I…I need a quiet moment with you. To feel this. To experience this reality as it's happening."

"Okay, honey," she murmured, then proceeded to hold me while I breathed through the vortex of feelings spinning around and around within my mind, body, and soul.

We sat there for several long minutes before I stopped trembling. I'd never experienced such a bizarre need before. The need to hold on and never let go.

"Talk to me," she urged.

I placed a kiss to her neck, then down to her shoulder. I lifted her left arm and brought her hand to my mouth where I pressed my lips to the wedding ring I'd placed on her finger earlier that night.

"It all just became so real." I interlaced our fingers, watching how intimate and mesmerizing that simple act was.

"What did?"

"Us. We're *married*. For real. Not just because of the auction. You're mine, Summer. My wife. *Min kone*. And we're parents."

She smiled wide, her eyes shimmering and reflecting the glow from the candles. "True. I agree it's a lot to take in. It's been a whirlwind, but the end result is us, right here, right now. Together. A family."

"It's all I ever wanted," I breathed, laying my heart wide open for her to take or stomp on if she chose. But I trusted Summer completely. Whatever she wanted to do with it was fine because it was hers from this day forward.

"What was?"

"You. I dreamed of you for years. The woman I'd marry and have kids with. As a foster kid, an orphan with no real home, it's all I could dream about. I wanted it so desperately, I threw myself into school and work in order to become a man a woman like you would want to share her life with. And I dated so many women I never felt so much as a spark with. I joined the auction because I'd given up on true love. Little did I know it would lead me to you. The very thing I wanted most. A woman I knew with my whole heart loved me and would never leave me willingly. And here you are." I cupped her beloved face. "Beautiful. Smart. Wise. Fun. Free-spirited. A goddess in bed. And already showing your ability as a devoted mother with a child that isn't even yours. I'm not worthy of any of this…"

"But Jack, honey, you are. You are exactly what I have been looking for. I'd given up on true love too. Joined the auction to get a man to help me run my business and throw me some orgasms once in a while. I didn't believe I could find what we have. Not in a million years, but that's the universe for you. That's fate and destiny doing their thing and bringing the right people together at the perfect time. And this is only the beginning, Jack. We have a lifetime to share, an eternity to explore this love to its fullest."

"You, me, TJ, we're family," I croaked pressing my forehead to hers.

"We're family," she agreed, dipped her head, and kissed me.

The kiss went on and on, neither of us wanting to separate for even a moment.

We kissed as she ground against my shaft and mewled, the sexual desire back in a flash.

We kissed as I held her tight and rolled us over on the bed until she was beneath me.

We kissed as I divested her of her lacey thong.

We kissed as I kicked off my pajama bottoms.

We kissed as I tugged down the cups of her bra, too eager to hold and caress her bountiful curves.

We kissed when I entered her for the first time as

husband and wife.

And finally, we kissed as we made gentle, slow, unhurried love to one another.

After we'd satisfied our need a few more times, my wife was sleeping soundly by my side, her face on my chest right over the heart I'd handed her on a silver platter. I finally closed my eyes, at peace knowing I had achieved it all.

I was one lucky man, and I'd never take her or this new life for granted.

Episode 105

Man to Man

RHODES

"You sure you're okay, Em?" Maia spoke into her cell phone as I led us out of the hotel room in Colorado. We'd touched down late Friday night, and were now headed to breakfast. I needed to give her the rundown of what Bruno's team had provided about her family. And it wasn't pretty.

"I know you're thirteen and very capable. Still, your uh, Dad and I wanted to check in." Her gaze flicked to me, and I smiled and shook my head at her tactic of adding my concern into the mix when in reality, Maia was devastated to leave Emily in California.

Of course, I, too, was concerned about Emily being with Portia for the weekend while we were in Colorado. However, I had a long talk with Marisol, the woman I technically left in charge. And Marisol was a Mexican American grandma who would take absolutely none of Portia's bullshit. She'd make sure Emily was safe physically and emotionally. Besides, she'd call at the slightest provocation. The woman hated my ex and would find every reason to rat on her in the hopes I'd kick

Portia out of all of our lives forever.

"Okay, okay, I'll stop worrying. Keep your phone and Apple watch on you at all times. Text me, I mean *us* when you get back from the spa." Maia closed her eyes and sighed. "I love you, too, Emily. We'll be home soon." She frowned and then hung up.

"You realize that was the third time you've checked on her since we left yesterday?" I grinned and looped my arm around her shoulders, keeping her close as we took the elevator down to the lobby. Colorado was beautiful. I could absolutely see why so many people made the state their home.

Maia pressed her lips together and shrugged.

"Hey, I'm not going to be mad about your concern over Em. She loves it and *you* as much as I do," I rubbed her arm.

"I don't trust Portia, and after everything Emily endured…"

I nuzzled her temple and placed a light kiss there. "I know. I agree. Under different circumstances, we'd have stayed home, but I made you a promise. And after reading the file Bruno's team gave me on your family, I knew we had to make our move now."

Her shoulders slumped as she leaned closer to me. "That bad, huh?"

I inhaled through my nose and let it out. "Baby, it's the worst."

"Fuck," she breathed and closed her eyes briefly, giving herself a moment. Then, as I was used to seeing from my little sprite of a fiancée, she steeled her spine and stood up straighter.

We walked to the restaurant and followed the host to the private balcony I'd reserved for a few hours. Once we'd finished eating, I asked the staff not to bother us further.

"Okay, Rhodes, lay it on me," Maia said as she sat back in her chair and crossed her arms over her chest protectively.

I flipped open the file.

"Let's start with your stepfather, Damon." I glanced up to see Maia nod, her eyes going glassy as she looked out at the landscape. "He's been the Chief Marshal of this county for over a decade. A decorated officer for fifteen years prior to that. There are reports of complaints from a variety of citizens over the years. Unnecessary roughness, assault and battery, things like that. Each charge never making it to court. However, there were a couple women who came forward and stated they'd had a one-night stand that ended in sex and them getting beaten. Again, those charges were dropped. Jonah, the tech guy on Bruno's team, pulled those women's bank records and found a couple hefty deposits right around the time the charges were dropped."

"Not surprised. He'd make sure to cover his criminal activity. My mother called the authorities for help a couple different times when I was younger and got zero assistance seeing as his father was the Chief back then."

I gritted my teeth.

"What about my mom? Do you have anything about her?"

"Yeah," I reached across the table for her hand. She put it in mine, and I held on. "Don't let go, okay?"

Her face paled, but she dipped her head curtly.

"Lena Burke has been admitted to the local hospital over a dozen times for a variety of medical concerns including but not limited to a shattered cheek bone, broken nose, ribs, arms, wrist, and more. The last emergency was supposedly for falling down a flight of stairs. She was in a neck brace and had to have surgery for that one."

"The house doesn't have a second story unless they moved." Maia's nostrils flared as her eyes filled with unshed tears.

"They've been in the same house for over fifteen years," I whispered.

"And my sister Maisie and brother Zach?"

"Zach has been hospitalized a few times. Mostly broken bones. Once for internal bleeding and a head wound from a car accident. All four of them were seen for various injuries after that accident. Says here your mother was driving and didn't realize how sharp the turn was."

"That's impossible. Damon would never have let her drive. She didn't even have a license or a car, otherwise she'd be able to leave him. Mom was forced to ride the bus or wait for Damon to come home to even do the grocery shopping. She wasn't allowed to have a bank account or her own phone. That's why we used the convalescent hospital to check in with each other."

Anger coiled in my stomach like a venomous snake ready to strike. I couldn't wait to take down this motherfucker.

I flipped through her records, noting Lena's name wasn't listed on the single SUV that was registered to Damon Burke. No insurance account for Lena either, only Damon.

"Mom has nothing in her own name. That's why I had to enter the auction. Secure enough money to ensure I could restart all of our lives." Her bottom lip trembled.

I squeezed her hand. "I understand completely, and you no longer have to worry about money or finding a proper residence. We'll have your mom and siblings move to California with us. They can live in the guesthouse for as long as they like. It's three bedrooms and two bathrooms, with a small kitchen, living room, laundry room, and its own entrance. They can stay forever if they want. Whatever your family needs, we're going to provide for them."

Maia gave me a small smile, and it settled the snake hissing within my gut. Nevertheless, I hadn't shared the worst of it. The next part was going to destroy my beautiful fiancée, and I despised being the one to have to share this news with her.

"What about my sister Maisie?" she asked.

"Maybe you've had enough for one day…" I tried to spare her the ugliness, protect her from the pain I knew was coming.

Maia stood up and cocked her head. "What aren't you telling me, Rhodes? I know that look. You're more than upset, which mean it's bad." Her voice shook as she hugged herself.

I swallowed down the sour taste threatening to make me vomit all the food I'd just eaten.

"What happened to my sister, Rhodes? Did he beat her too? Was she hospitalized for more than broken bones?"

"No broken bones." I cleared my throat. "Uh, last year, Maisie was admitted into the hospital for an elective surgery."

"Elective?" She rubbed her arms as though she were cold. "What type of surgery?"

"She received an outpatient procedure, a D&C."

Maia's arms dropped, and she bent forward, bracing them on the back of her chair. "A D&C on a twelve-year-old girl... No...she, she couldn't have..."

"She had an abortion, Maia. File says she was eight weeks along."

"What!" she screeched.

I held out my arm. "Come here, baby."

"My baby sister had an abortion at twelve years old," she croaked, tears falling down her cheeks so fast I wouldn't have been surprised to see a puddle of water at her feet. "My stepbrother Derrick did this," she hissed through her teeth, her eyes wild. "He hurt her. I fucking know it was him!" she sobbed. "I hoped since they were blood-related, he wouldn't touch her in that way, but that sick and twisted motherfucker did it anyway! Oh my god, Maisie!"

"Maia." My own voice was hoarse as I put the file down, got up, and pulled her into my arms. Her face went straight to my chest as her body convulsed, the pain flooding through her body like lava. "I'm so sorry. I'm so sorry," I chanted over and over as she broke within the safety of my arms.

"I'm going to kill him. I don't know how, I don't know when, but I'm going to kill him," she swore against my chest.

For the rest of the afternoon, Maia stayed huddled up in

the hotel bed, alternating between crying and asking more questions about her family's history.

Eventually, she asked about the disgusting piece of shit also known as her stepbrother.

"Where is Derrick now?"

I scanned the information we were given on Derrick Burke, and my stomach dropped to the floor. Sweat beaded on my forehead, and my hands became clammy.

"Rhodes?"

"Uh, it says here he graduated from Colorado State with honors in Physical Education. Fucking hell…" I cursed and then breathed through my need to be sick or punch this man in the face until there was nothing left but an unrecognizable mess of gore and bloody pulp.

Maia pushed up into a seated position, her back against the headboard. "Just tell me."

"He's teaching PE at the high school and coaches the girls volleyball team. He bought a house across the street from your mom and stepfather."

"Oh, sweet Jesus," Maia said, covering her face with both of her hands. "I should have gone to the police in another state and filed charges, but I was too scared. I didn't have a family or a home. I lived on the streets. I was filthy and half-starved most of the time. Who would believe some 'runaway' over a decorated member of law enforcement or his son for that matter? That's what I was classified as—a runaway. Even though he kicked me out and threatened to kill me if I ever came back. I…I should have done more. Then maybe Maisie…"

I tossed the file on the nightstand, then turned to Maia and pulled her into my arms. She came willingly.

"You were a child. A teenager yourself. Scared and alone. The fact that you aren't dead, a prostitute, or some junkie in the streets is a testament to your strength and will to survive. Since the moment I met you, your entire focus has been on finding a way back here. To help your mom and siblings. There's nothing more you could have done. Get that outta your head right now. I'll not have you, an innocent victim of multiple years of abuse, taking on the burden of their crimes. No way. All of this is on them, and they will be punished."

"You promise?" she whispered.

"I promise to do absolutely everything I can to get your family away from those men and to have justice served. They cannot use the law to protect themselves from the filthy crimes being committed behind the scenes any longer."

Maia clung to me as she buried her head between where my neck and shoulder met. The warmth of her breath was a comforting sensation battling against the fury boiling within my soul.

We stayed that way for a long time, neither of us talking, both simply breathing the other in and holding on tight.

* * * *

The funeral hall was mostly quiet as we entered. Only a dozen or so people, either sitting down in one of the pews or standing and chatting with one another, were in attendance. The door behind us slammed closed, causing most of the people in the funeral home to turn around at the noise.

A woman with the same face and beauty as Maia was the first to make eye contact. She was sitting in the first pew, with a few people beside her. When her teary gaze transformed into a look of sheer terror at the sight of Maia, my stomach lurched with concern. Sitting next to who I believed was Lena, Maia's mother, was a teenaged girl, hair down around her face. She glanced up long enough that I could see her face more clearly, eyes the color of warm caramel. But those eyes were vacant, devoid of any light or emotion. I assumed the girl was Maisie. To the young girls right was a young man, maybe in his mid to late twenties. His arm was locked around the girl. His lips curled in disgust when his dark gaze landed on Maia, putting me on instant alert.

Evil oozed from that young man's gaze as he glared in our direction. Maia held my hand so tight I was no longer getting any blood to my fingers, but I wouldn't dare let go.

"That's Derrick," she half-whimpered.

Lena, stood up and swayed, her hand over her heart, focus completely on Maia. That was when the man sitting next to her stood, a snarl on his thin lips. He had a too-long mustache, beady little eyes, and bushy blond eyebrows. When he stood, his rounded gut hung over his belt, the buttons of his dress shirt straining against the bulk. His stance and bravado screamed "I'm the man in charge," which pegged him as Damon, Maia's stepfather.

Next to Damon sat a young male teenager with light hair. He watched us approach with a curious expression plastered across his pale face. His eyes were the same color as his younger sister's but held an edge of despair. His bottom lip was scabbed over from what could only be a recent injury. When he lifted his arm to the back of the pew, I noticed his wrist was also in a cast.

Motherfucker.

I had to hold my breath in order to bank the anger that wanted to come out like a category five hurricane, obliterating everything in its wake.

"Maia!" The woman finally gasped and dashed toward us, her hands up in the air, her eyes wild with concern. "Honey, no, you shouldn't be here!" she cried on a sob, embracing her daughter. "I left a note," she whispered into Maia's ear, but I was close enough to hear every word.

"I know, Mama, but we need to talk."

"Well, well, well," came a sneering tone from behind the women. "Look what the cat dragged in from the garbage."

Lena dropped her arms from Maia and went straight to her husband's side on autopilot. "I had no idea she was coming. I'm sorry, Damon. They'll just be on their way…" she pleaded almost hysterically. In this light, I could now see the ring of bruises around her neck—as though someone had been strangling her. Not to mention the poor job she'd done covering up the black eye and swollen cheekbone she sported with makeup.

"Excuse me?" I interrupted. "This is the funeral for Evelyn Fields, Maia's grandmother, is it not?"

"It is." Damon practically spat, his eyes flicking from me to Maia.

"Then we're in the right place." I held out my hand, pretending to be civil. "I'm Rhodes Davenport, Maia's fiancé. When we heard about Evelyn's passing, we hopped on a plane to be with her family and mourn together. It's good to meet you."

Lena didn't say a word, nor take my hand. Damon reached out, a scowl marring his ugly mug, and took my hand, gripping it unnecessarily hard, not that I'd give him the benefit of showing it affected me at all. Instead, I tightened my own hold until he ripped his hand away, shaking it as though it were burned.

"Fiancé huh? You must not know her history…the filthy, little, lying slut," he sneered at Maia.

I took Maia's elbow and pushed her behind my considerable bulk. Her stepfather might be law enforcement, but I was taller, in shape, and knew without a shadow of doubt I could bring him to his knees with one punch if I were so inclined.

"What did you say?" I got up close and personal with Damon, my face only inches from his.

"You heard me," he sneered, but stepped back, then shifted his blazer to show his shiny badge. "You might want to settle down, Mr. Davenport. You wouldn't want to go to jail for threatening an officer of the law, now would you?"

"I asked you what you said, and I didn't so much as touch

you. How in the world could that be threatening?"

As I'd hoped, the four bodyguards I'd paid to travel with us appeared out of nowhere. Damn ninjas, though this time I was grateful for their agility and stealth.

"There a problem, Mr. Davenport?" the lead guard asked.

Damon clocked the guards one by one. "Is this an ambush?" he growled.

"Does it need to be? My understanding is we're here to lay Maia's grandmother to rest and have a few words with her mother before we head back to California."

"Lena talks to no one without my say so, and I'm going to have to not-so-politely decline your invitation for a chat. Anyone associated with her"—he hissed as he gestured to Maia—"is nothing but trouble."

"Okay, but that means I'll be forced to speak with Kate Bennings and Cheryl Kent, along with the dozens of lawyers I have on retainer, about a certain experience they had with an officer of the law. Hmmm…" I rubbed at my bottom lip. "Apparently, someone hurt those two young women, threatened their lives, and demanded they sign settlement agreements for a sum of ten thousand dollars to keep their assault quiet. That's blackmail, but as an officer yourself, I'm sure you already know about that."

Damon stepped forward, coming toe to toe with me. "You want play with the big boys, bucko, I'm game. Name the place and time, we can meet alone. Man to man."

I huffed a dry laugh. "Man to man? Is that what you think you are? Listen—" I dipped my head forward conspiratorially. "If a man needs to beat his wife and kids to feel like the king of his castle, he's no man at all. And if that said man allows another to repeatedly abuse his stepdaughter, well, I believe that is called an accessory to a crime. And I also believe that when a parent kicks their teenager out of the house at gunpoint after beating them up, it's another form of child abuse. What do you think?"

"I think there is a statute of limitations that we're well past. Besides, I am the law. What I say goes. And I want you and your two-bit whore to get the fuck outta my town before I put a bullet between both of your eyes and drop you over the side of a cliff where no one will ever find you."

That was when I pulled my phone out of my pocket and showed the front of the screen. "I recorded all of that. I'm sure a jury of your peers will be okay with you blindly using your badge as your personal golden ticket to commit whatever crimes you want and not suffer any consequences. Unless, of course, you want to shut the fuck up, sit down, let this family put their matriarch to rest and have a quiet little chat without you or your goons present."

"You're going to regret ever setting foot in my town," Damon sneered.

"Got that on record too. You're just digging the hole deeper and deeper. Now, Mrs. Burke, it's good to finally meet you. Please, if you will"—I gestured to a pew about twenty back from the front—"I'm sure your daughter would like to sit with her mother and siblings as they say goodbye to their grandmother. Your presence is not needed," I snapped.

"Yeah, well, I'll be back—with a warrant for your arrest. Derrick, you're with me!" He hollered over his shoulder. Derrick moved like a snake, not saying a single word as he followed his father.

I lifted my hand and waggled my fingers. "My lawyer is already waiting at the hotel. Do your worst."

Damon pointed at Lena. "You have no idea the hellfire coming your way."

I smiled as I watched him and his eldest son follow him out of the building.

"Mom, we have to talk. We don't have much time..." Maia started her spiel, delving straight into our plan to get them out of Colorado and away from the devil and his spawn.

Episode 106

Cat and Mouse

MADAM ALANA

"What is the meaning behind this?" I asked Angel Salazar, who stood, arms crossed, his chiseled facial expression set to "extreme focus" as he watched his technician place a glittery looking diamond on one of my red painted nails.

"It is a tracker. The highest tech available."

I frowned. "Why do I need a tracker when we're the ones setting the trap?"

Angel's deadly gaze flicked to mine, piercing straight through me like an arrow to the heart. His nostrils flared as he cocked his head to the side. "Plan B. Prepare for anything."

I licked my lips and shifted in my seat, uncomfortable with his intense scrutiny. "Have you..." I cleared my throat. "Have you ever needed the Plan B?"

His eyes flared with an instant fury, the likes of which the Devil himself would cower beneath before he spoke. "Only once," he clipped and then dropped his gaze back to his technician.

Conversation over.

I sat quietly as they made sure the diamond tracker was securely placed. It actually looked rather pretty sitting atop my wedding ring fingernail. Something I might consider under different circumstances, those being the opposite of putting myself up for bait to one of the world's most wanted criminals and his treacherous daughter.

"Here, make your call." Angel handed me a burner cellphone. "Do not provide more information than what is stated here but say it in a manner that Angus and his team will believe it's legit."

"It is real. We're sitting in the hotel as we speak…"

Angel looked at me with a stern, rather terrifying expression that said if I pushed him too far, he'd be the one to take off my head and not Angus.

"Madam, the one thing we have going for us is that Angus has no idea of your connection to us. Our people will not be on his usual suspect list. Our intel has his men scrambling to find you." He handed me the sheet of paper that detailed the exact location I was to give to my most trusted estate employee.

"I understand." I inhaled and let the breath out quickly, putting on a brave face. Celine and I had learned the American phrase, "Fake it until you make it," and that's exactly what I planned to do.

Christophe took my hand, lifted it to his mouth and kissed my palm. "I believe in you, Alana."

With his strength and faith, I could survive this hurdle as I had all the others in our thirty years together.

"*Merci, mon amour.*" I cupped his cheek, leaned forward and pressed my lips briefly to his.

He placed his hand to my knee and nodded in solidarity.

"I'm ready," I announced with confidence. It was only a phone call. It would be over soon.

The phone started ringing, and I pressed it to my ear.

"*La residence Toussaint. Aurélie parle,*" Aurelie, the exact person I wanted to speak with answered as expected.

"Aurélie, it is me." I answered.

"Alana! Thank the heavens above. Are you all right. And Christophe?"

"He is well. We both are."

"Where are you? The authorities have been calling nonstop to see if we've heard from you and taking the staff in for questioning. I had to go last night, and it was awful. They told me they believed you could be dead." She sniffed, her tone filled with emotion.

"I'm sorry, my friend. We had to escape to a safe place. Unfortunately, a criminal is after us, the same that kidnapped me and Emily. We've gone into hiding."

"Hiding? Where?"

"You cannot tell a single soul," I cautioned, setting the trap as instructed.

"I would never betray you or Christophe. You are my family," Aurélie gasped. I could almost visualize her placing her hand over her heart.

"We feel the same, *chérie*. Please keep this information to yourself. Do not inform the authorities of our location at this time. Can you do that?"

"*Oui*, for you I will take this secret to my grave."

"We are at Chateau Morena, an hour outside of Paris. If you hear anything from my friends and family in the States, please contact me at this number." I rattled off the number Angel's man had given me for another burner.

"Okay, I've written it down and will memorize it before I destroy it," Aurélie claimed. She was such a loyal member of my staff and a dear friend. I hated using her to further Diego and Angel's plan, but I didn't have a choice. People were dying, and my family had been hurt in a way that might not ever be repairable. My thoughts went to Brenden in a coma. He had been such a good boy growing up, the apple in his father's eye. Until Bianca Sokolov and her father's revenge plot changed him. And then there was Giovanni and Julianne's suffering…

I sat up straighter. "Please, stay at the estate and be safe. I will be in touch soon. Thank you for everything, Aurélie."

We hung up, and I handed the phone to Angel. "What's next?"

One side of his mouth lifted as though he was trying to smile, but it mimicked an evil looking snarl. I shivered and looked away.

"On to phase two."

"What happens in phase two?" I reached for Christophe's hand. He held mine with both of his. A solid support I knew I could always count on. Together, we could brave any storm.

"Tonight, you and Christophe have dinner in the hotel restaurant. We anticipate they will attempt to take you as you leave or when you are en route to your room."

"And then what? You swoop in and kidnap them?" I asked, not fully understanding all that being bait to a hardened criminal would entail. "What if they decide to kill me while I'm eating dinner or walking to my room? It would be nothing for one of their expert snipers to take my life in seconds."

"That is not how Angus works. If they'd wanted to kill you in your home, you would already be dead. He's playing with you." Angel's voice lilted with mockery. "You are his prey. He thinks you are the mouse about to be lured into his trap, when in reality, you are the cheese, luring *him*. He is the mouse in this scenario; he just doesn't know it."

"Then what are you?" I whispered, my voice quaking.

"I am the cat that eats the mouse and all his little friends," he murmured on a low purr, his slightly psychotic snarl/smile combo on full display.

Christophe stood abruptly. "Okay, well the bait has been set. I think it's time Alana gets some rest before we make our move this evening. Come, darling. Let's go to our room."

I stood on wobbly legs. Fear swirled in my gut, but I tamped it down. Diego and Angel were two incredible forces to be reckoned with; I didn't imagine much got past them. Alas, I also knew how crafty and revenge-focused Angus was. He wanted me to feel the pain he felt having missed ten years with his only child. Not to mention that I'd bought the auction right out from under him and was making far more than he ever did with the same product and a new business model. Something actually legally binding.

Christophe left me to my thoughts as he led me out of the hotel room they'd converted into their mini command center. According to Angel, their snipers were not on the roofs of nearby buildings as they assumed Angus would employ such tactics and they didn't want him to get wind of the trap. No, Angel put his snipers in actual rooms, their guns and scopes just barely peeking through the curtains and pointed at every rooftop so no one would be the wiser. According to them, they had twenty men surrounding the small hotel, not including the dozens inside, all in disguise.

Diego informed me they'd rented the entire 20-room hotel out. It was owned by a friend who owed Diego a marker. A very expensive marker, if I had to guess. The phones for the establishment were being redirected to an offsite customer service for future bookings. All of the people onsite were members of Diego's team in some form or another and had been given the necessary training to play their parts by the real staff before they were given a week off. They even had Mama in the industrial restaurant sized kitchen making meals for everyone pretending to have dinner tonight. Since we weren't sure what Angus planned, all precautions were being taken to ensure the best possible outcome, including no blowback to French civilians.

The whole thing was choreographed down to the nth degree. People came in and out of the hotel, carrying packages from local businesses, laughing, pretending to have been seeing the sights and so on. If I didn't know better, I would not have noticed anything out of sorts. Diego was leaving nothing to chance, which I appreciated more than I could ever say or repay. Then again, attempting to find a bride for life—for a criminal leading the Latin Mafia—was quite the challenge. One I still had no idea how to accomplish, but it was also pushed to the back of my brain to deal with when all of this was over. Provided we all came out of it alive.

* * * *

Christophe held my hand as we made our way out of our room, down the elevator, through the lobby and into the restaurant. I tried not to shake like a leaf, using my fear to control my body the way I wanted, instead of allowing it to swallow me whole. Fear could be a powerful motivator, and this situation was no exception.

A man called Javier, who I knew as another of Diego and Angel's "brothers" because he'd been at two of the meals we'd shared, plastered on a wicked smile when we approached the host podium in the restaurant.

He grabbed two menus, for show only, as we already knew the menu this evening was a variety of Mexican-French fusion dishes Mama was trying out. Of course, according to Christo, this was a highlight of our evening.

While the fake host led us to our table, I scanned the busy room. It was unbelievable how normal everything seemed. Those they'd hired or brought in to play the part of regular diners were doing a spectacular job. Everyone was chatting, telling stories, smiling, laughing out loud, or being flirty with one another. A couple seated directly to our right were canoodling in a little booth. When I looked at the beautiful woman, I was shocked to see eyes and a face similar to Diego and his mother. Did Diego have a sister? Diego often talked about his many brothers, but he'd never mentioned a sister. The woman I watched suddenly smirked at me before dipping her head and kissing the man she was with.

The detail in this entire tableau was miraculous. I wouldn't have suspected a thing if I didn't know otherwise.

We sat down, cuddled on one side of a table that sat four, facing most of the restaurant. We had a good view of every door, window, and person in the room. I scanned each one, terrified beyond belief.

I jerked when a male waiter approached with a bottle of wine. "To calm the nerves, Madam." He pointed at my empty glass.

I pushed it forward. "*Merci*." I gave a half-hearted smile and then continued to scan the room.

"*Mon coeur*, if you keep scoping out the room, our targets will know you are being monitored. Why don't you turn to the side and focus on me? Let's pretend we're just out on a nice weekend away and having dinner together." He lifted his wine glass, and I followed his lead.

"To justice, healing, and a bright future," he said.

I was just about to clink our glasses together when a familiar voice interrupted our toast.

"I couldn't agree more. May we join you?"

My entire body shook as I turned my head to find not only Angus, but his daughter, Bianca, as well.

Javier approached, still playing the part of host. "Welcome, new friends. Will you be joining them for dinner? The chef has a Mexican-French fusion cuisine special that is to die for." Javier smiled.

Angus pulled out one of two chairs across from where we sat. "That sounds wonderful, thank you. Bianca," Angus gestured to the chair, and she removed her coat, her baby bump accentuated by the tight-fitting dress she wore. She put the coat on the back of the chair and sat gracefully, but her cold gaze was that of a viper ready to strike. Angus did not remove his coat, his right hand firmly in his pocket, appearing to be wrapped around what I assumed was a gun.

My mouth went dry as Angus took his seat. Javier was

about to hand them the menus when Angus waved his free hand. "We'll both take the special. Now leave us." His voice was curt and straight to the point.

Javier nodded then left. I tried not to tremble—and failed—as I reached for my wine glass. Angus missed nothing, smirking as I dropped my hand to my lap.

"You should be terrified. Both of you. My hackers told me it was actually you, Christophe, who ratted me out to the authorities all those years ago," Angus scowled.

Christophe didn't so much as flinch as he said, "It was. Alana has nothing to do with any of this. Your anger should be directed at me, not her. Let her go and take me."

"No!" I whispered. "It's my fault. All of it. I should have left well enough alone. I was the one that bought your precious auction and promised to keep your involvement quiet. Take me and leave Christophe," I begged.

Bianca laughed heartily and then rubbed her belly. "You're both pathetic. I'm going to enjoy watching you take your last breaths."

"Bianca, settle down. Your bloodthirsty side is showing. Never let them see how eager you are to take their lives. It ruins all the fun." Angus scolded his daughter playfully and smiled in a predatory way that sent chills racing down my spine.

The man was evil incarnate. I'm not sure Angel or Diego planned for any of this—Angus and his daughter sitting down to have dinner with us. Why hadn't they just captured them when they entered? I should have asked more questions.

"It didn't ruin the fun when my beloved Dimitri sabotaged the small charter plane that took down Rachel and Lewis Myers and Valentino and Caterina Falco now did it?" Bianca cooed.

Both Christophe and I gasped in utter horror and shock, neither of us able to form a single word at hearing how our beloved friends had been ruthlessly murdered.

Angus sat back and rubbed his chin. "You are right, my dear, watching that happen was indeed fun."

"Why?" I breathed, tears filling my eyes. "They didn't do anything to you."

He lifted his free hand and wiggled his pointer finger. "Ah, ah, ah, but they did. At least, Lewis and Rachel did. If you recall, Lewis was my client, and Rachel one of my candidates. They were your first big payout from the auction, were they not?"

Dread flooded my veins at the truth he spoke. "They were."

"They were the catalyst to your success. Your first love match that came with a fat paycheck to fuel your business further. I considered that a personal slight. So when I spent ten years in prison, planning your demise, I had a lot of people to add to the list of suffering. When the Myers had children, well, you know how that went, seeing as both are now dead, along with Giovanni Falco. I consider him a bonus." Angus smiled wickedly.

"You planted that bomb." I gulped. "It wasn't an accident," I croaked. I knew Bianca had been responsible for the explosion in the office building, but I also knew that Angel and Diego were clever men. They'd have this place mic'd for sound. If Christo and I ended up dead, I wanted proof of all that Angus and Bianca had done in the hopes this conversation would make it back to the authorities.

"That was easy." Bianca yawned as though bored of this conversation already. "Daddy had me well-trained for the job."

"And you were the one that forged the legal documents for the Myers will and testament?" I asked.

"Guilty." She winked. "Criminals these days don't know how to play the long game. I've been trained to take over their empire since the age of ten. It was nothing to start with Giovanni, whom I knew was close to the Myers. He was a beautiful man and easy to wrap around my little finger." Then her expression contorted into irritation. "Until I realized the asshole was in love with Julianne. The second he introduced me as his girlfriend to Julianne, I knew he had a thing for her. It was in every look he gave her, every smile, every longing glance when she left a room. Which was fine with me, because the man I was after was his best friend, Brenden. Obviously, the money was way better with the Falcos, but that didn't fit into our plan, did it, Daddy?"

Angus pointed to her pregnant belly. "No, it didn't. You needed to be pregnant with the rightful heir to the entire Myers estate for our revenge to be complete."

"So the baby is…"

"Brenden's, as planned," Bianca confirmed, and my body lurched, the pain of knowing she carried my godson's child was all encompassing.

"And you killed him. A man who was completely in love with you. Ruined his friendship with Gio, ruined his relationship with his sister… What kind of monster are you?" I growled, the pain of all she'd done to my chosen family shredding my heart into a million tiny pieces.

"Casualties of war, I'm afraid." Bianca lifted her chin haughtily.

"This isn't war. This is revenge. Against me. Yet you hurt innocent people to achieve what? What is the end goal?"

"Ultimately, I want to see you suffer the way I did," Angus growled, pulled his hand out of his jacket, and pointed a gun at Christophe's head. "But it's not enough. I want to watch you as I destroy the one person you love above any other…"

"No!" I screamed at the top of my lungs as a shot rang out.

Episode 107

No More Secrets

GIOVANNI

The sun shimmered and reflected its glorious light across the top of the lake. I breathed in the crisp air, celebrating the fact that I could even do such a simple thing. A week ago, I'd been in an explosion. Not many people could claim such a thing and live to tell about it. The many wounds on my back and legs were proof of such a miracle. I should have died in that bombing. I'd been lucky.

The real miracle, though, was walking toward me. Her head tilted to the side, her long red hair flowing out behind her. She'd lost quite a bit of weight, which I hated. I loved her full-figure hourglass shape with curves for days. She still had them, but the strain and stress of everything that had happened over the past month had taken its toll in more ways than one.

"Hey." I reached my arm out.

She took my hand. "Did Maggie give you the sign-off to walk around outside?"

"It's more like shuffling slowly, but yes, she thought the

fresh air would do me some good. Did she send you out here to check on me?"

Jules grinned and shook her head. "No, I came looking for you after I found something concerning in your office."

My eyebrows rose of their own accord. "Oh?"

She pulled an envelope out of her back pocket. One that had her name written across it in my script. One I'd written years ago when I made my first million. I'd updated the information within as I'd aged and my wealth grew, but I certainly never expected her to find it while I was still alive.

My heart started to beat a million miles an hour as shame and worry filled my mind. "Jules, you weren't supposed to see that…"

She pursed her lips. "No? Then why was it in your, "When I Die" file in your desk? Hmm? Aptly named seeing as we did just fake our deaths."

"Jules." I put my hand out for the envelope. "That was private. You weren't supposed to see that until…"

"You died. Got it." She crossed her arms over her chest and glared.

"You read it," I whispered, fear in every word.

"Of course I fucking read it. It had my name on it and was in your *death* file. Horrible freakin' name, by the way. And it's your fault I found it," she snapped angrily.

"Mine?" I practically gagged, knowing what was in the file. Most specifically, knowing what I'd admitted to in a letter to Julianne that was included within that file.

"You're the one that told me to work with Muriel on keeping the business afloat yesterday. So today, when I thought you were napping, I got to work. Muriel told me anything current would be in the desk drawers. Imagine my surprise when I came across this." She waved her hand, the envelope flapping in the breeze like a big red flag.

"I'm…" I slowly walked over to the railing of the pier and braced my weight against it, worrying if I didn't, I'd fall over as all the truths I'd admitted in that letter scattered like confetti all around us. "I'm sorry."

"Sorry for what?" she growled. "For leaving me every penny of your fortune, going back as far as being the beneficiary of the trust your parents left you at eighteen?"

"Yes." I swallowed, knowing what was coming next.

"For telling me you are in love with me and always have been. Since we were kids?" She growled.

I cleared my throat as I croaked. "Yes."

"For taking my virginity that night and pretending you didn't know it was me!" she screeched, tears flowing down her face.

I nodded.

"Say it!" she demanded. "Say it to my face, you bastard!"

I firmed my jaw as all that I was, all that I would be, spilled out on the ground before the woman I loved.

"Yes! I took your virginity and pretended it never happened. Yes, I have been in love with you since we were children. Yes, I left you everything of mine, even when I'd planned to marry someone else. Anyone I ever dated, Bianca, all of them were a consolation prize to the one woman I could never have. You. It has always been you, Julianne. Always."

"And when we made love that night?" she croaked. "And the next morning when you rolled over and said another woman's name...*you destroyed me.*"

"I know," I admitted, the old shame-filled feelings rising back to the surface all these years later.

"I loved you too. From the very beginning. You were all I ever wanted. My brother's best friend. Giovanni Falco, the most beautiful boy, then man, I'd ever known. Inside and out. And that night, you ruined me for others. RUINED me for all other men, because I'd given myself to the only person I wanted to be with."

"Jules, I'm sorry. I was drunk, scared, but more than that, I was *terrified.* Of all of it. What it would mean to you that I took advantage while drunk. What it would mean to your family. To Brenden. You were the star of the Myers clan. The one person that shined brighter than any other, and I'd tarnished you. Taken something I could never give back. I hated myself. And then, when you also pretended it never happened, I stole that opportunity to do better. Be a better man. Let you flourish and shine without me."

"I went a decade thinking I was a loser because I'd given my virginity to the one man I loved—one who didn't love me back."

"I did love you. I *do* love you. I just didn't love myself enough to take the risk back then."

"You should have fought for me! You should have made it up to me." She sniffled and wiped at her tears as though they were pesky flies.

"Can I now?" I gulped and moved forward, coming one step closer to the woman I loved. "Can I make it up to you now? Prove that you are the only woman I could ever truly love." I took another step. "Show you every day that I am sorry for how I behaved. I am sorry for making you think even for a moment that you aren't exactly what I want and need."

Her bottom lip trembled. "Why did you even put that in a letter to me? I'd already forgiven you. Reading it today brought all of it back."

"What does the last paragraph of the letter say?" I made it to a foot away from her, where I gently went to my knees. My back and legs pulled at the movement, but I gritted my teeth and took the pain as I'd deserved.

"No, you'll hurt yourself." Jules reached for me, but instead, I took her hands and held them, the envelope crushed between us.

"Not anymore than I hurt you. Now please, what does the last paragraph say, Jules?"

Her bottom lip quivered.

I repeated it from memory. *"That night was the best and worst night of my life. The best because I now know what it feels like to have loved you. And the worst, because I know what it feels like to love you, knowing you'll never be mine."*

She fell to her knees before me, tears running down her face. "I wish I had been strong enough to talk to you about what happened."

"I wish I'd been strong enough to admit I was a fool and fight for you. I'm sorry, Julianne. I'm sorry for all of it. And if you can find it within yourself to forgive me, I'll spend the rest of my days making it up to you."

She shook her head and cupped my cheeks. "I have already forgiven you. I wouldn't still be married to you if I didn't. I knew what I was getting myself into when I signed that contract. When the officiant declared us as husband and wife, and I kissed you. But as we genuinely fell deeper in love with one another, I let the past go." She ran her fingers through my hair, easing some of the tension racing through me. "What happened when we were kids is in the past. We both have to let it go so we can move on. This is out in the open now for both of us. No more secrets. It happened. We both regret the way it went down, but we are smart enough and mature enough to leave it where it belongs, in our past. We're paving the way to a beautiful future, Gio. After all we've endured, we both deserve it."

Jules pressed her forehead to mine.

"God, I love you so much, Julianne. And I really am sorry for being such an idiot. You didn't deserve that. Especially from me. And the fact that you are being so graceful about it now shows how incredible you are. I promise to never keep anything from you again. No more secrets."

She shifted her head and kissed my lips. I cupped her face and kissed her back with all the love I had to give. My body started to quake; kneeling for so long had morphed into a full body ache.

"Are you okay?"

"Help me back up," I hissed in agony.

She jumped up and helped me to stand. I put my hands on her shoulders, feeling light-headed and dizzy.

"Breathe, baby, just breathe with me." She inhaled for a few seconds and then let it out slowly.

I paired my breathing with hers as my back felt like the fire had returned, licking across my skin and burning everything in its wake. Every time the pain meds wore off completely, I felt the flames again. At least, I no longer smelled the burning flesh. That had been the worst.

"We need to get you inside." She looked at her watch. "You're long overdue for your meds and a nap."

"I'm tired of fucking sleeping all day," I grouched through gritted teeth. The pain was worsening, making it difficult to hobble back up the path toward the house.

"Maggie says…"

"You heal when you sleep," we both said at the same time.

"Will you lay with me? After that conversation, I need you close." I didn't care if I sounded like a wounded animal—because that's exactly how I felt.

She pouted, and her mouth was so beautiful I wanted to kiss it, but the fiery heat tapping into my nerve endings was preventing me from doing anything but grinning and bearing it until I could take the meds.

"If you need me, I'm there. Doesn't matter what it is. Helping you run your empire while you're healing, yelling at you for the stupid shit you pulled in the past, or lying down with you so you sleep soundly. Gio, I'm never leaving you. This is our life now. I've got the one I've been in love with for as long as I can remember, and I'm never letting you go."

"Good," I managed through a wince.

Maggie stood inside the kitchen, waiting for us, hands on her hips. Today's scrubs were a plethora of rainbows with cute little bubble clouds on each end.

"I see you overdid it, just like I told you not to. Don't think I didn't catch you kneeling. Pffftttt!" She shook her head. "Come on now, Pookie. Let's get you sorted with your meds and back in bed. No more walkabouts today. No more begging to do some work. It is my job to help you heal, and by golly, I'm going to do it, whether you help me or not. Ya hear?"

"Yes, ma'am."

"Ohhh, ma'am. I like it. Very respectful. Maybe if you're good, I'll have your chef whip up your favorite dinner." She bolted ahead of us, allowing Jules to lead me to our room.

"What was the chef supposed to make for dinner?" I asked to keep my mind off the mind-numbing pain.

"Your favorite meal. I asked him to do it. She heard me. Now, she's playing you like a fiddle," Jules snickered. "Serves you right."

"We need to have a son," I griped.

Jules stopped us both in our tracks. "Um, come again?"

"So I'm no longer the only man in the house. Everywhere I go, I'm outnumbered and outranked by the females in my life."

That had her cackling. "It's cute you think you'd have a boy. I doubt the universe would be that kind," she teased. "I know we've sort of talked about it…but, you still want kids? After all of this?"

I started shuffling forward again, lifted her hand, and kissed her fingers. "I want everything there is to have with you, Jules."

"Okay," she whispered. "And, uh, when were you thinking about us trying for a family?"

I shrugged one shoulder and then gasped at the sudden burst of explosive pain. It made me sway on my feet while stars popped all around the edges of my vision, threatening to take me down.

"You're not looking good, Giovanni." Maggie appeared with a muscle relaxer in one hand and a syringe in the other. The doctor had prescribed some of the heavier pain killers that Maggie doled out sparingly as I'd requested. I wanted to get better and off the drugs as soon as possible, but it would take a lot more time.

Maggie and Jules helped me back into bed where I took the pill, and Maggie administered the pain killer. In what felt like an eternity but was only a few minutes, the woozy floaty feeling from the pain medicine coated the worst of it.

Jules got into her side of the bed, put her hand over mine, and smiled. "Sleep, Gio. I'll be here when you wake up."

I tried to say I love you, but it came out garbled to which she laughed.

Her response was, "I wub oooh too."

I fell asleep to the sound of her laughter and the memory of her forgiveness. I couldn't ask for better.

Episode 108

Redemption

NAOMI

My hands shook as I ran my fingers along the pristine white satin of my wedding gown hanging in front of the standing floor mirror. I was alone in my soon-to-be husband's apartment. His sister, Sydney, had just dropped me off from the rehearsal dinner. According to tradition, Memphis and I weren't supposed to see each other until I walked down the aisle. I found it an odd tradition, but who was I to balk at the Taylor's customs? They had been nothing but warm, inviting, and unbelievably understanding, given the situation with my father and him buying their house out from under them. Even though I bought it back and gifted it to them free and clear, it was embarrassing to say the least. Yet they handled the entire fiasco with grace and aplomb. I wished my family were as kind and considerate.

A knock on the door broke me out of my thoughts.

I grinned as I walked down the short hall and through the small living room to the front door. My man was a cheeky bad boy, coming to see me the night before the wedding. I fluffed my hair, pinched my cheeks, and bit my lips to give them some color. Next, I undid the robe I was wearing, leaving it open to the cute short nightie I was wearing underneath.

"He'll never see it coming…" I breathed as I set my pose, unlocked the door, and opened it wide. "Hey baaaabyyyyyy…" I cooed and then croaked, dropping my hands to my robe, and closing it as quickly as possible.

"I can see you were expecting different company," Abraham Shaw grunted. My mother stood behind him, her eyes wide in surprise, mouth open, looking like a fish out of water. The only fish out of water was me in that dreadful moment.

"What on Earth are you doing here? How did you even find me?" I clung to the lapels of my robe then quickly tied it tight.

The man—I would not allow myself to think of him as my father or dad—tilted his head. "Mrs. Taylor not only gave us this address, she actually encouraged us to come tonight while you were alone, after the rehearsal dinner."

I clenched my teeth, a sudden wave of anger pushing against my chest. I didn't want to believe Robin would do me so dirty. It wasn't in her nature. However, what was in her nature was healing family wounds, and I knew she was deeply hurt when she learned my family and I were not only at odds, but that I'd disowned this man completely.

"Can we come in?" His tone was gentler than his usual booming voice.

"I'm sorry, Mr. Shaw," I crossed my arms over my chest protectively. "I don't invite my bosses over to my house. Especially at this late hour."

His nostrils flared while my mother, who'd finally gotten herself together, practically whimpered, "Please, Naomi."

I thought about slamming the door in their faces for all of five full seconds. Abraham stood stoic, chin raised, gaze on me, unflinching. He had always been an immovable force.

Something I'd once admired about him, until he stopped using that power for good and, instead, became a controlling monster. Planning my life and future out piece by piece as if it were a business plan that had big checkboxes next to each line item.

"We'd like to talk to you." he started. "May we please come in and have a civilized discussion in private and not out in this breezeway where three other neighbors can listen in?"

I snarled. He made a good point. If Memphis and I were going to stay here on and off for the foreseeable future, we definitely didn't want our neighbors gossiping about us.

"Fine. You have fifteen minutes, but then I need to get my beauty sleep. I'm getting married tomorrow." I held the door open wide.

They entered, both stopping to take in the small apartment. I'm sure he found it lacking because it was simple, and homey, compared to his preferred palatial, opulent lifestyle.

"Have a seat on the couch. Would you like something to drink?" I asked, the courtesy coming out on autopilot.

"A nightcap would be preferred. Scotch, if you have it."

I rolled my eyes and padded to the kitchen. "Mrs. Shaw?" I asked pointedly.

"Naomi, please, I'm your *mother*. He's your *father*, and we both love you dearly," she croaked. Her eyes actually teared up, one of the handful of times I've seen my mother show genuine emotion.

As I poured three glasses with two fingers of Scotch in each, I really took in my mother's appearance. Purple smudges underneath her eyes, her skin paler than normal, and if my eagle eye was correct, she'd lost some weight since the last time I saw her in person a couple weeks ago. All of this concerned me, knowing she'd suffered a heart attack earlier this month.

I returned with the drinks, passed them out, and then settled primly in the chair opposite the couch. The three of us sat there like strangers, waiting for someone to break the ice.

Abraham cleared his throat. "Naomi, we're here to discuss the wedding tomorrow and our role in it," he muttered then ran his palm along his pantleg.

"As my future boss, you have no role in my upcoming nuptials."

"Naomi, please, we're here to apologize." Mother's voice cracked, then she set the glass down and stood. With hands on her hips, she glared at her husband. "Abraham, I swear to God, if you don't fix this with our only daughter, I will walk away from you for good."

Her target scowled. "I'm trying," he bit out through clenched teeth.

"Not very hard you aren't!" she snapped.

"I'm here, aren't I? I have never in my life cowered to another, yet here I am, sitting before my only child in what amounts to a hovel, to…" For a fleeting second, he looked like he might actually throw up. "…renegotiate!"

"I am not a business deal to be made," I growled. "This is my life we're talking about. *Mine*. Not yours. Not Mom's. I want to marry a man I'm in love with. A man who treats me as though I'm the only person in a room. Who loves me for me, not for what I can give him or the money I have, or the connections my family has. Me." I smacked at my chest for emphasis. "Memphis loves *me*. Do you understand how rare that is?"

Mom crossed her arms over one another. "Naomi is right, Abe. Just because we agreed to marry for status and wealth, doesn't mean our only daughter should. She's in love…real love with the young man. And he dotes on her, I've seen it with my own eyes. And his family have welcomed our daughter into their lives fully. We wouldn't have this opportunity if Mrs. Taylor hadn't urged us to come and make amends. I'll not have you squander our second chance at redemption to make things right."

She came over and knelt before me. I set my drink on the side table as she reached for my hands.

"Naomi, I am deeply sorry for putting pressure on you to live your life the way your father and I planned. You are your own person." She swallowed then took a breath as she stared into my eyes. "You are the bravest, strongest, most intelligent woman I know. You have become more than I could have ever hoped. I am proud of you for chasing after your dreams and making them come true. I love you and I want to be in your life, *desperately*. You're my baby, my little girl. I want to see you get married to the man you love and have children. Please, don't take that away from me…from *us*." She squeezed my hands, her honesty searing a path straight to my heart.

"I love you too, Mom." I croaked and then turned to look at my father expectantly.

"Abraham, I believe you have something to say to Naomi." Her tone cut like a blade. Even I trembled at the severity of her demand.

"Naomi, I am sorry. I'm sorry for pushing you so hard I pushed you away from me. I've always wanted nothing but the best for my child. Everything I've ever done was to ensure your future success. I realize now that I went too far. That meeting we had…" He shifted his shoulders as though shaking off a nasty chill. "That was the first time I realized I could lose you forever. I treated you and your future as a business deal. Thinking back on it, I am disgusted with myself." He ran his hand over his close-cropped hair then down over the back of his neck. "I may be the head of an empire, but I'm also your father. And I forgot that."

"And what you did to the Taylors? Buying their house, having their friend fired from the bank," I hissed, letting my anger show. "These are good people. They don't deserve your wrath because their son fell in love with your daughter. They've welcomed me fully into their family. Instantly, I have five sisters, in-laws, and a granny. I'm gaining so much by marrying into the Taylor family. You should be happy for me, not upset that they aren't as wealthy as you are. Their wealth is in their love for one another, and that can't be bought or sold. It's given. And they've given it to me. It's worth more than anything money can buy, Dad."

"Dad," he whispered and closed his eyes, a moment of true peace crossing his features. "I worried I'd never hear you call me that again."

Mom got up from her position on the floor and went to sit next to her husband.

"I'll make it right with the Taylors, Naomi. I've already contacted the bank and demanded they rehire their friend. He's now in a higher position."

"How did you manage that?" I asked.

He smirked. "I threatened to take my money elsewhere."

I gave him a half-smile. He really was ruthless in business, but he couldn't apply that same method to his daughter's personal life.

"Naomi, we're here because I want to be in your life," he grumbled, sounding exasperated.

Mom cleared her throat expectantly.

"*We* want to be in your life," he amended.

"And attend your wedding," Mom interrupted once more.

"Yes, and see our beautiful girl marry the man she's chosen."

"*A good man.* A man that loves me. A man who supports my success. The best man I have ever known." I drove the knife deeper into his ego, wanting him to realize the position Memphis truly has in my life. "I'm no longer daddy's girl who does and says what you want. I played that role for far too long. I am my own person. I am Naomi Shaw, soon to be Naomi Taylor. And if you have any chance of being in my life in any way, shape, or form, you need to accept that, right here, right now. No more discussion about marrying Malik or anyone else for that matter. No demeaning the man I love or his family for not being as wealthy as you."

"I understand," my father answered.

"If you mean that, you will apologize to the Taylors for the pain and suffering you caused them. You will also apologize to Memphis for being so incredibly rude to him and his kin."

My father's jaw tightened, a muscle ticking in his cheek with the effort to keep his mouth shut.

"Last, but certainly not least, I will not be working for you."

He tried once more; I don't think he could help himself. "You would excel at my company. Take it all and make it your own one day."

I slashed the air with my hand in a brutal manner. "I will *not* work for you. I will not be forced into a life I don't want. I'm happy. My company is extremely successful. Be proud of that. Train Malik to be your second. He wants the job more than anyone. He worships you. The only reason he even dated me was to get close to you. Make him the son you never had. I don't care. I want what I have right now. I'm happy with what I've created all by myself."

"I am a man that can admit when he is wrong. And you have done well. Your company is top notch, and the profit margins are extremely high. I am impressed. It may not be at the level of my own company…"

"Yet!" I smirked. "I'm still young, old man. I've got lots of time and support at my back."

He grinned fully, a genuine smile I hadn't seen in too long. "That attitude will get you far."

"I learned it from my dad."

He closed his eyes, his body vibrating at the praise.

"I am deeply sorry, Naomi," he stated as he shook his head.

Mom took his hand. "We both are."

"Can you forgive me?" He glanced at my mother then back to me. "Forgive us, for being so short sighted and controlling."

"And rude, revengeful, demanding, ruthless…I could go on and on."

"Yes. Can you forgive us for all of those things and let us back into your life?" The question was a plea.

"We'll do anything honey." Mom added.

I sat for a full minute, staring them both down, watching them squirm. The fact that they were both here, practically groveling, was an absolute first. Something I doubted I'd see again. But it also proved how much they truly loved me and finally understood how horrible they'd been.

"You can come to the wedding tomorrow. It starts at noon," I announced.

"Can I come help you get ready?" Mom pleaded, her pretty brown eyes filled with shimmery tears.

I nodded, my nose stinging at the emotion filling the room.

"Can I walk you down the aisle?" my father asked, his heart in his throat.

"Depends on how your apology goes with Memphis and his family. I suggest you arrive a bit early so that you can have a chat with them. Knowing how kind they are, I'm sure they'll welcome you with open arms. But I'll never allow you or anyone else to look down upon them. They are good people, and they deserve better."

"I will do whatever it takes to earn their favor and respect," my father said.

I stood up. "Then I'll see you tomorrow at the wedding." My voice shook as reality sunk in. My bottom lip trembled while Mom got up and came around the table to pull me into her arms.

"I love you, honey. So, so much. Thank you. Thank you for hearing us out and being so forgiving. We won't let you down." She held me tight, and I held on right back.

"It's time we let her rest. She has a quite the day tomorrow," Dad instructed.

Mom nodded and then let me go. She swiped at the tears that were falling down her cheeks, but the smile on her face was true beauty. I hadn't seen a genuine smile from her in a while. She moved to the side, and I stared at my father, the first man I'd ever loved, standing before me looking wounded and uncertain.

My breath caught at the sight of him, and that was all it took before he opened his arms, letting me choose if I wanted to hug him.

God, I did. I wanted my father to know me, understand me, and more than that, I wanted him to accept me for who I was.

I went into his arms, pressing my face to his chest.

"I love you more than anything in this world, Naomi. I'm sorry I lost sight of that for far too long. I understand what I've done, and I will change. You'll see. He hugged me tight, resting his chin on the top of my head. "I'll never lose sight of what's important again." He nuzzled my hair and then leaned back, and placed a kiss on my forehead. "We'll see you tomorrow."

I swiped at the stubborn tears sliding along my cheeks. "Tomorrow."

I followed them to the door and held it open as they exited.

Across the breezeway, leaning against the wall, was the most welcoming sight in the world.

"Memphis," I breathed, my entire being filled with joy at seeing him.

He winked at me as he stepped forward, hand out toward my father. "Mr. Shaw, Mrs. Shaw, I'm glad to see you both."

My man was the best in the entire universe. My heart pitter-pattered wildly within my chest, knowing he came here to ensure I was okay.

I watched as my father shook his hand. "I can see that you're here for my daughter, but if you would be so kind as to spare a shame-filled man a moment of your time tomorrow, I'd like to apologize."

"You being here and apologizing to her is enough for me. She's what's important." Memphis gestured toward me with a lift of his chin.

My father smiled. "That she is. I'd still like a word with you tomorrow, if possible."

"I'll see to it," Memphis nodded.

My mother was not nearly as chill. Still crying, she threw her arms around Memphis. "Please forgive me for being so rude. I was only trying to protect my daughter. I'm so sorry. I was wrong. About you, about all of it."

Memphis patted my mother's back. "I accept your apology. Both of you. I hope we'll be seeing you tomorrow?" One of his eyebrows rose in question.

"They've been reinvited," I stated softly.

"Good to hear. Now I'm going to make sure my fiancée is okay. Sleep well and we'll see you tomorrow." He let my mother go, who went right to my father's side. My father placed an arm around her shoulders and led her to the waiting limo.

A fucking limo. I rolled my eyes and sighed.

Memphis approached, and I held the door open for him. When I shut it, he spun me around and caged me up against the door.

"How are you?" he demanded instantly.

"Better now that you're here." I looped my arms around his neck and pressed my body against his.

"Honestly, Nay. That had to be some heavy shit, and right before our big day…"

I nodded and sighed. "It was, but you know what? It was needed. They apologized, and I believed it. I know when they are playing a part, and they were genuinely heartbroken."

"And that shit about you working for your dad?"

I shook my head. "Not happening. He understands I'm paving my own path. I suggested he hire Malik to be his second."

Memphis snarled. "Please don't speak that man's name while wearing next to nothing, the night before our wedding." He dipped his head and ran a line of kisses along my neck.

"How long do we have?" I pressed my body closer to his.

Memphis slid his hands down my body until he got to the robe's tie where he undid it, letting it fall open.

"Have mercy!" He groaned at the sight of my simple nightie. Then his hands went to my thighs where he ran them up and down and around to my ass. He gripped my butt and lifted me up until I wrapped my legs around his waist. "We have as much time as it takes for me to love you properly and make sure your mind is only on us for our big day tomorrow."

I took his mouth in a long, wet kiss. "I love you for coming to check on me." I nibbled on his bottom lip. "I love you for being so forgiving." I slid my tongue briefly into his mouth to tease him. "I just love you, Memphis."

"Prove it," he growled wantonly, pressed me up against the door and kissed me until I forgot my own name.

Then he let me prove it, all night long.

Traditions be damned.

Episode 109

Chickens and Ducks

SUMMER

I tiptoed back to bed and climbed in quietly after having checked on TJ by phone in the other room. Savannah and Erik had a full day of fun planned for my little boy, which meant I had a free day with Jack.

My little boy.

I still couldn't believe it.

Lifting my left hand I stared at the simple gold band. As of last night, when I'd said, "I do," to Jack in the most magical evening of my life, I also became mother to a two-year-old boy.

Motherhood wasn't originally the first thing on my agenda when I entered the auction, but I'm not mad or sad about it in the least. I've always wanted a house filled with children. Did I think I'd be getting married and taking on the parenting of a toddler within the same month I put myself up for auction? No I did not. Yet I was totally okay with it. I loved Jack. I loved TJ. I loved his whole chosen family. Everything felt so natural.

Including the arm that just wrapped around my waist as Jack rolled over and snuggled against my side, his lips pressed against the ball of my shoulder.

"Mmm…where did you go?" he mumbled, his eyes still closed.

"I used the restroom and then called Savannah to check on TJ."

He smiled against my skin. "And?"

"And he's perfect. Having a good time with his aunt and uncle. They have a whole day planned, and TJ's in good spirits."

He hummed against my skin. "Already checking up on our boy."

I cuddled closer and sighed dreamily. "It's like a switch was flicked on for me. Suddenly I became someone's mother. And of course, I know I'm never going to replace Ellen, and we'll make sure to share his parents' memory often, but when I really think about it, I'm his new mom."

"You are. How does it feel?" He kissed my arm again and nuzzled his forehead against me.

"It feels…" I thought about it for a bit, getting my thoughts together. "It feels like I'm on a roller coaster. There are highs and lows, twists and turns, scary drops, and the pinnacle of excitement, all rolled into one experience. But I'm loving the ride and looking forward to where it takes me."

He chuckled. "That's a good analogy. I'm terrified but know that, with you by my side, anything is possible."

"Awwww, you're being sweet again." I rolled onto my side so I could face him. Our noses were about six inches from one another.

Jack opened his sleepy eyes. "Hi, wife," he whispered.

"Good morning, husband," I said with a cheesy grin.

"I know we're supposed to spend the day making love and enjoying our first full day as husband and wife, but there are some things we need to talk about too." He yawned and stretched, displaying that sexy as sin body. I watched avidly as the sheet slid down his sculpted chest, over his bricklike abdominals and down toward the V at his hip bones. That V made smart girls stupid. My mouth watered as I tried to focus on what he'd said.

"Hmmmm," I reached out and petted that fine chest I could now touch whenever I wanted. "Let me guess. You want to discuss where we should go when we leave this snowy paradise?"

He turned back to the side and cupped my cheek. "Exactly. I want to do what's best for you and TJ but there's a lot to consider."

"Like your job, my job, and our families?" I supplied helpfully.

"Yeah." He let the word out in a sigh.

"I think I've been very clear on how my plan has changed." I reached for his hand and held it. "I'm going where you and TJ go. Whatever is needed to keep our little family of three together will be my first choice."

"And that is beautiful, Summer, but you had a life before me. A very successful business, the dream home you own, the one that allows your sister to have her metaphysical store…"

I shrugged one shoulder. "Humble Buds and The Pink Lady are important, but I'm not giving them up just because I've gotten married and became a mother."

"If we live in Norway, it would be impossible for you to be in both places all the time," he warned.

"True, but that's why there is this thing called an airplane. It traverses countries, big bodies of water, even continents in hours. It's like magic. You see there's this big engine…"

Jack cut me off with a laughing kiss that turned into a make-out sesh.

Eventually he rolled my naked body on top of him. I was really starting to get into it, rubbing my body across his much harder one, desire spreading through my veins at a rapid pace.

Suddenly he cupped my cheeks and eased my head back gently from his.

"I want to move to California," he stated pointedly.

"Okay, this is news to me." I frowned, thinking through all that was here in Norway. "Do you want to run through your thoughts with me?" I jostled my body until my hands were resting on top of one another on his chest, my chin on top of my hands.

"TJ is so young, he won't miss Norway," he started.

"This is true. What about Ellen's home? What will you do with it?"

"Sell it. She never lived there with Troy or anything. It was something I helped her purchase after his passing. We'll sell it and leave the money in a trust for TJ, along with their retirement accounts and any other financial holdings."

"That sounds reasonable. And what do you want to do with her things?"

"I think we box up anything important we might want him to have and bring it with us, including all of TJ's belongings. His clothes, favorite toys."

"That's a big decision. Do you want to give me your reasoning for this choice?" I asked, wanting to hear his rationale fully.

"As much as I'd love to raise TJ in Norway, you can't do your business here. It's illegal, and I don't see that changing for many years to come."

"True, but I also have my father…"

"Who wants only to do the science behind creating the perfect product. A man who is aging and will want to retire at some point in the near future."

"Yes, but we can hire people to run the business."

"I'm going to run it," he stated sharply.

I jolted to a seated position on his lap, tits out, surprise forcing my actions. "Wait a minute. You want to run Humble Buds?"

He nodded. "I think it's the best-case scenario. Johansen Brewing already has a great person running it in both Erik's and my absence. Erik is now back to being himself and is getting more involved with the daily comings and goings of the business. *His business.* Sure, I own a small portion and will ask to stay on in a consulting capacity, but I've done the work I need to do there."

"Yes, but it's been all on your shoulders for years. You've kept it running and are directly responsible for its success."

He nodded and put his hand behind his head, his gaze scanning my naked body. "All true. And I can do it again for Humble Buds."

"Why? You don't even use cannabis products."

"No, but if I believe in the product I'm selling and what it can do for its users, I can make it successful. Besides, Johansen Brewing doesn't need me. You and TJ need me. Humble Buds needs me."

I crossed my arms over my chest, covering my boobs, disbelieving what I was hearing. Was he about to give up his entire life for me?

Jack pouted at the disappearance of one of his favorite appendages of mine as he moved his hands to my hips. "Hear me out."

"Okay, but this better be good."

Jack chuckled and squeezed my hips. I dropped my arms and tried to make myself more comfortable.

"Yay!" he whispered at the sight of my boobs again.

I playfully smacked his chest. "Be serious. You were about to tell me why you're giving up everything in your entire life for me and my small business."

"I'm not doing it just for you. I'm doing it for us, for our future, and that of our child and future children."

"How so?"

"Well, for one, you have a huge, beautiful home you absolutely love that I'm also fond of. Your sister, our kid's aunt, lives right next door. That's babysitting ready to go."

I chuckled. "True. Autumn loves kids almost as much as my mother does."

"And that's another thing. Your mom. She wants to watch her grandchildren daily. And who better than a woman who's raised two wonderful women to love and guide our kids while we work."

"I told you I'm planning on taking some time away so I can raise TJ myself."

He waved his hands. "I know, *solskinn,* and I think that's beautiful. But having options is essential when you're a parent, right? Just think if TJ didn't have us, Erik and Savannah, or Irene and Henrik. He'd be in the system like I was. Like Troy and Ellen were. In California, he not only has us, he has your sister, your parents, and the entire small community you live in."

"My mom will teach him a bunch of things you may not want him knowing, such as which goddesses do what and why, how the moon affects our moods, that growing your own food is by far superior to what you get at a grocery store. Then, of course, there's tarot, crystals, vegan eating, tea leaves telling your future, Autumn and her sight...I could go on and on."

He chuckled fully. "And then there's Bernie, a scientist. And you, a horticulturist that knows everything about plants, and me who can teach him about business and financial independence or just being a guy who loves sports, and hiking, and cars."

I slumped forward, bracing my hands on his chest. "What about his roots? He's Norwegian."

"Which is why he'll have regular visits with Erik and Savannah and Irene and Henrik. Just because we live in California most of the year won't mean we can't spend time in Norway teaching him about his heritage. Plus, I was thinking at home, I'd speak to him in Norwegian, while you speak to him in English. He'll learn both languages simultaneously. And he can have calls with his extended family speaking Norwegian. We're not going to let him miss out on either. We have the means to live in both places, at least some of the time."

"And when he's in school?"

"We'll be in California. Then, when we're not, we can spend time in Norway. Or, apparently, in Montana since it sounds like homebase for Erik and Savannah will be there, near her sister and their family."

I nodded. "And you want to what? Become the CEO of Humble Buds?"

He grinned. "I was thinking I'd buy into the company. Invest in our future business. And yes, if you'd have me, I'd be happy to take the role of CEO."

"Are you kidding?" I screeched. "You're hired, baby!" I was about to jump off my husband and call my dad when he sat up, looped his arms around my body and rolled us until I was on bottom.

"That's it? I tell you I'm going to invest in your company and offer to be CEO, and that's all you have to say? You don't want to run numbers? Call your lawyers?"

"Pfffftttt. I was going to call my dad and tell him we were free to focus on the plants and science. He'll be so stoked."

Jack swept his nose across mine. "You are so easy to love. The absolute perfect woman."

I looped my arms around his neck. "I know, right?" I teased. "Honestly though, this solution solves a lot of our problems. If you run Humble Buds, that means I'll be free to just work part-time or whatever hours I want. Mom will lose her mind with joy if she can have a baby around the farm. Oh, I know! We should get chickens. Let TJ pick them out and watch them grow and provide eggs. Maybe ducks too."

"That's all you have to say? We should get chickens."

"And ducks," I added. "Don't forget the ducks. They're

so cute when they quack-quack and wiggle their feathered booties."

"So that's it. We pack up Ellen's house, put it on the market, bring the stuff we want to California, move into The Pink Lady, and I'll invest and start running Humble Buds?"

I let those facts run through my head until they added up to a fat, "Hell yeah!" However, maybe not say it quite like that, because I didn't want to sound like a dork, so I ended with a solid, "Sounds good to me."

"No more discussion. You're happy with everything I presented?"

"As long as it comes with you, TJ, chickens, and ducks, I'm one hundred percent on board."

"I won't forget the chickens and ducks." He shifted forward and kissed me. "So, we're doing this. Moving to California, raising TJ on the farm?"

"Yep! Now I think we should seal the deal by boinking each other's brains out, then ordering room service. I'm starving."

"You've got a deal, *Solskinn*. Now spread those legs. I'm suddenly famished too." He growled, kissing his way down my body. He paid special attention to each breast, sucking and nibbling on them until the tips were so erect they could cut glass and my body was undulating with pleasure. He ran his tongue down to my bellybutton where he circled the small indent.

When he braced his hands on either side of my spread thighs, teasing my core with his thumbs, he whispered, "Chickens and ducks," then shook his head and put his mouth on me.

After he made me see stars a few times, I thanked the goddesses that my life would be filled with a man who loved me, a little boy I adored, and bedtime discussions where we'd solve all our problems followed by a steady stream of orgasms.

I was finally living the life I always wanted.

Episode 110

A Few Minutes Too Late

MAIA

"Mom, we have to talk. We don't have much time." I ushered my mother into a pew. I waved at Zach and Maisie, then introduced myself. "I'm not sure if you remember me, but I'm your older sister, Maia."

"Mom told us all about you over the years. How you got away and started a new life," Zach mumbled.

"It took a while, but yeah, I finally found my true path," I glanced at Rhodes, who smiled gently.

"Are you here to help us?" Maisie asked so softly I could barely hear her.

"That's exactly what I'm here to do. Get you all out of Colorado and away from Damon and Derrick," I shared.

Mom shook her head, tears streaming down her cheeks. "It won't work. He'll find us. No matter where we go, he'll come for us, and he'll kill everyone before he allows us to escape for good. All the deputies at the marshal's office won't do anything. They believe his lies. I've tried…I've tried so many times. You have to leave," she pleaded. "He won't come for you because you're not his blood. It's the only reason you were able to get away all those years ago."

"You mean after I came clean about Derrick sexually assaulting me. I was beaten and thrown out of the house. I was a child, Mom. You have no idea the things I had to do and say to survive. Terrified every day. Looking over my shoulder, waiting for one of them to pop up out of nowhere. But I'm finally here with backup. Rhodes would never let anything happen to any of you," I vowed.

"Are you really taking us away? For good?" Zach scratched at his hand where the cast cut across his palm.

"That's the plan. If we leave now, he won't be able to stop us. Rhodes has a private jet at the airport."

"A private jet…" Zach's eyes bulged. "Who are you?"

Rhodes chuckled and put a hand on my brother's shoulder. "I hope to be seen as your brother-in-law very soon. But first, we have to get you all out of here and away from that maniac."

My mother jerked her head, her entire body shivering. "It won't work. He'll just find us," she rattled through her shivers.

I put my arm around her shoulders and rubbed her arm. "Mom, my fiancé is obscenely rich. He has a home in California that is like Fort Knox. Gated. Guarded at the front and a security team crawling the perimeter."

She shrugged. "Doesn't matter. He'll find a way. Besides, he'll demand custody of his children."

"Excuse me for being insensitive or blunt, Mrs. Burke," Rhodes interrupted. "Based on the kids' and your medical files, and written testimony by each of you of the repeated abuse, no impartial judge in Colorado is going to allow him anything. And I assure you we'll demand an impartial judge."

"I don't believe it. I can't even begin to hope that we can escape." She closed her eyes. "He'll eventually find us. He'll kill us all." She repeated it like a broken record. Something she'd likely been telling herself for years.

I cupped her cheeks, and she opened her teary eyes. "Mom. We won't know unless we try. Rhodes and I have the means to take care of all of you for the rest of your lives. You can move into his three-bedroom guesthouse and have your own space. You can heal. The kids can go to school and have friends. Live a life where they're not being hurt."

She still trembled within my grasp and groaned as though pained. "I don't know…I just don't know…"

Then my sister, who was as pale as a ghost, gaunt and rail thin reached out and grabbed our mother's hand.

"M-Mom…p-please. I can't sleep. I can't eat. Derrick comes for me…" She made a gagging sound.

Zach was by her side in an instant. "I told you, I won't let him in your room again," he growled.

"And what did that do?" Maisie spat. "It earned you a black eye, split lip, and a broken wrist. Neither one of them will stop the things they do," she croaked.

"That's it, we have to go," Rhodes demanded, his voice tight, his teeth clenched. "I'll not hear another word of what these men are capable of. None of that is ever happening again."

"If we're going to do this we have to go home first. Grab our things," Mom whispered.

"With all due respect, ma'am, I can buy you a department store full of essentials. We really need to leave Colorado as fast as possible and let my lawyers do their jobs to ensure your continued safety."

My mother stood up. "You don't understand. We have to go home!" she screeched and clawed at her own arms.

"Why? What's so important that can't be replaced?" I asked gently.

"I need to go home," she demanded. "And then, we'll go with you. We'll try." She reached out to Maisie and then to Zach, tucking them close. "I have to try for all of you." She nodded as though convincing herself.

"Fine," Rhodes growled, tension vibrating off the man in waves. "Let's go."

* * * *

We arrived within fifteen minutes of leaving the funeral home. Rhodes made the apology to the funeral director, claiming we had an emergency and to continue as planned with the few people in attendance.

Mom sobbed all the way to the car and all throughout the ride there, grief and fear taking its toll.

My stomach tightened painfully as I stared at the one-story home in the quiet suburban neighborhood. Pretty little flowers dotted the path leading to the stairs up to the front door. It was all to keep up with the Joneses. A perfect little lie for everyone to believe that the local Chief Marshal, his pretty wife, and kids all lived happily here together.

"We have to hurry. Grab whatever you can. We need to leave in the next ten minutes," Rhodes barked.

Mom and my siblings raced into the house. I wanted to help but was too afraid to go in, old demons wreaking havoc with my emotions.

"Do you want to wait out here?" Rhodes asked. "I can help your family gather what's necessary."

I nodded. "I…I…just can't go in there."

Rhodes cupped my cheek and then kissed my lips. "I've got this. You wait here. We'll be done in ten minutes." He turned to two of the four guards that came with us. We had divided into two blacked-out SUVs. "You guys check around back and keep watch. One of you with me inside the house, and the other out front, keeping an eye on Maia. Call out if you see anything or anyone approach."

"Will do, sir." The one in charge of the rest answered then pointed to positions for each man as Rhodes instructed.

I was left with the serious, big, beefy looking dude who

didn't speak often. He wore a buzz cut, black sunglasses and a scowl. If I didn't know he was in our security detail, I'd be terrified of him.

Pulling up my phone, I leaned against the SUV and called Emily.

She answered on the first ring, sadness in her tone. "Hey."

"What's the matter?" I asked instantly.

She waited several seconds before saying anything, but I could hear her sniffling.

"Emily, you're freaking me out," I snapped. "What's going on?"

"Mom left," she whispered.

"She left?" I pushed off the car and started to walk, moving away from the car and down the path a bit. "Where did she go?"

"Some job, or something." The sorrow in her voice struck like a fist to the heart. "Said it was an opportunity of a lifetime that she couldn't pass up," she croaked.

"Oh honey, I'm so sorry." I closed my eyes and gritted my teeth. That woman…there was a special place in hell for women like her.

"It's my fault. I believed that maybe,"—she sniffled— "just maybe she actually wanted to get to know me better. Be a part of my life. But nooooooo. Not when some designer, or photographer, or magazine or whatever comes along. Why are they always more important than me? Than her own kid?"

I could hear her crying, and my entire body became white hot. I wanted to strangle that woman so badly. Instead, I breathed in through my nose and out my mouth, calming myself down so that I could handle my devastated stepdaughter like an adult. My fury could wait.

"Em, sometimes people make really bad decisions. Your mom just made one. That's on her, and she'll have to suffer the consequences of her actions. All your dad and I have been able to think about is picking up my family so we could come back to you, because we love and miss you every second we're gone."

"You do?" she blubbered.

"Baby girl, your dad is a mess without you. He hates that we had to make this quick trip, but we plan to get on a plane tonight and come home. We're bringing my mother and two siblings with us."

"I'll get to meet your family?" she asked, a bit more chipper.

"Yeah, we're going to all be together. One big happy family. Very soon. And we'll be planning the wedding, and of course, you're going to be in the wedding."

"Really? As a real bridesmaid? Not just the flower girl?"

I chuckled. "That's right. And of course, I'll need your help with every detail, if you're interested…"

"Oh my god! I get to help plan your wedding and be a bridesmaid? My friends are never going to believe how cool this is."

"I'm glad, honey. Now you start looking online for dresses and keep a list of all the ones you like. We'll look at them when we get home. Deal?"

"I'm so excited!"

"I'm glad, Em." I smiled as I stared at my feet. "We will deal with your mother when we return, but are you okay? Dad's busy right this moment, but I could have him call you when we're on the plane."

"Don't bother, I'm fine," she gushed, her mother's drama pushed into a corner while this new shiny thing had her attention. "I have so much to research about weddings! Love you, Maia. Can't wait for you guys to get home."

I shook my head and toed the ground, my phone pressed tightly to my ear so I could enjoy her happiness for a moment.

"Okay Em. I'm going to let you go. Love you too. See

you soon."

"Bye!" she said and hung up.

Seemingly out of nowhere, a pair of dress shoes appeared on the ground in front of me. I moved to glance up and stared straight into the eyes of my worst enemy.

Derrick.

On my chest, I felt something hard and circular prodding me.

A gun.

"Scream and you die right here," Derrick grimaced. "Now be a good girl and start walking." He nudged me with the gun, gesturing for me to cross the street.

I looked over my shoulder as I moved forward, the gun now pointed at my head from behind. On the ground near the SUV about ten yards from where I'd been walking, I saw the big beefy security guard knocked out cold. His chest was still moving thankfully.

"Derrick, what are you doing?" I snarled even though my hands shook, and fear flooded my veins.

"What I should have done a long, long time ago. Taking care of our family's little problem."

"Which is what?" I glanced over my shoulder at the house where Rhodes was, hoping another of the guards might notice me missing or their colleague on the ground. No such luck.

"Move, you little slut. Even now in that dress. Showing your tits and legs off like you always did. Asking to be fucked."

"I'm wearing a perfectly respectable dress for a funeral, you asshole. It's men like you that think they can take whatever they want just because they are men," I bit out.

"Women are the weaker sex," he snapped. "Your kind are here only to serve us. Any propaganda otherwise is nonsense."

"You're so fucked up in the head. The only way you can get anyone into your bed is by force. Is that what gets you off?

Assaulting your sisters?"

"That space between your legs is just a hole to fuck, which I'm about to do before I put a bullet right between your eyes and solve all our problems for good." He pushed me through the back gate of what I assumed was his house.

Over my dead body would that man touch me again.

I searched the area for a weapon of any kind. Leaning against the wall near the back door was a rake. I knew if he got me into that house, I'd never make it out alive.

"Why are you doing all this? I've never understood why," I asked as we got closer to the door and the rake.

"Because I can." He laughed in the menacing tone that had filled my nightmares for almost a decade. "Get in the fucking house!" he barked.

I moved forward but pretended to trip, my hand flying out and catching the rake by the long handle. I spun around, metal prong side facing up and dragged it across his face.

He screamed like a stuck pig, the gun flying as his hands went to his face. I shoved him aside, but his foot caught mine and we both fell to the ground, me face first, scrambling for the gun. I'd just gotten my hands on it when his body landed on top of mine.

"You fucking bitch!" he roared, punching me with one hand while reaching for the gun with the other.

Blinding pain burst over my cheekbone and eye socket where he landed the first punch.

I just barely got my fingers on the weapon when I heard a gunshot ring out from behind us. We both spun to the side and rolled, grappling for the firearm. Big Beefy must have come to and found us because he had his own gun pointed at the sky, firing a warning as he barreled toward us.

"Let her go!" he demanded, another shot being fired in the air, but Derrick didn't stop. He punched me so hard in the nose I saw stars. But I'd gained some ground and had his body squeezed between my thighs. I may have even heard one of his ribs crack as I used all the strength in my legs to hurt him. Derrick cried out as he was suddenly lifted off of me.

I managed to rip the gun from his hold when his body was lifted, and I pointed it at him.

"You'll never hurt me, my sister, or another woman ever again." I stared straight into his evil eyes as he smiled.

Then I shot him three times straight in the chest. Both the guard and Derrick fell back, the guard rolling away. He ambled up, checked his own chest, patting at his bulletproof vest, and then came over to me and held out his hand.

I was still pointing the gun, my fingers on the trigger, my body poised to kill. Reality hadn't quiet caught up to me yet.

"Give me the gun, Maia," he said gently. "It's over now," Big Beefy claimed.

I shook my head. "Is he dead? If he's not dead, it's not over."

He wiggled his fingers. "Give me the gun, Maia."

I did as he ordered and let him help me up. My entire body hurt as blood poured from my nose, which I suspected was broken. My cheek was also blazing hot and swollen. My back felt ripped to shreds because we'd fallen on a gravel path as we'd fought.

"Are you going to have me arrested?" I asked as I leaned against Big Beefy and let him lead me out of Derrick's backyard.

"For what? I was attacked by the same man that held you at gunpoint and then threatened to kill you right before you got the gun and shot him. Looked to me like self-defense…"

When we exited the side gate from Derrick's house we were surrounded by cops.

Rhodes was on the ground, his hands cuffed behind his back.

* * * *

Ten minutes earlier....

RHODES

"Grab everything you need quickly," I pleaded, not wanting to scare them by shouting.

The three of them scattered to their rooms as I looked out the windows. Maia was on the phone walking in front of the house, her guard, Buddy, scanning the environment as expected.

I moved through the house to check on her mom and siblings.

Maisie had a bag already sitting on her bed. She was putting on a hooded coat. "I'm ready."

"How did you do that so fast?" I pointed at the large bag.

"I was waiting for my chance to run away. Everything I love is already in here. I just couldn't leave my brother..." she admitted, her eyes going to the floor.

I walked over to her and tipped her head up with a single finger while still keeping my distance. "That was very smart of you. And very courageous."

"But I didn't go and then last year..." she gulped.

"Hey now. You have done nothing wrong. And you're about to embark on a whole new life. One where you're safe..."

"And my brother and mother too?" she asked.

I nodded, swallowing down the bile that threatened to make me sick.

"Yeah, I'm going to make sure you're all safe."

"Thank you, Mr. Davenport," she said to the ground.

"You're welcome, Maisie. But you can call me, Rhodes. Seeing as I'm going to be family when I marry your sister."

"Maia's my hero," she whispered.

I smiled and dipped my head so I could look her in the eyes. "Mine too, sweetheart. Mine too."

Zach stumbled down the hallway with a duffle bag stuffed full and a backpack.

"Good. Run out front and get into the car with your sister. I'll help your mother," I instructed the teens.

The kids took off toward the front of the house. The guard that was inside was nowhere to be seen. He must have gone out front or checked with his team out back.

"Mrs. Burke!" I called out as I made my way to the back of the house.

She was in her bedroom trying to open a large safe.

"What are you doing? We have to go."

"Not without evidence. It's the only way…"

"What are you talking about?"

"He keeps videos of the women he assaults. Including me. He beats me with a camera on and then assaults me sexually. I've seen him watching the tapes. They are here. In here!" She smacked the side of the large safe.

"Do you know the code?"

"I know the first three numbers are 326 but I don't know the last two!" she cried.

"It doesn't matter, we'll deal with him after we get you all safe," I promised.

She shook her head. "No! I'll never be able to breathe fresh air unless he's behind bars or dead! We need the proof!" She kept typing in the numbers. "Think Lena, what does he love more than anything else?"

"Himself," I grated sarcastically.

Her eyes widened. "On the phone, what letters represent the three and the two?"

"Uh, DEF and ABC."

"And the 6?" she asked.

I did the alphabet quickly in my head and related them to the numbers on a phone. "MNO."

"Oh my god! I'm so stupid!" She typed in the 326 and then 66. "D-A-M-O-N" she said out loud. Then the safe clicked and popped open. Of course the number 666 would coincide with the name Damon.

Inside there was money, guns, ammo, files, and a box filled with individual flash drives, each with a woman's name taped across it. She grabbed the box and nothing else.

"Now I'm ready to go," she said as a gunshot blasted from somewhere outside. She spun around and went as white as a ghost. "Watch out!" she screamed.

I shifted to the side just barely avoiding being clobbered by Damon's gun. His arm came down on my forearm and I grunted, a shot going off and the bullet slamming into the wall across from us.

Lena screamed and ducked as I pushed forward and grabbed his wrist that held the gun. He rammed against me like a bull. I braced for the hit and punched him as hard as I could before we both fell to the bed.

At some point, he must have dropped the gun because his hands locked around my neck and squeezed, his heavy body pinning me to the mattress, making it almost impossible for me to move. I'd never felt anything so painful in my life. Still, I thrashed and kicked, punching him wherever I could get a hit in until he loosened his hold. Just as I was about to hit him again, Lena picked up the lamp on the end table and smashed it over her husband's head, knocking him out.

I shoved him off of me.

"Are you okay?" I asked as she stared down at her husband's limp body, blood spurting from a gash in his head.

Her entire body shook. She was clearly going into shock. Then we were both jolted by another gunshot blast going off outside.

"Fuck! Maia!" I roared and ran toward the front of the house.

A few county marshal's office vehicles rolled up, officers pouring out and standing behind their open car doors with their guns drawn and pointed...*at me*.

I instantly put my hands up as Lena ran to her children across the lawn.

"Get on your knees!" one of the deputies demanded.

I complied as we heard a series of gunshots going off across the way at the house listed in my paperwork as Derrick's. And I knew if Damon had come after us, Derrick certainly went after Maia.

"My fiancée! He has her!" I pointed to Derrick's house across the street, fear and uncertainty plaguing me. "Please, help her!" I begged.

"Face to the ground, now!" A marshal commanded, not a cop from a neighboring city, as I'd hoped, when I'd made the call on our way over here. I'd forwarded the information Bruno's team had gathered on Damon and Derrick to a local detective in the bigger city a couple towns over. They hadn't made it in time.

I was so fucked as one of Damon's deputies pointed his gun at me, cuffs already dangling from his fingers as he approached.

I didn't resist, even though my body and heart wanted to run across the street. That would only get me killed.

The marshal came up behind me and put my hands in cuffs and held me down. "Stay there!"

"Please help my fiancée. She's over there!" I said right as I heard Maia scream, "Rhodes!"

I shifted my face on the grass toward where I heard her voice and saw Buddy helping her cross the street. Blood was pouring down her swollen face.

"You have the wrong man!" she cried.

Before she could reach me, another gunshot went off.

I watched it all as if in slow motion.

Her stepfather stumbling out of the house, gun raised.

He fired.

"No!" I roared as I watched Maia's mother slump to the ground. She had used her body to shield her children.

Another shot went off, but Buddy had already put himself between Maia and Damon. His big body convulsed, as the bullet tore into his back. Maia tried to hold him as they both fell to the grass.

"Hold your fire!" The marshal that was closest to me hollered, pointing the gun at Damon. "Sir, what are you doing? Hold your fire now!" he demanded of his own boss.

That's when the local cops from the nearby city finally rolled up to the scene as planned... A few minutes too late.

Episode 111

One Down, One to Go

MAIA

"Ouch! That fucking hurts!" I blustered as a nurse poked and prodded at my fractured nose. Not even the pain of my injuries could hold my attention.

The emergency room in the small county hospital was a mess of people. Our security team had all been wounded by Damon or his son Derrick. One of them didn't make it as his throat had been slashed and he'd bled out on the scene. I added his name to the long list of people Damon and Derrick had harmed irrefutably.

Buddy, I since learned his name, thankfully had been wearing a bulletproof vest protecting him from Damon's shot to the back. The conk he'd received to his skull when Derrick knocked him out to get to me, was also going to heal fine. He acted like none of it had even happened, his big body a veritable wall between me and anyone else that got close.

Buddy stood next to me, my shadow, gaze scanning the room, big arms crossed over one another looking like one mean motherfucker. I suspected his ego had been bruised along with his head from where he'd been taken by surprise by Derrick.

He hadn't left me since the deputies demanded Rhodes be taken in to the station for questioning, while me, my mother, Buddy, and my siblings, along with the two other guards that survived were taken to the hospital. Derrick was pronounced dead on the scene.

The memory of hearing that news on the ride over gave me a modicum of peace.

One down, one to go.

A doctor approached, my siblings trailing behind her. The relief I felt at seeing them alive and unharmed was like a physical blow to the chest. I covered my heart and rubbed at the dull ache. Last I'd heard, they'd followed Mom's ambulance with one of the neighboring town's police detectives.

"Maia!" Zach hollered as they caught sight of me. He raced to my side, Maisie following at a quick clip behind him. "Are you okay?" His eyes were wild and scared as he looked me over.

"I'm fine, Zach. What about Mom?" I asked, gesturing to the doctor.

"She's in surgery. When the bullet entered her, it obliterated her gallbladder and created some damage and internal bleeding. We'll know more in a couple hours when the surgeon can give us an update. Once the doctor is done patching you up, you're welcome to sit in the surgical waiting room."

"Thank you," I whispered as Maisie came up to my side, reached out and took my hand.

"Are you going to be okay, Maia?"

"I'm okay, sis. We'll stick together and wait for the results of Mom's surgery." And between now and then, I hoped like hell Rhodes would be released by the authorities.

"What if she dies?" she croaked, tears shimmering in her

pretty eyes.

"Let's not think like that right now. We're going to be as positive as we can." I squeezed her hand, and she nodded.

Buddy's phone rang, and he pulled it out of his pocket and answered with a clipped, "Go for Buddy."

"What about Dad?" Zach sneered.

"And Rhodes? Why did they arrest him?" Maisie asked.

I shook my head, and the nurse who was treating me groaned before handing me an ice pack and a tiny paper cup with two pills inside. "Keep icing on and off for the next two days. Here's 800 milligrams of Ibuprofen. Take for swelling and pain. Follow up with your normal doctor when you get back to California. And try to rest. Be careful when touching it. If you get uncontrollable nosebleeds or excruciating pain, contact your provider immediately. Understand?" she snapped, clearly done with my lack of care for my own well-being.

"Yes, thank you." I popped the pills and took the water cup she handed me before I pressed the ice to my face. Pain bloomed across my cheek and nose, but I gritted my teeth and slipped off the bed. My entire body felt like it had been hit by a truck, and that truck had backed up and run over me a second time. Buddy settled me with an elbow for me to hold even as he spoke to whomever called.

"This is good news. We'll see you soon, sir," he clipped and then stowed his phone into his pocket. "Mr. Davenport is on his way. He says he has a lot to update you on, but they've released him and are dealing with his lawyers now."

I closed my eyes and slumped toward Buddy. "Thank you. Why didn't he call me?" I asked.

"He did, multiple times, but I don't see your bag here. I believe it's still in the SUV."

I nodded, relieved that Rhodes would be here soon.

"Come on, guys. Let's go wait for Mom to get out of surgery." I let Buddy go and wrapped both of my arms around my siblings' shoulders, letting them help me hobble toward the surgical ward.

Rhodes arrived not thirty minutes later, a flurry of activity as he rushed through the double doors, a wild energy surrounding him like a tornado.

"Maia!" He gasped, his head falling forward at the sight of me. His large frame bent over, hands going to his knees bracing himself. It was as though he'd just completed running a marathon and needed to catch his breath.

When I got to him, he stood straight and pulled me into his arms, one hand cradling my head against his heart. "I was so fucking scared. I can't lose you, Maia. I just can't."

I sobbed against his chest, tugging at his shirt. "You won't. I'm here. I'm right here."

"Thank God. That was a nightmare. None of that went as planned." He eased back and cupped my cheeks, wiping my tears as they fell.

"You're hurt." He took in my battered face, tracing my swollen cheekbone. "If he weren't already dead, I'd kill him myself. I'm sorry I wasn't there," he breathed, his expression tortured.

I put my hand over his on my cheek and nuzzled into it even though it hurt to do so. "I'm okay. What happened to Damon?"

That's when Rhodes gave me his first smile. It was glorious in its beauty.

"He's been charged with one count of murder for the security guard, two counts of attempted murder on you and your mom, and that doesn't include whatever they find in those drives your mom pulled out of the safe. I suspect he'll be in jail for the rest of his life. And cherry on top, the feds are now involved and investigating their entire outfit, their past cases, the whole lot of them are fucked royally."

I sobbed in relief. "So as long as Mom comes out of this okay, she and my siblings are free and clear to live their lives."

"Yeah. The feds are on their way to interview you and Buddy. One of my lawyers is parking the car he drove us here in and will be right up to provide you both with legal counsel."

I wrapped my arms around his waist and rested my head against his chest over his heart, letting his heartbeat soothe me. "Thank you, Rhodes." My voice shook. "Thank you for saving me. For saving them. For all of it. I don't know how I'll ever be able to repay you."

He cuddled me close. "That's what we do for the people we love. Anything and everything possible to ensure their safety. And no repayment is necessary. We're family."

I glanced over at my brother and sister. Zach was cuddling Maisie, whispering softly to her.

"Yeah, we are. Speaking of, did you talk to Emily?"

Rhodes' entire body went stiff. "Fucking Portia. She can't do the right thing for one damn weekend. I'm done. Emily's done. I talked to her on the way here from the station. She's hurt, but for some reason, her entire focus is on planning our wedding. She briefly told me about Portia bailing on her, then asked if I would be willing to wear a brown tux."

I grinned and sighed. "She was sad, I redirected that sadness to helping plan the wedding."

"You realize we were already supposed to be married by now. Based on the marriage contract," he whispered into my ear.

I shrugged. "I don't care about any of that, or the money. As long as you love me and continue to help my family, none of the rest matters. I want to marry you because you're the best man I know. The man I want to love and cherish for the rest of my life. Not because of some stupid piece of paper."

Rhodes held me close and laughed deeply. "Me, too, Maia. I'm so glad to hear you say that. I want to do right by you. Give you the wedding of your dreams."

I chuckled and patted him over his heart. "We have time for that. On our terms. I just want you, Emily, Mom, Zach,

Maisie, and a few friends and family like Alana and Christophe. Speaking of…have you heard from Alana since we left?"

He shook his head. "Last I heard they were leaving their French estate to go to a safe house. With everything that's happened, I haven't checked back in."

"And neither of us have heard from them?" I frowned.

"No," he shook his head. "I'll check in later. Tell me about your mom."

Gooseflesh rose on my skin as I gave him the short version of what the doctor shared.

"Come on, let's have a seat," Rhodes encouraged, bringing me over to where my siblings were settled.

"Glad you're back, Rhodes," Zach stated. "What's going to happen now? Did they arrest Dad? What about Derrick?"

I glanced at Rhodes, my entire being preparing to share the good and bad news with my brother and sister while we waited to hear if our mother was going to make it.

* * * *

I was awakened by a soft tap on my shoulder.

"Maia, the surgeon is here to update us," Rhodes whispered close to my ear.

I blinked away the sleep, realizing that I had been leaning against Rhodes. I looked to my right to find Maisie asleep against Zach who was alert and completely awake.

A woman wearing light blue scrubs approached. She looked tired, but her corresponding smile was all I needed to see to know everything was going to be okay.

"Your mother did very well. It was touch and go for the first couple hours, but she's strong. We removed the bullet and repaired the damage and stopped the internal bleeding. We extracted her gallbladder. She will have some dietary restrictions and bedrest for the next few weeks, but she is expected to make a full recovery."

I reached out and took the doctors hand. "Oh, thank God. Thank you for saving our mother."

"You're welcome. She was very lucky."

"Can we see her?" I asked.

The doctor shook her head. "She's in recovery and has been given pain medication to keep her comfortable. If you want to wait another couple of hours you can pop in for a few minutes. However, it's really late. I recommend you go home and get some rest and come back in the morning. We'll take excellent care of her."

Rhodes put his arm around my shoulders. "Let's take the kids to the hotel and get some rest. We'll come first thing in the morning," he encouraged.

"Thank you, doctor. We'll be back tomorrow." I waved my hand at my siblings who'd heard everything the doctor said. "Let's go guys."

Both of them stood silently and followed Rhodes and me out of the hospital. Buddy, my new shadow, of course led the way.

* * * *

"Mom, seriously, if you keep trying to move around, they're going to sedate you!" I warned, not knowing if that was true or not. "Be a good patient," I growled.

"I'm so stiff, Maia. I can't help it," she groaned where she lay, the top of the hospital bed propped up enough to ensure her comfort.

"Don't make me call in the nurse…" I threatened.

Mom glared. "She doesn't like me."

"No, she doesn't appreciate her patients disregarding her orders and trying to get up and walk to the bathroom unassisted when you're only ten hours out of surgery."

"I'm so uncomfortable. I want to go home."

I let out a frustrated, drawn-out sigh. This was going to

be a long, few days in the hospital if this is how she was on day one.

"Mom, just do what they say," Zach pleaded. "We want you to get better fast. You can't do that if you're not following the rules."

"Yeah! What he said," I pointed at my brother then looked around the room and realized Rhodes wasn't there. "Do you know where Rhodes went?" I asked Zach.

He grinned "He said he had a surprise for you."

I closed my eyes and groaned. "I hope it's coffee," I sighed dreamily.

"Nope, it's better!" Rhodes said from the door.

He stepped aside, and there was Emily.

"Oh my god!" I opened my arms automatically and the girl practically flew into them.

"Maia!" she cried with joy as she plowed into me.

I held on tight, even though my battered body throbbed and ached at the sudden tsunami that was Emily.

"Em, how…why…how did you get here?" I breathed, still clinging to the girl I now loved with my whole heart.

"Dad updated Mari last night. I demanded to be here. When family is hurt, we need to be together. Dad agreed. So, one of his rich friends flew us in their private plane. And here I am!"

I snuggled her close, allowing her familiar scent to wash over me. "I'm happy you're here. We missed you so much."

"I missed you guys too."

Zach cleared his throat, and I glanced over Em's head to see him straightening his shirt and sweeping his hair back.

Oh dear…

"Yo, sis, you want to introduce us to your stepdaughter?" Zach asked, his expression having changed from a concerned son to a cool guy with swagger the minute a beautiful girl his age entered the room.

I grinned and turned Emily to the side. She was all smiles,

long blond hair, pretty eyes and a stunning face. This was going to be interesting.

Immediately her cheeks pinked up as she laid eyes on Zach.

"Zach, Maisie, this is Emily, Rhodes' daughter."

Maisie gave a tiny wave and then dipped her head, staring at her shoes and fiddling with her fingers nervously. Rhodes and I had already spoken last night about getting the kids into some therapy when we were back and settled in California. They'd been through so much and it showed, especially on Maisie.

"Hey," Zach reached his hand out. "I'm Zach, and you're beautiful."

My mouth dropped open as Rhodes groaned loudly from behind us.

"Um, thank you. I'm Emily." Her cheeks went from rosy to lobster red in an instant.

"Gorgeous name too. How old are you?" Zach smiled.

"I'm turning fourteen in a couple weeks. You?" she asked.

"Just turned fifteen." He put his hands in his back pockets and puffed up his chest.

Oh, sweet baby Jesus...

"Okay, that's enough, Romeo," I clipped, pushing Em toward her father.

I looked at my mother for help, but she was sound asleep, little puffs of air leaving her mouth. The woman had been through hell and back and needed her rest.

"How about we all go get some lunch, get to know one another better?" Rhodes whispered.

"I'm game. I'll sit next to Emily." Zach suggested openly.

"You'll sit between me and Rhodes is what you'll do," I grumbled, and he laughed.

Emily stayed quiet, which was shocking. The girl normally spoke a mile a minute. She was clearly smitten with my brother flirting with her, still she went over to Maisie and held out her hand.

"Hi, I'm Emily."

"Maisie," my sister whispered, only glancing up from behind her overly long bangs for a moment.

"How old are you?"

"Um, I just turned thirteen."

Emily perked up. "We're the same age! This is so cool! We can have sleepovers every night if we want. I can introduce you to all my friends. They'll love you! And you are so pretty, just like Maia." She beamed.

Maisie finally lifted her head and looked deeply into Emily's eyes. "Why are you being so nice to me?"

My heart cracked in half.

Her default setting was people being mean to her. My hands shook with the need to pull her against my chest and hold on tight so nothing bad could ever harm her again, but I couldn't. She needed to see the world for what it really was. Filled with a lot of really good people. And Em was one of the best I knew.

"Well for one, you're Maia's sister, and I love Maia, so of course I'm happy to meet you. Plus, Dad says you three are coming to live with us. It's been me, Dad, and Marisol for so long…"

"Who's Marisol?" Maisie asked.

"Our house manager but she's mostly a nosey, bossy grandma."

"I heard that!" Marisol snapped from the door, carrying not only a backpack I recognized as Emily's, but also her purse and jacket. She set her load on a nearby chair and came over to me. She hugged me and kissed my temple then scrutinized my face while making a tsking sound. "I will fix this with holistic herbal medicine." She lightly grazed her fingers across my nose, black eyes, and cheekbone that was twice its size.

"Okay," I shrugged. I trusted Marisol with Emily's life; I'd trust her with mine. After she squeezed my hand, she looked at my siblings.

"*¡Vengan aquí!*" she demanded of them.

"Uh, what did she say?" Zach asked Emily.

"She wants you to come to her," she snickered.

"I want to get a good look at you both," Marisol murmured as they approached. She reached out and lifted Maisie's chin. "Too pretty for such sad eyes. No worries, we will wash away the sadness with time," she claimed then proceeded to look Zach up and down. She lifted his casted wrist, her eyes narrowing as she took in his scabbed over split lip and fading black eye. "Old injuries…" She reached out and pushed his hair from his forehead showing a nasty jagged scar.

"Hey! Don't." He shook his head and patted his hair back in place, until the scar was no longer visible. "I'm fine."

Marisol clucked. "You are not, but you will be under my house."

Her house meaning Rhodes' but neither one of us corrected her because she kinda was the boss. She made their lives work for them after Portia's repeat destruction, and I had faith she'd take in our ragtag crew and make them whole again too.

Marisol turned on her heel and announced, "The kids are too thin. We need to get them fed. Lunch time is now." She sauntered back to her stuff and picked it all up. "I'll get the car."

"I'll get the car," Buddy stated, my shadow hanging out in the hallway near Mom's room. Where I go, Buddy now goes. Rhodes was adamant about it. Even with the trouble no longer at our doorstep, he wasn't convinced I didn't need protection, and after all the hell we'd gone through, I could not care less if I was assigned a security detail for the rest of my life as long as my family was safe.

And I could finally say, as of today, hooking arms with

my fiancé while our three teenagers roamed in front of us, Marisol leading the way, that we'd finally be okay. And more than that, we were all together again and safe.

I couldn't ask for more.

Rhodes nuzzled my temple, his breath warm against my ear. "You're smiling."

"I'm happy. Truly happy for the first time in my entire life. Thank you for giving that to me."

He kissed my hairline. "Anytime, every time, Maia. Nothing but happiness from here on out."

I cuddled close and sighed. "I finally believe you."

Episode 112

Rest In Peace

MADAM ALANA

"Ultimately, I want to see you suffer the way I did," Angus growled, pulled his hand out of his jacket, and pointed a gun at Christophe's head. "But it's not enough. I want to watch you as I destroy the one person you love above any other." His corresponding smile was evil incarnate.

"No!" I screamed at the top of my lungs as a shot rang out.

Angus' body jolted, his eyes bulging with surprise as he dropped the gun, blood pooling at his shoulder. He covered his wound with his free hand as I watched Bianca stand, pull a gun from a thigh holster, and point it at me.

"You fucking bitch! Now, you die!"

Gunshots roared through the restaurant as men crashed through the windows. Every single waiter pulled out their hidden guns and started shooting at the invaders.

The room exploded with the sounds of breaking glass, gunshots, people fighting, tables being knocked over, chairs tossed this way and that.

It was madness.

Bianca turned from pointing her gun at me and started shooting wildly at Diego's men. She looked like a pregnant Tomb Raider as she pulled another gun from her other thigh and shot double fisted.

I watched in horror as she was hit at the top of her chest between her breast and clavicle, blood blooming across the front of her dress.

"The baby!" I screamed to anyone that would listen. The plan was never to kill Bianca or harm the baby. Brenden's baby.

Christophe heard my plea and tackled Bianca sideways, before she was riddled with more bullets, using his body to protect her.

Angus flipped the table, grabbed me by the ankle and pulled me toward him. I fell to the ground amongst the broken dishes and glassware. His bulky frame moved so fast, within a second, he'd straddled me and pinned me to the ground behind the table as gunshots blasted everywhere.

"You little cunt! You planned this." He pointed the gun at my face, pressing the nozzle straight to my forehead, digging the metal into my skull. "If she dies, I'll kill every single person you've ever known!" He swore, spit spattering my face.

"You did this! You and your revenge! You only have yourself to blame!" I screeched through my teeth, struggling against his hold. He battled me as I reached up to his shoulder where blood seeped out and pushed my thumb into the wound as hard as I could.

He roared in pain, his gun hand shaking. I pressed with all my might and used every ounce of strength within my body to roll him off of me, while screaming for help. His gun went off several times, blasting into the wall behind us.

Suddenly the table was shoved away, and standing there amongst all chaos was my savior. A halo of light shining behind his dark features.

Ángel de la Muerte.

The Angel of Death.

He pointed a massive, shiny silver gun straight at Angus. A menacing, dare I say handsome, smile on his face.

"Go back to hell, demon," he muttered and then fired.

The bullet went straight into Angus' forehead, right between his eyes.

I heard Bianca shriek like a wounded animal, fighting against Christophe's hold. Someone had divested her of her dueling guns and was currently zip tying her hands together.

I crab walked backward until I hit the wall.

Angel reached out his hand. Bullets were flying but not a single one came near him. It was a miracle.

I took his hand as though it were my lifeline, and he hauled me up and against his chest. He lifted me off my feet and ran toward the kitchen, bullets still flying.

"No! Christophe!" I roared, struggling against Angel's vise grip.

He got me to the kitchen and set me down on one of the metal counters.

"Guard her!" he snapped and then disappeared like a puff of smoke.

Mamá came over to me, gun in her hand. She put her free hand on my knee.

"You are safe," she said in heavily accented English while patting my leg.

My entire body trembled as gunshots blasted nonstop in the other room.

Someone pushed through the double doors and before I could even turn my head to see who it was, *Mamá* had already fired two shots, dropping the man like a hot rock.

"Safe," she patted my knee again and kept her guard. "*¿Hambrienta?*" she asked.

"I don't know that word?"

"Hungry?" she asked in English.

What in the world? She wants me to eat right now? The woman was nuts. Then again, she was the mother of a very violent mafia group. I didn't imagine much affected her. I shook my head numbly.

Another person raced in from a back door yelling, "*Mamá!*"

Mamá spun around just as a second person, this one huge, white, and armed with a big gun barreled through the door after the first person.

Mamá raised her gun like an expert marksman and shot right past one of her own son's heads and put two slugs into the attacker. He dropped right there. She pulled a gun from a kitchen drawer that had several more guns in it, boxes of ammo…and was that a grenade rolling around in the drawer like an old battery in a junk drawer? She tossed one of the guns to her son.

"*¡Gracias Mamá!*" he said, kissed her cheek, checked the weapon making a bunch of clicking sounds and then headed for the double doors, gun raised. I realized in my frightened haze that I recognized the man as Javier.

"Christophe! Please get him, Javier!" I begged.

He kicked the dead man aside and scouted out the restaurant, looking both ways before grinning at me and nodding succinctly. Then he also re-entered the shootout.

My entire body trembled, likely going into shock, as I clung to the edge of the counter where I sat.

Mamá started to hum, and then casually went over to a pot on the stove and stirred it. One hand holding a wooden ladle, the other a loaded gun.

What had I gotten myself into? I covered my face with my hands as the tears rolled down my cheeks.

The noises started to lessen, only a couple shots here and there.

My terrified mind went straight to better times.

Meeting Christophe at the auction over thirty years ago.

The view of the Grand Canyon.

Celine's laughter and smile.

Christophe's paintings.

The line of little rocks I placed all along the window sill in our ensuite bathroom back in France, reminding me of the places I'd visited that were special.

Rachel and Lewis Myers' wedding.

Emily's birth.

Brenden's first baseball game.

The day Maia tried to steal my bracelet, and I took her under my wing.

Savannah's wedding.

Hearing that Dakota was having twins.

Julianne's wedding to Giovanni.

So many beautiful moments I'd been given. None more beautiful than the love I shared with my husband.

"Christophe," I sobbed into my hands.

"I'm here!" he said as he pushed a bleeding, hobbling Bianca toward a small seating area. She slumped into the chair and promptly passed out, her head against the back of the wall, hand on her protruding belly.

I jumped off the counter and threw my arms around Christophe. "You're okay, you're okay, you're okay," I chanted, hugging him so tight my arms shook with the effort.

He rubbed his hands up and down my back. "I am fine, *mon coeur*," he whispered and placed a series of gentle kisses all over my face.

"We need to get Bianca medical help," I said.

Mamá pointed her gun at Bianca and shook her head. "No! She dies."

"She's pregnant with my godson's child!" I snapped, and shifted so that I was standing in front of her, *Mamá's* gun raised to take Bianca out once and for all.

"Bad seed." *Mamá* scowled and shook her head.

I held up my hand in a stopping motion. "I don't care!" I

pointed to Bianca's belly. "That child is *mi familia!*"

Mamá frowned. *"¿Familia?"*

"Sí." I shuddered. "No kill."

Mamá snarled. "Bad seed. Bad human." Then she let the gun fall to her side and went back over to her pot. She snapped her fingers, and Christophe and I turned toward her.

"Taste?" she ordered, pointing at Christophe and then her pot.

"Sweet love, she wants you to taste her food." I couldn't deal with *Mamá* anymore, rushing instead to grab at the stack of folded white towels I saw across the room on a shelf.

I brought the stack over to Bianca and pressed two of them over her bullet wound to stanch the blood flow. I could see she was breathing but it was labored.

"She needs a doctor!" I hollered.

We heard a commotion near the back door, then a single gunshot before a man entered.

Mamá had her gun up and ready to fire but didn't.

Diego grinned at his mother, holding up both hands, even the one with a gun.

"Oh, thank God!" I cried. "Diego, Bianca needs a doctor right now!"

His gaze went from his mother then to me and to Bianca. He had his gun drawn in a nanosecond, pointing straight at Bianca.

"No!" I screamed and once again put myself in the line of danger for a woman that didn't deserve to live. But that didn't mean her child wasn't innocent. "The baby is my family," I reiterated.

Diego's entire face turned murderous. "You want her to live? After everything she did?"

"The baby didn't do anything," I pointed at her protruding stomach.

"Bad seed." *Mamá* repeated with a cluck of her tongue.

"Shut up, *Mamá*!" I snapped, anger and fear flooding my

veins.

Diego's eyebrows rose as a couple men I recognized entered the kitchen through the double doors. Angel leading the way. He glanced at Diego who still had his gun pointed at me as I stood protecting Bianca. I stupidly had my arms and legs spread out as though my small body could do anything to prevent Diego from killing her if he truly wanted to.

"Stop him, Angel. He wants to kill Bianca and the baby!"

"Brother, since when do we kill children?" Angel rumbled, not a speck of emotion crossing his features. "Women we treat equally. If they commit the crime against us, they deserve it. *No bebés.* That is too far, my brother."

Diego let his gun drop to his side and nodded. "*Verdad.*" *True.* He muttered sounding unhappy with the reminder.

I could relate. I wanted the woman to cease to exist. But I also wanted her child, *Brenden's child*, protected even more.

"What do you want to do with her?" Diego asked while tucking his gun into his shoulder holster.

"I want her to pay for her crimes. I want justice. And when the time comes, our family wants that child," I demanded on a huff.

Diego rubbed his jaw back and forth. "Angel, what do we have on her?"

Angel leaned against the counter, arms crossed, his gaze never leaving Bianca. "Everything. My team wired the table. We have all of their confessions recorded."

"*Bien.* Patch her up and drop her at the hospital. Have your men watching from a distance. Send the recordings to…"

"I can bring them to Inspector Moreau." I offered.

"You're going to have to have a great story, *Reina de Las Vegas,* about how you came across this information." Angel smirked as he called me The Queen of Las Vegas.

Diego crossed his big arms over one another. "This is what will happen. We will clean up the hotel. There won't be a single trace of what occurred here today. You will tell the authorities that you were in hiding. They found you and shared all their nasty deeds. There was a scuffle, and you and Christophe ran away. You don't know how she got shot. Give us a week to accomplish this before meeting with the inspector."

I nodded. "What if she tells them what happened?" My voice cracked.

He shook his head. "She won't. That's not how this works. If she wants to stay alive in prison, she'll keep her mouth shut. As the daughter of a mafia boss, she knows better."

"That's it? She'll just keep quiet?" I scoffed.

"Trust me," Diego cocked an eyebrow.

"And what about the gunshots, the people that died here?" I pointed at the two dead bodies littering the floor.

"What gunshots? We heard fireworks for the wedding we were hosting. Did you not see them light up the sky?"

"You're kidding?" I gaped.

Angel offered me the slightest smile, practically non-existent. "You really must have been scared to not have heard them. The entire neighborhood watched them, cheering during the finale," he ran his thumb across his bottom lip.

I shivered as my teeth started clacking.

"She's going into shock, we need to get her out of here," Christophe stated.

Diego whistled loudly, and a couple more of his men entered the kitchen. "Take the pregnant woman to the hospital and notify the authorities that she's there through an anonymous tip. They have a warrant for her arrest as she fled the US after being let out on bail. Then keep an eye on her."

"*Sí jefe*," they responded unanimously.

One of them gestured to me to let go of the pressure I was putting on Bianca's chest wound and took over. The other lifted her bottom half as they carried her through the back door.

Christophe pulled me against his side. "Where do we go now?" he asked Diego.

"There's a car and two of my men that will take you to my estate," Diego said. "Clean up, rest, and we'll discuss things in more detail when I'm done here."

We were led through the back of the restaurant, and as promised, Javier and another man I didn't recognize were waiting for us. Javier held the door open. Blood was spattered across his white dress shirt, and I winced at the sight of it.

"Are you hurt?" I asked.

He shook his head and gave me a soft smile. "No, Madam. Please, let me take you home."

"Home is outside of Paris," I mumbled.

"Then let me take you to our home to heal."

"I'm not hurt…" I croaked, tears spilling down my cheeks.

"Your mind is." He pointed at my forehead and then to my heart. "Your heart is."

"I guess you're right."

He grinned. "I always am, but don't tell my brothers." He winked and then held the back passenger side door open for us.

Christophe urged me inside the vehicle, and I reacted on autopilot, my entire existence feeling wired and raw. I was having trouble going over all that had happened today within my own mind, including my part in all of it.

All I knew for certain was that Angus was dead.

He could never hurt us again.

Bianca had been shot but was breathing when they left to take her to the hospital.

I said a silent prayer the baby would make it. If Bianca survived, she'd go to jail for the rest of her life.

It was finally over.

The Myers, the Falcos, and my dearest friend Celine could finally rest in peace.

Episode 113

Epilogue 1: Memphis & Naomi

MEMPHIS

I stood under the wooden arbor my father made with his own hands, my gaze set at the end of the short aisle between the seated small crowd of people here to witness me marrying the woman of my dreams. I scanned the first rows. My mother dabbed at her eyes, tears already falling, and we hadn't even started the ceremony. Next to her my father sat, pride evident in his puffed-up chest, wearing his favorite suit. Granny was all smiles sitting in the very first seat wearing a new dress and her favorite pearls and church hat. Each of my sisters wore their Sunday best, Sydney per usual dressed to the nines looking like she'd just walked out of a fashion magazine.

We didn't have bridesmaids or groomsmen because we didn't feel it necessary with such a small event, not to mention the fact I had a handful of sisters. Picking between them would have been a nightmare. Still, my family had gone above and beyond, making my mother's lush garden even more glorious by adding twinkling lights, mason jars filled with glowing candles and pots of blooming flowers throughout. In the back, there were a handful of large round tables, already decorated for the reception, using flowers from the garden as the centerpieces.

Beyond my family, I saw some of my friends. Faith and Joel Castellanos were present, their two little girls sitting quietly between them. In the same row were Ruby and Nile Pennington who'd flown in from London just for the event. Ruby winked and flashed me a thumbs-up in encouragement. Next to her was Jade, wearing a chic black suit, her hair slicked back, and bright red lipstick adorning her lips. At first glance I would have mistaken her for Alana, but I knew better. As much as Jade didn't want to admit it, she was enamored with Alana, and being her protégé for The Marriage Auction was a position she didn't take lightly.

I had finally received a text from Alana stating they were indeed okay. She said they had been in hiding from the same person that had blown up the office building in New York that belonged to Julianne and her crew. Instantly, I started to give her my condolences on losing her family members, but she told me that the three of them were actually okay and that announcing their deaths had all been part of a bigger plot to catch the person behind it. Which supposedly they did. I looked forward to hearing the full story when Nay and I returned from our honeymoon.

Thinking of Naomi must have conjured her because the acoustic guitarist my sisters hired started playing a soft melodic tune and requested everyone rise for the bride.

My palms started to sweat, and I tugged at the collar of my suit and tie trying to loosen it enough to get a full breath of air. It didn't matter. The minute Naomi appeared at the end of the small aisle, I lost my ability to breathe.

She was the most beautiful thing I'd ever laid eyes on in my life.

Her father looked stoic at her side, but there was a new softness to his features. I think almost losing his only daughter had truly changed him. We even had a sit-down this morning where he apologized for his behavior and promised he'd support our union and future moving forward. After he spoke to me, he had a quiet minute with my parents and my granny, too, which I was told by my mother ended in forgiveness and well wishes for both of their children's future together. Honestly, I thought then that I couldn't be happier, everything was finally working out.

I was wrong.

Nothing prepares you for the moment the woman you love walks down an aisle toward you, ready to enter into forever by your side. I'll never forget it.

The sheen of the slinky, elegant satin gown that glided along her curves, flowing with her movements.

The rosy hue of her cheeks.

Her slow blink as our gazes met and I stared in open awe of her glory.

How her glossy pink lips shifted into the most stunning smile…just for me.

It was all for me.

For us.

For this day where we would become one.

My gaze never left hers when they approached, her father passing her hand to mine before going to sit with her mother.

I interlaced our fingers and I held on.

I wanted to hold her hand forever.

It all passed in a blur of I do and I will, whispered words of love and commitment, and sultry sweet kisses.

Through it all, I held on.

I wanted to hold her hand forever…and now I could.

"It is my pleasure to introduce you to Mr. and Mrs. Taylor."

* * * *

NAOMI

Married life was not what I expected.

It was better.

The best even.

I grinned as I watched my footballer walk up the sandy beach, his muscled body dripping with salt water and looking good enough to eat. All I needed was a shot of tequila. I'd lick the salt right off that gorgeous body and go back for seconds.

"You keep lookin' at me like I'm lunch, and you'll never eat a full meal again," he warned.

I looked at him over the rim of my sunglasses, eyebrows cocked. "Who needs a full meal when I've got all of that to feed off of?" I gestured to his perfect chest.

He smiled shyly and shook his head. I loved it. I loved him. Learning that my man was actually rather shy about his body was a delight. He had one of the best bodies I'd ever seen but was rather prudish about showing it off. I'd tried to get him to go skinny-dipping with me last night, and instead, he tackled me the moment I'd ripped my top off on the beach and hauled me back to our private cabana. He claimed my tits were his to look at, and no perv was going to get in on any of his action.

Turns out, he also felt the same about himself. Already he was reaching for his t-shirt and slipping it over his head, cutting off my view.

I pouted, which earned me a wet, salty kiss.

"Food first, then dessert." He nipped at my bottom lip, and I groaned, my gaze on the massive private beach and miles of ocean beyond.

"I can't believe Joel & Faith gifted us this for our wedding. You've got some cool friends, baby."

"Yeah," he said while rubbing a towel over his head. "It was kind of them for sure."

"I think I'll gift Faith something special from my Mother's Day collection. Can you find out what month the girls' birthdays are in?" A pendant with both Eden and Penny's birth-stones would be beautiful. Maybe an infinity symbol with each loop wrapping around one of the children's gemstones.

"Nay, just because someone gave you a gift doesn't mean you have to return the gesture right away," Memphis noted.

"I know, but they're your friends, and I want to build a relationship with them. Joel doesn't need anything in life. He's made it clear that all he cares about is Faith and those girls. So a present that represents both kids would be nice, don't you think?"

Memphis shrugged. "Sure. But what happens when they have another baby?"

"Are they trying?" I asked, wanting to hear all the tea.

"Joel claims he wants another baby asap. Faith wants to wait a bit because she's working on setting up an authentic Italian restaurant like the one her father had in Las Vegas that burned down. Only this one will be in Greece."

"They're going to stay in Greece most of the time?"

He nodded. "Faith says there's too many bad memories in the States. She was in hiding and on the run from that douche Aiden for a long time."

I turned onto my side on the lounge chair to face him and get more comfy. "Ooooh, tell me more?"

Memphis burst out laughing. "You're as bad as my granny."

"No, I aspire to be as well informed as granny. That woman knows everything about everyone. Nothing gets past her."

He chuckled. "True. It's not a happy story though," he frowned.

"Okay, well we can discuss it later. Let's talk about how in two days we are going back to New York where my man will be finishing up his degree and starting work at Columbia."

I watched a gorgeous smile spread across his face. "I'm really excited about it. Football, the players, the game, all of it has always been my passion. Getting to help college kids live out their dreams?" He shook his head. "It's my dream job, baby. Well, if it turned into me coaching for an NFL league, that would be the ultimate."

I reached out and covered his hand with my own. "You're young. You have years of experience ahead of you to learn, but I believe if you work hard, focus on that ultimate goal, one day you'll get it."

He sat down next to me and played with my fingers, turning my wedding ring from left to right, toggling it as he seemed to enjoy. "Sometimes I think I can't dream any bigger because finding you, marrying you, my family being set..." He let out a long breath. "It's all better than I could have imagined. More isn't needed. I've already got everything I ever truly wanted. And it's all because of you. I love you, Naomi Taylor."

"I love you, too, Memphis Taylor."

He leaned over and we kissed for so long he ended up pulling me up and over onto his chair, straddling his large frame where we made good use of the outdoor private patio facing the ocean.

When the night fell and we were cuddled in bed, whispering about the things we wanted to do in the future, I thought back to when all of this began.

I'd lost faith in men.

I'd lost faith in my family.

I'd lost faith in myself.

Now here I was, in paradise, married to the best man I'd ever met and happier than I'd ever been.

I didn't originally believe The Marriage Auction would lead me to my one true love, but I was wrong.

Life is filled with the unknown, and sometimes you have to leap off the side of the cliff into murky waters to find your truth.

Or in this case, bid on a footballer from Georgia with a great family, a fantastic body, and a beautiful soul.

Episode 114

Epilogue 2: Summer & Jack

SUMMER

Jack held my hand as we walked back from the indoor grow houses to my parent's farmhouse. I could already hear TJ squealing with glee in my mother's patio garden. I glanced at Jack to find him smiling peacefully.

"The last couple months have been a whirlwind, huh?" I swung our locked arms playfully.

He inhaled deeply then let the breath out while taking in the landscape. Eureka is a magical place for those who live in it. My family's farm, though, was true beauty. The only peace I knew before I married my soulmate.

"It has been the highest highs and the lowest lows of my life," he shared truthfully.

"I know, but look at what we've already built." I pointed to TJ and my mother who were sitting in the middle of her garden. Baby ducks and chickens waddled freely around them, curious about their new home. The scent of flowers and growing vegetables filled the air with their earthly aroma, serenading our senses.

We watched as my mother showed TJ a sprig of rosemary she'd plucked from a nearby bush.

"Smell it." She lifted it to her nose and inhaled, then passed it to our boy. "Rosemary," Mom shared.

"Ro-mary" he repeated gripping the entire spring in his meaty toddler fist as he shoved it against his face and hummed, "Mmmm".

"Be careful, grandson." Mom chuckled then proceeded to pick up a fluffy baby chick and present it to him.

"Chicken," she cooed to TJ while petting the small animal gently. "Here, pet him, but be gentle," she warned.

TJ attempted to comply with her request, his little tongue pressed to the side of his cheek as he reached out with his entire hand, fingers spread like a starfish.

Mom laughed while protecting the chicken from being bashed in the head by a two-year-old.

As we stood to the side of the garden watching them, Dad burst out of the house with a plate of cookies in one hand and a bottle of bubbles in the other.

"TJ, my boy! Look what grandpop has!" he called out as he approached Mom and TJ.

My parents were living their absolute best lives. Not only was the business they'd started from scratch doing amazing, I was happy, in love, and married. Autumn's store was doing even more business with some helpful suggestions Jack gave her, and boon of all time...they had a grandchild.

And my parents loved having a little one around. At any given time, one or both of them were off with TJ, teaching him something or playing games with him like they were now.

"Coming here was the right choice," Jack said without a hint of melancholy or sadness.

Jack was just starting to smile more often and finding his footing in California. The cannabis business was all new to him, and as expected, he'd thrown himself into it with both feet. Already he was implementing a new business strategy that would double our profits in the next three years. He also believed getting involved in the political landscape around the use of cannabis medicinally and recreationally was important to the future of our business, so we'd hired a lobbyist.

When Erik found out Jack wanted to leave Johansen Brewing as an employee, there was a bit of a battle. Erik had just come back from the dead, so to speak, and wanted his best friend, his chosen brother, to work with him. Jack wanted to be here with us while putting all of his focus on TJ, me, and Humble Buds. Jack was being challenged in ways that excited him both personally and professionally. Of course, Erik eventually understood and accepted that Jack would continue to hold a position on their board, and in turn, Jack asked Erik to consider investing in our company and consider serving on our board. Last I heard, he was genuinely thinking about it.

I was grateful that it had all worked out, and both men were happy, healthy, and building their futures with families of their own.

"Hey," I knocked his shoulder with mine. "You know what I did last week and didn't tell you about?" I teased.

His brows furrowed, and he turned completely toward me. "Summer, I don't want any secrets between us." His tone brooked no argument.

I grinned and waggled my eyebrows. "You'll be okay with it once you hear this one," I taunted.

His lips compressed into a flat line as he crossed his arms over his chest. "Tell me," he grumbled, sounding worried.

I rolled my eyes. "You act like what I'm going to say is a bad thing." I laughed. "Relax, baby. It's good news, I promise."

"What?" He let his shoulders drop and tilted his head.

"I got my IUD removed. That means from here on out, nothing is going to prevent me from getting pregnant."

His eyes widened at first, then shifted to desire, and then went pedal to the metal, barreling straight for lust. He moved so fast I didn't even realize it before I had my back against the house and Jack's mouth on mine.

Our tongues tangled as his hand traced down my side, then over my breast, where he gave an encouraging squeeze, and then down to the curve of my ass in my booty shorts. His fingers teased the crease of where my ass cheek met my thigh, and my mind fizzled out. My entire focus became every feather light touch, every intense grip, every gasp as our tongues tangled and he pressed me harder against the wall.

Jack had just slipped his hand between my shorts and underwear when we heard, "You two realize you have your own house, right?" my mother called out clearly having spied us from where she was playing with TJ about thirty feet away.

Jack's hands froze on my ass as though he suddenly realized what he'd done and where we were at that moment.

I laughed. "Hey, Ma, can you watch TJ for a bit longer? We're gonna go try and make a baby." I called out, not taking my eyes off the blazing dark gaze of my husband.

Jack shook his and head laughed out loud. The man wasn't used to my shamelessness or shenanigans quite yet. I hoped he never got used to them. I liked the idea of keeping my man on his toes.

"Whoo hoo! Did you hear that, Bernie?"

"I sure did! I think that's cause for celebration. Fresh squeezed OJ for everyone!" He clapped.

Mom continued to blather on while I jumped up and locked my legs around Jack's waist. "I'm going to need to consult the cards and do a fertility ritual."

"You think we can make it to the car, or should we hit the shed out back real quick?" I asked.

Jack ground his very large erection against me and grunted, almost sounding pained. My lower region throbbed and ached, ready to finish what we started against the wall.

"The she-shed it is!" I lifted my arm and made a roping gesture. "Giddy-up cowboy. This cowgirl wants a ride."

Jack carried me all the way down the side path as I kissed his neck, sucking hard enough to leave a fat hickey. He'd bitch and moan about it later, but also secretly love it.

The second he got me through the rickety door, he kicked it shut with his booted foot, and I let my legs drop to the floor. I'd just barely unbuttoned my shorts and shoved them down to my ankles before he spun me around and bent me over the wooden workbench.

He cupped my center from behind and sank two fingers deep.

I arched back on a loud moan, forcing those fingers deeper, my entire body aching for more. He fucked me properly with those fingers, working me into a frenzy until I begged for more.

"Jack, please…"

I heard the sound of his belt being undone and his new jeans sliding down his narrow hips. He removed his soaked fingers, and then I was rewarded with the sound of him humming.

I glanced over my shoulder to see his fingers being licked clean.

"Fuck, that's so hot," I moaned, the temperature in the shed becoming balmy and humid with our rapid breaths and beating hearts. "Fuck me," I demanded, waving my bare ass in the air.

His hand came down hard against my bare skin, blistering my ass like a fiery brand. "That's for the hickey!" he rumbled like thunder, then lifted his hand and swung again, reddening the other cheek. "That's for keeping me in the dark about your doctor's appointment."

I gagged on a moan, my entire ass aflame, arousal coating my thighs and dripping down my leg. The need for him to fuck me was so strong it was carnal, no *primal*.

"Please!" I begged.

I didn't have to wait.

Jack centered the fat head of his cock at my entrance, gripped my hips, and plunged all the way to the hilt.

We both cried out in a mixture of pleasure and pain. He pulled back and then thrust home again, his balls slapping my pussy.

I pushed back as he rode me hard.

One of his hands threaded through the roots of my hair, and I arched into the pressure, going up onto my toes as he impaled me over and over with his thick cock.

"Jack, Jack, Jack...I'm gonna..." I gasped as he jackhammered into me, stretching my channel brutally, hitting that sweet spot inside of me until I was keening and wailing as I came.

"*Jeg elsker deg.*" *I love you*, Jack hissed through his teeth as he thrust home. His entire body convulsed against mine, his chest falling to my back. "*Jeg elsker deg,*" he whispered, breath fanning my ear as we both panted.

"I love you too." I smiled and then closed my eyes, sated and happy.

He eased off my back and swiveled his hips, almost as though stirring the pot.

"What are you doing?" I chuckled, amused at his actions.

"Making sure it's all in there," he whispered distractedly, still working his softening cock within me.

"I don't think that's how it works," I snorted and then pressed my forehead to the wooden worktable he'd bent me over.

"I think we should go home, shower, make dinner, put TJ to bed and continue working on this," he said, still swirling his hips.

I sighed, enjoying the feeling of him gently playing with my body.

"Okay." I snapped my hips back hard enough to dislodge him. Then I pulled up my underwear and shorts not giving a shit I was going to be a mess when we finally did make it home.

He did the same.

"Let's go get our boy," I hooked my arm with his.

We made it back to the patio where Dad was in full bubble blowing mode. TJ was split between running after the chickens and ducks or popping the bubbles.

Mom's head rose as she pointed at one of them and then her gaze landed on us. "You didn't even make it to the car, did ya?"

I shook my head grinning. "She-shed."

"Nice," mom praised me with a wink.

Jack's entire face was beet red as he crouched and opened his arms calling for TJ.

"Dada Yak!" TJ screeched and then ran into him. "*Boble*," he pointed to a shimmering, glistening orb, which popped the second he touched it. "Booobbllleee!" TJ squealed.

"Bub-ble" Jack corrected in English. "*Boble*, in Norwegian. Bubble in English," he explained.

We'd agreed to speak both English and Norwegian to TJ. We didn't want him forgetting anything he'd already learned in preschool, nor did we want him forgetting his own language. So most of the time, Jack explained what things were in English and Norwegian which helped all of us learn more.

"Well, thanks Mom and Dad. We're gonna take TJ home and make dinner."

"Oh, Autumn wants to talk to you more about entering the auction. She said she wasn't getting a response from your friend Alana."

"Alana's on break," I said, not wanting to share all we'd heard about what Alana and Christophe had gone through with that Russian psycho and his daughter Bianca. "Jade's running the next auction. I'll give her Jade's information."

"Say bye to grandmom and grandpop," Jack instructed.

TJ waved. "Bye, bye."

"We love you, grandson," my mother said, waving wildly.

My father put his arm around her, and they both waved as we left.

"Maybe this time next month we'll be announcing our pregnancy?" I said dreamily, imagining our future and loving every second of it.

"That's why we need to practice. A lot," Jack murmured, nuzzling my neck.

TJ grabbed my face and tried to kiss my cheek, doing everything Jack did.

"Well, they say practice does make perfect. Last one to the car is a rotten egg!" I cried out and then sprinted toward our vehicle.

Jack and TJ let out a silly war cry and came running after me.

* * * *

Nine months to the day we banged in the she-shed, I gave birth to Ellena Ann Larson named after two amazing women. One who we lost too soon and my mother.

But we call our little princess…Ellie.

Episode 115

Epilogue 3: Julianne & Giovanni

JULIANNE

The prison bars clanked shut behind us, sending a shiver of nerves racing up my spine.

"I can't believe we're doing this." My voice quivered as a guard led us into a small room. The walls were cement blocks and gave a foreboding feeling. I'd never even been to a regular jail, let alone a prison.

"We can leave any time. It is not our responsibility, Jules. Not a single soul would question us if we decided against this plan. It's our lives too," Gio reminded me for the tenth time today.

We'd been contacted by the State's child services. When Bianca had put Brenden Myers as the baby's father, the system immediately started to work on finding a next of kin for the baby. Bianca was serving back-to-back life in prison sentences. Once she had the baby, the system needed someone to give that baby to, or it would go into foster care. We'd been debating our options ever since that call.

I closed my eyes and counted to ten while breathing in through my nose and out through my mouth. "I just...my parents. If they were here, they'd tell us this is the right thing to do."

He pulled me into his arms and held me close, his face pressed to the side of my head.

"Jules, if you want to leave, it's not too late." He shifted his body and put a hand over my abdomen where our 'little pea' was growing safely. "We have more than just us to think about. And Alana and Christophe are an incredible second option. They offered to become the baby's guardians."

I shook my head, clearing the fear away as I swiped at my tears. "No. Even though my brother was an asshole in the end, he'd want us to take care of his only child."

Giovanni cupped my cheeks. "Look at me, Jules."

I frowned and slid my gaze up to his. His eyes were a dark, beautifully stormy gray blue today, but I'd walk through that storm to be by his side…anytime every time.

"Brenden is dead." Each of those three words was like a knife wound to my heart. "You do not owe him anything. We tried to save him. We tried. The doctors tried. The burn center did everything they could, but after a month of fighting, it was just too much for his body to handle."

I choked on a sob as I clung to his shoulders.

"His child is not ours. You do not owe anyone anything," Gio was firm but kind.

"But the baby is all I'll have left of him…of my parents," I gulped.

Gio closed his eyes, his nostrils flaring as he inhaled sharply. "I understand. You know, I loved him like a brother. Even after everything, I loved him."

"I know," I lifted up onto my toes and kissed him gently, pressing my face to his. "I know."

"We don't have to do this."

I swallowed, opened my eyes and focused on my husband. "Do you not want to?"

He shook his head. "Jules, I told you I'd love any baby we

had. Ours, our niece or nephew. I'd have a house full of them with you. It's not about the child. It's about what pieces of you and me are going to be cut up and destroyed by taking on this responsibility. That's what I'm afraid of. We've already been through hell and back."

"I'm more afraid of the pieces of myself and my soul I'd lose by not taking this child into our home. The baby is my blood. The only blood relative I have living besides our baby," I covered my growing bump protectively.

"So you are one hundred percent sure you want to raise Bianca's child?" His voice was a low, scratchy rumble.

"No, I want us to raise *Brenden's* child. Teach him or her about who Brenden was before Bianca ever entered any of our lives. I want the child to know the real Brenden. The loving, caring, protective brother. The funny, zany, silly jokester. The baseball lover. The young man that was happier boating on a lake than anywhere else in the world. The man who claimed his favorite color was purple because it was rad."

Gio chuckled, his shoulders relaxing. "He was the funniest man I ever knew. I always told him he should do standup comedy as a hobby."

I patted Gio's chest. "Exactly. I want his child to know that. I want his child to know the brotherhood you had before it all went to hell in a handbasket."

"And this isn't the grief talking? Because once we make this decision, Jules, we can't go back. If we adopt this child, it will be *our* child. Our responsibility for life. And it will be hard. Having two under the age of one at the same time will not be easy."

I shrugged. "We can afford the help. Besides, when Maggie found out we were not only having a baby but planning to take over guardianship of another, she offered to transition her role from nurse to nanny."

Giovanni's eyes lit up. "Really? Just last month we were looking at vacation homes in Florida for her."

"Turns out Maggie would rather be a grandma. And that best friend of hers found herself a retiree at their monthly bingo game and bailed on her ass. She's planning to move in with him, leaving Maggie in the dust." I snarled thinking about how crappy it was.

Maggie had become a staple in our lives and anyone going against their word to her could suck on rotten eggs in my book. Maggie might be rough around the edges and have a take-no-shit type of personality, but she was good people. The best actually. She'd forced Gio to do everything his doctors instructed, and he healed beautifully. Sure, he was stiff and would need physical therapy for years, and future surgeries if he wanted to remove the worst of the scarring, but he was alive, mobile, and happy as a clam to become a daddy.

"You're kidding?" Gio scoffed. "Maggie must be pissed."

"Oh, she's mad. Isn't talking to her best friend at all and hasn't for a month. Says she's got another couple months of being angry with her before she is willing to talk it out. Though her bestie calls her every day begging for forgiveness."

Gio smiled. "I'll bet Maggie lives for the groveling."

"You know it!" I chuckled.

Just then our social worker entered with a small bundle cradled in her arms.

"It's a boy." She smiled and passed the bundle to me.

I cuddled him close and stared into his sweet little face. "Hi, little one. I'm your Auntie Jules. Your daddy would have been so proud to meet you." I let out a shuddering breath, doing my best to hold back the overwhelming need to clutch this baby to my chest, fall to my knees, and cry my eyes out. The baby had already suffered so much loss in his young life, and he didn't even know it. Yet I knew I needed to be strong right now, for Gio, for the baby, and for my brother Brenden. May he rest in peace.

Giovanni cupped the baby's small head. "What's his

name?"

"Angus Myers-Sokolov," the social worker claimed.

Giovanni shook his head. "We'll be changing that immediately. We will not utter that name again in his presence. What do you want to name him, darling?"

I thought about all the years with my brother, my parents, and the love we all shared. Knowing the real Brenden would want to honor our father in some way.

"I think we should name him Myers Lewis Falco. That way he'll always know where he came from."

"Myers it is," Gio smiled, dipped his head, and pressed his lips to the baby's forehead. "I'll be a good father to you. Protect you from harm, teach you right from wrong, and love you as if you were my very own."

Tears fell as I looked at my brother's baby. His son. No…he was *my son* now. I'd never have him feel as though he was second place to our child.

He was family. Our family.

* * * *

Exactly six months to the day, I gave birth to our daughter Caterina Rachel Falco, named after our mothers.

* * * *

To my beloved son,

Every day I conspire to make it back to you.

Every day I find new ways to survive in this hellhole your fake parents put me in.

Every day I dream of getting out, of escaping…one day I will.

One day we'll be together again.

One day…

All my love,

Bianca

Episode 116

Epilogue 4: Maia and Rhodes

MAIA

"Maia!" I heard Emily scream from the entrance to our home. Buddy had just picked up the kids from school. Mom and I were in the kitchen with Marisol, learning how to cook.

The tone of that scream made gooseflesh rise on my skin.

"Maia!" she screeched again, as the sound of multiple pairs of teenaged feet came clomping through the house to the kitchen like a herd of horses.

Emily was a mess of rosy cheeks, wild hair and streaked mascara.

"What the fuck!" I dashed over to her and cupped her cheeks. "Did someone hurt you? Where's Buddy?"

"Right here. And I already asked. I'm going outside to patrol. I did not sign up for this shit," he grumbled and bailed out the kitchen side door to the backyard. Buddy often bitched about the teenagers but was also the first to volunteer to pick them up. I think he was still dealing with what happened in Colorado and being overly protective of everyone in the family. The kids and their drama drove him up the wall, which I thought was hilarious. Most of the time.

"You!" Emily spun around and pointed at my brother Zach. "You ruined everything!" she roared.

The noise apparently interrupted Rhodes because, within moments of them arriving, I could also hear his feet pounding down the back staircase off the kitchen that led to his office.

"Maia, Emily!" he called out as he rushed into the kitchen, his gaze going from Emily's angry red face to Zach, and then to Maisie who was leaning with her back against the wall quietly watching the show.

"Dad! You tell him he is not the boss of me!" Emily yelled at Zach.

"Zachery, what did you do?" Mom approached him. She was moving around great now that it had been six months since we left Colorado. For the most part, she spent her time helping Marisol and learning how to be an independent woman. It wasn't easy going, but she was a champ, and I believed in her. Plus, I loved having our entire family in the same place.

"That slimy jock had his hands all over you!" Zach snapped.

"He's my boyfriend!" Emily shrieked, the pitch rather piercing to the rest of us.

"What boyfriend?" Rhodes asked.

I let out a deep sigh. "Babe, I told you she was dating someone. A guy on the wrestling team."

"He sucks though. I took him down in one punch. A little bloody nose and he went whining away to his dumb-as-rocks friends." Zach smirked, clearly pleased with his actions.

"You are not allowed to hit my boyfriend! You are not allowed to hit anyone!" Emily stomped her foot with petulance.

Zach maneuvered around Mom and pointed in Emily's face. "Then you should keep your kissing in private! And he should have kept his hands off your ass!"

"Oh my god! He kissed you?" I started bouncing up and down on the balls of my feet. "Jeremy Joplin?"

Emily smiled huge. "JJ for short. It was so awesome!"

"Eeeek!!!" I hugged Emily and we jumped up and down together. She'd wanted to catch the eye of the hot wrestler since high school started months ago.

"Who kissed you? Maia, stop celebrating for chrissake," Rhodes rumbled and rubbed at the back of his neck.

"It was so dreamy, Maia," Emily breathed. "I thought I was going to die. He was so romantic!"

"It was so dreamy..." Zach imitated in a high voice while snarling and making quacking motions with his hand.

"You shut up!" Emily pointed her finger at Zach's face. "Maia, tell him he's not allowed to hurt my boyfriend. Or any other guy I date!" she added for good measure.

I patted her back. "Bro, what's up? Why did you fight him?"

"Did you miss the part where he was kissing her and touching her ass?" Zach deadpanned.

"Kid has an excellent point..." Rhodes cut in.

"Daddy! Not cool." Emily's eyes narrowed as she glared in his direction. "All I know is that you need to lay off dude! I am not your girl, I'm never going to be your girl, and you can't go around beating up the boys I like. Period. I'm going to my room. Maisie!" she called out like my baby sister wasn't hiding in the corner as all this went down.

She pushed off the wall. "I'm here, Em."

"Our room. Now. We have to do damage control because somebody may have ruined my entire life!" She growled in Zach's direction then did an about-face and stormed out of the kitchen and toward their room.

After about a month of Maisie living in the guesthouse, the two of them asked if they could share a room. Since the bedrooms in Rhodes' house were ginormous, and Mom was cool with it, they bunked up and became best friends.

"Hey," I put my hand to Maisie's shoulder. "Don't forget, you leave for therapy in an hour."

Maisie smiled. "I won't."

"Besides all this drama, therapy is going good yeah?" I liked to check in every couple weeks.

She nodded. "I like her very much. Right now, we're working on the idea of me making one friend that wasn't given to me by Emily."

I tilted my head. "I don't understand."

She dipped her head and her cheeks turned red. "All of my friends are Emily's. And they are nice, but the therapist wants me to make a friend of my own. She says it would be good for me to put myself out there."

"Oh honey, that's a great idea," Mom interrupted.

"I think so too," Maisie agreed. "Today I actually complimented a girl sitting next to me in math class on the dress she was wearing. Turns out it was one she made herself. She says one day she's going to be a famous designer. I told her she was definitely on track. Then she asked for my cell phone number, but I don't have one."

I blinked, standing there like a stupid idiot. I remembered getting Mom one. And when we went to the store, we'd taken Zach because he was learning to drive. He'd straight up asked for one.

"Honey, shoot. I'm so sorry. We'll get you one on the way home from therapy. I don't know why it didn't dawn on me sooner," I apologized.

Maisie shrugged her shoulder. "I didn't have anyone I needed to call before. Now maybe I will."

Behind Maisie I could hear Mom sniffling. Rhodes went over to her and patted her back. "It's an oversight, we'll take care of it right away."

"But you shouldn't have to," Mom croaked. "I'm supposed to be providing for my children, and it's my child and her husband doing all the heavy lifting."

Husband.

I loved hearing Rhodes called that. We'd married three months after getting home from Colorado. None of us had ever seen the ocean, so that first weekend we were all home together, we went to the beach. Every last one of us felt the calming healing vibes of the ocean, finding the experience so uplifting and freeing. I'd decided there and then that I wanted to get married right where I'd felt free. Rhodes thought it was a wonderful idea. We'd only invited a handful of people to witness it. My best friend Sam of course, Alana and Christophe, Marisol and her family, and us. It was perfect. After the ceremony, Marisol and her kids cooked us a Mexican feast, and we drank margaritas and danced under the stars until our feet were too tired. It was one of the most beautiful nights of my life.

"Maisie, go on ahead but be ready for therapy," I instructed.

"Okay, Maia. Love you, Mom!" she called out and then headed to her room.

"I'm outta here," Zach snarled.

"The hell you are!" I hollered. "Zach, you cannot beat people up at school. Not Emily's boyfriends, not anyone. You are not that person."

"Bullshit. Dad made sure I was. Taught me exactly how to take a punch and return it double-fold. And if anyone lays a single finger on Emily or Maisie, I'll do what I have to do."

"You are not the law." I growled under my breath.

He recoiled at those words, likely remembering how his father claimed to be the law all the time. Look where that got him. Serving life in prison and likely becoming some inmate's bitch. Served him right.

"Like I said, I'll do what I have to do to protect what's mine," Zach crossed his arms over one another defensively.

"Emily is not yours," I said as calmly as I could muster.

"One day she will be." And on that note, he stormed out

the back patio door all teenage angst. "I'll be in my room," he said as he slammed the door.

Rhodes left Mom and came over to my side. "That boy has a lot of anger coiled in him even with regular therapy visits. It still doesn't take much to set him off. I can see why he'd react the way he did, especially since he's made it no secret he is enamored with my daughter. But he's going about it the wrong way," he sighed.

"Can you maybe, talk to him? Try to show him a better path to channel his anger?" I asked.

He nodded. "I talked to Buddy about this the other day. He thinks we should get him into boxing or some form of mixed martial arts. Put a heavyweight bag in the gym, sign him up for some classes or a league."

I closed my eyes. "I hate the idea of him using his fists for a hobby though," I said, not saying what I truly feared, that he'd end up like Damon one day.

"That's why he has to channel it. He lived in that house with that man for fifteen years. Using his fists is his first go-to. We need to teach him a healthy way to do what he's already good at."

"Mom?" I knew it was technically her decision, but she'd been deferring to me and Rhodes on anything involving the kids since they got here. It's like the woman I remembered had been beaten down so badly she didn't know what was right or wrong, healthy for the kids, or what even was good for her. But she was learning, and I'd do everything I could to help her transition into being the mom those kids needed. The mom I needed.

"I have to agree with Rhodes," she wiped at her teary eyes. "Zach was taught to use his fists to solve a conflict. It's his default, just like it was Damon's. Finding a positive outlet for that could be the best bet."

I nodded. "Okay, I trust you." I lifted my head and Rhodes planted a kiss on my lips.

"I'll go talk to him. You'll sort out Emily?" Rhodes clarified.

I waved my hand. "She's easy."

"Just for the record, I can't say I'm mad about Zach protecting our girl like that." He grinned.

"Rhodes, don't you dare encourage him. He already thinks he's going to marry her one day. You want the kids getting hitched right outta high school?"

"She despises him." He frowned. "Doesn't she?"

I rolled my eyes. "If she didn't care what he thought, or what he did, she wouldn't be fighting so hard now would she?"

"So she hates him, but that means she actually likes him?" he asked.

"Exactly. She likes him, likes him, but she doesn't want to. Therefore, she hates him. For now. Could last a week. A month. A year. Or more. Depends on how it all goes."

"Likes him, likes him....what?"

"God," I groaned. "Men. Just go talk him off the ledge and approach him about the boxing idea."

He pecked my lips again. "On it. You ladies cooking?"

"Mari is teaching us the art of making the perfect homemade sopes and tortillas. They are way harder than they look."

He grinned. "Looking forward to eating it, *and you* later." He whispered that last part just for my ears. Now my cheeks turned pink, but I busied myself with picking up my chunk of dough and giving it a few smacks.

"So, back to our lesson. Mari?"

Shockingly, Mari had not gotten involved in our family argument, letting us handle it all ourselves, continuing to cook or pretending to, and listening in I'm sure.

I went over to her side and bumped her shoulder. "How'd we do?" I asked, genuinely curious about her opinion.

"I agree with the boxing. Teenage boys need things to

punch once in a while. All those pesky hormones." She made a sour expression.

"And Emily?"

"She'll soon learn she can't string one boy along while kissing another."

I snorted and chuckled. "True. And Ma?" I whispered.

"She'll be okay in time. More time is needed. A lot more. We will help her heal."

I loved Marisol even more for saying that. She'd become a solid resource for my mother, who questioned everything. When a person lived over twenty years with a vile, violent man who didn't let them be a true adult, it wasn't surprising that Mom was extremely awkward around other women. Marisol wouldn't allow anyone to feel awkward around her. She'd push and pull until the person gave up and accepted her bossy, nosy version of love.

"And me?" I added just to see what she would say, never having asked her thoughts on Rhodes and me before. Not that it mattered. We were a done deal. But I was a little curious.

"You, my dear, are the best thing that ever happened to our little family. Alas, you are a bad cook. You lose points for that."

"Mari-sol," I enunciated her name. "That was soooo mean!" I laughed. "If I'm a bad cook it's your fault because you're the one teaching me." I skipped right over her love-bomb of a message and went straight into easier waters. Marisol loved a good bickering sesh, which she always won.

She hit me with rapid fire Spanish that I had absolutely no hope of translating when she spoke so fast, but the results had Mom and me laughing like hyenas just the same.

* * * *

RHODES

Later that night, after I'd fucked my wife to the point where she could barely move, I asked the burning question I'd been worried about for months. We'd had so much going on in our lives, it never came up, and I certainly wasn't getting any younger. I was coming up on thirty-nine while my wife hadn't even turned twenty-five yet.

I threaded my fingers through Maia's now shorter hair. After we got married, she chopped her curls to chin length. I loved it. The shorter length made her curls look even more enticing and I adored running my fingers through the silky spirals as I fell asleep.

I started our nightly conversation focused on the day's events. "Today was a bit rougher than we've experienced since your family moved in with us, huh?"

She sighed, her breath puffing against my bare chest. "Yeah. Teenagers are a lot of work."

I chuckled. "They are. Speaking of teenagers or children in general…"

Maia didn't say anything or even breathe, but her body did go stiff in my arms.

"We never talked about us having kids." I threw it out there, wondering where the conversation would lead.

Maia shifted off me and sat up, holding the sheet to her chest. "You already have a kid."

I crossed my arms behind my head and rested my head in my hands. "Yeah, but you've never had one of your own."

"Emily's mine," she responded instantly, making my heart swell to the size of Texas. It was the leeriness to her tone I didn't like. "Are you about to drop a Portia situation on me? Is that why you went for the third O? Buttering me up for some new drama she has going?" she frowned.

I grinned. "No. And I know Emily's yours, baby. No one is suggesting otherwise. I'm grateful you've taken on the role of mother to her so well. But what about you?"

"What about me?" She pressed her hand to her chest.

"You haven't experienced being pregnant or caring for a baby."

"And?" Her entire face scrunched up into one of disgust.

"Well, I just thought we should talk about the future. About whether or not you wanted to have a baby together. I'm not getting any younger."

"And I am?" She scoffed. "What about our busy life says, let's have a baby? Honey, do you want another child?" She winced.

Winced.

"I want what you want," I chose my words wisely. If she wanted to expand our already large circus, I'd be happy to share that experience with her. Did I want it? Not particularly.

Maia reached out and ran her hand up my abdomen to rest it on my chest over my heart. "Rhodes, I do not want to have more children. I do not have any desire to ever become pregnant. Honestly, before Em, I didn't even want children in my life. Now, I'm good with them, but I certainly do not want to add more to the equation."

"Are you sure? You're so young."

"I've lived a harder life in my twenty-five years than most will ever in a hundred. I do not need to add a baby to feel fulfilled. I'm happy as it is. Knowing all of them will be out of the house and going off to college in a few years is a true blessing I do not look down upon."

I couldn't help it. I burst out laughing, lifted up to a seated position and yanked my wife up and on top of me. She came with an *oomph* and a cute little giggle.

"God you're the perfect woman for me." I cuddled her small frame.

"Do you want more kids?" she asked.

I shook my head. "No. Would I willingly make a baby with you? Absolutely. I have room in my heart for anything that comes from us and our bond. But I love the idea of being empty nesters in a few years. You and me, alone…" I ran my hands down to her juicy bottom and gave it an encouraging squeeze.

"Down boy!" She playfully swatted at me. "We need sleep. It's your turn to take the kids to school tomorrow."

One of the things we'd agreed upon was that if we were busy, Buddy would pick up the kids from school, but one of us always drove them for drop-off. They needed to see how much they were loved and cared for, and part of that, in our opinion, was checking in with them at the start of their day. Making sure everyone was okay and ready to roll with whatever life threw at them.

I kissed Maia deeply and with my entire body and soul. Then I slid her off me, and she cuddled in close to my side in her normal sleeping position. She hadn't had a single nightmare since we'd come home from Colorado. Which was weird, but I kept vigilant in case she did. The bathroom light was always on, the door cracked so she could see in the dark if the fear returned.

"Goodnight, Maia."

"Goodnight, Rhodes. And just so you know, I love our life just as it is. Hormonal teens, fights, slumber parties, Mexican cooking classes with Marisol, teaching Zach how to drive, and looking after all of them. Thank you for giving me everything I could ever want."

"All I ever wanted was for Emily and me to have a woman in our lives we could both love and who would see our love as something to cherish. You show me that every day. So I think we both got what we wanted."

"Yeah, we did. Love you."

"Love you."

Episode 117
Epilogue 5: Madam Alana

MADAM ALANA

"Alana, he's absolutely beautiful," Julianne whispered with awe. "Brenden would have been beside himself with love."

I pressed the phone closer to my ear. "And…" I waited with bated breath to hear their decision.

Prior to this call, Christophe and I'd had long conversations about Brenden's child. We then had them with Julianne and Giovanni. We were both in agreement that we didn't want the baby to go into child services. However, my goddaughter and her husband had many concerns about being the guardians to not only Brenden's biological child, but to Bianca's, and with good reason. Just the stain of Bianca's misdeeds, and the trauma she caused weren't easily forgotten. Bianca and Angus were the catalyst of most of the couple's personal losses. Their parents. The sexual assault. The explosion. Brenden.

It wouldn't have surprised anyone if they'd chosen not to raise Brenden's child. Which was why Christophe and I offered to become the child's guardians. We weren't exactly young, but we'd always wanted children and would love the child as our own, regardless of who was his biological mother. Christophe warned me not to get my hopes up, because he felt strongly that Julianne and Giovanni would take the baby under their wing. And since Julianne was officially next of kin, they were contacted first regarding guardianship of Bianca's child.

"We're going to raise him as our son," Julianne said with confidence.

My heart swelled and also cracked at the seams. It was the right choice for them and the baby, but that didn't take away the fact that a kernel of hope had taken root within me that I might become a mother. Alas, it was not meant to be. And I was okay with that. Had made peace with that fact over twenty years ago.

"I'm elated to hear that, *my petite fleur.*"

"Gio's already in love. To be honest, we both are, but it's hard…" She let her voice fade away.

"I know, my darling, but it is what Brenden would want. The brother you knew and loved before Bianca got her claws sunk into him."

"That's what we think too. I miss him. The him he was before her."

I smiled sadly while thinking back to the precocious young boy, then gangly teen, and later, driven businessman. Somewhere along the way, he lost himself.

"At least now he can be at peace, knowing his sister is raising his son. What did the she-devil name him?"

"Oh, she tried to name him after her father, but Gio's already contacted our lawyers. His name will be changed to Myers Lewis Falco."

"Lewis would be so pleased." My voice cracked just a bit with the emotion I wasn't able to hide.

I thought back to Lewis Myers. My first client. A busy businessman with big dreams, an even bigger bank account. None of that compared to his desire to find a mate for life. He laid eyes on Rachel that night, stood up and waved his paddle like he was an air traffic controller. Then he dared anyone in the room to bid against him and the woman he would marry. It was rather romantic and obnoxious at the same time, as I was trying to hold a respectable auction and he'd ruined it with his impatience.

In the end, he got the girl and the life he wanted. It was unfortunate that a revenge plan, connected to me, was what cut their lives short.

So much tragedy and loss.

I wasn't sure I could ever do it again. After all that we'd endured, not to mention all the people I loved who'd been hurt or I'd unknowingly put at risk, for lack of a better word, I was now gun-shy. And here we were, six months after the shooting in France, and I still hadn't hosted an auction. Jade had gladly stepped into my shoes and had done well in the last auction with candidates we'd already vetted and bidders we were familiar with. So far, all of those candidates had been chosen, had gotten married, and were happy with their partners.

Everyone was happy but me.

Lately I'd accepted the reality that there was an inherent dark side to the auction I might never understand, and that frightened me to my core. However, it also made me wiser and more thoughtful about the entire process. Which was why I was back to sitting behind my desk in my Las Vegas office. I could no longer hide from the job I loved or the company I'd built.

Christophe was on the couch in the corner, reading. I hadn't been able to be away from him since what occurred in France. He understood and took my neediness in stride. But it concerned me because he hadn't made art since then either. I tried to question his lack of interest in creating new pieces, but he shook his head and told me to, "Leave it." So I did. We were both working through our feelings on all that had occurred, and he was no different.

The sound of a baby crying in the background reminded me I was on a call, my thoughts having run rampant into the past. "I'll let you go. Send my love to Gio and please forward us pictures of our new nephew when you have a moment."

"I will…and thank you, Alana. For everything. Come visit us soon?" her tone held expectation within it and that mended my cracked heart instantly.

"We will evaluate our schedules and plan for a time to visit," I promised.

"I love you, Alana. Very much. Please don't be a stranger. I need you in my life now more than ever."

My throat went completely dry, a bushel of cotton wedged into my esophagus. I cleared it and smiled. "We will be there for whatever you need. *Je t'aime aussi. Au revoir.*"

"Bye," she said and hung up.

"They're going to raise Brenden's child," I announced loud enough for Christophe to hear and look up at me from the pages of his book.

"I'm proud of them. It was the right call."

"Me too." I agreed.

"It's okay to be a little sad."

"I'm actually happier than I am sad. They needed to do this. Prove that Bianca hadn't won in the end. And they'll be great parents. Plus, their own child is due in six months. The boy will have someone to play with.

"Boy?" He smiled so sweetly his eyes crinkled at the edges in that way I adored.

"Myers Lewis Falco."

"Lew would be so puffed up with pride you wouldn't be able to fit him through a doorway," he said of his old friend.

I chuckled, allowing the rest of my anxiety over the situation to dissipate along with our laughter.

"Okay," I let out a sharp breath. "Time to get back to work."

"Who's your first client?"

"Diego Salazar." I shivered at the mere mention of the man's name.

We hadn't seen Diego since he put us in a blacked-out SUV after everything had gone down and sent us back home. True to his word, we gave the authorities the exact information Angel's team had trained us to say. I didn't enjoy lying to Inspector Moreau, but since Bianca never spoke a word of what had occurred, we were only questioned regarding the kidnapping, the snipers shooting us at our home, and our dinner conversation between her and Angus, sans the shootout that occurred. True to his word, not a single peep had been mentioned about the bloodbath that we experienced in that hotel. I had no idea where or what they did with all the wounded or dead, but Diego made it clear it was not our problem to consider.

For once, I listened, did what I was told, and both Christophe and I walked out of the police station and never looked back.

The body of Angus Sokolov had also not been found and I suspected that it never would be. I did know that one of Diego's younger brothers, Xavier Salazar, had taken over Angus' empire. I hadn't the slightest clue what that entailed, and I didn't want to know. The further I was from their dealings, the better.

Only I couldn't exactly escape one hundred percent because I owed Diego a marker, and he intended to cash it in today.

He wanted a wife for life.

My phone buzzed, and Jade's voice came through crystal clear on the speaker.

"Mr. Salazar is here. Shall I bring him in?"

"Yes, Jade, I am ready."

I was nowhere near ready, but if I was going to go back to living my life, running the business I'd put thirty years of my soul into, I had to make myself do scary things.

Jade entered with Diego a few paces behind.

I stood up as Diego approached, a huge smile on his face.

We shook hands, he nodded at Christophe, and then clapped as if this was a celebration.

"So, who am I going to marry?"

"Please take a seat. Jade, this was your idea, and I've decided you will be running this new side of our business."

Jade blanched but adjusted to the change in stride, standing taller, nodding, then took the seat next to Diego. She sat primly, crossed her legs and put her tablet on her thigh.

"Have a seat, Mr. Salazar. I'd like to introduce you to our new division: The Marriage Auction: After Dark."

"Sounds intriguing." He sat and turned to face both me and Jade. "Please explain."

"The concept is a bit different than what we have now. You see, the current Marriage Auction offers a three-year period of marriage. Bidders bid on individuals and the highest bidder wins. Everything is on the up-and-up. We meticulously vet our bidders and candidates, ensuring there are no hidden skeletons in either of their closets, no previous entanglements with the law, and that their finances are as they say they are."

"I'm guessing I don't fit into one of your approved bidders categories." He smirked but didn't say more.

"No. As the leader of the Latin Mafia your alleged crimes…"

"*Alleged* is the key word, Ms. Lee," Diego interrupted with conviction.

"I understand, and I, for one, believe everyone deserves a chance at true love. The difference in your situation being we cannot in good conscience prepare a list of candidates that are not already familiar with your—how should I put it—"

"Lifestyle choices," I added.

"Thank you, Alana. Yes, your lifestyle choices."

"What you're saying is you don't want to put some

innocent woman into an auction lest she end up with a man who allegedly runs a criminal empire?" Diego supplied.

Jade smiled. "Exactly."

"This does not make me happy, Alana." His dark gaze cut to mine. He started to remind me of my commitment. "You owe me a marker of my choosing—"

I lifted my hand. "Diego, I have every intention of providing you with exactly what you desire. Please continue, Jade."

"As I was saying, we cannot enlist our normal crowd. What I propose is we hold a private auction for you. This will be held "After Dark" or immediately following our normal auction. We'll have selected a series of women all willing to be tied to a man of your..." She tapped her lips. "Caliber and lifestyle."

"Noted. I like where this is going." Diego eased back in his seat, making himself more comfortable.

"We'll choose women who have a history of similar tastes," Jade shared.

"Meaning criminals."

"Allegedly," Jade continued. Then she pulled out a list of women she'd already vetted specifically for this job. Not only did it show pictures, but it was essentially each candidate's rap sheet. Some longer and more detailed than others, as they had a darker history, or more smaller convictions. All of them were free of any current sentencing, all of them having been to jail or arrested in their past, and all of them were interested in marriage for life, provided they got a lot of money out of it. None of them had even flinched at hearing Diego's name.

"I sat down personally and spoke to each of these six women. I showed them your photo. Two of them recognized you." She pointed to one on the top of the list and one at the bottom.

"Ah, yes," he rubbed at his chin. "This one," he pointed to the woman on the bottom named Christy. "She was one of my informants. Remove her from the list. Too many people are aware she's a snitch. She wouldn't last a day in my family."

"Okay, done. I'll attempt to replace her prior to the auction. Are there any others?" Jade was doing a phenomenal job running this meeting. I couldn't have been more proud or grateful.

"Do all of the women understand what they are getting into? I want a mother for my three children. A life partner that will stay faithful, or risk ending up in a body bag. Not that I need to remind you," Diego's gaze flicked to mine. "My world is dangerous. The woman for me should not shy away from it. She must be comfortable in it."

"These women thrive on danger. They are perfect for you," Jade's tone was confident as she lifted her chin haughtily.

Diego stood abruptly and buttoned his blazer. "Set it up. I'm ready for the auction whenever you are. Excellent work, ladies. I look forward to being part of The Marriage Auction: After Dark."

I stood as did Jade. We shook hands and then Diego held up a finger to Christophe. "*Un momento*," he said then walked to the door. He opened it and snapped his fingers. One of his guards handed him a plastic container. "*Gracias*," he mumbled to his man then went over to my husband. "Tamales from *Mamá*. She wants you both over for dinner soon."

Christophe's eyes lit up as he rubbed his hands together, practically licking his lips. "Homemade tamales?" he breathed as if Diego had just offered him a plate of precious diamonds.

"Pork *and* chicken, *mi amigo*." Diego waggled his brows and grinned like a lunatic. It would have been scary if he wasn't so handsome.

"That woman is a saint. Tell *Mamá* she holds a piece of my heart." He took the container and practically hugged it.

Diego smiled. "She will be happy. And if *Mamá* is happy, everyone is happy. Dinner soon?"

"Absolutely. We'll bring the wine," Christophe agreed instantly, signing us up to become actual friends with the mafioso and his family.

Goodness gracious, we needed to have a very stern talk about who we allowed into our inner circle.

"Well, that went really well," Jade breathed excitedly after Diego departed.

"It did. You were phenomenal, Jade. I'm impressed. You've proven yourself as my protégé. I want you to run this new side of the business with an increase in pay and a new title, Madam Jade. Something tells me Diego isn't going to be the only morally gray character that wants to find love in the darkness."

"I mean, bad boys deserve love, too, right?" Jade grinned, genuinely excited about this opportunity.

"Agreed. Bad boys deserve love too."

"Can we talk about the next quarterly marriage auction? I've received a couple calls from Autumn Belanger. She's Summer Belanger, now Larsen's, sister. And from what I understand, a complete hippie."

"And Summer wasn't a hippie?" I recalled the woman entering my office, taking off her shoes and pulling her legs and feet up onto my couch. People at business meetings didn't remove their shoes unless they were extremely comfortable in their own skin and unbothered by societal norms.

"She's not our normal candidate. She doesn't *need* to be in the auction, she wants to be, and not for the money."

I frowned. "Then what's her angle?"

She smiled. "Love, of course. Plus, she claimed to have seen the future, and in it, she was being bid on at our auction."

"She claims to be psychic?" I asked.

Jade shook her head and chuckled. "Not exactly. I actually clarified it with Summer. She claims it's wild and unusual but that her sister has "the sight", which is what she called it. Apparently, Autumn also envisioned Jack before she met him and asked where his son was. He didn't have one then, but within two weeks he became the legal guardian of his friend's toddler when she suddenly passed away. I don't know if I believe it, but Summer and Jack both agreed she's harmless and well meaning."

I let out a long breath. "Okay, let's schedule a meeting with her to discuss the finer details. If her sister has already been in it and is happy with her match, there's really no reason not to allow her in the next batch of candidates provided she's vetted and her record is clear."

Jade scribbled notes on the tablet. "The next new bidder we have is a female and you'll recognize her. In fact, everyone will. We may have to host a private auction for her too."

"Who is it? Taylor Swift?" I chuckled, appreciating my own joke.

"No, but not far off. Juniper Ross."

"Stop it," I waved a hand at her trickery.

Juniper Ross was a Pop-Rock princess. Much like Taylor was a Country-Pop princess, Juniper had her own thing going for her. She was very much an Lzzy Hale meets Taylor Swift meets Tori Amos type of artist. Everything goes with her. She had a bad girl attitude, showed a lot of skin, hated the media, and was known for being spoiled rotten because she came from money. And not a little money, but a dynasty of music legends in her family. Her music reached far and wide, and she had several Grammys to prove it. The good girls loved to hate her but listened to her music anyway. The bad girls worshipped her because they wanted to be her. And men, well, she was every man's sex symbol. A role she excelled at and leaned into much of the time in her stage performance and music videos.

"Alana, I'm not kidding. Juniper Ross wants to choose a husband at the next auction."

"Seriously? How did she even find us? It's not as though we advertise. Everything is word of mouth."

"Yeah, and that word of mouth got back to her publicist who contacted me. Juniper wants a man in her life that is willing to go on tour with her, attend red carpet events, and let the public see their romance play out live."

"Is that what Juniper wants or her publicist? Is this one of those fix her image type of deals? Because that's not the business we're in."

Jade shook her head. "Nope. I spoke to Juniper myself. She claims no one knows the real her and she wants true love. She says she doesn't believe it's possible for her to find it, so she's going to buy it."

"Hmmm, I'm not sure about this one. Set up a meeting between me and Juniper and her publicist. I'd like to speak to them personally."

Jade jotted down the request. "The last thing is The Christmas Auction. You said you had a candidate in mind but didn't share any details."

I smiled remembering the bartender I'd met at that dive bar I happened upon by accident when the car I'd hired had blown a tire. The driver who'd picked me up had barely made it to the rickety locale. While he'd dealt with the car and waited for assistance, I went inside to have a drink.

Holly was her name.

She was incredibly beautiful with long blonde hair, big brown eyes, and a buxom body. When I sat down, she took one look at me and said, "We don't have fancy cocktails or martinis here. If that's what you want, you're in the wrong place."

I smiled and ordered a double shot of her best tequila. She added the lime, for which I was grateful. Then she asked me what a classy woman was doing on that side of town. We talked, and I found out she was a native to Las Vegas, having been born and raised in the desert. Her father was a card dealer. Her momma a waitress in the same casino.

When I asked why she bartended, she said it was the best money she could make that wasn't shaking her ass or climbing a pole. But she aspired to own her own bar one day. Then she playfully asked if I wanted to be her fairy godmother and bankroll her.

I told her not that day, but one never knew what awaited them in the future.

She was perfect for the Christmas auction.

And Bruno Castellanos would be the perfect bidder.

I tapped my pencil on my desk and played out a scene where I'd force the two to meet in advance. Some people thought my matches were all luck of the draw, or luck of the bidder. And in some cases, that was true.

Other times, like with this special auction, I knew exactly who to pair, I just needed to do some old-fashioned reconnaissance like I did in the past.

What was the first way to get back into the saddle if you've fallen off? Go back to what you know best.

And the best thing I knew how to do was matchmake.

"*Mon Coeur,* I'm feeling like a drink. Shall we head out?"

"Can I eat my tamales in the limo?" He gave me puppy dog eyes. Food was one of my husband's love languages. I'd never deny him.

"Of course, *mi amor.* Jade, you've got things handled. We'll see you tomorrow."

I linked my arm with my husband's and smiled as I mentally started planning in my head how I was going to finagle a meet and greet between Bruno and my soon-to-be new candidate Holly.

"I love my job." I sighed and cuddled next to my husband as we headed to a filthy dive bar on the outskirts of Las Vegas.

Holly and Bruno had no idea their lives were about to change forever.

The End of The Marriage Auction Season 2.

If you want to read more right away, with pop-ins by your favorite Season 1-2 characters, you can read Season 3 as it publishes by episode, on Kindle Vella.

Intrigued by Holly and Bruno's story mentioned above? Read A Christmas Auction, a 1001 Dark Nights novella, that releases October 15, 2024.

Want to read how it all started, read Madam Alana, a 1001 Dark Nights novella featuring the owner of The Marriage Auction. Available now.

If you want to read the grittier side of The Marriage Auction, including Diego, Angel, Javier, Xavier and Mama, check out my new spinoff series *The Marriage Auction: After Dark*, on Kindle Vella.

Acknowledgements

This has been a wild three years my friends. I had no idea when I told my agent Amy Tannenbaum that I wanted to write a filthy soap opera that she'd actually find a way for me to do just that. This series started on Kindle Vella exactly three years from when The Marriage Auction 2 releases. In that time, I had no idea what I was getting myself into or that I'd find an entirely new way to approach storytelling. I'd always been known for my serials such as Calendar Girl and International Guy, but I wouldn't have expected that skill would transition into having eight full-length novels and two novellas all in the same universe...and counting! I'm so grateful to all of you TMA readers who read every episode week by week as it releases as well as to those of you that binge read the series when it's done and published in book format. Thank you, thank you, thank you. I endeavor to continue to give you the absolute best story possible while continuing to keep it fresh and engaging. And there is so much more to come! Follow me on my socials and my newsletter to stay up to date with the most current TMA news.

To **Team AC**, for those of you that don't know, these women read everything I write in DRAFT format at the same time it's being edited professionally. They receive no less than two chapters a week, read it, write out their feedback, suggestions, concerns and send it to me within a day of receiving it. They are the baddest, coolest, most talented, loving, and supportive women I know. And they are NOT paid. They do all of this out of their love for the stories, me, each other, and the sisterhood at large. I am nothing without them. I love each and every one of you to the deepest depths of my soul.

Tracey Wilson-Vuolo – Alpha Beta, Disney Freak, Proofer, ADA Expert

Tammy Hamilton-Green – Alpha Beta, Rock Chick, Plot Hole Finder, Educational Expert

Elaine Hennig – Alpha Beta, Brazilian Goddess, Medical Expert

Gabby McEachern - Alpha Beta, Dancing Queen, Spanish Expert

Dorothy Bircher – Alpha Beta, Mom Boss, Sensitivity Expert

Dannica Chiverrell – Admin Assistant, Niece, Gen Z Expert

To **Ekaterina Sayanova,** can you believe I roped you into editing another serial? Lol I just want to thank you for being a constant source of advice, intelligence, and always being willing to help me out of a writing corner I've put myself in. Your knowledge of the written word and my voice as a writer is unmatched. You get me, you get my storytelling, you just get it. You are one of a kind, my friend.

To my literary agent, **Amy Tannenbaum** with Jane Rotrosen Agency, you are my rock. You protect me, encourage me, and see my storytelling as something special. I think you're special. I wouldn't want to do this job without you at my back. I am constantly impressed by your business prowess, tact, and exceptional ability to find my babies homes. Let's do this together until we're old and gray. <wink>

To **Liz Berry, Jillian Stein,** and **MJ Rose** from Blue Box Press, you ladies are a triple threat of badassery and class. I've told you before and I'll say it again louder for those sitting in the back, you are a dream publisher to work for. On a personal note:

Liz Berry – I have never known a woman whose sole purpose on this Earth was to lift other women up and make them shine. Not only do you excel at it, you make it look easy when I know for a fact it's not. You set a beautiful example for the rest of us of what it means to be classy, confident, and successful. All of which you've done without walking over others to get there. I am in awe of you. You are true beauty inside and out.

Jillian Stein – I'm not sure I've ever known a cooler chick in my life. I aspire to be everyone's friend, but you just are. You have an uncanny ability to connect to people on a business and personal level that is genuine and everlasting. I aspire to be as well-rounded, hip, and considerate as you are with everyone you meet. Your ideas and excitement for the books you publish is as infectious and endearing as you are. Never change.

MJ Rose – At first, I was a little scared of you…in a good way. You're such a veteran of the industry I wanted to bow before the Queen upon meeting you the first time. Having the benefit of speaking to you about writing books and promoting them was like receiving a masterclass by a guru. Your knowledge and intellect is a gift to behold, and I'm honored you share it with me. One day, I hope to have such business savvy with the reputation to match. (Also, you remind me of Stevie Nicks and that's just cool AF.)

Last but not least, thank you to **Stacey Tardif** and **Suzy Baldwin**, you make sure my stories shine as brightly as possible. Thank you for your editing prowess and considerate feedback and suggestions. Knowing I have you two at the finish line making sure my stories read well is an enormous relief. I'm grateful for both of you. Our team ROCKS!

About Audrey Carlan

Audrey Carlan is a No. 1 *New York Times*, *USA Today*, and *Wall Street Journal* best-selling author. She writes stories that help the reader find themselves while falling in love. Some of her works include the worldwide phenomenon Calendar Girl serial, Trinity series and the International Guy series. Her books have been translated into over thirty-five languages across the globe. Recently her bestselling novel Resisting Roots was made into a PassionFlix movie.

NEWSLETTER
For new release updates and giveaway news, sign up for Audrey's newsletter: https://audreycarlan.com/sign-up

SOCIAL MEDIA
Audrey loves communicating with her readers. You can follow or contact her on any of the following:
Website: www.audreycarlan.com
Email: audrey.carlanpa@gmail.com
Facebook: https://www.facebook.com/AudreyCarlan/
Twitter: https://twitter.com/AudreyCarlan
Pinterest: https://www.pinterest.com/audreycarlan1/
Instagram: https://www.instagram.com/audreycarlan/
Tik Tok: https://www.tiktok.com/@audreycarlan
Readers Group:
https://www.facebook.com/groups/AudreyCarlanWickedHotReaders/
Book Bub:
https://www.bookbub.com/authors/audrey-carlan
Goodreads:
https://www.goodreads.com/author/show/7831156.Audrey_Carlan
Amazon:
https://www.amazon.com/Audrey-Carlan/e/B00JAVVG8U/

Discover 1001 Dark Nights Collection Eleven

DRAGON KISS by Donna Grant
A Dragon Kings Novella

THE WILD CARD by Dylan Allen
A Rivers Wilde Novella

ROCK CHICK REMATCH by Kristen Ashley
A Rock Chick Novella

JUST ONE SUMMER by Carly Phillips
A Dirty Dare Series Novella

HAPPILY EVER MAYBE by Carrie Ann Ryan
A Montgomery Ink Legacy Novella

BLUE MOON by Skye Warren
A Cirque des Moroirs Novella

A VAMPIRE'S MATE by Rebecca Zanetti
A Dark Protectors/Rebels Novella

LOVE HAZARD by Rachel Van Dyken

BRODIE by Aurora Rose Reynolds
An Until Her Novella

THE BODYGUARD AND THE BOMBSHELL by Lexi Blake
A Masters and Mercenaries: New Recruits Novella

THE SUBSTITUTE by Kristen Proby
A Single in Seattle Novella

CRAVED BY YOU by J. Kenner
A Stark Security Novella

GRAVEYARD DOG by Darynda Jones
A Charley Davidson Novella

A CHRISTMAS AUCTION by Audrey Carlan
A Marriage Auction Novella

THE GHOST OF A CHANCE by Heather Graham
A Krewe of Hunters Novella

Also from Blue Box Press

LEGACY OF TEMPTATION by Larissa Ione
A Demonica Birthright Novel

VISIONS OF FLESH AND BLOOD by Jennifer L. Armentrout
and Ravyn Salvador
A Blood & Ash and Fire & Flesh Compendium

FORGETTING TO REMEMBER by M.J. Rose

TOUCH ME by J. Kenner
A Stark International Novella

BORN OF BLOOD AND ASH by Jennifer L. Armentrout
A Flesh and Fire Novel

MY ROYAL SHOWMANCE by Lexi Blake
A Park Avenue Promise Novel

SAPPHIRE DAWN by Christopher Rice writing as C. Travis Rice
A Sapphire Cove Novel

IN THE AIR TONIGHT by Marie Force

EMBRACING THE CHANGE by Kristen Ashley
A River Rain Novel

LEGACY OF CHAOS by Larissa Ione
A Demonica Birthright Novel

On Behalf of Blue Box Press,

Liz Berry, M.J. Rose, and Jillian Stein would like to thank ~

Steve Berry
Doug Scofield
Benjamin Stein
Kim Guidroz
Tanaka Kangara
Asha Hossain
Chris Graham
Chelle Olson
Jessica Saunders
Stacey Tardif
Suzy Baldwin
Ann-Marie Nieves
Grace Wenk
Dylan Stockton
Kate Boggs
Richard Blake
and Simon Lipskar